WARSAW CONCERTO

Also by Dennis Jones

Rubicon One
Russian Spring
Barbarossa Red
Winter Palace

WARSAW CONCERTO

Dennis
Jones

Macdonald

A MACDONALD BOOK

Published by arrangement with Stoddart Publishing Co. Limited, Toronto, Ontario, Canada

First published in Great Britain in 1990 by
Macdonald & Co. (Publishers) Ltd,
London & Sydney

British Library Cataloguing in Publication Data

Jones, Dennis, *1945–*
Warsaw concerto.
I. Title
813'.54[F]

ISBN 0–356–18682–2 H/B
0–356–19104–4 P/B

Printed and bound in Great Britain by
Richard Clay Ltd, Bungay, Suffolk

Macdonald & Co. (Publishers) Ltd
66–73 Shoe Lane
London EC4P 4AP
A member of Maxwell Pergamon Publishing Corporation plc

To Helene and Larry Hoffman

Glen Cove, New York
5:45 A.M.,
Sunday, September 29

"THERE'S the turn," said the driver. He peered through the rain-speckled windshield as though trying to read the street sign, though he could have driven the route with his eyes taped shut. His companion didn't answer; he was gazing steadily into the side mirror, watching for lights behind them.

The headlights of the TV mobile unit swept across the sign, illuminating it for an instant: Dosoris Lane. Only half a mile to the first checkpoint. The driver shifted down to second gear and pulled the vehicle into the turn, looking into his own side mirror as the reflection swept an arc across the road behind.

"No one?" he asked. Like his passenger, he wore blue coveralls with the NBC logo stencilled on the left breast. A laminated identification card bearing his photograph was clipped to the flap of the breast pocket; according to the tag, the driver's name was Robert Dalton.

"No. No one," his passenger said.

"Good," said Dalton, although he hadn't expected any surveillance. The preparations had been sound, and his low voice reflected his confidence. He was a nondescript man, with short blonde hair receding from a widow's peak; his eyes were pale blue under sparse eyebrows. Only his hands were out of the ordinary: they were broad for his frame, with thick, strong fingers that lay lightly now on the rim of the steering wheel, directing the mobile unit with small, economical motions.

Dalton's companion was taller, with dark-brown hair and a face as nondescript as his own. His ID tag bore the name James Wheatley.

The radio under the dash crackled. Wheatley unclipped its microphone. "Unit seven."

"There's been a delay," was the reply.

"Acknowledged," Wheatley said, and put the microphone back. Dalton nodded in satisfaction. They couldn't reasonably be more than ten minutes early at the checkpoint, so the other mobile unit had to be delayed to give them the time they needed. They'd calculated that the checkpoint wouldn't be told about the deliberate accident to the other vehicle for a good half hour, by which time they'd be well away with their purpose accomplished.

Both men watched the wet road ahead as their van neared the dogleg that bent off to the right, concealing the checkpoint. Rain whipped against the van's cab, driven by a strengthening wind from Long Island Sound; the raindrops made short bright lines in the headlight beams.

"Checkpoint," Wheatley said, as the mobile unit came out of the dogleg.

Up the road, yellow lights were blinking on and off: the US Secret Service barricade, a hundred yards from the main gate to the Killenworth mansion.

"There won't be any problems," Dalton said. "We're expected."

A floodlit barrier had been erected across the road. Just beyond it on the shoulder stood a Cadillac-Gage Commando armored car, the twin machine guns in its turret pointing straight down the road at the mobile unit. Dalton took his foot off the accelerator and let the truck slow to a crawl. The Commando's crew and the Secret Service men would be touchy, and well-armed.

Four of the latter, clad in yellow rain slickers, were watching from behind the striped barrier. They were holding submachine guns. A big German shepherd, the explosives sniffer, sat disconsolately next to a wind-whipped puddle. Dalton stopped the vehicle six yards from the barricade, and waited. The engine ticked over softly, barely audible above the noise of the wind.

One of the agents walked over to the mobile unit's cab. Dalton rolled down the window, admitting a gust of cold, damp air. The agent was carrying an electric lantern, and splashed its beam over the lettering on the van's side: NBC NEWS MOBILE UNIT 7. Then he checked the license plate number. Satisfied, he stepped up onto the running board, and played the light over Dalton's and Wheatley's badges, then their faces.

"You're ten minutes early," he said to Dalton.

Perfect, Dalton thought. Exactly on time. "Sorry," he said, with exactly the right amount of apprehension and subservience: civilian confronting armed government man. "We made better time than the dispatcher bargained for. No traffic. Do you want us to wait?"

The agent didn't answer. The ID on his slicker said Polanski. Under other circumstances, Dalton would have smiled at the irony.

"May I see your identification, please?"

Dalton and Wheatley showed their NBC identity cards, duty sheets, passes for the KGB checkpoint and driver's licenses. Polanski inspected each one, fastidiously, and then returned them. "Open up the back," he ordered.

Dalton got out of the cab and went around to the van's rear. The door slid up with a rumble and clatter, to expose the mobile control room with its consoles and monitors. Stacked between the consoles were coils of thick camera and lighting cables, as well as several cases of equipment.

"Open the boxes," Polanski commanded. One of the other agents had come over, and was watching Dalton and Polanski. His submachine gun was cradled loosely in the crook of his right arm, not quite in firing position.

Dalton opened the equipment cases to reveal cameras, lights and other odds and ends of gear. Polanski studied it all with a flicker of interest. "Not very big cameras."

"Nope," Dalton replied. "Everything's small, these days. Ten years ago you'd have needed a unit three times that big to get the same quality."

"You going live with the press conference?"

"No. Taping at nine, for rebroadcast at one o'clock this afternoon."

"You got a generator for all this stuff?"

"Yeah. But we won't use it unless we have to. Depends on how much power's available up at the house."

Polanski gave a short bark of laughter. "You shouldn't have any trouble with power. The Russians have got so much monitoring and communications equipment up there, they probably swallow as much juice as the town does. Aerials all over the roof."

"A lot of guards?"

"A few."

Polanski's reticence didn't matter to Dalton. He knew exactly how many KGB personnel were on the Killenworth grounds.

Polanski started poking around behind the equipment consoles, tapping the floor, the walls. Outside, Dalton knew, at least one other man would be checking the cab and the underside of the truck, using the dog to smell for explosives. Polanski finished his search, went to the tailgate and said, "Get the nose up here."

The dog handler coaxed the shepherd into the cargo space, and followed it. The animal stood uncertainly for a moment, black nostrils twitching. Then it worked its way around the compartment, guided by the handler.

"Clean," the handler said after perhaps two minutes. Dalton started closing up the equipment cases. They'd used up as much time as allowed, and they had to get moving. "Everything okay?" he asked.

"You can go on," Polanski said.

"Thanks." When they were all out, Dalton pulled the door down and locked it. "By the way," he said to Polanski as they headed toward the cab.

"What?" The agent's voice was neutral.

"I noticed your name. You related to that film director?"

"Everybody asks me that. No."

"Okay, just asking." Dalton put the van into gear as the Secret Service men swung the barrier back from the road. The van rolled past them and Dalton waved briefly to Polanski, who didn't respond. The dog was sitting by the puddle again, tongue lolling.

"We're through," Dalton said to Wheatley. "Do you think they were suspicious?"

"No. They were careful, but routine. We're on schedule."

"Good."

The gate at the road into the estate was just ahead now. Dalton could see the two KGB men standing just outside the gate's ornate ironwork; the barrier was all of twelve feet high. The guardhouse was just inside it. Farther up the main road, beyond the gate and this time pointing away from the mobile unit, was another Commando armored car.

"Next step," Dalton said. He swung the mobile unit up to the gate and stopped. A third KGB man, wearing a beige raincoat, stood inside, looking through the metal filigree. Cameras were fixed to the tops of the gate supports; inside the estate's perimeter there were motion sensors and more cameras, both visible light and infrared, as well as buried ground-vibration detectors. The protective network was monitored from the security office inside the mansion; the building itself had its own separate, interior security system.

One of the guards came around to the cab and inspected the special passes issued to the television crew. He spoke heavily-accented English. Like Polanski, he also studied the license plates. The man inside the gates stood quite still, a few feet from the guardhouse, observing the proceedings. Dalton had to open the cargo space again, and the second KGB man searched it, this time without a dog.

They finished quickly enough to suit Dalton, and one of the KGB men called to the man by the guardhouse. This man took a small transmitter out of his raincoat pocket and spoke into it. The guard told Dalton, "That person will take you up to the house. He will stay with you while you are there. Do not leave the main road."

"Okay," Dalton said.

The gate swung open; Dalton drove through it and stopped. The guide climbed up onto the running board and hung on to the side mirror supports. "Up the lane," he said, in English. "I will show you where the service entrance is."

The truck rumbled along the lane, which was almost a tunnel under the trees; the dawn light did not penetrate the leaves overhead, and the headlights bored twin yellow beams through the darkness. Dalton kept the speed down, watching out of the corner of his eye the pale blur of the KGB officer's face.

The trees ended at a vast expanse of lawn. On a knoll ahead rose the mock-Tudor mansion, Killenworth, its half-timbering dark against the paler brick, even in the early dawn. Dalton recalled the mansion's history: built by George Dupont Pratt at the turn of the century; forty-nine rooms on thirty-seven acres, no outbuildings except the garages, bought by the Soviets in 1946 for their AMTORG trade mission, and then used as a retreat and secure enclave for their UN personnel based in New York. The lines of the roof were spoiled by antennas and satellite communications gear; the mansion served also as a base for spying on the local US aerospace industry. Grumman Aircraft Corporation, for example, was only a few miles away.

Pratt couldn't have imagined what would become of his estate when he built it, Dalton thought. Nor what history would be made here today.

''Take the right turn around to the back,'' the KGB officer said. ''The service entrance is there. You will see a light over it.''

I know, Dalton told him mentally. I know.

Even in the poor illumination, Dalton could see that the rear of the house was in poor repair, the grounds overgrown and the half-timbering eroded by rot. One of the mullioned windows on the ground floor had been broken, and was covered with a sheet of plastic, which flexed and thumped in the wind. The service entrance was at ground level at the west end of the house, near the garages. The security office was inside, near the service entrance, five yards along a corridor leading off to the right. Beyond that, the corridor made a couple of bends past the servants' stairs and the kitchen and ended at the dining room; beyond the dining room was the main entrance hall and the main staircase leading up to the second and third floors.

''Stop here.''

The mobile unit drew to a halt about ten feet away from the service door, and parallel to it. This was important; the camera above the door must not be directed into the cargo space. The door itself was a blank steel panel, with a touch-pad set into it. The single bulb lighting the area was placed well away from the camera, and above it.

''I will open the door while you get ready to bring the equipment in,'' said the KGB man.

''Okay,'' Dalton answered. Everything was ready. He glanced at the digital dashboard clock, which he had set precisely before starting out. By now the NBC dispatcher would have received word from his crew that their mobile unit had broken down, but it should still be awhile before the Secret Service checkpoint was told that the unit would be late. Everything would be over by then.

Dalton and Wheatley got out of the cab, went to the back of the truck, unlocked the door again and slid it up. Dalton climbed inside, leaving Wheatley to watch the KGB officer. The next sequence was timed at sixty-five seconds, brief enough to keep the guide from becoming suspicious. Dalton hurried to the front wall of the cargo space and tapped on it twice.

A crack appeared where the wall joined the roof. Dalton stepped back and took the weight of the false partition as it swung down. Behind it, in the eighteen inches of hidden space, were three men. One was tied to ring-bolts set into the real wall, and had a gag in his mouth; his wrists were secured tightly with padded shackles. The eyes above the gag betrayed a mixture of fear and rage.

The other two men also wore NBC coveralls and ID tags bearing the names Roger Blake and Peter Thorpe. Black ski masks covered their faces; both carried silenced Ingram machine pistols. They moved swiftly from the concealed compartment and reached back inside for a TV equipment case and a small stainless-steel canister, which had prevented the dog from sniffing out the explosive charges and detonators inside it. Thorpe closed the compartment door on the prisoner while Blake shoved the canister into the pocket of his coveralls. Both men nodded to Dalton.

Dalton checked his watch. They were on schedule.

"Ready for the first one," Wheatley said from the tailgate: the all-clear signal.

Dalton dragged the case to the open doorway, keeping count in his head. He let go of the box and dropped to the ground. Sixty-five.

He helped Wheatley lift the case out of the truck. With his free hand Wheatley turned on an electric lantern, shining its beam ahead to guide his footing on the rough flagstones. The KGB officer was standing impatiently at the service door, now wide open with yellow light spilling through it.

"Do you need help unloading?" he asked as they approached him.

"No," Dalton answered. "Jim, just a minute. I want to make sure we put the transformer in this thing."

They set the case down. Dalton knelt beside it and snapped back the latches. Wheatley idly moved the lantern to and fro, its beam hard and white in the dimness. The plastic sheeting over the nearby window flapped sharply in the wind. Dalton couldn't have asked for a better covering sound. He opened the case. Inside were two ski masks, two more Ingrams and a Browning 9mm automatic pistol; all three weapons had silencers.

"Keep that light clear of the camera," the KGB officer snapped. "It will blind it."

"Right," Wheatley said, and shone the beam full into the lens as Dalton's hand, holding the pistol, came up from the case. The KGB man's eyes widened and his mouth opened. Dalton put a bullet through it, the soft pop of the gun sounding just like the flap of the plastic sheeting. The Russian fell over backward, the back of his skull blown out by the ascending bullet.

Dalton dropped the Browning into the case and pulled out the two ski masks. He tossed one to Wheatley, who had already positioned the light so that it kept shining into the camera lens. The two men yanked the masks over their heads and grabbed the machine pistols.

Now.

Blake and Thorpe burst from the truck after them as Dalton and Wheatley rushed through the open service door into the corridor beyond it. They turned right and moved silently along the corridor to the security office. Its door was standing open; music drifted out: a radio playing. The duty officer and a second security man inside were just beginning to react to the blinding of the camera, the duty officer half out of his chair in front of the security control console, his companion reaching under it for the general alarm button. Wheatley shot the junior man through the head with a burst of three rounds; his skull dissolved into fragments of blood and brains that sprayed over the monitor screens and the control console. The duty officer threw his hands into the air. Dalton slammed him facedown on the console, holding him there with the Ingram's muzzle rammed into the side of his jaw. The music had stopped and the radio announcer was introducing the next song. Outside the house, wind whistled and howled.

"Turn off the systems!" Dalton hissed into the officer's ear, in English. "Inside and outside! *Now*!"

The duty officer reached out a shaky hand and punched codes

into a keypad. The monitors flickered and went blank; elsewhere in the mansion, the motion detectors and infrared beams died silently, and out in the grounds the sensors and cameras went blind. For the moment, Dalton and his men were safe.

That's done, he thought. He drew the Ingram's muzzle away from the duty officer's neck, aimed with exquisite care, and squeezed the trigger. There was a soft *phutt,* almost inaudible under the noise of the wind and the radio playing. The duty officer dropped heavily to the floor as Dalton let go of him.

Twelve seconds had passed since they entered the security office. Dalton followed Wheatley back into the hall. Blake and Thorpe were surveying the corridor's end, where it turned at right angles toward the kitchen. Five yards past the bend, a servants' staircase led up to the second and third floors; there would be a guard there, but Dalton was confident that the man would have heard nothing. He walked calmly to the bend in the corridor and stepped past it, the Ingram already aimed. The guard was there, all right, sitting on a wooden chair at the foot of the narrow staircase, staring blankly at the opposite wall. Dalton shot him three times at close range, before the man even realized he was in danger. The four raiders were in motion again before the guard hit the floor.

Dalton, followed by Wheatley, ran past the staircase; Thorpe and Blake ascended it to deal with the communications staff on the third story, along with the other KGB guard shift that would be asleep up there. Dalton's target was on the second floor.

He saw the kitchen entrance just ahead, on the right. At this hour, the room was empty. The kitchen corridor ended in a double-leafed door; the right-hand leaf was standing open. On the other side of the door lay the cavernous dining room, and on the far side of that was another double door of carved oak that opened into the main entrance hall. The two men hurried across the dining room and stopped just inside the doorway. On the far wall of the entrance foyer, and perhaps two yards toward the huge iron-bound front doors, hung an enormous gilt-framed mirror. In its reflection Dalton could see a suit of armor whose breastplate glinted dully in the light from above, where the staircase curved up to the second floor. He could also see a KGB guard sitting on a wooden chair facing the front doors, his back to the hallway. He couldn't shoot him; there'd be two more KGB men up on the second floor, and Dalton dared not risk the clatter the chair might make as the guard toppled over. This one would have to die another way.

Dalton moved carefully into the hall, his soft-soled shoes noiseless on the polished oak. The guard didn't stir, and there was more than enough noise from the wind outside to mask any sound Dalton might have made. He reached striking distance and leaped forward, circling the man's throat with his forearm, clamping tight to prevent a shout. The guard stiffened, and then relaxed as he felt the muzzle of the Ingram pressing into his jawline.

"On the floor," Dalton whispered. "Facedown."

He kept his arm clamped around the guard's throat until the man had complied. Then Dalton put the Ingram down and struck the guard with the edge of his stiffened hand, delivering a killing chop to the back of the neck. Wheatley, who had been watching in the mirror, joined Dalton as he retrieved his gun and stood up.

The two men started up the broad carpeted staircase, as silent as mousing cats. Near the top of the stairs, Dalton paused. Very carefully, he peered around the newel. The hallway was empty.

He and Wheatley dashed the rest of the way up the stairs and ran along the dimly-lit corridor, Wheatley behind. At the bend in the corridor Dalton stopped. This was the delicate part.

He braced himself mentally and signalled Wheatley. They stepped past the corner, out into the open. Two KGB men were posted at the door to the target's suite, ten yards away. They saw the intruders simultaneously and reached for their weapons, which were lying on the floor beside their chairs. Aiming very carefully, Dalton shot the man nearest him, the gun's reports only a soft stutter. Beside him, he heard Wheatley's Ingram whisper, its bullet stream catching the other guard in the chest and throwing him onto the floor. The guard's chair fell over with a barely audible thump.

The way into the target suite was clear. Dalton and Wheatley raced to its entrance, stepping over the guards' bodies, and stood at each side of the double doors leading into the suite. Dalton looked at his watch. Three seconds early; not bad.

He heard a faint sound, almost inaudible under the rush of the wind outside. It came from the far end of the hall, near the landing for the servants' staircase. Blake and Thorpe stepped into the corridor, weapons ready. Dalton gave them the success signal, and tested the handle of the door to the suite. It turned easily and silently, as though recently oiled. He pushed, and the heavy wooden panel swung open without the hint of a creak. Inside the door was a sitting room; just enough light filtered in from the hallway to make out the shapes of furniture. At the far side of the sitting room was another door, which was standing half open.

The four men slipped across the carpet to the doorway. Dalton looked through it. The room was very faintly lit as dawn crept through the mullioned windows, and he could see the shape of the sleeper hunched under the counterpane on the huge canopied bed. He nodded at Wheatley. Together they entered the bedroom. Dalton stood above the sleeper and looked down.

The covers were half over the man's face. Dalton pulled them back gently, to confirm that the sleeper was the person they were after. Dalton put the muzzle of his Ingram under the side of the man's jaw and clamped his other hand over his mouth.

The man's eyes flew open; he tried to say something before he realized that his mouth was sealed and that there was a gun muzzle at his throat. His body went rigid.

This was the most dangerous moment so far. "Be quiet!" Dalton hissed in Russian. "Or I will kill you."

The man's eyes flicked toward the foot of the bed where Wheatley stood, his Ingram clearly outlined in the gray light from the window. Rain beat at the glass. After a second's hesitation, he nodded.

"Gag," whispered Dalton.

He kept the gun muzzle at the man's throat until Wheatley had secured the gag. Then Dalton prodded the man onto his stomach and Wheatley clamped handcuffs around his wrists. The target was wearing blue silk pajamas.

"On your feet."

He struggled erect. Wheatley grabbed him by the back of his collar and propelled him toward the door, the Ingram's barrel jabbing into the small of his back. The target stiffened when he saw Blake and Thorpe; he had probably hoped there were only two raiders.

Along the corridor to the top of the stairs. "Communications?" Dalton softly queried Blake. He spoke in Polish now.

"As scheduled. We got everyone we could find."

"Good." In less than four minutes, the mansion's radio links with Moscow would be broken. Plenty of time for everything.

The target almost stumbled going down the staircase; it might have been on purpose, to make a noise. Wheatley grabbed his shoulder and stabbed him viciously in a kidney with the muzzle of the Ingram. The target winced and gave a soft grunt. Dalton glared at him. The man's eyes above the gag glared back; if he was frightened, he wasn't showing it.

He'd be a handful if we allowed it, Dalton thought. But we knew that from the beginning; he didn't get where he is by being weak.

As they hurried him along the corridor toward the security office and the service entrance, the expression of fury on the man's face took on an anxious edge; he must have been hoping to encounter at least some security staff on the ground floor, despite the danger of such a meeting. The thought that all his men might be dead or incapacitated obviously hadn't occurred to him until now.

They passed the security office; the prisoner glanced in and saw the bodies. Dalton met his gaze for a moment. The man was thinking, as clearly as if he had said it: *How could this have been allowed to happen*? Dalton wondered briefly how long their captive would take to figure it out. Probably not long; he was a clever man.

Blake and Thorpe had gone on ahead. When Dalton and Wheatley emerged into the dark wet of the morning with their captive, Blake was bending over the dead KGB officer, pulling the man's PSM pistol out of its shoulder holster.

One more detail to take care of, Dalton thought. Apart from getting away. That could still be tricky. Their best ally was surprise. Nobody would be expecting a team of raiders to be fighting their way *out* of Killenworth.

They heaved the target into the back of the van and snapped cuffs around his ankles. Then Dalton opened the false partition, cut the other prisoner loose from the ring bolts, and helped Thorpe and Wheatley drag him out into the cargo space. From the compartment Dalton then removed a second canister of explosives, and a larger protective metal box containing a pair of tubular devices as long as his arm: M72A2 LAWs, light antitank weapons.

While he unpacked the LAWs, the other two raiders hauled their first prisoner out of the van and over to the dead KGB officer. They sat the prisoner down on the wet flagstones in front of Blake, who was holding the PSM. The prisoner's eyes widened in terror, and he made futile efforts to escape Wheatley's grip. Blake slipped a silencer over the pistol muzzle, put the gun into the dead KGB officer's hand, and shot the prisoner twice, once in the heart and once in the right lung. Wheatley lowered him to the ground and removed the padded manacles, which he stuffed into his coveralls.

Dalton was already in the cab with the second canister of explosives and the LAWs. As he started the engine he heard thumps from behind as Blake clambered into the back and closed the door on himself, Thorpe and the target. Wheatley climbed into the cab.

"No marks on him?" Dalton asked as he put the mobile unit into gear and started it moving. They were exactly on time.

"No. There's no sign he's been bound."

"Good."

It was still far from light, and the rain was becoming heavier, decreasing visibility even more. Dalton heard a muffled *thud* overhead: the explosives detonating in the radio room. It was a small charge, just enough to wreck the transmitters.

Everything was going perfectly.

Polanski looked at his watch. He'd be going off duty in a few minutes, and he was glad of it. The rain and the wind off the Sound had chilled him until he ached with cold and fatigue. The shelter tent next to the barricade helped a little, but if he'd known the weather was going to be this miserable, he'd have bought a Coleman stove. Even the coffee in the thermoses was lukewarm.

"Alex!"

Conroy was calling from the tent flap. Something in his voice made Polanski's skin tingle. "What?"

"Call from HQ. They say the NBC mobile's been delayed."

"*What?*"

Polanski ran for the tent entrance and darted inside. Grabbing the radio microphone he said, "Pinnacle here. Over."

"Pinnacle, this is Blue Tower. We have an advisory for you. NBC News just told us their mobile unit broke down on the freeway, and they're sending another one. It will be there by seven A.M. Please prepare to copy personnel and document data. Over."

This can't be happening, Polanski thought. Ohmigod. "Blue Tower, this is Pinnacle. The NBC mobile unit passed this checkpoint and the Soviet one approximately fifteen minutes ago. Over."

A silence. Then: "This is Blue Tower. Are you sure? Over."

Polanski forgot radio discipline. "Of course I'm sure, goddamn it. I was inside the thing myself. Full of TV equipment. Are you sure NBC hasn't got its wires crossed? Over." Please let that be true, he thought.

"This is Blue Tower. The NBC mobile broke down, repeat broke down. Over."

"This is Pinnacle," Polanski said. Conroy and the other agents in the tent were staring anxiously at him. "Emphasize we had an NBC truck pass this point. All ID details cleared, license plates, personnel, NBC documentation. NBC dispatcher must be wrong. Over."

"This is Blue Tower. Pinnacle, we repeat, NBC has positive ID on broken-down mobile unit. Assume you have intruder. What in hell's happened out there, anyway? Over."

"This is Pinnacle. We don't know yet. Will advise. Over."

"This is Blue Tower. Will keep this channel open. Contact Red Tower security and report. Over."

"Acknowledged, over," Polanski said. He spun to face Conroy. "Alert the perimeter units. See if the chopper can get off the ground. I'm calling the Soviet security HQ up there."

He heard Conroy getting onto the perimeter communications band while he keyed for the Russian security office in the mansion. At least the man up there spoke good English.

Two minutes later, he realized that it was worse than he could have imagined. The Russians weren't answering.

Something had gone horribly wrong at Killenworth.

The ground was rough with fallen branches and undergrowth, but there was more than enough room for the mobile unit to pass among the trees. The windshield wipers slapped at sodden leaves.

"There's the fence," Dalton observed. He could barely see the iron bars in the darkness beneath the trees. "Knock it down." He stopped the van.

He could have saved his breath; Wheatley was already halfway out the door with the explosives. He ran to the fence, knelt and opened the metal case. Inside were four shaped explosive charges, one for each end of the two horizontal iron girders supporting the fence. Wheatley fitted the charges around the girders, set the fuses and ran back to the cab. Both men ducked below the dashboard, in case of fragments. Six seconds ticked by, then there were four sharp cracks. Something struck the windshield, but not hard enough to damage it. Dalton surfaced from beneath the dashboard in time to see the fencing topple forward; the way to the beach was clear. Wheatley readied his Ingram, with the side window open; the woods should have muffled the bang of the shaped charges, but it was possible that one of the Secret Service men was near enough to have detected the noise. That could pose a problem; if they were suspicious enough to put a helicopter over the Sound, the escape would be that much more difficult in spite of the firepower provided by the LAWs. But the bad weather was an unexpected ally; it would make air surveillance difficult, even if the authorities could get a helicopter aloft in this wind.

The van lurched forward, tires skidding on the grillwork of the fence. On the other side of the estate boundary, the land sloped gently northwest toward a small body of water called the West Pond, which was connected to Long Island Sound by a shallow channel. One road to cross, and they'd be within a hundred yards of the motor launch.

"Get ready with a LAW," Dalton said. Here was where they were most likely to encounter an armored security patrol. He slowed the van so Wheatley could open the door and climb out onto the running board with the antitank weapon. You couldn't fire a LAW in a confined space like the van cab, because of the rocket projectile's backblast.

The trees thinned; ahead was the road. Dalton caught a glimpse of headlights on its shoulder. A vehicle was approaching from the right. It was a Commando armored car.

The van lurched out from under the trees, engine laboring in low gear. A man, mouth wide open in a shout, appeared in the Commando's turret hatch, pointing to the van as it climbed onto the pavement. The turret's machine guns began to track the mobile unit.

Wheatley didn't hesitate. He jumped to the ground from the slowly moving van, aimed and fired. There was a blinding flash as the antitank rocket leaped from its tube, shot across the space between Wheatley and the Commando, and struck the armored vehicle squarely beneath the turret overhang. The detonation blew the turret clean off the Commando's deck, and shredded the crewman inside it. Flames rose from the gaping hole in the armor. Wheatley ran to catch up with the mobile unit, and jumped onto its running board just as Dalton accelerated into the undergrowth on the other side of the road.

Shit, Dalton thought. They found out sooner than we'd expected. Have to trust the weather and bad visibility, now. Something always goes wrong, no matter how well you plan.

The van lurched into the open, with Wheatley clinging grimly to the side mirror supports. Ahead was the shore of the West Pond, and beyond the Pond the channel that led to the Sound. A dark shadow near the shore: the motor launch. The dinghy was waiting, drawn up on the beach; the launch's captain stood beside it.

Dalton stopped the van and jumped out of the cab, leaving the engine running. Blake already had the cargo door up; he and Thorpe hauled the prisoner roughly out of the back, and dragged him down the sand to the shoreline and the dinghy, while Wheatley, ready with the other LAW and his Ingram, scanned the woods behind.

"How's the sea?" Dalton asked the captain.

"Rough. But not dangerous," the captain replied. He bent over the small outboard. It was warm and fired immediately. Dalton pushed the prisoner into the bottom of the dinghy, and helped the others shove off. Wheatley, as rear guard, was last in.

As Wheatley scrambled aboard, Dalton glanced at the man they had taken. Rain was soaking into the blue silk pajamas, and had plastered the thin strands of the captive's hair to his balding scalp. He was shivering violently in the chill September wind.

Mikhail Sergeyevich Gorbachev, general secretary of the Communist Party of the Soviet Union, head of the Politburo and leader of the Union of Soviet Socialist Republics, was obviously very cold.

Orchard Harbor, Maine
September 29

SEAN BRENNAN strolled by the sea, watching the sun come up. The bad weather had blown away to the southwest just before dawn, and the sky was slowly lightening to an unclouded blue. It would be hours before the Atlantic calmed, though; long and slate-gray, streaked with bubbles in the troughs, the rollers broke and formed and broke again, driving sheets of foam far up the shingle of the beach where Brennan walked.

It's fall, he thought, stopping at the path that ascended the clay bluffs to the house above. Where did the summer go?

He imagined he could feel the breakers' vibrations though the soles of his running shoes; even this far from the tideline, droplets of spray brushed his face. Half a mile northward, the lighthouse at the mouth of the harbor was still blinking rhythmically. As he watched, the automatic machinery registered that day had come, and the light was extinguished.

Another bad night, Brennan thought. Goddamn it. Why now, of all times?

He put two fingers in his mouth and whistled to a dog, which was sniffing with far too much interest at what could only be a dead gull at the bottom of the path. The dog ignored him.

"Haig, dammit!" Brennan yelled. "Get out of that! *Bath?*"

The dog, a gray-and-white bearded collie mixed with terrier, promptly left the corpse and trotted toward him, tail drooping apprehensively. Brennan bent over and rubbed the animal behind the ears. ''No bath,'' Brennan said reassuringly. ''Just keep out of the garbage, okay?''

The dog, relieved, sat down and scratched. Brennan straightened up and pulled the collar of his white nylon windbreaker closer around his neck. He was a little over average height, broad-shouldered and solid-boned after the pattern of his Irish ancestry, with reddish-brown hair, brown eyes and a straight nose with slightly flared nostrils. His mouth was a little too large for his face, and some muscular oddity made it turn up at the corners. This quirk made his usual expression that of a man cheerful with himself and the world around him. It was as good as a poker face, in its way, and Brennan knew it. He had been concealing himself behind that deceptive smile for most of his life.

It's a good thing Molly understands, he thought, watching the breakers tumble in and out. That it's not Jane haunting me, not she herself, but the way she died. My helplessness in it. Jane's gone. I did what I could, afterward. I have to stop being afraid that it might happen again.

He looked farther out to sea. A huge roller was forming out beyond the surf, one of those freak storm waves that gather the energy of a dozen smaller waves. The roller towered over the broken water before it, devouring the foam of the previous breaker, until the land began to drag at its base; the friction of water and sand increased until crest outran trough, and the wave peak collapsed in a crash that shook the gravel beneath Brennan's feet and exploded in echoes against the face of the cliff above him.

The echo of a bomb.

They'd gone to Munich for the *Fasching*, the carnival, at Jane's insistence; she'd been worried for some months that he'd been driving himself too hard. In those days he was a case officer at the CIA station in Bonn, during the crisis over Reagan's decision to install American cruise and Pershing missiles in Europe, to offset the threat of the Soviet SS20s. They'd been married for six months, and he'd hardly been able to spend a weekend with her. She was the daughter of an English diplomat, the first woman who had been able to reach through the armor of his self-sustaining smile and remain there.

They'd arrived Saturday morning; Saturday evening they

started off for the Augustiner-Keller beer hall — Jane had a fondness for German beer — and, just as they were leaving the hotel, it started to snow. She'd insisted he go back up to the room and put on a scarf; he was recovering from a touch of bronchitis. Grumbling, he did so, while she waited on the hotel steps.

He was about to enter the elevator when the terrorists' car bomb went off on the other side of the street. The blast smashed his wife through the glass doors of the hotel entrance, and then drove her thirty feet across the lobby into a marble pillar. Brennan was protected from the flying glass by the same pillar; when he reached her she was, somehow, still alive, although so ruined that she was unrecognizable as the woman he had left on the hotel steps seconds before. She lingered in the hospital for four days, never regaining consciousness, and then died with Brennan beside her. For the eight years that followed her death — until he met Molly, and even for a time after that — not a day had gone by without his imagining that she'd come back to the elevators with him, that the pillar had protected them both. Even now he remembered clearly how the beep of the heart monitor descended into a steady tone as she left him.

The broken water from the great roller was receding. Brennan's lips tasted of salt and his cheeks were damp from the spray. The dog had been frightened by the wave and was looking apprehensively out to sea, nose twitching. Brennan absentmindedly patted him on the head.

It doesn't make any sense to still feel this way, Brennan thought. There was nothing I could have done. I didn't know what was going to happen. What kept me awake last night . . . ? It's not guilt so much as the feeling of powerlessness her death left me with. Vulnerability. That there's nothing you can do, finally, to protect anyone, even someone you love. That the world's arbitrary, without purpose, that there's no reason for anything to happen, or not to happen.

Three years hunting them down. The station chief watched me like a hawk for the first year, didn't want me going off the rails and doing something reckless. But I wasn't reckless about it, and he never knew what I'd done, nor did anyone until I told Molly. Three years it took, but I found them.

West Berlin, January. The temperature was well below freezing, and a bitter wind whipped snow into Brennan's face as he hailed a cab at the taxi stand outside the Tegel airport terminal.

"Hotel Hamburg," he told the driver. The taxi set off through the early winter evening.

He checked into the hotel, using the Fritz Kellerman passport, and went up to his room. He didn't unpack the overnight bag, but left it on the bed next to the attaché case containing one hundred thousand deutsche marks, in small bills. Half an hour until the call was due. He sat at the window for a while, looking out at the lights of West Berlin. Then he put his coat back on, picked up the attaché case and went outside.

The designated telephone kiosk was half a block away, at the corner of Kurfurstenstrasse; hard flecks of snow ticked against the kiosk's plastic shell as he entered it. He pretended to busy himself with the telephone directory, waiting.

The telephone rang. Brennan picked it up.

"Herr Kellerman, please." Through the earpiece, Brennan could hear traffic noises: Dieter Mack was also calling from a kiosk.

"This is Kellerman," Brennan said. He wasn't worried about being taken for a foreigner; his German was flawless.

"Are there any problems?"

"No."

"Good. Twenty minutes."

Brennan hung up and went back out into the snow. A few minutes' walk took him across the canal — frozen and white under the streetlights along its banks — to Corneliusstrasse. He went up Lichtensteinallee, which ran along the edge of the Tiergarten park, and past the café that stood on the banks of the tiny lake Berliners called the Neuer See.

Mack was waiting for him at the end of Lichtensteinallee. He was bundled up against the cold, a scarf pulled across his mouth so that only his eyes and cheeks and nose were exposed; frost condensed from his breath clung to the scarf. He was shorter than Brennan, and stocky, with a big round lump of a nose that protruded almost horizontally from his face. He had once been a terrorist.

Mack's right hand was in his pocket. In this pocket, pointed at Brennan, would be a gun. During their one previous meeting, the German had taken similar precautions. "Did you bring the money?" he asked.

"Yes. In the bag here." Brennan had cleared out half his personal account to put the cash together; there had been no possible way to use CIA station funding.

"Let me see it."

Brennan opened the case a little, shielding it from the wind with his body. Mack looked briefly inside and then nodded. "Good West German marks, comrade," Brennan said, closing the case. "We use their own money against them."

"Yes," Mack replied. "There will be more, though?"

"Of course," said Brennan. "This is only to establish goodwill. We're prepared to finance you much more fully than this. Depending on results."

"There'll be results," Mack said. "We'll put some more capitalists against the wall, soon. We'd like to go after more of the war industrialists, like Schleyer. But it will be expensive."

"If we are financing you this directly," Brennan said sharply, "we'll designate targets."

"We can talk about it," Mack responded. "Come with me."

He'd be taking Brennan to a safe house. There, Mack would expect to start negotiating the cooperation of his Red Kommando urban terrorist group with the organization he thought Brennan represented — the East German security and espionage service, known as the SSD. Reaching this point had taken all Brennan's skill and resources, especially since he was working alone; the files and contacts of the Bonn CIA station had been a tremendous help, but he'd been limited in their use by the need to hide what he was doing from his superiors. Nevertheless, he had been able to piece together from the files a pattern that no one else had had the time or the persistence to identify.

Mack, as he walked beside Brennan, was no longer a terrorist; at least, he himself no longer killed, robbed, kidnapped, or exploded bombs in busy streets. But he was a conduit, or so Brennan was convinced. The West German police had suspected the same for a time, but they had been able to prove nothing and eventually lost interest. And they had never connected the now thirty-three-year-old Frankfurt businessman with another man named Gerd Fichte, who was known to be leader of the Red Kommando team that had exploded a bomb during the Munich *Fasching* of 1980. Fichte had gone underground and stayed there. Mack hadn't needed to; he appeared to be a good West German capitalist, with absolutely no connection to Red Kommando or to the bomb deaths in Munich.

From studying the Bonn files, Brennan was certain of all three of Mack's connections: to Fichte, to Red Kommando and to Jane's death. Had Brennan passed his conclusions and his evidence to the station chief, Mack would have been in deep trouble, but Brennan had long ago decided to settle his accounts personally with Jane's murderers. He wanted not only Mack but Fichte, now rumored to have taken over the leadership of Red Kommando.

The problem had been to get Fichte into the open. Politics had played into Brennan's hands.

The Bonn station had known for some time that the KGB and SSD were looking for ways to halt or delay the installation of Pershing II and cruise missiles in Western Europe. A week before this encounter, Brennan had called Mack in Frankfurt and requested a meeting "to discuss a business arrangement of mutual interest." Mack assented, not without suspicion, which had been doubly apparent when the meeting took place two days later. Using a selection of carefully forged documents and his inside knowledge of SSD organization and techniques, Brennan convinced Mack that he was indeed who he was pretending to be: an SSD lieutenant-colonel assigned to foment trouble for the Americans and the West German government. The act wouldn't have fooled a professional intelligence officer for very long, but Mack wasn't one. Brennan told the German that there would be an immediate payment of one hundred thousand marks, "for operational expenses," on one condition: Brennan was to meet the field commander of Red Kommando, to coordinate planning.

That went over, although with some difficulty. Now Brennan was hoping that the field commander would indeed be Fichte.

He followed Mack back to Corneliusstrasse, where the German stopped beside a black Opel and fumbled in his left pocket for his keys. "Is this your car?" Brennan asked.

"No, of course not." Mack opened the passenger door and gestured Brennan in. "It's someone else's."

Brennan put the case containing the money into the back, closed the car door behind him and settled into the seat. Mack slipped behind the wheel and started the engine. The windshield began to fog as the moisture of their breath reached it, and Mack turned on the defrosters with quick, efficient movements.

"Are you quite certain there is no surveillance on you?" Brennan asked.

"Yes," Mack said, as he put the Opel into gear and pulled away from the curb. A trace of irritation crept into his voice. "I am extremely careful. I always have been. That's why I continue to be free."

"Good," said Brennan. "Where are we going?"

"Somewhere."

Within a few minutes it became clear that they were heading northwest. Mack checked his mirror regularly but with a routine air; he seemed quite satisfied that no one would be following them. Brennan studied the German inconspicuously: the prominent bulb of a nose, the pudgy cheeks, the round chin nestled in the expensive silk scarf. Some portly men looked cheerful and good-natured. Mack did not; his eyes were too watchful by far. Killer's eyes, Brennan thought. I've waited a long time for this. This is the man, one of the men, who smashed my wife, a woman they'd neither seen nor heard of, into a stone pillar, without carring what they did to her, or to me, or to anyone else.

Mack turned the Opel into Mullerstrasse. Brennan guessed that they were heading for Reinickendorf, a neighborhood populated by transients and foreign workers. A good place for a safe house; police weren't popular there.

Mack said, "Open the glove compartment. There are special glasses in there. Put them on. You are not to see where we are going."

Brennan obediently found the glasses. They were silvered, like sunglasses, but coated black on the inside. Shields attached to the earpieces prevented the wearer from seeing to the sides. They were as good as a blindfold, but much less conspicuous.

He tried to use the Opel's movement to judge the overall direction Mack was taking, but lost track very quickly. The man was following a circuitous route to their destination. After a few more minutes the car stopped.

"Wait," Mack said. "I'll open the door."

Brennan heard him getting out of the car, and then the crunch of his boots on snow as he came around to the passenger side. Brennan's door clicked, and swung open.

"Out," Mack said. "I will take your arm. Here's the money case. Carry it. Keep the glasses on until we are inside."

Brennan obeyed. The traffic noises were distant; they were well away from any main streets, then.

"Three steps up," Mack said. "Right here."

Brennan went up the steps, feeling Mack's grip through the sleeve of his overcoat. He heard a key slide into a lock, and the creak of a hinge. Warmer air puffed over his cheeks. He stepped forward under Mack's guidance, and heard a door thud closed behind him. The door sounded heavy.

"Take the glasses off now," Mack said. "Give them to me."

Brennan did as he was told, and looked around. They were standing in a medium-sized room, with a stone floor and crumbling brick walls. The room was dimly lit by a low-wattage overhead bulb suspended from a rusted metal beam high overhead; three or four wooden crates were scattered about the floor. In front of Brennan was an open doorway, about nine feet high and twice as wide. Through the doorway he could see a large, dark space with more wooden and cardboard crates stacked inside. He and Mack were in a warehouse.

Mack was slipping the glasses into his left pocket; his other hand had disappeared into his right pocket again. He looked tense.

"I have to search you," he said. "Raise your arms."

"Very well," Brennan said. He put the attaché case on the dusty floor. "Although it is not necessary for you to treat me like an enemy. You know who I am."

"I know who you say you are," Mack told him. He ran his left hand over Brennan's torso, then his legs, and under his arms. Brennan submitted patiently.

Mack stepped away from him, removing his gloved hand from his right pocket. "He's not armed," he called into the dimness beyond the doorway.

A man slipped around the edge of the door. He wore a leather jacket, faded jeans, leather boots and a dark wool scarf. His hair was thinner than it had been in the photographs that Brennan had studied, but there was no mistaking the pointed chin and the broad, thin mouth. Fichte.

"Herr Fichte," Brennan said. "Good evening."

Fichte looked at Mack. "Did you tell him who I was?"

"No," Mack said. He looked worried. He's afraid of Fichte, Brennan thought.

Fichte returned his attention to Brennan. "You're the SSD man, then."

"Yes."

"You've brought the money?"

"Yes. It's in the case here." Brennan gestured at it.

"I've seen it," Mack said. "It appears to be all there."

Fichte was studying Brennan intently, as though trying to look through his skull to the thoughts within. "What do you want?" he asked.

"We need to come to an understanding about targeting," Brennan said. "We are more than happy to finance the revolutionary struggle against the capitalists, but there must be firm direction from the center. Otherwise our efforts will be dissipated and ineffective."

"I see," Fichte said. He sat on the edge of a crate, a body's length from Brennan. "Why do your people believe they know more about targeting than we do? *We* are the people in the center of things."

"That's true," Brennan replied. "But we are able to acquire information you can't. Movements of prominent people, for example. It will enhance the revolutionary struggle, make it much more effective, if we cooperate fully."

Mack had moved away from Brennan a little, and was standing just a few feet to Brennan's right. His gloved hands hung loosely at his sides.

"Explain," Fichte said. He seemed interested, despite his clear suspicion of Brennan.

"I brought more than money," Brennan said. "We have a target we think you will be delighted with. I have with me a dossier on this man."

"Who?" Mack asked.

Fichte scowled at him. "Where's the dossier?"

"With the money, in my case."

"Let me see it."

Brennan picked up the attaché case and walked over to the crate

Fichte was sitting on. This was a critical moment; the man might perceive the movement as a threat, and drive Brennan off while he looked at the dossier. It was essential that the three of them be close together.

The moment passed smoothly. Fichte moved aside and let Brennan put the attaché case on top of the crate. Brennan unlocked it, and swung it open and began removing the bundled stacks of deutsche marks. Underneath the bills was a manila folder.

"Look in it," Brennan said. He sensed Mack moving up on his right side. Mack first, then.

Fichte removed the folder and opened it. Inside were several sheets of typewritten paper. The German began to study it. After a moment or two, his eyes widened. He looked up at Brennan. "What is it?" Mack asked.

Brennan stepped back to give Mack room to look. They were unprofessional, all right. "You should be able to guess who it is from his daily itinerary," Brennan said. "Look at the routes, and the destinations."

"*Gott in Himmel,*" Fichte breathed, studying the file. "The West German Minister of Defense."

Mack was crowding in, excited. "But is he vulnerable?" he said. "We might know all his movements, but not be able to touch him —"

"On the next page," Brennan said. "There *is* a vulnerable point that no one has noticed."

Fichte turned the page, intent, distracted.

Brennan raised his right arm and smashed his clenched fist onto the back of Mack's neck, the short cylinder of lead concealed in the palm of his glove converting his hand into the equivalent of a blackjack. Bone crunched as the vertebrae collapsed inward, severing the spinal cord. The German collapsed onto the crate and the dossier; papers scattered. Fichte jerked upward in shock.

Brennan was already recovering from the blow that had killed Mack, spinning on the ball of his left foot, his weighted glove driving toward Fichte's larynx. The German was quick. He twisted his head away and the blow slammed into the left side of his jaw, smashing it inward. He emitted an agonized croak and stumbled sideways, his face suddenly misshapen. He fumbled at his jacket.

He shouldn't have gone for the gun, Brennan thought as he drove his left hand forward, the fingers stiffened into a battering ram of flesh and bone, and struck Fichte in the right tricep. The gun clattered to the stone floor.

"You shit!" Fichte screamed, blood sputtering from his broken mouth, as he clutched his numbed arm. "*Traitor —*"

He was defenseless.

Jane had been defenseless.

Brennan didn't hesitate. He hit Fichte across the bridge of the nose as hard as he could, smashing bone into the frontal lobes of the brain. Fichte dropped, his voice suddenly sliced off . . . .

The warehouse was instantly very quiet. Brennan looked down at the two men he had killed. He felt nothing; he hadn't expected to. That would come later, perhaps.

He gathered up the false dossier, set a match to it and rubbed the ashes into the floor. He stuffed the money back into the attaché case. He found the keys to the Opel in Mack's overcoat and slipped out of the warehouse; the snow had stopped and above the narrow street the sky glowed dull orange.

He drove the car as far as the Birkenstrasse U-bahn station, and abandoned it there.

Brennan whistled at Haig, who was pretending not to be making another try for the dead sea gull, and started up the path along the face of the bluff. The exercise slowly pushed Berlin to the back of his mind, where it belonged, and he began to notice his surroundings again. The hard clay of the path was eroding in two or three places; next spring he'd have to do some maintenance to keep it usable. It was the shortest way down to the shore from the house, and if it wore away completely they'd have to start going round by the village.

Halfway up he paused to look at the view. Orchard Harbor was built at the mouth of a small river that opened into a naturally sheltered bay protected by breakwaters. A small white lighthouse stood at the far end of the south breakwater; upstream, where the main village road crossed the river, was a lift bridge to allow the fishing boats passage from the harbor to the freezing plant that processed their catch. The river wasn't, in fact, called a river at all; it was named Thorn Creek, after the first family to settle in the area. Local residents referred to it simply as The Creek.

Brennan started climbing again. He was slightly out of breath by the time he reached the top of the bluff, and the lawn in front of the house. Standing fifty feet or so from the cliff edge, the two-story frame house had weathered gray siding and a veranda across the front, facing the ocean. Its nearest neighbor was two hundred yards away, toward the main village. Orchard Harbor was itself rather isolated; there was only one paved road leading into the place, and the nearest commuter airport was an hour away, at Portland. The isolation suited both Brennan and Molly. They had bought the house in March, and she'd moved before he did, at the beginning of July; Brennan had been coming up from Washington on weekends. This weekly separation would end on Tuesday, the day after his resignation from the CIA took effect, when he would move their last odds and ends out of the Washington town house and bring them home to Orchard Harbor.

Brennan liked living near water. Before retiring, Brennan's father had been an officer in the New York Police Department; usually, he could scrape together enough money every year for the family — Brennan had a younger sister, Kathleen — to spend a week's holiday by the seashore at Cape Cod. Even in New York, when he was growing up on the edge of Queens, Brennan had spent hours on weekends haunting the shoreline, riding his bicycle (to his mother's despair) as far as Manhasset Bay and Kings Point to watch the freighters pass through Long Island Sound. Occasionally he saw the lean gray shapes of naval vessels, and a few times the huge flatiron silhouette of an aircraft carrier. He had promised himself that someday he'd live where he could look out the window in the morning and see the ocean. He had finally managed it, to his deep satisfaction.

He paused at the top of the path and looked across the lawn. The sun was well up now, striking gold reflections from the windowpanes of the house. Haig trotted ahead of him to the steps, nosed the screen door open, and disappeared inside. Brennan heard a clink of china, and Molly stepped out onto the veranda. She was carrying a coffeepot and cups on a tray, which she set down so she could wave to him.

"Morning!"

"Morning!" he called back, unzipping his jacket; the wind seemed to be dropping and the air had a hint of Indian-summer warmth in it. The day promised to be a perfect one.

"Out for a walk?" she asked as he mounted the veranda steps. There was a trace of concern in her voice; she always knew when he was troubled.

"Yeah. I saw one hell of a big wave. I thought it was going to wash me all the way up the cliff and in the front door."

"I'm glad it didn't. Salt water's not good for the floors."

He smiled, looking at her as he flopped down in one of the deck chairs. Molly Carpenter was the daughter of a retired air force colonel, and had grown up at military bases all over the world, an air force brat. She had been widowed at twenty-three when her husband, a pilot, died in a helicopter crash in West Germany. Now thirty-six, two years younger than Brennan, she was a strikingly attractive woman. The morning sun accentuated the reddish highlights in her heavy brown hair, worn short with a slight curl. Her eyes were blue, set off by dark eyelashes under arched eyebrows that gave her a quizzical look, as though she found the world, and the people in it, odd and faintly astonishing. She had clear skin, flawless even in strong sunlight, although there were tiny wrinkles at the corners of her eyes. As usual, there were traces of oil pigments on the cuticles of her fingernails; she was a talented landscape painter.

"Worse than the floors," he said, "it would have ruined the coffee."

She poured and handed him his mug. "Seriously, though," she said, "you ought to be careful down there, when the sea's up."

"Mm," he responded. "I know." She had added a dash of cinnamon to the coffee; the fragrance of the spice made him realize he was hungry.

"Since we didn't sleep in after all," she said, "I suppose I ought to go and put the phone back on the hook."

"Leave it. If anybody wants to talk to us, they can wait."

"Good idea," she agreed. They both watched the sea, sipping coffee.

"Is it bothering you again?" she asked suddenly. "Munich?"

There was no point trying to hide it from her. "Some."

"Can I help?"

"You already have. It's going away, bit by bit."

"You were dreaming last night."

He looked out at the line where the dark blue-gray of the Atlantic met the lighter blue of the sky. The line was broken by the horizontal black stroke of a tanker's hull. "Yes, I was."

"What about?"

"I can't remember. As usual."

Her palm pressed hard into the back of his wrist. He put his hand over hers. "I'll be glad to get out of Washington," he said, trying to change the subject. "Out of Langley. Tomorrow's the last Monday. I really am tired of it, you know. Once it seemed fascinating, knowing what the Poles were doing, the Czechs, the East Germans, what the Warsaw Pact general staff was planning to do tomorrow, next week, whenever. None of it seems to have made any difference. The world's still the same damn place."

"Not all of it. Not here."

"No," he said. "Not here." Suddenly he shaded his eyes, peering south along the coast. He had detested the faint thrum of a helicopter's engine. The sound reminded him of Viet Nam. There it was, the tiniest of specks, just over the headland five miles away. He heard the clock striking eight in the living room: four pairs of chimes, eight bells. It was a distinctive chime based on the nautical watch system: two bells for one o'clock, four bells for two o'clock, and so on.

"I wish you'd stop worrying," she said. "I can tell when you're worrying."

He looked over at her. "Sometimes," he said, "I'm afraid you'll feel I'm disloyal. To you."

"I know how you felt about Jane," Molly said. "But I don't see her as a ghost hanging over us. I'd think less of you if you were ready to forget her because of me. You're actually a very loyal man, Sean. That's part of your attraction for me."

The helicopter was closer now. "That chopper's coming this way," he observed.

He narrowed his eyes against the brightness of the sun. The machine was dipping toward them, beating shoreward with sunlight gleaming from its canopy. It carried civilian markings. They watched intently as it flew nearer.

About sixty feet from the edge of the cliff it stopped and hovered, almost level with the veranda. Brennan could see the pilot inspecting the house. Apparently satisfied, he pulled the chopper up and made a wide swoop to the right. Brennan stood up as it settled behind the line of hawthorn trees that separated the yard at the side of the house from the meadow beyond. Oh, Christ, he thought. What now?

The noise of the helicopter's turbines subsided as the pilot switched off the engine. Molly looked up at Brennan.

"It's come for you?"

"I think so." A cold weight had settled in Brennan's stomach. They had sent a helicopter, probably from Boston. That meant that something very bad had happened. He wished he'd listened to the news that morning. Maybe Knight had tried to call. But the phone was off the hook.

"Dammit!" Molly exclaimed. "Tomorrow's your last day. Can't they leave you alone?"

"Apparently not," Brennan said. He leaned on the veranda rail, waiting. He caught sight of the pilot struggling through the hawthorn bushes. To hell with them, he thought. Let them come to me.

The pilot extracted himself from a clutching branch and hurried across the lawn. He was panting slightly as he approached the veranda.

"Mr. Sean Brennan?"

"Yes. Who are you?"

"H.K. Enterprises. I'm to take you to New York right away. We're supposed to be there by ten-thirty."

H.K. Enterprises was the cover for the New York CIA station.

"New York? Why New York? What's happened?"

The pilot's eyes flickered to Molly and then back to Brennan. "I'm afraid I don't know, sir. All I know is, I'm supposed to get you there as soon as possible."

New York. Gorbachev was in New York. Brennan looked at his watch: it wasn't even ten past eight yet. The Soviet leader's press conference was supposed to be aired at one; he'd been intending to watch it. "Where in New York, exactly?"

"Glen Cove," the pilot said. "I'm supposed to put you down on the high school football field."

"Oh, shit. Killenworth." Brennan turned from the man and said, "Molly, I've got to go."

"But —" She saw his face, and stopped. "Okay," she said. "I'll help you get your things."

"I'll be back in a minute," Brennan said to the pilot.

She was putting his suitcase on the bed as he entered the bedroom. He could tell from the way she moved that she was angry.

"I'm sorry," he said.

"So am I. Does this mean you're putting off your resignation?"

"Not if I can help it." He went into the adjoining bathroom to get his shaving gear.

"What is Killenworth?"

"It's the Soviet compound they use for their UN VIPs. Out on Long Island, at Glen Cove. Gorbachev's staying there. He's supposed to be addressing the UN General Assembly at two. And his summit with the president is tomorrow."

"Something's happened to him?" She brushed a strand of hair from her forehead.

"Could be. Molly, I'm sorry."

"I'm not angry now. Just disappointed. I was looking forward to the rest of the day."

"So was I." He dropped a few articles of clothing into the suitcase and snapped it shut. "Listen, if it's possible, I still quit tomorrow."

"And if it isn't possible?"

"Then I'll have to stay on until whatever it is, is over. But after that, I'm finished. Promise."

She looked down at the suitcase, and then her eyes found his again. "Okay. Promise accepted. I'm on your side, remember."

"I know. Thanks."

She put her arms around him; the anger had evaporated. "Take care of yourself," he said. "I'll be back soon."

"You'd better be," she mumbled into his shoulder, and then, as though a door into the future had opened for an instant and she had glimpsed something terrible through it, she urged: "Sean, please be careful. *Please.*"

"I'll be careful," Brennan said.

Outside, beyond the hawthorn trees, the pilot had started the helicopter's engines.

Budapest – Warsaw
September 29

THE RECEPTION LINE was easing slowly along. Yuri Isayev sneaked a glance at his watch as he shook hands with the Hungarian minister of light industry; it was just before one o'clock. Good. Isayev was hungry, and lunch, however hampered by the protocol and formality of a state visit, would be welcome.

The minister passed on, toward the rest of the Soviet delegation. The rotunda beneath the great dome of the Hungarian Parliament building was filled with echoes; Isayev heard Nikolai Koblov make a small joke to one of the Hungarians, and the Hungarian's answering chuckle. Koblov, vice-chairman of the USSR's Council of Ministers, was good at this sort of thing, which Isayev felt he was not. Isayev, a theorist, was chairman of the Secretariat of the Central Committee of the Communist Party of the Soviet Union, and carried out a critically important mandate: as well as Secretariat chairman, he was responsible for ideology and Party cadres. It was an immensely powerful post, to which Gorbachev had promoted him after getting rid of the antireformist Ligachev.

For a moment, Isayev wondered how Mikhail was managing in New York. Raisa Gorbachev hadn't gone with him this time. She'd had an operation for an ovarian cyst a couple of weeks previously, and the doctors hadn't wanted her to travel. It would be just before eight A.M. in New York, and Mikhail would be getting ready for the press conference. Isayev was glad he himself didn't have to face a horde of American journalists. Journalists were an annoyance at the best of times, and Americans were the worst of the lot.

He had three people left to greet, among them the camel-faced woman who was the Hungarian minister of culture. Then lunch, and after that, off to the Hungarians' Central Committee building to inform their secretariat of the latest ideological thinking in Moscow. Isayev's words would provide the signals the Hungarians needed to direct their own reforms, showing them just how far they could safely proceed. After Poland, Hungary was the Warsaw Pact country most ripe for a political explosion; there was a lot of muttering about allowing "loyal" socialist political organizations to exist in opposition to the Party itself, and that was only a few steps away from a bourgeois multiparty system. Such a system was not permissible, and such talk only misled the people. They were in a bad enough mood as it was, given the austerity measures the Hungarians had introduced to try to put the staggering economy back onto its feet. Many people were holding down three, even four jobs, to maintain what was essentially a bourgeois style of living. And yesterday, another round of price increases had been announced.

It's their own fault, Isayev thought irritably. If they weren't so materialistic, they wouldn't have to spend all their time working. They ought to be more like Russians. We're not afraid to make sacrifices. Heaven knows we made enough, more than enough, under Stalin.

He was greeting the camel-faced woman when he noticed, out of the corner of his eye, a disturbance at the head of the reception line, where Koblov was standing. The steady procession of dignitaries stopped. Isayev dropped protocol for a moment and looked toward Koblov.

One of the Russian aides was whispering in Koblov's ear. The aide's face was stark white, as though he'd been drained of blood. As Isayev watched, the color also seeped out of the vice-chairman's face.

Like a man who's been shot, thought Isayev suddenly. My God, what's happened?

Koblov whispered something back to the aide, who almost ran from the rotunda. The Hungarians looked on, astonished at first and then with mounting concern. Koblov dropped all formality, left his position at the head of the line, and moved toward Isayev.

He seemed to be having trouble controlling his legs. From the other side of the rotunda, the general secretary of the Hungarian Party, Karoly Grosz, watched Koblov's shaky progress with an expression of disbelief.

"Yuri," Koblov whispered as he reached Isayev. "We have to go back to Moscow. Immediately. I've sent for the cars."

"What's happened?" Isayev demanded, keeping his voice low. The camel- faced minister of culture was scutinizing the two Russians, alarm in her eyes. Koblov drew Isayev to one side. "Mikhail —" he stammered "— Mikhail's gone."

"Gone?" Isayev gasped. It was happening, as he'd always feared it might. His mind seemed to be working very slowly. "Dead?"

"No. I don't know. Gone. Someone attacked our compound outside New York. Mikhail's missing."

Isayev suppressed an urge to shout "What?" at the top of his voice. Instead, he asked evenly, "Whose information is this?"

"It comes from Ivan Zotin, in Moscow. He wants us back immediately. That's all I know."

Ivan Zotin was chairman of the Council of Ministers, and Koblov's superior. "Was it the Americans?" Isayev asked, realizing as he spoke that the question was ridiculous. The Americans would never attempt such a thing. It would be tantamount to a nuclear attack against the Soviet Union.

"How could it be?" whispered Koblov. "Come, we have to go. The Hungarians —"

"We can't tell them."

"Of course not." Koblov was regaining his composure. "I'll deal with Grosz."

"What will you tell him?"

"Nothing. That's safest."

"Rumors," Isayev warned.

"Any rumor would be better than the truth," Koblov replied grimly. "Make sure the cars are coming, and get everyone together."

"Yes."

Koblov turned away and strode toward the Hungarian general secretary. Isayev pasted a neutral expression on his face and, bowing politely to the minister of culture, headed for the main doors of the parliament building.

The limousines were already pulling up to the foot of the great ceremonial stairway as he reached open air. Bright September sunlight streamed down onto the stone lions on either side of the stairs, and onto the statues and monuments of Kossuth Lajos Square. Isayev hurried down the steps to the first limousine; the bottom of the steps was already cordoned off by the security detachments — Hungarian AVH men, and the KGB Ninth Directorate guards, who had accompanied the delegation from Moscow. The aide whom Koblov had spoken to a few minutes earlier was with them.

"We're heading for the airport immediately," Isayev said to the aide. "Is the aircraft ready?"

"I've already given instructions," the aide told him. He'd regained his color. "Everything will be ready."

"Good. I'll ride in the third car with Vice-Chairman Koblov. Some of the others can use the second vehicle, behind the security limousine. No one in the third car except myself and the vice-chairman. Anybody who's left over, put in the fourth car."

"Yes, Secretary."

Isayev turned to look back up the stairway. Koblov was descending it rapidly, flanked by the rest of the Soviet delegation and trailed by the Hungarians, except for Grosz, who was hurrying beside the Russian. Grosz was talking quickly, waving his arms, but Koblov didn't answer him. The Hungarian fell silent as the group reached the limousines.

"Third car, Vice-Chairman," Isayev announced. "I'll ride with you."

He left Koblov to salvage what could be salvaged of the diplomatic niceties, and got into the limousine. Koblov joined him less than a minute later. The door slammed behind him and the car departed immediately. Koblov slumped back into his seat, mumbling as he sometimes did.

"What?" Isayev asked. The motorcycle outriders were thundering toward the head of the convoy, which was led by a limousine full of security men. There would not have been time yet for the militia to clear the streets on the way to the airport, but it couldn't be helped.

"I don't want to have to do that again soon," Koblov said.

"Grosz thinks we've lost our minds. I think he's afraid the Americans are about to attack."

"I don't think they will," Isayev said. Although, he thought, if they wanted to, this would be a good time to do it. We're momentarily leaderless. Let me see. Chairman Zotin can take over as figurehead, for the moment; he's head of the government, after all. Party leadership. What of that? Myself, obviously, there's no one else. Except, perhaps, Dmitri Averin. The chairman of the Party Control Commission might be able to make a case for interim leadership . . .

No, I don't think so. He's resisted some of Mikhail's more radical ideas too strongly. He couldn't muster enough support in the Secretariat and the Politburo to overcome that.

Thank God this didn't happen three years ago, when Mikhail's control teetered on a knife edge. It's still not absolute, even now. If he's gone, the dogmatists, and the Stalinists, and the regional Party bureaucrats who are afraid of losing their perquisites and opportunities for corruption, will try to turn back the clock, no matter what the cost. We're going to have to be very careful until we find out what's happened.

What *has* happened? Who could have done it? Not the Americans, surely. They think better of him than a good many Party members do. Mikhail is hated more in the Soviet Union than he is in the West.

Who, then?

Terrorists?

The security organs?

Did Oleg Chernysh find out that Mikhail intended to deprive him of his full Politburo membership, and make the KGB chairman a non-voting Politburo member, the start of a long slide from power? Even if he knew, would Chernysh risk a direct, physical attack on the general secretary? No one, in all Soviet history, had ever dared that. Political removal, yes, like Khrushchev, but never violence.

It was unthinkable. There had to be another explanation.

Isayev glanced at Koblov. The vice-chairman was staring out the window, watching the buildings rush past. Sirens howled in front and behind, although the racket was muffled inside the armored limousine. "Do you think —" Isayev began, and then stopped. Koblov had known nothing of Mikhail's plan to demote the KGB chairman. It wouldn't do to bring that into the open, not yet.

"What?" Koblov turned away from the window. Like Isayev, he had been deep in thought.

"Do you think Mikhail's dead?"

"I don't know."

"What do you think the KGB and the army will do?"

"I don't know that, either. But we'd better be ready for anything."

"Yes. . . . Where are we?" Isayev didn't know Budapest. Koblov did, though; he'd been the ambassador to Hungary ten years ago.

"Nearly to Engels Square. That's St. Stephen's Basilica on our right. After that, it's almost a straight run to the airport."

The limousine slowed abruptly. Isayev jolted forward in his seat. "What —"

Koblov pressed a button and the smoked glass partition dividing them from the driver's seat slid down. Through the windshield, Isayev could see that the car ahead of them had also braked suddenly. The KGB guard in the front passenger seat had his radio microphone to his lips; he was speaking urgently into it.

"What in hell's happening?" Isayev snarled. They couldn't afford any delays.

"Secretary," the security man explained nervously, "there's some kind of demonstration just ahead, in the square. It began suddenly, about fifteen minutes ago. We didn't get word till just now —"

"Go around it," Isayev ordered. "Contact the lead vehicle and tell them. We have to keep together."

He realized then that the limousine ahead of them, which was following the security squad's car at the head of the convoy, was driving into a mass of people that had spilled off the sidewalks and onto the pavement. One of the escorting motorcycles had come almost to a halt, its rider struggling to keep the heavy machine upright. Isayev couldn't see the security squad's car, because his view was blocked both by the limousine ahead of them, and by the crowd. Placards floated above the mass of people, red or green lettering on stark white, the colors of Hungary, vivid in the bright autumn sunlight. A Hungarian flag snapped in the breeze; someone was climbing the basins of the Danubius Fountain with it, intent on raising the banner as high as possible. Memories of the uprising of 1956, when thousands of counterrevolutionaries fought Russian tanks in the streets, flashed through Isayev's mind.

The price increases, he thought. They're rioting over the price increases. Why couldn't Grosz have announced them after we left, damn him?

"Turn around," he commanded the driver, keeping his voice clear and level. "Nikolai, is there another quick route to the airport?"

"Try to turn right just ahead," Koblov instructed. His wide, flat face was anxious, although not yet frightened. "Go down to the Danube bank as far as you can, then turn right on Belgrad Rakpart."

The driver started edging the car to the right, but the crowd had become extremely thick; the limousine slowed to a crawl. Isayev had lost sight of both the motorcycle escort and the convoy's other vehicles.

The driver turned to look at him, desperation on his face. "I can't go much farther without running some of them over, Secretary . . . .

"Stop, if you have to," Isayev responded. "The car's armored." The demonstrators didn't seem hostile yet, just curious at the sight of the long black Zil caught in their midst. But the crowd could turn into a violent mob if someone was hurt. Isayev noticed that the KGB man was unclipping an AKR machine pistol from under the dash.

"Leave the gun alone," he growled. "If they see it, it'll provoke them. Get back on the radio and find out what's happening ahead."

The KGB man reluctantly stowed the gun away, and picked up the microphone again. An interchange full of static followed, involving codes Isayev couldn't follow. His inability to understand made him nervous. We're in cocoons, he thought, insulated and almost blind. We can't even be sure what the people who are supposed to be protecting us are doing. No wonder Mikhail wants to curb the KGB.

"The lead car is stopped as well, Secretary," said the security officer. "AVH riot police are on their way. They want us to wait and do nothing."

"This is fucking awful security," Koblov snarled. "Do you mean to tell me the security organs here didn't have any idea this was going to happen?"

"*Glasnost,*" Isayev reminded him. "The Hungarians are trying not to react to provocation. Let the people have their demonstrations, and then go home. It's better than what happened in 1956."

"It's lack of discipline," Koblov grumbled. "Openness is all very well, but a riot —"

"They didn't know we were going to be here," Isayev pointed out. "And it doesn't look like a riot. Yet."

Something struck the thick glass of Isayev's window, hard.

"It doesn't?" Koblov almost yelled. "What was *that*?"

Isayev looked out the window. Three young men, students perhaps, were peering at him through the tinted glass. One of them was holding a length of metal pipe. He was yelling something, the words obstructed by the thick window, and in Hungarian anyway, which Isayev didn't understand.

"He's telling the Russians to go home," Koblov translated. There was more than anxiety in his voice now; there was fear. "He's saying we're responsible for the food prices. He's saying Grosz sends everything to Moscow, there's nothing left for the workers."

Isayev saw a sudden movement in the front seat. He leaned forward. The KGB man had grabbed the AKR from its clips and was cocking it. The driver had drawn a pistol.

"*Put those away*!" Isayev roared.

"Pardon, Secretary," the KGB officer responded. "But it's too dangerous. We have to scare them off."

It was too late, anyway. The student with the pipe had seen the weapons. He backed away from the car, pointing and shouting. The shouts were taken up by the people around him, and hysteria began to spread. Someone climbed on the back bumper and the car began to rock to and fro.

"The fucking little *shits,*" Koblov shouted. "Where in hell are the riot police?"

Not here, Nikolai, Isayev thought as the car rocked more and more violently. The crowd, which had surged away from the Zil when the guns were first exposed, was now flowing back, pressing hard against the vehicle. Someone started pounding on the rear window with a brick. The bulletproof glass resisted the blows at first, but then began to star. The to-and-fro rocking stopped, was replaced by a violent sideways motion.

They're trying to overturn us, Isayev thought, as he grabbed the armrest. How heavy is this thing?

The KGB passenger was training his machine pistol ineffectually at the attackers. Idiot, Isayev thought. He can't use it unless the windows are down; bulletproof glass works both ways.

The radio was crackling; Isayev grasped just enough of the codes to realize that the other cars were also under attack. This wasn't a demonstration anymore; this was a riot. He glanced over his shoulder at the rear window. The student with the pipe, as well as the brick-wielder were hammering on it. Designed to absorb the impact of a bullet without allowing penetration, the glass could not withstand a steady battering. The cracks were spreading, and pebbles of glass were flaking off the inner surface.

They're going to get in, Isayev realized. Then what?

"Move aside, please, Secretary," said the man with the AKR, aiming the weapon so that it covered the Zil's back window. "I may have to shoot." Isayev did as he was told; at this point it was useless to argue.

The heavy Zil lurched back and forth, while the hammering at the rear window persisted. Isayev felt the limousine's left wheels lift off the ground and then slam back onto the pavement. The crowd might in fact succeed in flipping them over. Suppose some demonstrators had bottles of gasoline . . . . Isayev clung desperately to the armrest as the car plunged up and down.

The window finally gave way in a shower of glass fragments. Realizing what was coming next, Isayev threw himself onto the floor. Koblov's heavy bulk slammed across his back as the vice-chairman did the same.

The machine pistol banged deafeningly above Isayev's head. Explosive fumes roiled about him. He heard a scream from outside the car, and a deep roar surged from the crowd.

That's done it, he thought. They'll drag us outside and beat us to death.

The car stopped lurching. Over the din of shouts and screams, Isayev heard the grind of heavy engines, accented by a series of pops. The wind blew something acrid through the shattered window of the Zil. Tear gas. The pops were gas grenades. Then there were three rifle shots, followed by a full volley. The thunder of the engines drew closer, accompanied by a hissing roar. Isayev shoved Koblov aside, and raised his head to look out the rear window. A blast of water hit him in the face. The riot police were using water cannons.

Gasping, he dashed the water out of his eyes and looked again. The demonstrators were streaming away down the side streets, followed by clouds of tear gas and iron-hard jets of water from the water cannon. Half a dozen inert forms lay on the pavement, shot or trampled.

Koblov was scanning the scene, as well. "They got here in time," he managed. "It's over."

"No, it's not," Isayev said. He'd inhaled some tear gas and was laboring for breath. "It's not over yet. Far from it."

Four hundred twenty miles to the north, KGB Major-General Anastas Vlasov was presiding over the final stages of an interrogation. Juisdictionally, operationally and diplomatically he had no business being where he was, in the basement of the Public Security committee headquarters in the Mokotow District of Warsaw, but here he was, anyway. It was not the first time he had graced the Sluzba Bezpieczenstwa headquarters with his presence; as head of the Eleventh Department of the First Chief Directorate of the KGB — the department controlling the security and intelligence services of the Warsaw Pact nations — he had vast power over the secret police of Poland, East Germany, Hungary, Bulgaria and Czechoslovakia. No legal instrument gave him this power, but he had it nonetheless, for a very simple reason: the Polish SB, like the StB of Czechoslovakia, the DS of Bulgaria, the AVH of Hungary and the SSD of East Germany, all had much more in common with the KGB than they had with the regimes of their individual countries. Suppression of dissent was important, but at least as important was institutional survival. Alliance with the KGB was an essential defense against occasional Party efforts to reduce the power of the secret police, and this fact kept the Polish SB and its sister services firmly under the direction of Moscow, no matter how independent they were on paper.

Especially in a case like this one. Vlasov swayed forward, hands clasped behind his back, his small round eyes glimmering in the office pallor of his face.

"Ask her again," he said. "We have to be absolutely certain." He glanced at the tall Pole next to him. Witold Jurys, chief of the SB, was sweating this one out, too; Vlasov could tell by the way he kept fingering the moustache on his too-long upper lip. If CONCERTO had been compromised by his organization's negligence, Jurys would be in very serious trouble. So would Colonel Adam Kaminsky, who was Jurys's subordinate, and who was responsible for CONCERTO's internal security. Kaminsky was sitting in a chair near the door, observing the proceedings in his usual detached manner.

The interrogator bent over the motionless form of the woman. She was naked, strapped to a metal table under a light whose concentrated white beam left the rest of the room in semidarkness. On the far side of the table, the doctor began observing the heart and blood pressure monitors again. He'd warned the interrogator ten minutes ago that the woman was on the edge, but there was no time to let her recover. They, and she, would have to take their chances.

"What were you going to tell the Americans?" the interrogator asked the woman, very softly. She was thirty-three years old, and with a bath and her hair combed she would have been attractive, despite the three days of interrogation; there were no external marks on her, except where she had bitten through her lower lip. Vlasov was beginning to believe that she was really no more than she claimed she was: a junior clerk from the SB registry downstairs, who last week had taken it into her head to defect, and had made a mess of it. It had been unlikely from the first that she knew anything about CONCERTO, but Vlasov had to be absolutely sure. She *could* be a CIA spy, and she *might* have been able to crack the partitioning that separated CONCERTO from all the other operations controlled from SB headquarters. The timing of her attempted defection might have been coincidental, but then again it might not.

Her words were barely audible now. "I've told you . . . please. Don't do it again."

"You must tell me everything."

" . . . don't know . . . ."

It would be fortunate for both the interrogator and the doctor if she didn't mention CONCERTO. Neither of them knew about it. If she did blurt out something, Kaminsky would have to neutralize both of them for at least as long as the operation was underway.

"Tell me more," the interrogator threatened. "Or you will be hurt again."

The woman screamed, wordlessly. The interrogator hadn't even touched the electrical transformer positioned on the lower shelf of the metal table on which the woman lay.

"Careful," the doctor warned. "Adrenalin." He wielded a hypodermic. "Go on."

"Tell me what you were going to tell the Americans," the interrogator urged, his voice very gentle.

Her voice was stronger. "I don't . . . know. Oh, please, let me go. I don't know anything else. Please."

The interrogator looked sadly down into her eyes and touched the fine wire that led into the corner of her mouth. The wire ran down her esophagus into her stomach, and at the end of the wire was a small clump of electrically conductive beads. The other end of the wire was connected to the transformer. This arrangement administered much deeper discomfort than the older technique of applying electricity to the genitals; it also left no external traces.

The woman hopelessly returned his stare as he reached down and twisted the transformer control. Her body convulsed against the straps as the current slid into her, but she remained silent. This was not from a determination to resist; one of the bizarre effects of the treatment was that the victim was unable even to scream.

"Look out!" the doctor yelled. The interrogator instantly switched off the current.

"Damn," said the doctor. "She's gone." He stood up from his stool and began applying CPR.

The interrogator turned to Vlasov and Jurys. "In my opinion, sir," he said to Jurys, "she's told us everything. I can usually sense it."

Vlasov looked at Kaminsky. "Your opinion?" he said to the man in the shadows.

"He's one of our best," the Pole told Vlasov, referring to the interrogator. "I don't think she knew anything of further interest."

Vlasov, who had been present only during this last hour of the interrogation, nodded judiciously. "If you say so," he concurred. "Comrade Jurys?"

"I agree with Colonel Kaminsky."

"That's all, then," Vlasov concluded.

Jurys turned to the doctor, who was still trying to revive the woman. "You can quit that," the Pole said. "She's not needed anymore."

The doctor stopped the cardiac massage and began packing up his instruments. "What're you going to do with her?" Vlasov asked.

"Suicide," Jurys responded briefly. The Polish SB had to maintain strict secrecy about rigorous interrogations like this one; a few years back, four SB men had killed a counterrevolutionary priest, and much to everyone's surprise, the four had been arrested, convicted and imprisoned for it. That was just after General Jaruzelski imposed martial law and formed the Polish military government; the authorities had been trying to prove to the population that the police were as subject to the law as anyone else. It was only during the past year, after Jaruzelski had had that massive stroke and had been forced to retire, that the SB had begun to regain its freedom of action. Nevertheless, Jurys still had to be careful. Vlasov knew Jurys was looking forward to the day when he wouldn't have to be.

It wouldn't be long in coming.

"I have to contact Moscow," Vlasov commented. "They're waiting."

"Please come upstairs," Jurys said. "Colonel Kaminsky, get rid of her."

"Yes, Comrade Jurys." Kaminsky motioned for the interrogator to begin loosening the straps from around the body.

Jurys and Vlasov rode the elevator to the top floor, to Jurys's office. Jurys closed the door and made sure the antisurveillance equipment was functioning properly. He was a meticulous man.

Vlasov sat down behind the Pole's desk and picked up the receiver for the direct Moscow line. After a moment the call went through. Vlasov heard Vadim Besedin's voice, scratchy from the descrambling.

''Yes?''

''Dove,'' Vlasov announced, giving his code name. ''We're clear. She didn't know anything.''

''Good. Anything else to report?''

''No. All is in order here,'' Vlasov reported with satisfaction. The instant the New York dispatch came into operations headquarters here in Warsaw, he'd relayed it to Moscow. That had been seventy-five minutes ago. The matter of the woman had been the only rough spot so far in the operation, and that had been cleared up. Besedin, head of the KGB's First Chief Directorate, and Vlasov's boss, would be pleased. So would Oleg Chernysh, head of the KGB and Besedin's own superior.

They'd kept the chain of command as short as possible, from Chernysh through Besedin to Vlasov and then to Jurys. The operational people were a mixture of Poles, like Kaminsky, and Russians; Vlasov would have preferred that they be entirely Russian, but that would have made the internal Polish component of CONCERTO too difficult to manage. Like it or not, the operation depended heavily on the Polish secret police. That was one reason it was being controlled from Warsaw; the other, which was unstated but equally significant, was damage-limitation. If CONCERTO went awry, Chernysh could try to blame the SB.

''You are absolutely sure?''

''Yes.''

''Good,'' Besedin said, and rang off.

Concerto, Vlasov thought as he also hung up. Aptly named, but not big enough. It's a full-scale symphony.

Washington
9:10 A.M., Sunday, September 29

THE COLD AUTUMN RAIN that had been falling on Long Island earlier in the morning was now drenching Andrews Air Force Base. The heavy drops stippled the sheets of water that lay on the concrete hardstand where the two black limousines waited, engines running and windshield wipers swishing rhythmically. A third Lincoln was rolling to a stop beside the other two; several hundred feet from the car, a Marine helicopter waited in the rain. Its rotors turned slowly and steadily, throwing a fine spray from the tips of the whirling blades.

Simon Parr, national security adviser to the fortieth president of the United States, and chairman of the National Security Council, peered through the rain-flecked window as his limousine drew to a halt. The end of the east-west runway obscured by the downpour; Air Force One should be in its final landing approach by now. They'd all be in the helicopter within five minutes, and on the way to the White House.

Then it'll start to hit the fan, Parr thought. I wonder how President Halliday's going to take it?

Parr's breath had fogged the window; he rubbed it with his palm, leaving damp smears on the glass. He was a wiry man of average height, with a narrow face that implied intelligence while revealing little of the character behind it; although a careful observer might find in the eyes behind the steel-framed glasses the look of someone who has forced himself to work too many hours for too many years. He was forty-two.

A blurred figure appeared outside the window. Parr pressed a button and the bulletproof glass hummed open. Paige Martin, secretary of state, was holding an umbrella over his head against the pelt of the rain.

"Morning, Paige. You want to join me?"

"Good idea. Got any coffee?"

"A thermos." Parr slid across the seat to make room for the secretary of state. As the door slammed Parr said, "I just got here. What's the president's ETA?"

"Only a minute or two. I better skip the coffee, now that I think about it. There won't be time. Jesus, what a mess."

"That's an understatement. Who's in the other limo? Reid?" Stephen Reid was Halliday's DCI — director of Central Intelligence and head of the CIA.

"Yeah. He got here a couple of minutes before I did."

"Where's Hugh?"

"He's still over at Defense. He'll meet us at the White House." Hugh Ormerod was the defense secretary.

"Okay. Here comes Reid." Parr opened the door for the DCI, thinking: that's a step in the right direction. He comes to my car, not me to his.

Reid didn't have an umbrella, and rainwater was dripping from the brim of his hat. His face, despite its pink roundness and the white hair visible beneath his hat, conveyed severity rather than good humor. Like Parr, he was a slender man, but he shared nothing else with the national security adviser. Parr — in the usual manner of bureaucratic infighting — had been vigorously trying to extend his influence over the American intelligence community ever since the election, and Reid had been just as vigorously fending him off. Parr's office had no specific legal right to direct intelligence matters — the office was supposed to be purely advisory, and Reid, like Parr, was responsible directly to the president — but with a weak DCI, and with presidential backing, the national security adviser could acquire effective control of the entire structure of US intelligence.

Unfortunately for Parr, Reid was not a weak DCI, and President Halliday's backing was not something one could always depend on.

"Join the not-so-happy throng," Parr remarked easily, making room for the DCI. He made a point of showing affability toward Reid, not that it fooled the intelligence man for a moment.

Reid, however, was staring across the limousine roof toward the end of the runway. "Not now," he said. "Here comes the plane."

"Here we go," said Parr, climbing from the car. "Paige, can you spare me some of that umbrella? I don't wear hats."

The Secret Service escorts also emerged from the limousines — they'd been riding in the front seats — and collected in a small, unobtrusive group where they could watch Parr, Reid and Martin, as well as the approach of Air Force One. Parr could now discern the blaze of the landing lights as the Boeing touched down, although the plane itself was obscured by the mist and rain. After a few moments the aircraft loomed out of the veils of water, engines roaring as it swung onto the taxiway toward the waiting men. A yellow utility truck with two Secret Service men crouched in it scurried out to lead the jet off the taxiway onto the hardstand, while a motorized boarding ramp trundled from the direction of the airbase terminal. Parr and Martin huddled under the single umbrella; Reid stood by himself in the rain, as though he didn't deign to notice it.

The Boeing rolled to a stop and the pilot switched off the engines; the door behind the cockpit opened as the boarding ramp swung up to meet it. Parr heard the helicopter turbines begin to spool up as President James Halliday descended the stairway, followed by a collection of aides and the air force officer who carried the Football, the case containing the release codes for the nation's nuclear arsenal. The aides would have to be left behind, to return in the limousines.

Parr was first to greet the president; Halliday regarded his security adviser with a plaintive expression. One of the aides held an umbrella over Halliday's head.

"Simon, what the hell's happened?"

"Very bad news, Mr. President, I'm afraid," Parr replied. They started toward the helicopter, the aide with the umbrella hurrying to keep up with Halliday's long strides. Parr had to scurry as well; he noted with satisfaction that Reid had to do likewise. The secretary of state, who was almost as tall as the president, had less difficulty.

"What's this about Gorbachev?" Halliday shouted, competing with the noise of the helicopter turbines.

"We don't know, exactly, sir," Parr shouted back; he then fell silent as they all hurried under the whirling blades to the door of the helicopter. The aide with the umbrella dropped back at the foot of the steps; Parr, Martin and Reid, followed by the Football, clambered into the helicopter at the president's heels. The door slammed shut behind them and the noise subsided abruptly. The helicopter swayed as it lifted off. Halliday threw himself into one of the deeply upholstered seats — the helicopter betrayed its Marine origins only on the outside — and said to his advisers, but mostly to Parr:

"Okay. What's going on with Gorbachev? What in hell is with this Russian alert?"

Halliday had been on a three-day vacation at his Iowa farm; he'd already been on the way back to the capital aboard Air Force One when the news — that there'd been some kind of terrorist attack on Killenworth — reached Washington. Parr had contacted him aboard the plane at seven o'clock, to give him what meager information they had had at that time. They still had little more.

As Parr opened his mouth to speak Halliday interjected, "Does this mean Gorbachev won't be in Washington to see me tomorrow? Simon, run it all past me again."

Parr winced inwardly. Despite the short time the new administration had been in office, Halliday's ignorance of foreign affairs was already becoming legendary, at least within the inner circles of power.

Never mind, Parr thought. If Halliday weren't so ignorant about everything outside Iowa, he'd be making his own foreign policy, and that could be disastrous. This way we're in control, and the president isn't, although nobody outside this helicopter cabin would ever guess it.

"Well, Mr. President," Parr began. Halliday stopped pulling at his earlobe, and gazed at Parr hopefully. The president was an exceptionally handsome man, with electric-blue eyes and an unruly shock of blonde hair that (according to the psychological surveys) rendered him irresistiby appealing to female voters; they supposedly wanted to run their fingers through it. He also looked like an Anglo-Saxon male's fantasy of an older brother; his face was sufficiently rugged under its blonde thatch to suit a cigarette advertisement, the kind of ad featuring saddles and horses and dusty corrals in the background. Halliday's voice had a relaxed resonance overlaid by a midwest twang; when he spoke, the listener assumed strength and competence.

Unfortunately, as far as Parr could tell, Halliday had never had an original thought in his life. He'd been selected — for his stereotypical appeal — as the vice-presidential running mate for the Republican presidential candidate in the last election. The candidate had seemed like a perfect choice until a *Washington Post* reporter leaked the fact that he was not entirely faithful to his wife. The Democrats had then shot themselves in the foot by choosing an overintellectual Easterner as candidate, and the Republican campaign manager took advantage of the string of disasters to promote Halliday. He'd won by a landslide.

Although Halliday's ignorance was a potential national disaster, Parr knew that that same ignorance gave Halliday's advisers enormous influence over foreign policy. One of the constants in Halliday's ideology was his knee-jerk reaction whenever communism was mentioned: despite the changes taking place in Mikhail Gorbachev's Soviet Union, Halliday still felt that communism was godless, immoral, murderous, evil, subversive and warlike — all the things that American democracy presumably was not. Halliday's preconceptions made him impatient with the reasoned analyses of secretary of state Paige Martin, who was now folded into the seat next to Parr's. Halliday preferred to listen to Parr, whose neat simplifications were much easier to understand than Paige Martin's subtleties. Parr could foresee the day when his influence in foreign affairs would outweigh that of the secretary of state.

"This is what we know has happened," Parr said. "At a quarter to six this morning, a mobile TV unit went into Killenworth, where Mr. Gorbachev was staying, to set up for his press conference. Just before six, the Secret Service guarding the estate was informed that the NBC van had broken down before it reached Killenworth. The van that went in was bogus. The Secret Service raised the alarm. Within a minute of that, the fake mobile unit broke through the rear fence of the compound. Whoever was in it was armed to the teeth, because they blew up an armored car that tried to stop them. The van was found at twenty past six on the beach north of Killenworth, empty."

"We monitor all of Killenworth's radio communications. At six, the Killenworth transmitter went off the air. At ten past six, the Secret Service agent in charge of the guard detachment tried to telephone the Russian security office in the mansion, but couldn't get through. He warned the KGB guards at the gatehouse that something was wrong, and one of them went up to the house. He didn't come back. At twenty past six, a couple of dozen Russians, including the Soviet ambassador to the UN, left their UN mission building in Manhattan and went roaring off to Killenworth as fast as they could. They got there at half past seven. Just before eight, the Killenworth transmitter went back on the air. At ten past, the Soviet armed forces went on alert. As of half an hour ago, the Russians at Killenworth weren't letting anybody onto the grounds. But the Soviet UN ambassador has cancelled the press conference, and Mr. Gorbachev's address to the UN as well."

"The Secret Service headquarters called me at six-thirty," added Paige Martin. "I contacted Simon here, the DCI and the FBI, as well as yourself, Mr. President. The FBI was on the scene at Killenworth by seven. But there's been no further information, other than what Simon's told you. The Russian's Washington ambassador isn't talking. We have absolutely no idea whether Mr. Gorbachev is alive or dead."

"So who the hell did it?"

"It looks very much like a terrorist attack," said Reid. "A very well-planned one. Judging from where the van was found, it's likely they got away by boat."

"*Looks* like a terrorist attack?" Halliday queried. "Who else would want to kill Gorbachev?"

"*If* he's dead, Mr. President. We shouldn't make that assumption until we know for sure."

"You didn't answer my question, Director."

"I'm sorry, Mr. President. I think we have to entertain the possibility that this has been done by Gorbachev's own people."

"*What*?" Halliday's expression was bewildered. Even after months in office, he still thought of the Soviet government as one monolithic entity dedicated to the destruction of freedom; specifically, the freedom represented by the United States. He couldn't fathom the idea that the Russians might be divided amongst themselves.

"Yes. Mr. Gorbachev has many enemies at home. Some of them may be desperate enough to remove him by force. We know that the KGB, and others, are not entirely happy with his reforms."

"But why would they do it *here*?"

"He has friends in the Soviet Union, as well as enemies. Here, he would be isolated from his friends."

"But why would they stage a performance like this? Why not just . . . poison him, or something?"

This was something the DCI obviously hadn't wanted brought up. "We don't know, yet," he admitted. "It's too soon to tell."

"I see," Halliday said, without conviction. "Simon? What do you think?"

"If I may add something, Mr. President," Paige Martin broke in.

Halliday gave the secretary of state a long-suffering look. "Go ahead," he consented. The helicopter swayed in a downdraft as it began to lose altitude. Simon Parr, who disliked flying, felt his body tense. He consciously forced his muscles to relax.

"I have to agree with Stephen," the secretary of state was saying. "We have to remember, Mr. President, that there are powerful people in Russia who don't like Mr. Gorbachev's reforms. They think the reforms will weaken the Soviet Union, perhaps tear it apart. They point to the ethnic riots in the southern Soviet republics, the agitation for freedom in the Baltic states, the attacks on Stalin and the possible dismantling of collectivization, as well as the unrest in Poland that's lasted from the birth of Solidarity in 1980 right up to the present. The conservatives are terrified that the Polish unrest will spread to the other satellites, particularly Hungary, resulting in a full-scale revolt against the Kremlin."

Halliday was looking increasingly lost. Martin ploughed on.

"These people are also afraid that Mr. Gorbachev's restructuring of the Soviet State will diminish their power and privileges. We know the KGB leadership is worried about the KGB being reduced to no more than a police force, and the KGB has always regarded itself as the preserver and protector of the Russian Revolution. It doesn't want to lose the immense power it's always had. Oleg Chernysh is KGB chief, the man who helped get Gorbachev into power. But Chernysh was part of the group around Mr. Brezhnev, from 1964 to his death a few years ago. Many of that group were very corrupt. Chernysh was part of it, although he himself wasn't corrupt. Now, Mr. Gorbachev has been working very hard over the last few years to discredit Brezhnev's regime. In the process, he's also eroding Chernysh's position. If I were Chernysh, I'd be worrying about both the position of the KGB, and my own personal power."

"Goddamn it," Halliday said, "I can't follow all this Russian politics. Simon, what in hell's really going on?"

"There's an alternative explanation," Parr said. "It's horrifying, but we have to consider it."

"What, for God's sake?"

"Paige mentioned the unrest in Poland, and elsewhere in Eastern Europe. The Poles and the Czechs and the Hungarians all want freedom, and they hate the Russians. I believe the attack this morning could have been carried out by a group of freedom fighters who want to strike a blow against communism. Gorbachev may be reforming things over there, but he's still a communist, we mustn't forget that. And I do *not* think the KGB would have dared to do something like this. Mr. Gorbachev is far too popular among the Russian people. Moreover, the KGB has never removed a Soviet leader by force. They just don't do that."

"Freedom fighters," Halliday said, savoring the words, which Parr had chosen carefully. "That makes a lot more sense than that other stuff."

"But, Mr. President," Reid objected, trying to keep annoyance out of his voice, "it wouldn't make any sense for the Hungarians or Czechs or Poles, or the East Germans, to try to pull this off. Gorbachev's their best hope for at least a measure of independence. They'd be crazy to attack him."

"But maybe they don't all see it that way," Parr countered. "It's quite possible that there's a group working on the principle that a reformist leader like Gorbachev will make it *harder* for Eastern Europe to regain complete independence. They'd realize that most people over there would rather not fight Russians in the streets. So they'd reason that if they killed Gorbachev, the Soviet reprisals would be so savage that the satellite peoples would rebel out of sheer desperation."

"They'd have to be quite irrational to start something like that!"

Martin snapped. He always became irritable when Halliday ignored his careful explanations.

"I'm not saying it's rational," Parr replied. "All I'm saying is that we have to look at the possibility. It's too dangerous to ignore."

"Maybe," said Martin. He still sounded annoyed, but Parr could tell that he was considering the likelihood.

"*Could* it be freedom fighters?" Halliday asked Reid. The idea seemed to have struck his fancy. Parr squinted out the window again. They were nearly at the White House; the helicopter flew much lower now.

"There's a faint possibility," Reid said, reluctantly. "Although how they could have breached Russian security at Killenworth without help, I can't imagine."

"I can tell you one thing," said Martin. "If it *was* a group with East European links who attacked Killenworth, we may have one hell of a mess on our hands. The Russians will crack down on the satellite governments, and there's always a chance that could trigger revolts against the Kremlin. And if the Russians get really paranoid and blame us for encouraging the revolts —"

"But that would be good, from our point of view, wouldn't it?" Halliday asked. "We've always wanted the Soviet satellites to be free."

Christ, what a nitwit, Parr thought. "Mr. President," he observed, to divert Halliday from any further idiocies, "we're landing."

The helicopter bobbed, swayed and settled onto the White House lawn. Parr got up and opened the door. The shrill of the engines poured into the cabin, cutting off all conversation. Outside, the rain had diminished to a light drizzle. The four men, trailed by the colonel with the Football, hurried toward the White House entrance. Just inside, Secretary of Defense Hugh Ormerod was waiting for them.

"Mr. President," he announced as they trooped in from the drizzle, "the Soviet ambassador is here to see you."

"Jesus Christ," Halliday muttered. "It never rains but it pours." He turned to an aide who had appeared from nowhere. "Get him up to the Oval Office in three minutes."

"Is this wise, Mr. President?" Martin inquired anxiously, as they hurried up the stairs. "This ought to be handled through the State

Department, not through the presidency, at least not yet. We don't even know exactly what has happened to Mr. Gorbachev. Until then, I think you ought to keep yourself aloof. . . ."

Halliday raised a hand to silence him. "The buck stops here," he intoned. Parr wondered whether the president knew that he was quoting Harry Truman. "This is a serious business, as you've all been so eager to tell me. If something's happened to a foreign leader, it should be me who deals with it. What's the ambassador's name again?"

"Arkady Tretiakov, Mr. President." Martin was clearly smelling political disaster if the president involved himself this early, but there wasn't much he could do about it.

By the time they'd shed their coats and reached the Oval Office, the three minutes were almost up. With a groan, the president threw himself into the chair behind the great desk, and ran his fingers through his hair. "Where's that Russian?"

As if in answer, there was a gentle tap at the door. The aide stuck his head in and said, "Ambassador Tretiakov, Mr. President." The aide looked flustered. Protocol's gone all to hell this morning, thought Parr.

Everyone stood to greet the Russian. "Ambassador Tretiakov," Halliday said. "We are very glad you came. Please sit down and tell us what has happened. We are extremely concerned."

When he doesn't have to think, Parr reflected, Halliday can charm the skin off a snake. If he had the brains to go with it, he could be Roosevelt's equal.

"I prefer to remain standing," the ambassador said coldly.

Despite himself, Parr blinked, as did Martin. The Russian's response was an appalling breach of diplomatic manners.

"Very well," Halliday replied smoothly. "I hope Mr. Gorbachev is safe. We know there was an incident at Killenworth, and two of our Secret Service men are dead."

"Have you apprehended the assailants?" Tretiakov demanded. Despite his calm formality, his face was as white as chalk.

Halliday was taken aback at the abruptness. "No," he apologized. "But we will, soon. We would appreciate it enormously if you'd tell us what has happened at Killenworth."

"I am speaking for the collective leadership in Moscow," Tretiakov said, his voice not warming by a fraction of a degree. "Our Chairman of the Council of Ministers, Ivan Zotin, is guiding events in the absence of Mikhail Sergeyevich Gorbachev. Minister Zotin wishes to inform you that at this time, we do not hold the United States responsible for what has happened, except for laxness in allowing the attackers to reach Killenworth. Our military alert, which you doubtless know about, is purely a precaution."

"What *has* happened?" Halliday asked. "Is Secretary Gorbachev all right?"

"The assailants killed all but two of our security men inside Killenworth during their attack," Tretiakov remarked, ignoring the president's question. "There were also civilian casualties. We are assuming at the moment that the attackers are counterrevolutionary terrorists."

Parr glanced at Reid. The DCI was looking out the window. His expression was indecipherable.

"Oh," said Halliday lamely.

"This is extremely serious, as you can imagine," Tretiakov continued. "My government requests that the United States refrain from any precipitate action until the situation is resolved."

"You have our assurance," Martin replied.

Halliday glared at him, then returned his attention to Tretiakov. "Where is Secretary Gorbachev?" he asked.

"We don't know," said Tretiakov. "We have searched the grounds at Killenworth from end to end. He is not there. He has been kidnapped."

There was a long silence, which Halliday finally broke.

"Surely you're kidding," he said.

Glen Cove — New York
September 29

THE HELICOPTER transporting Brennan swept low over the shoreline of Long Island Sound and flew inland, just beneath the sullen clouds. The pilot gestured. ''Killenworth's over there,'' he explained, his voice clear in Brennan's headphones. ''I'm setting you down on the high school football field, like I said. It's ten thirty. You're right on time.''

''Okay,'' Brennan replied. The pilot changed radio frequencies and began alerting the ground. The machine was flying straight down Dosoris Lane, the road leading past the mansion. There were at least twenty cars parked on the road's shoulders, including five or six police vehicles. Lights blinked and flashed. A crowd had gathered beyond the southern barricade and Brennan could see a dozen TV news vehicles parked as near the barrier as their crews could position them. Half the reporters in the New York area had to be down there.

Hardly surprising, Brennan thought as the helicopter dipped toward the school grounds. Anything to do with Gorbachev attracts them like wasps to jam.

''There's a car for you,'' the pilot's voice instructed over the earphones. Brennan spotted it, parked near the fifty-yard line, a neutral brown sedan. Frank Knight might be in it, unless he was staying put at Killenworth and had sent a driver.

The fact that Knight had come up from Langley showed that something catastrophic had happened. First, Knight was head of the Soviet/Warsaw Pact Division of the CIA's Clandestine Operations Directorate, and divisional heads didn't usually involve themselves directly with the field for any threat short of Armageddon. Second, it was the FBI's responsibility to deal with attacks on Soviet nationals on American soil; the CIA wasn't legally permitted to become involved, and the Bureau guarded its preserve jealously. Knight had spoken with Brennan for a minute or two during Brennan's flight from Orchard Cove, but unfortunately it was an unsecured transmission and he'd been able to give Brennan little information except what was already on the newscasts: Gorbachev wasn't going to hold his press conference, and there'd been some kind of trouble at Killenworth. Serious trouble. Worse, an American military alert had been activated, although the Pentagon was disclaiming it as a major, unannounced training exercise. The media obviously didn't believe the generals.

The helicopter bobbed in the wind, settling closer to the ground, and then a sudden gust deflected it away from the still-wet grass. The pilot swore, trying to keep the machine steady. Brennan had discarded his seat belt and headphones and was out the door by the time the helicopter had finally landed. He slammed the door behind him and squinted against the blast of the rotors as the pilot lifted off again.

The brown sedan was hurtling toward him. Knight was behind the wheel. He stopped just long enough for Brennan to scramble inside with his suitcase, and then accelerated toward the field exit, the car fishtailing on the wet grass. "I tried to let you know the chopper was coming," Knight explained as he wrestled with the wheel, "but your line was busy."

"Phone was off the hook," Brennan said. "What's happened here?"

Knight regained control of the car and said, "According to what the Soviet ambassador told the president, Gorbachev's been kidnapped."

"*What?*"

"You heard me. Kidnapped."

Brennan stared at his superior in disbelief. Knight was an unusually tall man, and thin as a bean. His bald head brushed the roof of the car as the wheels bounced over the grass. "It's not possible," Brennan said. "There must be some mistake."

"The Russians've said it, so we've got to believe it's true," Knight said, glancing at Brennan through outsize rimless glasses that made him look perpetually surprised. ''They think it's true enough to go on a major alert.''

They had reached the road and Knight maneuvered the car onto it, slowing down amid the crowd of reporters and news van. ''Jesus Christ,'' Brennan sighed.

''Yeah.'' Knight leaned furiously on the horn to clear a path through the mob, which parted reluctantly. He stopped the car at the barricade. The police must have recognized the vehicle, because they raised the barrier to let it through. Knight accelerated toward the Killenworth gates.

''Are we going to be directly involved?'' Brennan asked.

''This time, yes. Under Reagan's old presidential executive order. It'll likely raise hackles at the FBI, but the DO says the president will back us up.'' The DO was John Barlow, director of operations. ''Reid was in a meeting with the president up until a few minutes ago and Barlow routed the decision through to me. They can't make up their minds whether the kidnapping's terrorist work, or an inside job. Anyway, Reid persuaded the president to call in a couple of Soviet and East European experts — that's us — to help the Bureau figure it out.''

''What's the FBI think of that?''

''Don't know. We'll have to wait and see.''

Knight pulled up behind a line of unmarked cars a hundred feet from the mansion's gates. ''Nobody's been inside yet except Russians,'' he said as they got out of the car. ''The Soviets have been stonewalling, as usual. Maybe the State Department's arranged something by now. I hope. We can't do much unless we get a look in there. Come with me, we've got to see the FBI guy in charge. Lee Ennis. You know him?''

''No.'' Brennan splashed through a shallow puddle. At least the rain had stopped.

''You will. You've been tapped to be liaison with him in the New York area. If Gorbachev's anywhere at the moment, it's New York.''

''So much for my resignation,'' Brennan commented.

''Tough luck. We need you to handle the East European end. If it was terrorists who snatched Gorbachev, they might have been an emigré group. You know more about that than anybody else with recent field experience.''

"Jesus Christ," Brennan complained. "You're putting me back into the *field*?"

"You got it," said Knight. "Your resignation's not accepted. And as for the fieldwork, I don't think you'll find out much sitting behind a desk."

They had almost reached a group of men standing just outside the iron gates. One of the men caught sight of them and turned to greet them. He appeared to be in his late forties, with that impassive, observant face that FBI men seemed to cultivate. From the way his companions turned as he did, he appeared to be in charge.

"Hello, again, Lee," Knight said to him. "This is Sean Brennan. The man I told you about. Sean, Lee Ennis. Lee's Special-Agent-in-Charge, New York Field Office. Counterintelligence and internal security."

Brennan tried to suppress his anger and to recollect the FBI structure in New York. The office was big enough to rate an Assistant Commissioner to run it, and there were at least four SACs like Ennis.

"Hello, Brennan," Ennis said. The voice was neutral, the look appraising. He's prepared to dislike me, Brennan thought: he thinks I'm an Agency spook. But it doesn't matter whether we like each other or not, as long as we work together. I hope he realizes that.

"Hello," Brennan said.

"What's happening?" asked Knight.

Ennis gestured toward the gate. "There's been some kind of arrangement worked out. The State Department guy says the Russian ambassador will be out in about five minutes to take us up to the house. They're going to give us criminal jurisdiction, even though it's diplomatic territory."

"Good. They letting in a forensic team?"

"Yeah."

"We've been given clearance to go with you."

Again the appraising look. "Okay. I figured you might be. The press know you guys are going to be working with us?"

"It's not being hidden," Knight said, "but on the other hand we're not going out of our way to announce it."

"Okay. That's the way we'll play it."

"Here comes somebody," observed one of the other FBI men.

Brennan looked past them, through the ornate iron filigree of the gate. A Soviet embassy limousine was gliding down the tree-shaded drive. It stopped just inside the entrance and two men got out.

"The passenger's the Soviet ambassador to the UN," Ennis remarked. "The one driving, I don't know. One of the UN embassy KGB people, probably."

The KGB officer pulled back one leaf of the gates, leaving a gap wide enough for the vehicle to pass through.

"You coming up with us?" Ennis asked. "Or in your own car?"

"We'd better come with you. Make like we're FBI."

"Suit yourself." Ennis gestured at a nondescript sedan. "Climb in."

They started up the long drive, the Russians leading them in the embassy car. "Any idea how the attackers got in?" Brennan asked.

"Bogus NBC van," said Ennis. "We found it down on the beach at West Pond. Motor still running. There was supposed to be a real one coming here for the press conference. The real one broke down on the expressway on the way out here, and their radio transmitter went dead. We suspect sabotage, but we're still checking out how it was done."

"Documents?" Brennan asked.

"The Secret Service man who was in charge here says they all checked out perfectly. TV crew names, authorizations, the works. Somebody had inside information from NBC. Professionals wouldn't have had any trouble. They probably tapped into the NBC computers."

"The equipment in those mobile units isn't cheap," Knight said. "You can't just buy it over the counter. We ought to be able to get traces on who bought it."

Ennis shook his head. He didn't appear annoyed at Knight's use of the word "we." "The equipment was all mock-up. It looked perfectly real, but it was obsolete stuff dressed up to look high-tech. It could have come from anywhere. If they were being careful, from outside the country. We'll have to check Canada and Mexico as well as here."

"Dammit."

''You found the van by the water?'' Brennan asked. ''How did they get away?''

''High-speed launch, most likely. The Secret Service chopper went up, but they couldn't see anything. It was still almost dark, and raining into the bargain. Even if there hadn't been rain they had a twenty-minute start, and there's a lot of traffic out in the Sound. Somebody did a lot of planning, and lucked in with the weather, too.''

''Really professional,'' Brennan said. ''I'm not sure terrorists — *any* terrorists — are that professional.''

''The thought's occurred to me, too,'' Ennis said. ''Maybe it was an inside job? Pretty weird, though.''

Knight remarked, ''That possibility might be clearer after we have a look at the house.''

''There it is,'' Ennis said.

The car was out of the trees, now, and the half-timbered walls and gables of Killenworth loomed ahead of them. With the low gray clouds and the faint mist it looked ghostly and haunted, even in the daylight.

''Quite a place,'' Ennis said. ''I'd hate to have to heat it.''

The Soviet limousine stopped outside the front entrance. Ennis drew up behind it and the three men got out. There were two other cars in the procession, and a van with the forensic equipment. Ennis's men climbed out of the other vehicles and stood in a loose group, waiting for orders.

The UN ambassador marched over to them. ''Colonel Yefremov speaks English,'' he said. ''He is chief of our UN embassy security. He has spoken with the survivors of the attack. He will tell you where to start, and where to go. I will accompany you. Please follow Colonel Yefremov's instructions.''

''Let's get one thing perfectly straight, Mr. Ambassador,'' Ennis responded. ''I am responsible for this investigation. If Colonel Yefremov has suggestions, he's welcome to make them. But they're suggestions, and that's all. Not instructions. If you have difficulty with that, please call the State Department before we begin.''

He stood, waiting. The ambassador shot him a virulent look. Yefremov, who was about Brennan's age, waited also. The man's broad Slavic face looked worried, surprisingly.

"You said there were survivors?" Ennis asked the Russian.

Yefremov nodded. "The head of compound security. He was shot in the head, but, miraculously, is in no serious danger. The other was the chief communications officer."

"We'll want to talk to them both," Ennis said.

"As soon as we've completed debriefing them. They have been sent to our Manhattan compound. Our doctors are treating the security officer."

Stonewalling, Brennan thought. How very Russian.

"Do you have a floor plan of the house?" Ennis asked Yefremov. "We don't want to miss anything."

"In the security office," Yefremov said. "We can go in through the front door."

"Wait here," Ennis called to his men. He, Brennan and Knight followed Yefremov to the huge, nail-studded oak doors, the ambassador trailing glumly behind. The entrance hall was vast; a suit of armor stood at their left as they came in. Overhead, carved oak beams arched against white plaster. A wide curving staircase led upward. At the bottom of the staircase was a wooden chair. On the floor beside it was a body, facedown.

"One of Mr. Gorbachev's guards?" asked Ennis.

"Yes. One that came with him, not permanent staff."

"Shot?" Brennan asked. There was no blood.

"No. His neck was broken. They didn't want to make any noise at the bottom of the stairs, I think."

"Okay." Ennis turned to the ambassador. "Have you been through the place?"

"Only the house. Colonel Yefremov and others have searched the grounds."

"Any luck outside?" Ennis asked Yefremov. Brennan had a momentary vision of the leader of the USSR lying under a dripping bush, with a bullet through his head.

"No," Yefremov answered. "He is not inside the compound perimeter anywhere."

"We'll look anyway. Has anything been touched or moved? In the house?"

"No," replied the ambassador. "We were thinking our own people would investigate first." Annoyance had crept into his voice. Brennan wondered whether what had happened had really sunk in.

"How many people were in the house when it happened?" Brennan asked Yefremov.

"There are — were — eight permanent inside staff. With Mr. Gorbachev in the house were six security officers, the head of protocol, his press adviser and two aides. Nineteen."

"How many casualties?" Ennis asked, stopping to look up the stairway.

Yefremov looked pained. "Everyone except the security head and the chief of the communications unit. And, of course, Secretary Gorbachev."

Even Ennis was jolted. "*Everyone*?"

"Yes. Sixteen people."

"Why didn't you —? Never mind. Go on, please."

The Russian led the way along the hall to a set of double doors on the right. "Dining room," he said. "They would have come through here."

He trudged ahead of them across the huge room, around the end of a table that could easily seat a hundred guests. One end of it had been set for breakfast. Five place settings: Gorbachev and his four assistants. A huge crystal chandelier, obviously part of the original fittings of the house, was suspended over the middle of the long table. There were more oak beams arching from the walls up to the ceiling; the beams were deeply carved. Ennis stopped again, looking around carefully.

"Where was the radio officer when it happened?" Brennan asked.

"He told me he was getting up to check on his men and saw the attackers as they came from the direction of the servants' quarters. They'd probably already killed everyone in there. The corridors were dark, but he saw the guns, and got out onto the roof by one of the windows, the ones that come out of the roof — "

"Dormers," cued Ennis.

"Dormers. He says he called out, but it was too windy for anyone to hear. He was probably too afraid to call loudly, if he did at all."

"How many attackers in all?"

"The security head saw only one. The communications officer saw two. But I think there must have been more than two, to have done this."

"It's likely," Ennis agreed. "Where do we go from here?"

"Through the far doors." Yefremov led them to another set of double doors, only one leaf of which was open. They stepped through into a dimly-lit corridor. At its far end, another body lay huddled on the floor.

"The guard at the servants' stair," Yefremov said. "Another one that Secretary Gorbachev brought with him."

They stopped by the dead guard. He was lying on his side in a pool of dark clotted blood. Several bullets had hit him; his jaw had disintegrated and the right side of his suit jacket was in ribbons. A few feet farther on, the corridor turned right. Ennis stopped and looked back.

"The perpetrator would have fired from here," he said. He examined the floor. "No cartridge cases. Very cagey. They must have had catch baskets on the weapons. Didn't want brass clattering all over the place . . . . Did anyone get a look at the weapons?"

"The security officer described the one he saw. It was a machine pistol. Silenced. Very small, square, with a big clip."

"Sounds like an Ingram," Knight said. He'd been quiet for so long that Brennan was startled.

"Faces?" Brennan asked.

"No. They all wore masks, the kind that goes over the head except for eyes and mouth. The security officer did say the one he saw had blue eyes and a thin mouth."

"Ski masks," Ennis said. He glanced at Brennan. Brennan knew exactly what he was thinking, because he was thinking it himself: If these people were so good at their job, why was the security officer still alive?

"Okay. Is that the security office along there?"

"Yes."

They went on to the office. The monitor screens were blank; none of the infrared sensors or motion sensors were registering. Blood and tissue had sprayed over the console. The body of the other Russian was lying next to a swivel chair, his legs under the console. Half his head was gone.

"Another head shot," Ennis said. "Very good marksmen, these people." The ambassador, who had been looking pale since the first body, abruptly turned on his heel and hurried back the way they had come.

"How did they defeat the security?" Knight asked Yefremov.

"They put a gun to the security officer's head. They had already killed the other man. The security officer turned the systems off."

And he shouldn't have, Brennan thought. His job was to protect his man at the cost of his own life. He lost his nerve.

But they didn't kill him. At zero range, and gunmen like these missed?

I suppose it's possible. They were in a hurry.

"Where did you say they came in?" queried Ennis.

"This way. Through the service entrance."

Yefremov led them to the steel door and opened it. Cool, damp air rushed in. Outside, one the flagstones, lay two more corpses, and what looked like a small trunk upon which was sitting an electric lantern.

"That," Yefremov said, pointing, "is one of the terrorists."

"You mean you *got* one?" Ennis exclaimed.

"Petrosian must have killed him before he died. Petrosian is the dead man over there. Responsible for external security at this compound. He brought them up from the gate."

Ennis leaned over the dead Russian, but didn't touch him. "This is his gun?" he asked, pointing to the dead hand.

"Yes. PSM pistol. We in the security units all carry them. Petrosian opened the door for the terrorists, then they blinded the surveillance camera with the electric light. It gave them time to get inside. They were very quick."

Brennan had gone over to the dead terrorist — if that was what he was — and was staring down at the pale face. The eyes were open, appearing to examine the low gray sky.

"Okay," Ennis concluded. "Give me the map, and I'll get my people started. I'll want to talk to the radio officer." He turned to Knight. "You two coming?"

"Frank," Brennan said, "I think we ought to stay out here and look around for a minute."

"Okay," Knight shrugged. "Lee? That okay with you?"

"Suit yourself," Ennis replied. "I'll get this show on the road. It's going to be a long day."

As they departed, Yefremov looked doubtfully over his shoulder. Brennan waited until he was sure they were gone.

"What's up, Sean?"

Brennan looked down at the terrorist's body again. "I know who this is," he said.

"What? Who?"

"I was called in to help debrief him eight months ago," Brennan said. "It was just before you took over the division, so you wouldn't have met him. He's a Polish SB colonel, a defector. His name's Jerzy Galeski."

New York
Monday, September 30

ENNIS WAS WAITING for him when Brennan stepped out of the elevator. The FBI man's chunky face betrayed anxiety. It was the first time, since meeting him yesterday, that Brennan had seen anything in Ennis other than the normal Bureau impassiveness.

"The tape's here?" Brennan asked, as the elevator doors slid closed behind him.

"Yeah. We're just setting it up for a look. Did you get one?"

"Langley did. They'll have it by now. Thanks for sparing me a trip to Washington."

"No trouble," Ennis said, leading the way along the corridor. He'd called Brennan at the New York CIA field office at 8:10 A.M., an hour ago; the FBI had received an anonymous telephone call directing them to a drop point down in Battery Park, where a videotape would be waiting for them. Knight had called a few minutes later from Langley to tell Brennan that they'd had a similar call down there. Brennan was to use the FBI facilities to look at their tape, if the FBI didn't mind.

The FBI, at least in the person of Ennis, didn't mind, although Brennan wasn't so sure that Cyril Ranelagh was of the same opinion. Ranelagh held the rank of assistant director, only one step down from the chief of the FBI himself, and was head of the New York field office. Knight and Brennan had been in the office for three hours yesterday afternoon, pooling information with the

Bureau counterintelligence personnel; Ranelagh had been there, and his rising annoyance with CIA involvement had been plain, especially as it became clear that the cooperation between the two agencies wasn't providing any leads to Gorbachev's kidnappers. Ranelagh clearly suspected the CIA of holding back information.

Which was precisely what it was doing. The FBI was not to be told that the dead terrorist at Killenworth was Jerzy Galeski. That policy had come from Barlow, director of operations, maybe all the way from Stephen Reid, the head of the CIA. Brennan had greeted the decision with disbelief; the Russian security officer at Killenworth would have been smart enough to photograph Galeski's body before it was taken away, and it was only a matter of time before they determined who he was. Barlow and Reid were apparently hoping the Russians wouldn't make it public. If they did, there'd be nothing to do but stonewall, and Ranelagh's suspicions would be more than justified. By the end of the three hours Ranelagh was taking no trouble to be polite.

Knight had left New York for Washington as soon as yesterday's meeting was over, and Brennan went uptown to the CIA field office near the UN, where he pulled Galeski's current, background and debriefing files from the Langley computers. He'd spent the rest of the day and most of the night working through the files and waiting for the black bag team Knight had sent to Galeski's boarding house. About three A.M. they turned up with all the papers they'd been able to find in the Pole's room; they'd got in and out without being detected. Brennan searched through the material they'd brought, but, as he'd expected, found nothing useful. It proved nothing; Galeski was an intelligence officer and would have been careful to keep his residence clean. That left personal checking, which Brennan had been about to start this morning despite his fatigue, when Ennis called about the videotape.

"Did the caller identify his organization?" Brennan asked as they neared the glass door to the FBI field office. For a Bureau man, Ennis needed a haircut; his curly graying hair had almost reached the back of his shirt collar.

"No," said Ennis. "But he said they'd sent copies of the tape to the *Times*, the three main TV networks and the Russians. They're not being coy."

"No," Brennan said. Ennis shoved open the glass door at the

end of the corridor. Inside was the reception area. There were a few not-very-comfortable chairs, a poster of the Ten Most Wanted Criminals, and a tapestry on one wall with the FBI seal woven into it. On the wall opposite the Ten Most Wanted, as though keeping an eye on them, hung a portrait photograph of the current FBI director, and a picture of J. Edgar Hoover. A tired yucca plant stood next to an end table stacked with FBI public relations pamphlets. A clock above the tapestry showed 9:16 A.M.

Ennis nodded to the receptionist and went past her, Brennan following. Beyond the reception area lay the field office proper: interview rooms, SAC and Assistant SAC offices, the squad rooms, gun vaults, radio and computer rooms, mountain ranges of files in rotor cabinets, secure areas for cryptographic and communications gear, the stenographic pool. There was also an audiovisual room, fitted out with motion picture and videotape display equipment. Brennan hadn't been in it yesterday; it was about twenty feet long and ten feet wide, with a pair of TV monitors at one end under a roll-up movie screen, and a couple of videocassette players. Down the middle of the room ran a formica-topped table on collapsible steel legs, surrounded by ten or so folding chairs. Except for two vacant seats, the room was already full. Ranelagh was sitting at the far end from the entrance; he was a large man, like a lot of Bureau people, paunchy, with a receding chin under an ill-tempered mouth. He glanced up and saw Ennis and Brennan enter.

''Finally,'' he said. ''Maybe we can get started, if the CIA's ready?''

''The CIA's ready,'' Brennan responded calmly, sitting down beside Ennis in one of the empty chairs. ''Thanks for the invitation.'' He thought: the bastard's had all night to brood about me. I wonder how he's going to handle it?

''Turn it on,'' Ranelagh said. The other agents had taken their cue from Ranelagh; they all, not quite pointedly, ignored Brennan.

Somebody dimmed the lights and switched on the VCR. The television screens flickered, grainy black on white, and then cleared. Two white blurs appeared against a gray background, then came into focus. A pair of naked feet. The ankles were shackled to the legs of what appeared to be a wooden chair.

The camera tilted upward, following the legs to the knees. No trousers, just white undershorts. Now it was possible to see the arms of the chair, and the forearms of the person sitting in it. The wrists were secured to the chair. The camera moved farther up. The abdomen and stomach were hidden by a newspaper. The camera went in a little to show the date: the *New York Times,* Sunday, September 29. Still no voice-over.

The newspaper disappeared, and the camera leaped up to the prisoner's face.

It was Mikhail Gorbachev, naked from the waist up. He stared blankly at the camera, but he was clearly alive. His face was haggard and the pupils of his eyes, which should have been contracted against the strong light, were dilated. Drugged, Brennan thought.

The camera held on the expressionless face, and a voice began to speak. Instinctively, the men in the room leaned forward.

''We are the Jan Paderewski Cell,'' the voice said. Good English, only a slight accent. ''We have arrested the criminal Bolshevik, Mikhail Sergeyevich Gorbachev, for crimes committed against the Polish people by both him and his predecessors.''

Oh, Christ, Brennan thought. Not the Poles again.

''We have certain demands, which must be met before he is released,'' the voice continued. ''First. Immediate withdrawal of all Soviet military and security forces from Poland. Second. Immediate withdrawal of Poland from the Warsaw Pact, and establishment of armed neutrality. Third. Immediate release of all political prisoners held by the Moscow-puppet Polish Union of Workers Party. Fourth. Immediate dissolution of the Polish Union of Worker Party, and the institution of free multiparty elections in Poland. Poland.''

''These demands cannot be negotiated. The Bolsheviks in Warsaw and Moscow have ten days to comply. If the demands have not been met by that time, the criminal Mikhail Sergeyevich Gorbachev will be executed by the soldiers of the Jan Paderewski Cell. That is all.''

The picture on the television screen broke up, and went black.

The room was silent. Then someone said, very softly, ''Jesus H. Christ.''

''Who in hell was Jan Paderewski?'' Ranelagh asked. ''I thought he was a musician, not a terrorist.''

Nobody answered.

Brennan said, "Paderewski was also president of the first Polish republic just after the First World War. It was the first time Poland had been free for several centuries."

Ranelagh shot him a look of intense dislike. "Okay," he said. "That's it. Ennis. I want to talk to you in my office. Would *Mr.* Brennan please come as well? Maybe he can tell us some more Polish history. If we need to know it."

There was a discreetly embarrassed silence as Ennis stood up. Brennan waited just long enough to see Ranelagh's color start to rise, and then got up as well, very slowly.

"We'll go on with this in a minute," Ranelagh said to the others. "Watch it again. See if you can pick *anything* up."

Ranelagh's office was a suite of two rooms tucked away at the back of the field office. Framed citations covered the walls, with the obligatory pictures of Hoover and the current FBI director. There was a picture of a much younger Ranelagh shaking hands with Hoover.

"Siddown," Ranelagh commanded. "This won't take long." He didn't sit down himself, though; he leaned back against the front of his desk and crossed his arms above his paunch. Intimidation technique, Brennan thought as he dropped into a leather chair. He must have enjoyed interrogations.

"I'll only say this once," Ranelagh said. "I don't like spooks on my turf. Ennis went over the line, inviting you here today. I don't want you frigging around here, wasting my agents' time. I've had to pull everybody off everything else, every other case, to look for goddamn Gorbachev; he should have stayed home. I haven't got time to nursemaid the CIA, too, just because you schmucks want a piece of the action. Terrorists or spies on US soil, that's the Bureau's business. Langley's got no legal footing for domestic operations. Get me?"

"President Reagan's Executive Order 12333," Brennan countered instantly, "allows CIA domestic operations to collect significant foreign intelligence, as long as the operations aren't directed against US citizens in the US. This matter deals with significant foreign intelligence. Or don't you think so?"

"This isn't foreign intelligence," Ranelagh snarled. "This is some terrorist bunch out to make a name for themselves. You can collect whatever you want, bottle caps, I don't give a flying fuck. But you haven't got the resources here to do the job, or you're not supposed to, and I don't want you using *mine*. Get me?"

"The president has ordered cooperation between the CIA and the FBI," Brennan said formally.

"Fine, we'll cooperate. I'll define cooperation. Right now, you can cooperate by getting the hell out of here. You want to set foot in this place, or talk to one of my people, you go through me. Nobody else. Get me?"

If he says that one more time, Brennan thought, I'll kick him in the crotch.

"You —" he began, but was cut off by the trill of one of the telephones on Ranelagh's desk. Ranelagh snatched it up. Brennan took the opportunity to glance at Ennis. The SAC was poker-faced, but Brennan could see a vein pumping in his temple.

"What?" Ranelagh barked. He eyed Brennan. "Yes, he's here. You want to talk to him?"

A silence. "Okay," Ranelagh said. He covered the mouthpiece. "It's your friend who was here yesterday. Knight. You can talk to him, but I'm putting you on the speaker phone. Whatever you've both got to say, I want to hear." He thrust the receiver at Brennan, who had to stand up to take it, and flicked a switch on the telephone cradle.

"Sean here, Frank. What's up?"

"You saw the tape?" The voice rang tinnily around the office; Ranelagh turned the volume down a bit.

"Yes. It's bad."

"It's worse than bad. I have more information for you."

"I'm not sure this is a secure line."

"It's secure!" Ranelagh snapped.

"It's secure," Brennan repeated.

"So I heard. You've got an FBI audience?"

"Yeah. Assistant Director Ranelagh, Lee Ennis."

"So much the better, they'll be hearing this soon from the Bureau director. The president's agreed to let the Russians send over a specialist team to help look for Gorbachev. They can't work independently, but they're to be allowed to participate."

"He's *what*?"

"You heard me. Russians are on the way. They'll be in at McGuire Air Force Base at seven this evening. I want you to talk to them. Get whatever information they're willing to give you. Depending on circumstances, if you know what I mean, it may be disinformation, but we need it anyway. Okay?"

"Okay." Now that Brennan thought about it, it made sense. If the president were kidnapped in Moscow, Washington would insist on American involvement in the search. "Who are they? KGB?"

"The Russians swear they're straight police, a special Moscow antikidnap squad."

"Bullshit."

"Yeah, well. The leader's name is Timoshkin. Any bells?"

"No."

"None here, either. Could be a cover legend. Anyway, go out to McGuire with the FBI and talk to this Timoshkin. See what he wants to do. The Bureau will want the same information, so you might as well kill two birds."

Ranelagh was listening with an expression of suppressed fury. "Fine by me," Brennan agreed. "Who's responsible for putting them somewhere?"

"They're staying at the Soviet UN mission there in Manhattan. You and I won't be having much to do with them. Jurisdiction."

"All right."

"Keep me posted," Knight said. "All hell's going to break loose down here pretty soon. One of the TV stations got a copy of the tape. They say they're going to air it, and I don't think we can stop them."

"Not much point, anyway," Brennan said.

"I suppose not. Good-bye."

Knight broke the connection. "Thanks," Brennan said to Ranelagh.

Ranelagh was nearly speechless. "Russians?" he managed. "*Russians*?"

"You thought you had problems with *us*," Brennan said blandly. "Good luck working with the KGB."

"You bastards," Ranelagh spat. "You set this up. Hand me the

Russians to worry about, on top of everything else. Ennis, get this goddamn spook out of here, before I lock him up for trespassing."

Ennis stood up silently, and opened the office door. Brennan followed him out.

"And get back to the AV room as soon as you've got rid of him," Ranelagh yelled after them. "We've got work to do."

They went through the reception area and out into the empty corridor. Neither of them spoke. Brennan punched the elevator button furiously.

"Sorry," Ennis said, as they waited. "He's a rancid bastard."

"He's a little short on common courtesy," observed Brennan.

"He wouldn't know courtesy if it bit him on the dong," Ennis said feelingly. "You know what's behind it, don't you? The director retires next year. Ranelagh figures if he pulls this one off by himself, rescues Gorbachev, he'll be in line for the director's chair in Washington. That's what he's after. He doesn't want to share the credit."

"Yeah. But if he balls it up, he won't have anybody to share the blame with, either."

"He doesn't think like that," Ennis said. "He figures if he wants something, he ought to have it. If I didn't have to work for the son of a bitch, I wouldn't give him the time of day from his own watch."

Brennan glanced at the FBI man. "Are you in shit because you gave me a hand?"

"No more than usual. He doesn't like my style."

"It's tough, sometimes," Brennan said.

The elevator door slid open. Ennis put out a hand to hold it there. "Look," he said, "it doesn't make any sense for us to cut each other out. No matter what Ranelagh wants. He can't see past the end of his nose. The leader of the Soviet Union has been kidnapped, for Christ's sake, he may be murdered, and all Ranelagh can see is the directorship. You want to keep working together?"

"There's nothing I'd like better," Brennan said. He found himself liking the man. "But you could get into trouble."

"Ranelagh doesn't know everything that goes on here," said Ennis. "Look, hold the door. I'll give you my home number." He pulled out a pen and notebook and scribbled on the back page.

Tearing it off, he handed it to Brennan. "You can call me here, too. Use a code name, my informants do. Use, let me see —"

"Figleaf," Brennan suggested. "It's a good cover-up."

"Very funny," Ennis said, although Brennan thought he saw a trace of a grin. The smile, if it was one, vanished. "You really think it was Poles who did this?" Ennis asked.

"I don't think so," said Brennan. "But it'll be a hell of a job proving it."

"Have you guys got anything on the dead terrorist yet?" asked Ennis.

"Have you?"

"No. Not a thing," Ennis said. "Not yet."

Brennan felt slightly guilty. Ennis was risking a career-damaging reprimand to help him, but the orders from Langley were clear, even if they made no sense: Galeski's existence was not to be revealed to *anyone* without authorization.

It's cover-your-ass time, Brennan thought. Langley has to figure out, and in one hell of a hurry, how to explain taking in a defector who blows a couple of spy nets for them, and then cheerfully goes out and kidnaps the leader of the Soviet Union. Everybody'll say we should have known. Hell, maybe *I* should have known, I helped debrief him. But Langley isn't going to *have* the time to cover its ass. Even if the KGB isn't behind this, they'll identify Galeski soon enough. Yefremov's sure to have taken pictures of the body. And they won't keep it quiet, either, no matter what Barlow or Reid or anybody else wants to believe.

"Lee," he said, "I know who the dead man is. Was."

Ennis didn't look surprised. "I thought you might," he said. "What about him?"

"He was a Polish defector, an intelligence man. I helped debrief him. There will be a lot of awkward questions as soon as people know who he was."

Ennis gave a quiet whistle. "I see. What're you going to do?"

"Try to find out if he was planted on us. I don't think it was the Poles, the Jan Paderewski Cell."

"What do you want me to do?"

"Nothing. I may need your help later, but at the moment, I have to play a lone hand."

"But you'll keep me briefed?"

"As much as I can."

"Okay," Ennis said after a second's pause. "We'll work it that way. See you out at McGuire tonight."

Brennan left the Federal Building, went back to the parking lot and retrieved the car; it was the CIA vehicle Knight had been using yesterday at Killenworth. The cloud cover that had dulled the sky earlier in the morning was breaking up, and fitful, watery gleams of sunshine drifted down among the towers of Manhattan and bounced around among the glass facades: a city of mirrors.

As he drove north, Brennan started worrying about Galeski again. The Pole had been an SB major in the Polish embassy in Bonn, Brennan's old station, running under the cover of a trade attaché. He'd been a walk-in; he hadn't been spotted by the CIA station and there had never been any attempt to recruit him. He had also been a very frightened walk-in. He'd realized, in the three months previous to his defection, that the SB Internal Security Office had started to take an unhealthy interest in him; they obviously suspected him of some kind of antistate activity, although he'd been unable to identify for his debriefing team (of whom Brennan was a member) what that activity might have been. He'd been ordered to return to Warsaw before his tour of duty expired, and this had sent him over the edge. He'd gone straight to the CIA, with a case full of documents he'd collected over the previous six weeks.

Brennan and the two other debriefing officers began on him with deep suspicion; given the circumstances of his flight, he could all too easily have been a plant, sent over to carry a load of disinformation. But the documents weren't disinformation at all. With their help, six SB agents operating in West Germany and West Berlin against American targets were identified and neutralized; one of them had even managed to recuit a captain in Eighth Army military intelligence, an espionage coup if it had lasted. Galeski was real.

They never did find out why the SB was suspicious of him. The seeds might have been planted by another security service, the West German or the British, in the hope that Galeski would defect to them. If this was the case, they'd received little return for their efforts.

Galeski also had extensive training in the Polish Special Service Unit, the equivalent of the British SAS or the Soviet Army's

SPETSNAZ troops, whose specializations included sabotage, penetration of defended targets, demolition, assassination — and kidnapping. If there had been a war in Europe, Galeski would have been ordered to go underground and join others like him to operate behind the NATO Front line, spreading as much mayhem, alarm and devastation as possible. If anyone outside the KGB could have planned and carried out Gorbachev's abduction, it was Galeski.

He realized with a start that he had driven almost as far as Bellevue Hospital without being aware of his progress. He couldn't even remember stopping for red lights, although he must have.

On automatic pilot, he thought. I'd better watch it. He was only a few minutes from the field office.

But would Galeski, even if he'd defected, go so far as to revenge himself on the Russians? His psychological profile had shown a very reserved character; he was unmarried, an only child, and seemed to have few social graces. But there had also been a great deal of anger in him; he had felt he belonged to the SB, and it had rejected him. For this, irrationally, he blamed the Russians, specifically the KGB. And his latent Polish patriotism had become extremely evident during the debriefing.

It fit, if you were inclined to believe it. A Polish defector from the SB gathers a few like-minded patriots, and strikes at the most potent symbol of his country's subjugation: the general secretary of the Communist Party of the Soviet Union. It was heroic, and ultimately futile, like so many of Poland's rebellions over the centuries.

The more Brennan thought about it, the more he didn't believe it. Galeski wasn't a leader; he lacked the charisma. But if you hadn't met him, talked with him for hours and days on end, you wouldn't know that. And if you didn't, the rest of it — Killenworth, the sixteen dead, the tape of Gorbachev — became plausible.

I'm going in circles, Brennan thought. Time to get some hard information. Where Galeski went after we finished with him, what he'd been doing, the people he saw, friends if he had any. Although he wasn't the kind to make friends.

He'd reached 101 Park Avenue, the skyscraper's angled black glass shooting like a vertical oil slick from its granite plaza. Inside was the New York field office of the Central Intelligence Agency.

Reversing usual practice, its telephone number was publicly listed, but its address was not. The field office was little more than a listening post; its number was listed only to give people a contact with the agency if they wanted to find out how to apply for a job, or wanted to report "suspicious incidents." There were a lot of crank calls. There would have been crank visitors, or worse, if the address had been publicized. Once in a while, the office provided logistical support for intelligence-gathering operations against foreign nationals, but it didn't normally furnish a base for such operations, and it only maintained four permanent staff.

Brennan parked the car in the underground garage and took an elevator to the thirty-seventh floor. Corridors upon corridors, then suite 3731. The sign on the bland panelled door read merely: H.K. ENTERPRISES, INC. Brennan had no idea what the H.K. stood for, if anything. A small camera lens glinted unobtrusively near the ceiling; he looked up into it and pressed the buzzer. A moment later the electric lock clicked open.

Inside was a reception area as bland as the door. Dorothy, the receptionist, was putting the telephone back in its cradle as Brennan entered. The instrument immediately rang again.

"I'm going to quit answering it," she said to Brennan. She was in her early fifties, plainly dressed, with gray hair drawn severely back from her narrow face. "It's been ringing off the hook all morning. Every nut in New York wants to lead us to Gorbachev. Either that or claims to be one of the kidnappers."

"You can disregard those," Brennan said. "We've heard from the real ones. Is Bill here?" William Partington was in charge of the field office, with two assistants.

"No. They've all gone out," she responded, as she picked up the telephone again, with a gesture of irritated resignation.

Brennan nodded, and went past the reception desk into the office area. Partington and his two juniors weren't Operations Directorate people, and wouldn't be much use in the search for Gorbachev, anyway. Knight was selecting a team down at Langley, and the men were supposed to arrive at the field office late int he afternoon.

He reached the suite that had been set aside as an operations headquarters when the field office was established a few years ago. According to Partington, it had never been used. The largest of the rooms contained three desks, each with telephones, a computer terminal and printer, a teletype, a couple of filing cabinets, a safe and not much else. The window had been sealed up with opaque plastic. Adjoining the working area were sleeping quarters, with an attached bathroom. It was spartan, but Brennan didn't expect to spend much time in it.

He tried to call Molly, but there was no answer. She might be out on the cliffs, sketching. He opened the safe, removed the thick printout he'd pulled from the Langley computer last night, and read through it again.

After his debriefing had ended, Galeski had demanded — as defectors at his level often did — a position as a CIA consultant, with a large salary. Langley had, as usual, refused. The CIA resettlement service gave him a new identity and found him a job with a private security firm in New Jersey, but he hadn't lasted; apparently he had disagreed with the firm's operational techniques. He'd appealed to Langley again, and they'd found him work at the shipping container port at Howland Hook on Staten Island. The Pole had then moved from New Jersey to a rooming house in Port Richmond, not far from the container terminal. Brennan ran through the printout until he found the address of the rooming house, and the name of its proprietor: Mrs. Elizabeth Petty. There was no significant information about her. The black bag team had found nothing in Galeski's room in the rooming house, so it was time for Brennan to start making personal inquiries, beginning with Elizabeth Petty.

First, though, he had to let Knight know about Ranelagh's behavior. Ranelagh couldn't refuse a presidential order to cooperate with the CIA, but there were plenty of ways to appear to cooperate while doing quite the reverse.

He got on the direct Langley line and dialled Knight's number. The answer was immediate.

"Knight."

"Sean here. We have a problem."

"What?"

Brennan told Knight about Ranelagh, but left out the agreement with Ennis. There was a longish pause. "Frank?" said Brennan.

"That's not the only problem," Knight said. "The Russians have identified Galeski. They passed the information to the *Post* half an hour ago. The whole shooting match. Defection, the fact that he went to us, everything."

"I hate to say I told you so, but I told you so."

"Yeah. It was a bad decision to keep it from Ranelagh."

"No kidding. It leaves me nowhere with him."

"That doesn't matter."

"What do you mean it doesn't matter?"

"We're being pulled off. No participation in looking for Gorbachev. No running operations on US soil in connection with Gorbachev, even against foreign nationals. No nothing."

"What in hell for?" Brennan realized that he was almost shouting into the telephone, and lowered his voice. "I thought the president ordered us to help. He was backing us up. That's what you told me yesterday."

"He was. But apparently his favorite national security adviser, good old Simon Parr, made him get cold feet because of the Galeski thing. It makes the CIA look bad already, and if Gorbachev gets killed, Parr says he doesn't want the CIA involved in any way, shape or form. If anybody screws up, it's going to be the FBI."

"Who's running the Company? Parr or Reid?"

"Reid fought it. But Parr persuaded the president. There's a direct presidential order now. No involvement. We can provide information for the Bureau, but only if asked."

"Jesus Christ!"

"Yeah. I know."

A pause. Then Knight added, "On the other hand, it couldn't hurt if we knew a little more about Galeski. Who he'd been seeing lately, for example."

"You mean I can actually ask questions?" Brennan didn't try to hide the sarcasm. "What'll happen if the president finds out?"

"Things could change in a hurry. The president might see things differently."

"Okay," Brennan said, after a moment. "I'll have a look. Are you sending the team? There could be a lot of digging."

"No team, Sean. This has to be low-profile. One person asking questions we can get away with. Two's a problem. More than that, impossible."

"Check on your desk. My resignation's there somewhere."

"Look, I promise, if you come up with something, we'll find a way to work it. But for the moment, all we can do is try to stay in."

"And I don't see the Russians tonight?"

"Christ, no. And keep clear of the Bureau. You know what Ranelagh could do with this."

"All right."

"Good luck, Sean. Talk to you soon."

"Thanks," Brennan said to the dial tone. He hung up, thinking: Why in hell didn't I tell him I'm through, that I won't work under these conditions, that my resignation stands?

Misplaced loyalty?

No, it isn't.

It's because somebody's trying to get me to swallow a pack of lies, starting with Jerzy Galeski, and I won't stand for it.

As he drove across the Verrazano Narrows Bridge toward Staten Island, he listened to the one o'clock news on the radio. Not surprisingly, Gorbachev's abduction was the story overshadowing all others. The newspeople were already reporting the Soviet-released information about Galeski — they were using his real name, not the one the CIA relocation people gave him — as well as the existence of the Jan Paderewski Cell, and its demands for Polish independence. They'd already begun to refer to the group as the JPC, its full name probably being too much of a mouthful. By tomorrow the media commentators would be asking pointed questions about the CIA's handling of Galeski, and first among the questions would be why Langley had let an assassin loose against Gorbachev. There weren't any answers to that one, yet.

At least Brennan was one jump ahead of the FBI. As far as Brennan was aware, they'd never known about Galeski, and they'd need time to pry information about him out of Langley.

This time, he thought, as the Ford glided down the long slope of the bridge toward Staten Island, the bureaucratic wars are working in my favor. With luck, I can slip through the cracks, for a while anyway.

Fort Wadsworth and the dull brick trapezoid of Battery Weed passed by on his right as the bridge swooped toward the land. Out here the sky seemed much larger. The sun was sending a real Indian summer warmth now; he opened the driver's window to admit a rush of wind that carried with it the brackish scent of the ocean mixed with unidentifiable chemical odors.

At the end of the bridge he got onto the expressway and followed it as far as Clove Road, where he turned off toward the north shore of the island. He hadn't been on the island for over fifteen years; at that time, the originally rural nature of the borough was already being overwhelmed by the flood of newcomers brought in by the opening of the Verrazano Bridge, much to the disgust and despair of the long-time residents. A lot of the middle class moved out of the North Shore area when that happened, leaving the old mansions and big Victorian homes to begin the slide from apartment conversion to rooming house to slum. The people who stayed had been fighting back, though, and seemed to be holding their own; there were some good shops, now, a few reasonable-looking restaurants, and quite a number of old buildings that had been renovated, rather than torn down.

But there was still a patch of desolate and declining real estate almost under the approaches to the Bayonne Bridge. Galeski had come to live and work here, for reasons Brennan couldn't guess at. A lot of Poles had settled up in Maspeth over the years, but Galeski hadn't gone to join them. Perhaps his past kept him away.

The rooming house was on a side street off Richmond Terrace. Brennan managed to find a parking space about fifty feet from the entrance, and studied the house for a moment. Before the Bayonne Bridge was constructed in the early '30s, the house must have been something of a showplace: a late-Victorian three-story with steeply pitched gables and a round tower at one corner, the porch once elaborate with gingerbread now paintless and decayed. It would have been set farther back from the road, too, when Richmond Terrace was narrower; now the porch steps reached almost to the sidewalk, and later building had eaten away at what must have once been a spacious yard. The hard ribbon of the Bayonne Bridge soared almost overhead.

Brennan got out of the car, locked it and went to the front door of the house. The porch floorboards creaked ominously under his feet. The glass in the upper half of the door had a lace curtain behind it; the interior was dim.

He had a choice between an electric doorbell and a vintage handrung one set into the door at waist level, and coated with half a century of brown paint. To be on the safe side, he tried both, and then waited. No one came.

He tried again. Still no one. The door lock was relatively new, a dead bolt. Presumably the roomers would have their own keys. Brennan tried the knob. The door swung open.

Pretty sloppy, in this neighborhood, he thought. He stepped into the foyer. After the outside of the house, it was a shock. The bannister of the staircase gleamed with polish and the black-and-white tile floor was spotless. A crystal chandelier gleamed in the dimness high above his head; the ceiling was a good twelve feet up. A mirror, its silvering cloudy with age rather than dirt, hung on the wall above an ornate mahogany table on which lay a copy of the *Staten Island Advance*, its headlines proclaiming Gorbachev's abduction. A pair of Queen Anne chairs flanked the table; from their patina of polish and the delicate faded tapestry of their seats, Brennan judged that they weren't reproductions. With a flash of nostalgia he remembered similar pieces in his grandmother's house up in Connecticut. He was fond of antique furnishings.

There was a panelled door on the left side of the hallway, and another at its far end; both were closed, and the house was silent. Maybe the doorbell wasn't working. Brennan reached back to the open door behind him and tried the button again. This time he heard it chime, far away at the back of the house.

After a few moments there were footsteps behind the door at the far end of the hall. Hastily, Brennan slipped back out onto the porch and closed the front door again, peering through its panes and the lace curtain. Light fell into the hall, outlining a slender figure moving in his direction. After a moment the curtain was drawn aside and Brennan found himself looking into the lined face of a very old woman. She was looked hesitant. Brennan nodded and smiled reassuringly. After a moment's consideration she fumbled with the lock; Brennan caught her expression of alarm as she realized the dead bolt hadn't been shot across.

Don't make assumptions, Brennan warned himself. She might have a Police Special in her apron.

She opened the door two inches and said, "Yes?"

"Mrs. Petty? I'm Sean Brennan, a friend of Mr. Sobiewski." Sobiewski was the name the relocation people had given Galeski, when they cut him loose. "Could you spare me a few minutes of your time?"

Her face remained neutral. It was an old face, but it was now very calm and alert. There was something in its poise that hinted at grace and breeding fallen on hard times, as the foyer suggested about the house itself.

"Mr. Sobiewski is not here," she said. Her voice wasn't strong, but it was very clear.

"I know," Brennan said. "He —"

"Who are you? May I please see some identification?"

If and when the FBI caught up with her, they'd find out he'd already been here. Too bad. Knight could say he'd gotten to Mrs. Petty before the hands-off order went out. He showed her his CIA identity card.

"Oh," she said. "You'd better come in. Is Mr. Sobiewski in some kind of trouble?"

He followed her into the foyer, where she stopped by the mahogany table and waited for him to answer.

"I'm afraid he's been killed," Brennan said.

Her eyes widened. "Oh, my God! How?"

"He was shot. I'm sorry, Mrs. Petty."

"That's terrible," she said. "He was only here for two months, but —" She stopped. "Who did it?"

"We're trying to find out. That's why I need to talk to you."

"Come this way." She opened the door leading to the left of the hallway, and led Brennan into a sitting room. Heavy nineteenth-century furniture, fireplace, bric-a-brac, scent of patchouli, antimacassars over the backs of the brocaded chairs. The drapes were dull-green velvet and half closed. She sat down on a sofa and gestured him to a seat across from her. "How may I help?"

"Did he have any friends that you knew of? Did anyone come here to see him?"

"There were no women, if that's what you mean. I have six rooms. My roomers are all men, very quiet. They have all been here for several years, except for Mr. Sobiewski."

"Male acquaintances?"

"There was only one. He came here, let me see, three or four times. I think Mr. Sobiewski met him before he moved here. But I don't know."

"What was his name?"

"Kepa. Stefan Kepa."

"Did he tell you his name?"

"Yes, the first time he came. He was very friendly, joking. He said that most Polish names were hard, but his was easy. He even spelled it for me."

The bastard, Brennan thought. Making sure we'd find another Pole, when we went looking. "Did he and Mr. Sobiewski get along well?"

"As far as I could see. I only saw them together twice, really. I was glad that he had a friend. He seemed so morose, most of the time. Except for working, and when he went out with Mr. Kepa, he spent most of his time in his room."

"Could you describe Mr. Kepa?"

"Let me try to remember." She leaned on the arm of the sofa, absentmindedly smoothing the folds of her dress as she searched her memory. "He was about forty, I'd judge. Average height. His hair was blonde, but he was losing it. Blue eyes, I think. There was really nothing that stood out about him. Except his hands."

"His hands?"

"They were really too large for his arms. Very wide. Big fingers."

"Anything else?"

"No. As I said, he was quite nondescript. His English was very good. If I hadn't heard him speaking Polish to Mr. Sobiewski, I wouldn't have known he was a foreigner."

He questioned her for another half hour, but she could add nothing else. She had never seen anyone else with Galeski, and he almost never went out. Where he went when he did, she had no idea. At the end, Brennan warned her that she might be visited by the FBI, and might perhaps have to go through this again. The prospect didn't seem to worry her.

She offered him tea or coffee before he left, which he had to refuse, although he felt vaguely that he was being discourteous. In the foyer, she stopped and looked down at the newspaper lying on the hall table under the mirror. "This has something to do with Mr. Gorbachev, doesn't it?" she asked suddenly.

"Yes."

"Thank you for being so honest."

He paused at the open front door and looked back over her head, into the foyer and its fading elegance. "Your house is wonderful," he said simply.

"Thank you," she said. "My grandfather built it. My father was born here, and so was I. I try to keep it up, but the outside is too much for me, I'm afraid. We can fall on hard times through no fault of our own, Mr. Brennan."

"I know." *Jane.*

"Good day, Mr. Brennan."

He made his way back to the car, feeling oddly as though he had just stepped into, and then out of, the previous century. With some effort he put the sensation out of his mind, and pondered his next move. Start checking on Kepa, to begin with. The Ford had both a radio and a cellular telephone; he called the field office on the phone and told Dorothy to request a file check on Stefan Kepa and to call him back. If the Russians were monitoring, they'd be quite happy that he'd found another Pole.

He drove to the container port. Galeski had worked there driving a forklift, but questioning the men he'd worked with and his foreman produced no result: the Pole's English was good enough, but he kept to himself, never went drinking with them although he often seemed to be hung over, ignored Polack jokes. Nobody'd seen him with anyone named Kepa. A complete blank.

Brennan slumped in the car in the parking lot, thinking. He'd have to backtrack to the security firm where Galeski worked before, and to his previous residence. He was already suspecting he wouldn't find much. More Kepa, if the man was laying a trail on purpose.

The car telephone dinged. Brennan picked it up. Dorothy was on the line.

"Mr. Brennan. Nothing on any Kepa, Stefan."

"Nothing at all?"

"No. I'm sorry."

"Okay."

There was another possibility. He dialled Ennis's direct line. After a moment, the FBI man answered. He sounded harassed.

"Figleaf. I have a name for you. Nothing in our files."

"Name?" asked Ennis.

"Stefan, Kepa." He spelled it.

"Okay. Where can I get you?"

Brennan gave him the number of the cellular phone. "Or at the other place," he said, meaning the field office. "Is our mutual friend still in a snit?"

"He's grinning. Didn't you know you guys were called off?"

"Never heard a thing about it. Maybe they'll tell me when I go back to the fort."

"Maybe," Ennis said, his tone indicating he didn't believe a word of Brennan's denial.

"Any luck at your end?"

"Zip," Ennis said. "The victim's disappeared into thin air. We've put everybody on the streets, but no dice yet. We'll try this name."

"One favor," Brennan said. "Let me know what you find before you take it any farther. I'll pay back."

"You're asking a lot."

"I know."

"I'll see what I can do."

"Thanks."

Brennan hung up and headed toward Manhattan.

He got back to the office at twenty after eight in the evening, hungry and tired. Everyone but Partington had gone home. The head of the field office was eating a pastrami sandwich, his feet up on his desk. Business as usual, by Langley's orders, with the general secretary of the Soviet Union hidden somewhere out there, likely within a radius of twenty miles.

"Any luck?" Partington asked as Brennan passed the open office door.

"Not much." As Brennan had expected, the security firm had nothing to offer, and no one in the apartment building where Galeski had lived knew anything about him. The man might as well have been a hermit. Brennan wished fervently that Langley had taken more interest in the man after they'd drained him. The agency had a poor reputation when it came to supporting defectors after their services were no longer needed; he sometimes wondered why anyone came across at all. The British were far more attentive.

"You been listening to the radio?" Partington asked.

"Yes." Brennan had kept it on whenever he was in the car. There were bulletins every half hour, each one reporting the continuing bafflement of the authorities, and the rising temperature of the political climate. Moscow was apparently crawling with heavily armed troops, and westerners had been advised to stay off the streets, for their own safety. The Soviet media was accusing "Polish counterrevolutionary terrorists" of the kidnapping, and was demanding a full investigation by Polish authorities into any links between the JPC and the Solidarity union. A statement issued in the name of Solidarity had somewhat desperately condemned the abduction, and insisted that the JPC was acting against the will and interests of the Polish people. But a street march in Gdansk, which had actually started as a protest against the shutting down of one of the shipyards there, was taken by the authorities to be a pro-JPC demonstration, and was broken up by riot police, with an uncertain number of casualties.

The only bright spot was that the Kremlin had not, so far, accused the United States of complicity in the kidnapping. Both superpowers, however, were maintaining a high level of alert. Some Soviet army divisions near the Polish, Czech and Hungarian borders had gone over to full mobilization, but had not yet moved from their base positions.

"Has there been an official response to the JPC demands?" Brennan asked. "I've been running around all day."

"Joint statement from Warsaw and Moscow. They say there might be some negotiations, but not on the basis of the demands already made. The statement gave the reasons you'd expect. There are no Soviet security organs working in Poland. There are no political prisoners in Poland. The Polish Party has the loyalty and trust of all Polish workers, so there's no need for a multiparty structure. The Warsaw Pact and the Soviet military forces in Poland are there to protect Poland from aggression by NATO and to preserve world peace."

"How can you argue with that?" Brennan said.

"I presume you're being sarcastic," Partington rejoined gloomily, taking another bite of his pastrami sandwich. "Why in hell would anybody, especially Poles, kidnap Gorbachev? He's loosened up on the East Bloc satellites more than anybody expected the Russians ever would."

"Good question," said Brennan.

"You think it *was* the Poles?"

"No," Brennan answered, and continued along the hall to the operations center. Still no word from Ennis; he'd be out at McGuire, likely, or on his way back, shepherding Timoshkin and the Russian tactical team to the Soviet mission building.

He logged onto the computer terminal, to be greeted by the message:

YOU HAVE MAIL.

READ MAIL, he typed back. CODE: responded the screen.
Brennan typed back: BLUEBOY.
The screen cleared and displayed:
FROM KNIGHT 19:42 09/30
PLEASE FILE IMMEDIATE REPORT ON MATERIALS ACQUIRED TO DATE. SPECIFICALLY, WHO IS STEFAN KEPA AND WHY ARE YOU INTERESTED IN HIM? BUREAU NOW ASKING QUESTIONS ABOUT GALESKI. PREZ ORDERED RELEASE OF THAT DATA ASAP, SO THEY'LL HAVE IT TOMORROW MORNING. PREZ ALSO FURIOUS ABOUT US LETTING GALESKI LOOSE WITHOUT BETTER CHECKING, SAYS CIA IS SCREWING UP AS USUAL. SO THE NONINVOLVEMENT ORDER STILL STANDS. REID SAYS PREZ WON'T LIKELY OVERRULE PARR ON THE ORDER UNLESS WE CAN SHOW KGB INVOLVEMENT WITH THE ABDUCTION, I.E., THAT GALESKI WAS AN UNWITTING INSTRUMENT. ANALYSTS' OPINION HERE IS THAT THAT SCENARIO IS UNLIKELY. KEEP YOUR HEAD DOWN.

* * * * MAIL ENDS * * * *

"Jesus Christ," Brennan muttered to the terminal screen. He typed I QUIT, deleted it, and started to file the report.

He was half finished when the telephone rang.

"Ennis here. Working hard, Figleaf?"

"Reports. How are our friends?"

"There are six of them. The head honcho, you know what his name is, he's a hard case if I ever saw one. Six foot three and built like a railroad tie. Anyway, I've got something for you. You want to pick it up?"

"Very much."

"You know where The Back Step is?"

"Yeah. It's that overhauled luncheonette on 2nd Ave. I thought they'd have torn it down by now."

"It's still there. They close at eleven. Can you be there by then?"

Brennan glanced at his watch. "Yes."

"See you."

He'd have to leave almost immediately. Call Molly first. He logged off the computer, and dialled. A sleepy voice answered.

"It's Sean. Sorry, did I wake you up?"

"It's all right. . . . I was just drifting off. Are you still in New York?"

"Yes. I'm going to be here for a while. Gorbachev."

"I thought as much. No resignation for the moment, then."

"I'm afraid not."

"Okay. Is it really bad? Worse than in the papers?"

"I think so."

"Are you in any danger?"

"Only from lack of sleep. Don't worry."

"That's a dumb thing to say. You know I'm going to worry."

"I called this afternoon. I figured you were out sketching."

"The light was good," she said. "I did some good work. You'll like it."

"I will," he promised. "Look, I've got to go. Love you."

"Love you. Be careful."

"Yes."

He rang off and went out to Partington's office. Partington was writing in a looseleaf binder. He looked up.

"Don't you ever go home?" Brennan asked.

"Paperwork," Partington explained. "What can I do for you?"

"I need to draw a weapon."

"Okay. What flavor?"

"Browning, nine millimeter."

"No problem. Just a minute."

He came back from the armory with the gun. Brennan signed for it, put it in his pocket and went down to the car.

He reached the restaurant at twenty to eleven, parked a little way down the street and locked the car. There weren't many people on the street, but enough to discourage muggers. He walked back to the restaurant, trying to spot Ennis's car. For a long time the Bureau's vehicles had been black and shiny and unmistakable, but over the last few years common sense had prevailed, and the cars were usually much less conspicuous now. There was a gleaming black vehicle near the luncheonette, but it was a Bentley. Brennan didn't think the Bureau had taken to using Bentleys.

He went into the restaurant. Ennis was in one of the back booths, eating a hamburger amid a smell of onions, frying meat and hot grease. Brennan sat down opposite him. "You want anything?"

"Yeah," Brennan said. "I haven't eaten all day." He still had to finish the report. It was going to be a long night.

"Fries and a burger and coffee?"

"Sounds good."

"Another burger and fries and two coffees over here," Ennis called in the direction of the counter. To Brennan he said, "The Russians told the world about Galeski."

"I know."

"Ranelagh was really pissed. Why did you keep it back?"

"Orders. It was stupid."

"Galeski connected with this Kepa?"

"Yes." Brennan told Ennis about the results, or lack of results, of his day's searching. "Did you have any luck with Kepa?" he ended.

"Yes, I did. Just a minute."

The waitress had arrived with the food and two cups of coffee. Brennan dosed his fries with ketchup and salt while Ennis chewed and swallowed the last of his hamburger. "Kepa," Ennis said, "is supposed to be a Polish seaman who jumped ship here eleven months ago. He was handed over to us, of course, got political asylum, went off to do whatever ship- jumping Polish seamen do in the land of the free. I've got an address and phone number for his apartment, but the landlord says he moved out a week ago. He was living in Yonkers. No forwarding address. Just vanished. Even left his car behind."

"He drove a car?"

"Yeah. It was a clunker, though, in character for somebody in his position. I had the plate number run through the NYPD computers. Nothing except an unpaid parking ticket, issued on September 22.''

''Where?''

''Emmons Avenue, in Brighton Beach.''

''That's odd. That's full of Russian emigrés and Russian Jews these days. Why would a Pole be down there? Especially if he was living as far away as Yonkers?''

''Dunno. Unless he likes Russian food. You can get stuff imported from the Soviet Union down there. I don't know why a Pole would like to eat ethnic Russian, though.''

''Unless he wasn't a Pole,'' Brennan said.

''Yeah. Unless. Anyway, as soon as I go through the motions of talking to your Mrs. Petty, for Ranelagh's benefit, I'm going to put a search team into Brighton Beach. That is, if Ranelagh lets me have anybody from the men already looking for Gorbachev. The Bureau and the police are tearing the city apart, but you know what it's like looking for somebody here, when they don't want to be found. . . . I've got a photograph of Kepa for you. It was taken when he applied for asylum. I pulled a copy for you.'' Ennis fumbled in his jacket. ''Here it is.''

Brennan studied the picture. Bland, uninformative face, but quite possibly the face that Mrs. Petty had described. ''You'll verify the photo with Petty?'' he asked.

''Soon as I can. What're you going to do next?''

''Check this picture of yours with Langley. After that. . . Start slogging through Brighton Beach, I suppose. See if I can trace him any farther.''

''You people have been pulled off,'' Ennis warned. ''Shit will fly if our men report a spook's been asking the same questions they are. With the same photograph. Most of the shit will hit me.''

''Damn,'' Brennan said. ''I hadn't thought of that. Sorry.''

''Let me do it,'' Ennis said. ''I'll tell you what we've got, as soon as we've got it.''

''All right,'' Brennan said reluctantly.

Ennis took a sip of coffee and leaned back in his seat. ''You from New York?''

''Uh-huh. Grew up in Queens. How did you know?''

''Irish name. Figured it was likely. Your father wasn't a New York cop, by any chance?''

Brennan grinned. He was warming steadily to Ennis.

"Stereotyping. But, yes. He's retired to Florida, with my mother. My grandfather was on the force, too."

"How come you didn't end up there?"

"It looked like I was going to. Dad said I'd better get some college in if I wanted to get past patrolman, so I went to State University of New York at Stony Brook. Politics and history. That was in the late sixties."

"How'd you make out on campus, with your background? Protests, and so on?"

Brennan chewed, remembering. He'd avoided the protest movement, partly because of his rather conservative ancestry, and partly because he was not, by nature, a joiner of causes. Most of his fellow politics students at SUNY were proclaiming more or less radical brands of Marxism and Maoism; when they discovered that he was not interested in their posturing, they treated him with derision. Toward the end of his freshman year, one of his classmates smeared his notes with dog excrement while Brennan was eating lunch in the college cafeteria. Brennan, with a half-smile on his face, nearly drowned the man in his own bowl of chicken noodle soup, after thoughtfully adding a couple of sheets of the fouled paper to the bowl. After that, they left him distinctly alone.

"I got along," he said. "I didn't pay much attention to it. I was on scholarship. Too busy keeping my marks up."

"How'd you end up in the CIA?"

"My draft number came up when I graduated. I was good at languages and I ended up in Army intelligence."

"Nam?"

"Yeah. I was up-country when the NVA rolled over the border in '75."

Ennis whistled softly. "Not a good place to be."

"Were you there?"

"Marines. In '65. You remember that *Life* picture of the Marines charging ashore at Da Nang?"

"I remember."

"If you look real careful, you can see my helmet in the back row."

"No kidding!" Brennan exclaimed. "On the cover of *Life*, yet."

"My only claim to fame," Ennis said. "I was rotated home a year later. Decided not to re-up, and joined the Bureau after I got out. Were you in Saigon at the end?"

"No. I missed that. I got out by boat."

"Lucky break."

"I was pissed off. We'd kept reporting the buildup, everything pointed to a big offensive. Nobody above the rank of major wanted to know. Especially, they didn't want to know from a lieutenant with a field promotion to captain, like me."

"That war was run by assholes," Ennis said. He put his empty cup down, too hard.

"It was," Brennan agreed. His coffee was lukewarm, as warm as the sea off Da Nang had been. When the North Vietnamese offensive started, he'd been in Da Nang for two weeks, working with his network of agents to try to pin down the exact date and time of the attack. The city was in chaos; Brennan had tried to get two of his people out, but by the time he'd located them it was impossible to leave by air. He and his two men had taken a sampan, loaded it with refugees and tried to get away by sea. The sampan was a hundred yards off the beach when a platoon of North Vietnamese tanks appeared on the shoreline and proceeded to shoot the boat to pieces. Brennan survived, although with a hold in his calf from a shell fragment. He was plucked out of the sea an hour later by a South Vietnamese patrol craft, but he'd lost both his agents. He never saw Saigon again.

"So exactly how did you end up with the CIA?" Ennis asked him again.

"I reverted to lieutenant back in the States. After I got out of the army I was going to go to graduate school, but the CIA made me an offer. I spent some time in Europe, specialized in East European and Soviet intelligence operations. So here I am." Brennan decided not to mention the fact that he'd already submitted his resignation. The coffee was finished.

"You married?"

"I was. She was killed in Europe several years ago."

"Sorry," Ennis said. It was clear that he meant it. "Open mouth, insert foot."

"It's okay."

There was a brief silence, while Ennis took money out of his wallet and shoved it under his coffee cup with the bill. "I'm buying," he said. "Look, I'd better get a move on. If you find out anything else. . ."

"You'll be the first to know," Brennan promised.

New York
Monday, September 30

THE LIGHT SEEMED to be coming closer, as though he were ascending very slowly from the bottom of a very deep well. After an indefinite length of time, while he studied the light with a detached curiosity, he began to be aware of physical sensations: the dryness of his mouth, first, and then the rhythm of his pulse. The light started to hurt, in syncronization with his pulse.

My eyes, he thought, formulating words at last. My eyes hurt.

More sensation returned: the pressure around his ankles and wrists, the weight of his body on a slightly yielding surface, the awareness that he was lying on his back with his bound hands clasped on his chest.

As though I were praying, he thought. And then: ridiculous.

He opened his eyes. The room was exactly the same as it had been when they gave him the last injection of the drug: smooth gray walls, smooth gray ceiling with the light set into it behind a heavy wire mesh, the steel door, the metal table and stool bolted to the concrete floor, the yellow plastic bucket in one corner, the cot on which he lay. A light chain ran from the padded manacles around his wrists to one of the legs of the cot, which, like the table and stool, was secured to the floor. The chain was just long enough to allow him to sit at the table and use his hands to eat, or to reach the bucket. It would not let him go as far as the door.

He wondered how long it had been since they'd taken him. It was astounding, that they'd been able to do it. He'd always accepted the possibility of the assassin's bullet, the chance of the bomb aboard the aircraft, but never abduction, not seriously. It simply didn't happen, not to the leader of a superpower.

But it had. They'd somehow defeated all the circles of protection around him, human and electronic, and dragged him away. Whoever they were.

They'd spoken to him very little, and then only in accented Russian; among themselves they'd used what he recognized to be Polish, although he did not speak it himself. He didn't know whether they were Polish or not, but one thing he did believe: they hadn't done this without powerful help. Not the Americans, though; they'd never dare *this*. It would be an act of war.

Oleg Chernysh, he thought. Did it reach that far up, all the way to the top of the KGB? Or was it someone I trusted, like Yuri Isayev? Or the minister of defense and the army? Or some combination of these? Not Yuri, surely. He's been with me too long. He believed in what we were trying to do. Unless . . . could he have been persuaded, somehow, that it wasn't going to work, and decided to join others in ending it? Men change their minds, change their dreams, give up the dreams from timidity or fear or greed. . . .

When I get out of here, some people are going to be in very serious trouble indeed.

If I get out of here. . .

He sat up on the cot, suppressing a groan of discomfort; his muscles had set in the position in which he had been lying. At least he now had clothes. They had left him almost naked when he faced the camera; he remembered that, despite the drug they'd given him beforehand. He was surprised they hadn't stripped him entirely, to complete his humiliation. But then, the Americans might have been unwilling to show the tape publicly. His captors would want all the publicity they could extort.

The headache was receding, but he was dreadfully thirsty. He wondered where he was. For all he could tell, he might be back in Moscow. They might have kept him drugged for days, weeks, and fed him intravenously. Up above — for some reason, he found himself thinking that he was in a cellar — there might have been a coup, somebody else might be in charge, purging the men and women who worked with him. . . .

Raisa. Irina, my daughter, my granddaughters, what would they do to you? How many people would they have to kill, to turn Russia back into the past? But I started something that can't be stopped. Wouldn't they realize that? The people were finding their tongues and their courage again, it had to be carefully controlled, but we were coming out of the dark, facing the mistakes and the tragedies as we never dared face them before, and all because of me.

Perhaps it was too much, too fast. Is Moscow up there above me?

He looked at his arms. No sign of intravenous-needle marks. It hadn't been that long, then.

He heard a sharp double click and the door swung open. Two men, dressed in black and wearing ski masks, stood in the opening. One carried a tray with dishes and a water pitcher on it; the man behind him cradled a machine pistol.

Not the executioners from Dzerzhinsky Square, he thought, seeing the tray. Not this time. He looked at the man with the gun. "Are you so frightened of a chained man," he asked, "that you need to come here armed?"

Neither one answered. The man with the machine pistol remained in the doorway while the other placed the tray on the table. "Eat," he ordered.

"How long have I been here?"

"Not long. You will be freed, soon."

This was the most they had spoken to him since his capture. "Who are you, and what do you want?" he asked.

Long ago, when he was just starting out, he had learned the complete and precise self-control he would need to achieve the task he had set for himself. He was conscious now of all the emotions that his captivity had aroused in him: rage at his captors, fury at the possibility that he would not be allowed to complete his work, dread of what might happen to his family and the people who had believed in him, fear for his own physical survival; but he kept these emotions in the place he had made for them, where they could not prevent him from seeing clearly what was possible and what was not.

"Freedom for Poland," said the man who had brought the tray, also in Russian. "We are the Jan Paderewski Cell."

"Ah," Gorbachev said. "I see. That is my ransom."

"Yes."

"Do you think you will succeed?"

The man shrugged indifferently. "If we don't, at least we'll have shown that not all Poles will lie down in front of the Bolsheviks."

Gorbachev burst out laughing. "You're living fifty years ago," he exclaimed. "What you're doing will destroy your hopes more effectively than we ever could."

He did not intend to engage seriously in an ideological argument; he was convinced that these people were no more working to free Poland than he was. But it couldn't hurt to let them think he believed in children's stories like the Jan Paderewski Cell. On the other hand, would they really believe him to be so naive?

Not likely. But the charade would be played out. The reality it exposed, though, was that they weren't worried about what he would do when he was released and returned to Moscow. He did not think they would kill him; they would have done so by now, if simple assassination had been their intent. It was his political destruction someone wanted, not his death.

"Eat," the man commanded again.

"I refuse to eat. I will not be drugged again." He said it simply to see what they would do. His thirst was almost unbearable. The water pitcher had cold beads of condensation around its lip.

"If you don't eat," the man said calmly, "we will feed you by force. You might as well enjoy yourself. There will be no drugs, in any case."

"When will I be released?"

"We have given a limit of ten days."

"And if your ransom hasn't been met?"

"It will be."

"You are very sure."

The mouth in the ski mask's opening twitched into a smile. "Yes. You don't need to be afraid for your life."

"I am not afraid for my life," Gorbachev said brusquely. It was the truth, at least now.

"Eat. I will return in half an hour." The man turned toward the door. His hands, Gorbachev noted, were strikingly too large for his arms.

The door closed and locked behind him. Gorbachev stood up,

his chain jingling, and went to sit down at the table. The food was still warm, although unfamiliar. He recognized it, though, from the time the first American specialized eating place opened in Moscow.

McDonald's, like the KGB, was everywhere.

Warsaw
Tuesday, October 1

COLONEL ADAM KAMINSKY felt the seat belt tug at his midriff as the Mi-3 observation helicopter jolted through an air pocket; the binoculars, through which he had been studying the crowd down in Parade Square, jabbed at his eyelids. He put the glasses on his lap and watched the vast sunlit bulk of the Palace of Science and Culture, two hundred thirty-four Stalinist meters of Corinthian porticos and sham Renaissance finials, slide by on his left. The pilot was keeping well away from the palace building; there was a strong southeast wind and they didn't want to risk being blown against the building's sheer upper facades.

"Hold it here," Kaminsky ordered. The helicopter slowed and stopped, bobbing in the gusty air. He looked out of the canopy at the crowd far below; a few white faces looked back up at him. Mostly, though, he saw the tops of heads. The crowd's attention was fixed on the man who was standing at the top of a stepladder in front of the main portico of the palace, and shouting at them through a bullhorn.

Kaminsky calculated. There must be at least sixty thousand people in the square, with more joining them every minute. They'd start moving toward the Party headquarters building within the next few minutes, and then his operation would start. His agents had been carefully briefed; they'd have an excellent chance of turning a more or less orderly demonstration into a furious and violent mob, while getting away safely themselves.

The man on the stepladder had climbed down, and another had

taken his place. They were both radical Solidarity members and the organizers of the demonstration, which was supposed to culminate in the declaration of a general strike. The Solidarity leadership was confident that the strike would work; the population at large had been growing more restive since Jaruzelski's stroke and the weakening of Party-military control that had ensued after his departure from power. Now they were frightened as well. Any Pole of average intelligence knew that Gorbachev's demise — if it came — would probably result in a new age of repression and deprivation for the country; all the more so because Gorbachev's abductors appeared to be Poles. The feeling in the air was that the country should make a break for freedom now, while the Kremlin's leadership was in disarray.

The man on the stepladder was gesticulating violently. Kaminsky knew exactly what he was shouting through the megaphone: freedom now, neutrality, independence, an end to price increases and the shortage of food, give the revolution back to the workers. Kaminsky knew this, because these were the things the man was supposed to say: he was a Security Bureau agent who had infiltrated the Solidarity leadership, and he worked for Kaminsky.

The SB colonel, six hundred feet up in his helicopter, did not feel any professional pride in what was about to happen below, and for which he was responsible. He was nauseated, although no observer could have guessed what he felt. His face, which was dominated by a large straight nose above a wide straight mouth, was expressionless. Kaminsky's eyes were dark brown and set deeply into their sockets; there were two short straight furrows between the eyebrows, although his rather high forehead was unlined. His ears protruded slightly from the thinning brown hair at his temples. He was forty-three.

A crackle of static in his headphones was followed by:

"Control to Air Post One. Are they starting? Over."

That was General Jurys, back at headquarters. Kaminsky imagined them in the secure radio room, the communications nerve center of CONCERTO: Jurys hunching over the microphone, nibbling at his moustache; Vlasov, the Russian head of the KGB's Eleventh Department, watching silently out of his little warthog eyes as he always did, waiting to step in if he didn't like what was going on. As the Russians always did.

"Air Post One to Control. In two minutes," Kaminsky said. It might be one, or three, but it was always better to be precise when you were dealing with Jurys.

"Keep this link open," Jurys said. Kaminsky thought he detected nervousness in the SB chief's voice.

"With respect, General," Kaminsky said. "I have to be able to monitor ground operations."

A pause. "Very well. Keep it open until they start to move. Then report the situation every five minutes."

"Yes, General," Kaminsky answered. Jurys must really be getting rattled, at least for Jurys.

He left the radio set to the HQ command frequency and looked down at the square again. Nearly a hundred thousand people by now, he guessed.

Suddenly, the man on the stepladder jumped down from it, and the crowd surged, like thick oil flowing across a smooth sheet of metal. Bright noon sunlight poured down on the roofs of Warsaw and the mass of human beings as it began to push toward Jerozolimskie Avenue. Placards rose and banners unfurled above the crowd. Kaminsky used the field glasses to read some of them: SOLIDARITY, BREAD NOW, the usual things except for one that said REMEMBER KATYN FOREST. Home-grown anti-Russian, that one. It wasn't in the stock that Kaminsky's men carried, and that wouldn't be raised until the fighting started. Those said things like RUSSIANS OUT and GIVE US OUR REVOLUTION NOW and LONG LIVE THE JAN PADEREWSKI CELL. Kaminsky's leaflet-distributors would soon be starting elsewhere in the capital, and in Cracow, Lublin, Gdansk and the other major urban centers; although not too near any military bases, just in case the soldiers took the leaflets' demands for armed revolt against the Party too seriously. The leaflets were signed by the Jan Paderewski Cell. It was going to look like the beginning of a full-fledged counterrevolution by the time Kaminsky's men were finished, which was exactly how it was supposed to look.

The crowd flowed into Jerozolimskie and turned northeast, toward Party headquarters. The bureaucrats over there would be quaking in their shoes in a few minutes, wondering whether they were going to be hanged from their own window ledges before the security forces intervened. The thought gave Kaminsky a considerable, if highly illicit, sense of pleasure, although the ones he'd really like to frighten — the very few who were helping the Russians with CONCERTO — wouldn't likely be there. They'd have made sure their skins were safe, just in case something went wrong. Kaminsky didn't yet know who they were; it was extremely dangerous even to try to find out, but he was working on it.

The demonstration slithered around the corner below the helicopter, and started for the intersection of Jerozolimskie and Nowy Swiat, where the Party building stood. From his vantage point, Kaminsky could see down into the side streets where the Militia Motorized Reserve, the ZOMO troops, were lying in wait. He'd been given every ZOMO man available in Warsaw; they'd be the shock force of the attack. They were a brutal crew, many of them violent criminals promised a remission of sentence for their service. Their officers were equally hard; necessarily, or they wouldn't be able to control the men. But they were all well-trained and followed orders to the letter; much better-trained and a lot tougher than the regular police, the Citizens' Militia.

The flood of demonstrators reached the intersection with Krucza Street. The attack would begin when the head of the procession was well in sight of the Party headquarters, and the tail was mostly out of Parade Square. The ZOMO troops would have the civilians bottled up in a long column along Jerozolimskie Avenue, unable to move forward or back, and the side streets would be sealed off. With its escape routes blocked, the crowd would fight; Kaminsky's provocateurs were present to make sure it did so, violently.

He switched from the central command to the operational frequency. Down in Rutkowskiego Street he could see armored cars, trucks mounted with water cannon, BRDM armored personnel carriers, the dark-blue uniforms of the ZOMO men looking almost black in the bright sunshine. The leading ranks of the demonstrators were less than a hundred meters from Nowy Swiat. Away to the northwest, the waters of the Vistula glittered cheerfully.

Kaminsky spoke into the microphone: "Air Post One to Broadsword. Move now. Keep this channel open. Acknowledge. Over."

The headphones crackled. "Broadsword to Air Post One. Moving. Channel remains open. Over."

Kaminsky looked over the side of the helicopter as it banked to sweep over the Jerozolimskie-Nowy Swiat intersection. He glimpsed figures at the windows of the Party building and wondered what they were thinking. Almost directly below, the first wave of ZOMO vehicles was pouring into the intersection. The riot troops were leaping out of the BRDMs and running to deploy even before their vehicles had slammed to a stop.

"Other end," Kaminsky ordered the pilot. That was where the violence would break out first, as the riot police cut their way through the tail of the procession to seal it in.

He could see the attack beginning even as the helicopter straightened on its southwest course. The water cannon had opened up to clear a way for the armored cars and the personnel carriers full of troops; spray from the jets formed transitory rainbows in the sunlight and the street's asphalt turned darker. Dozens of demonstrators were knocked over and bowled into the gutters by the shafts of water. A gap widened rapidly in the procession, and the ZOMO men plunged into it, insectile in their body armor and visored helmets. The avenue was sealed off in less than a minute. The three or four thousand people who hadn't yet entered the street were breaking away, fleeing back into Parade Square or into the gardens behind the main railway station, pursued by the truncheons and rubber bullets of the militiamen who were providing backup for ZOMO.

"Go back a hundred meters and stop," Kaminsky directed. "Then give me a sweep."

Obediently, the pilot swung the helicopter about and flew back up the street. Kaminsky took a few seconds to report to Jurys what was happening. Then he switched back to the operational frequency. The next phase would be starting very soon.

The machine stopped and the pilot turned it on its axis so that Kaminsky could see up and down the length of what was fast becoming a riot. ZOMO troops were trying to battle their way into the wide street from the side avenues; truncheons rose and fell and water cannon spurted into the crowd. Behind the advance rank of armored men stood a second rank; these were armed with rifles and riot guns that fired rubber bullets or tear gas grenades. Under normal circumstances, the demonstrators would be breaking up by now and running away down the side streets, but the side streets were full of police. The mob began to compress. Kaminsky saw a woman go down, her placard waving above her for a moment as she fell and then disappearing beneath trampling feet. The mob was beginning to throw things now: wire trash baskets, curb stones, anything. The glass in the front window of the Praga Restaurant sleeted to the sidewalk in a bright glitter; other windows followed it. Smoke billowed from the rear of a parked car.

Because of the roar of the helicopter's engine, Kaminsky couldn't hear the sound of the shots, but he knew approximately when they were to be fired. The exact instant revealed itself to him when the leading rank of ZOMO men fighting around the entrance to Krucza Street drew back suddenly from the crowd, and the armed rank behind them shouldered their weapons. He was able to hear, just barely, the crackle of the volley as it ripped into the mob.

The ZOMO men delivered a second volley, and the front-rankers waded in again. Even with the engine noise, Kaminsky could hear the screams rising over the crowd's roar.

Time to let off a bit of pressure. ''Air Post One to Broadsword,'' Kaminsky said. ''Clear Parkingowa Street on the south side of Jerozolimskie, and Bracka Street as well. Get the collections started in both places.'' There was a limit to how long the crowd could be kept bottled up; Jurys and Vlasov — and who else? — wanted some casualties to be attributed to the counterrevolution, but not too many. Kaminsky planned to release the trapped human beings little by little, starting from the front and the rear of the demonstration. As they fled, the militia would collect a sampling for imprisonment and interrogation.

He looked toward the Party building and what had been the leading edge of the procession. There was heavy fighting up there as well, and two more fires were smoking away. Kaminsky wondered how many shooting deaths there'd be at that end of the battlefield. He saw puffs of tear gas as grenades exploded; the troops up there must have already fired their allotted two volleys. Of all Kaminsky's men, the provocateurs who fired the shots in the direction of the riot police were in the most danger; the police didn't know about them, and they had to get rid of their pistols in a hurry. As well, they ran a risk of being attacked by the mob itself, if any of the demonstrators suspected they might be provocateurs.

''Hover over the Bracka intersection,'' Kaminsky ordered. ''Come down to a hundred meters.''

The crowd was beginning to bleed away into the side street as the ZOMO men pulled back from its entrance. Not many of them were staying to fight, not after facing live ammunition. Kaminsky could see the militiamen grabbing some of them as they ran, clubbing them to the pavement and throwing them into the backs of the police vans. The jails would be full tonight.

The helicopter banked. Damn, Kaminsky thought, I should have reported to Jurys by now. He reached out to change the radio frequency.

The pilot's side of the canopy starred and shattered. The helicopter lurched, throwing Kaminsky hard against his seat belt. Red flecks and splashes appeared on the plexiglass in front of him. He turned to yell at the pilot, but never got the words out. The pilot was looking back at him, eyes wide with horror. Half the man's lower jaw had been shot away. Kaminsky saw white gleams of teeth and jawbone in the wreckage.

Somebody else had a gun, too, Kaminsky thought. Not one of mine.

The helicopter was almost on its side. Kaminsky was looking up at the tower of the Palace of Science and Culture, half a kilometer away. He felt no fear; only an enormous surprise that this should be happening.

He snapped into action and grabbed for the controls. But the pilot had recovered just enough to realize what had happened and was somehow pulling the machine level.

He doesn't feel pain yet, Kaminsky thought. Not enough time to go into shock. If he can just get us down.

"Land in the intersection!" he shouted. "I'll get help to you —"

The man wasn't listening; he'd already figured it out for himself. But he was struggling to remain conscious. Blood poured onto his flying suit. Kaminsky saw faces below, staring whitely upward as the helicopter thundered down upon them. Then they were only a hundred fifty feet up, and dropping fast.

The machine hurtled over a BRDM personnel carrier, forcing the three ZOMO men standing on top of it to throw themselves onto the pavement below. Kaminsky could see right down into the open hatches of the vehicle. Involuntarily, his body tensed for the impact of the crash. But the pilot, nearing the end of his strength and rapidly slipping into shock, managed to halt the helicopter's rush just before the machine collided with one of the riot-control vehicles. The helicopter jerked violently upward, stopped, bobbed ten feet above the pavement at the center of the intersection, and then slammed hard into the ground as the pilot collapsed over the controls. The undercarriage buckled; one rotor tip hit the pavement and the blade snapped away from the hub. The engine shrieked under the unbalanced load until the next blade swung around and struck the ground. This time the impact stalled the engine. Kaminsky, sitting dazed in the cockpit, smelled aviation fuel. He reached over the pilot's motionless back and switched off the ignition.

"Holy Madonna," he whispered. Miraculously, the radio was still working; the headphones crackled in his ears. "Air Post One! Air Post One! Report! What is your situation? Report!"

The microphone had fallen to the floor. Kaminsky rooted and found it; it was smeared with the pilot's blood. "Air Post One reporting," he said. "We are on the ground. Struck by ground fire. Pilot is wounded. Rioters are being allowed to disperse. Operation proceeding according to plan, except for this incident. Danger of fire. Will report as soon as possible. Over."

A ZOMO major was wrenching at the door on the pilot's side. With the door open, Kaminsky could hear the crowd's roar mixed with screams, the pop of gas grenades and the roar of heavy engines. He rammed his own door open, staggered out onto the pavement and ran around the shattered nose of the helicopter to help with the pilot.

"She's burning!" the ZOMO major yelled at him as he arrived. "Help me, quick —"

The pilot's intercom lead was somehow tangled in the flying controls, and his seat belt latch was slippery with blood. The impact of the crash had jammed the door so that it would open only halfway; Kaminsky and the major couldn't both get at the pilot at once. Kaminsky smelled burning fuel and felt a burst of heat on his face. "More men over here!" he screamed over the uproar around them; he glimpsed uniformed men racing toward the wrecked helicopter.

"Try the other side!" he yelled at the major. "The door opens—"

They raced around the smashed windshield. It was too late. Kaminsky heard a soft *whoosh* as the fuel-drenched engine compartment ignited. A tongue of flame reached out for him; he turned and ran, the major beside him. Well away from the fire, he stopped and looked back.

The fuel tank blew up with a sullen thump, sending a gout of flame five stories into the air. The cockpit was on fire inside. Kaminsky could see the pilot, somehow conscious again, struggling first with the door and then with his seat belt and then with the door, in a mad rhythm. His face above the shattered jaw turned bright red, and then brown, then black. His hair caught fire. He stopped beating at the door and started on the plexiglass; first one wrist bent back at right angles as it broke, and then the other.

Then the flames covered him.

Kaminsky heard the major being sick into the gutter. He turned away from the inferno and looked along Jerozolimskie Avenue. The crowd was dissolving, leaving behind it a jetsam of bodies. Several feet away from Kaminsky, a young woman lay faceup on the pavement, her arms moving feebly back and forth, as though she were trying to make a snow angel. Her body from the waist downward had been crushed flat; except for the blood, the bottom half of her looked a little like one of those cutout fashion dolls that little girls play with. Kaminsky thought: She must have fallen and been run over by one of the riot vehicles.

Much to his surprise, since he had thought he was perfectly all right, he also bent over and began to vomit.

''Let me say,'' said KGB Major-General Vlasov, as he wound up the post-mortem on the operation, ''that colonel Kaminsky's planning and execution of his task today were exemplary. He has maintained the tradition of our revolutionary cadres, leading from the front here in Warsaw with complete disregard for personal danger. We are very fortunate that he survived the vicious attack on him today.''

Kaminsky nodded, but without smiling. Jurys wouldn't like it if he did. Personal pleasure and advancement were not supposed to be part of CONCERTO: CONCERTO was a necessary, although unpleasant, task, designed to defend and purify the Revolution. Not that Kaminsky felt like smiling, anyway. He was, in fact, feeling numb and exhausted. His throat still burned from retching, although the nausea was gone.

''Furthermore,'' Vlasov went on, ''his cadres in all the subsidiary operations, in Gdansk, Lublin, Wroclaw and elsewhere, performed flawlessly. We have drawn out and identified the deep penetration of counterrevolutionary forces into the social fabric, and are now in a position to liquidate those forces. Unfortunately, because they have infected the people's consciousness so virulently — we see an example in the attack on Colonel Kaminsky here — an extensive people's reeducation program is going to be necessary, as soon as the situation here and elsewhere is stabilized.''

The last phrase, Kaminsky had come to recognize over the last few weeks, was KGB code for disposing of Gorbachev and all he stood for. And the fact that it was Vlasov, a Russian, rather than General Jurys, a Pole, who was having the last word at the postmortem, symbolized the Russians' — or, rather *some* Russians' — determination to reimpose total control over the Warsaw Pact nations. The ''reeducation program'' would be the realization of that symbol. Once Vlasov's kind of people were in control in the Kremlin, the avalanche would fall here in Poland, in Hungary, in East Germany, in Czechoslovakia. The arrests in the night, the labor camps, the denunciations, the political trials, the distrust of neighbor, wife, parents, children, the constant dread: the monstrous gray apparatus that Stalin had perfected, and which men like Vlasov (and Jurys) remembered, instinctively, how to use.

Neither Vlasov nor Jurys had mentioned the man who had really died for their cause, if it was a cause: the helicopter pilot. But he was dead, a broken tool and a minor one at that. It was unnecessary to refer to him; he was no longer of any consequence.

Kaminsky, to his self-disgust, couldn't even remember the young lieutenant's name. And if I had died, he thought, it would have been the same. Because of my rank, maybe a word or two. Then nothing. The revolution eats its children. Who had said that? Bukharin? Kamenev? He didn't know.

How could it be happening again? he wondered, as Vlasov droned on. It was a brilliant, vicious plan, reaching, Kaminsky suspected, all the way to the top of the KGB and possibly into the Politburo itself. Gorbachev's new centralist democracy was taking root, the newly elected soviets and the new Congress of Peoples' Deputies were finding their feet. In a year or two at most, it really would be too late to turn back the clock. It wasn't possible, even now, to simply depose Mikhail Gorbachev and reexert

Party and KGB control over the new political institutions. They had had to find some other way, and they had succeeded.

Kaminsky didn't have access to all the details outlining how CONCERTO was supposed to work, but he was confident that he understood most of it clearly. Its centerpiece was Gorbachev's abduction. While the leader was powerless in the hands of his captors, the conspirators had a free hand to provoke violent unrest in the key Warsaw Pact states. With a little effort, this could be made to appear the vanguard of a widespread counterrevolution, something even Gorbachev's staunchest supporters wouldn't be able to stomach. It would be easy to lay the blame for the impending catastrophe on the liberalness of his reforms. See, the conspirators would say, what this man's ideas have brought: revolts in the Warsaw Pact nations; ethnic violence and unrest at home; weakening of Soviet military power around the globe; the Americans rubbing their hands with delight; the world ready to believe that the Revolution, that Leninism itself, are sham and false, that they do not, cannot work.

Then they would bring him home, discredited and defeated, his work in ruins. They would probably make him confess that his ideas were "serious distortions of socialism, major errors," as they liked to put it. They would send him somewhere for reeducation. When he came back, if he ever did, he would agree with all they had done, and their victory would be complete.

And to create a false counterrevolutionary force, the Jan Paderewski Cell, and make it responsible for the kidnapping — that was a brilliant touch. At one stroke it diverted suspicion from the conspirators, and raised the old specter of Polish counterrevolution, revolt and betrayal. And there were Poles in the SB and the Party who were more than willing to cooperate with the Russians, to commit their countrymen to a hideous future for the sake of their own privileges and power. They knew what they were going to lose under Gorbachev's brand of socialism; the shadows in which they had prospered would disappear, and perhaps they would vanish with the shadows.

Kaminsky looked at the other men in the narrow room. He loathed and despised them all: Vlasov, the Russian who carried the orders from Moscow; Jurys, head of the SB; Lieutenant-General Landau, chief of the CONCERTO logistics support group;

and Colonel Deribas, the other KGB man, who controlled the task force that had actually seized the Soviet leader.

And himself, Colonel Adam Kaminsky, chief of domestic provocation, disinformation and subversion, as well as of CONCERTO's internal security. A dirty mouthful. Soon he was going to spit it out.

He'd been recruited for CONCERTO by Landau, who was head of Department 1 and had already been pulled into the plot by Jurys himself. Kaminsky had been the obvious choice for the task he'd later been given; outside of CONCERTO, he was head of Branch 7 of Department 1 of the SB, the branch responsible for counterintelligence. They were called the *dziurkacze*, the keyhole watchers, and they tracked every form of dissent and counterrevolutionary behavior in the country, from the mutterings of drunken mine workers, to the subterranean maneuvers of Solidarity, to the telephone conversations of the Catholic Primate of Poland.

Landau would not, of course, have approached him if his credentials as a Party member and SB officer hadn't been impeccable. Kaminsky's father had been among the expatriate communists brought back to Poland from Moscow after the war, and had managed to stay out of trouble by switching his support judiciously just before the start of each internal crisis. He'd survived the Bierut, Ochab, Gomulka and Gierek regimes, and had died just before the onset of the Solidarity crisis. Kaminsky had inherited much of his father's political astuteness; when Landau floated by him the idea that Gorbachev's power was not as solid as it might be, he'd displayed polite interest, and waited. His superior had given him a little more and then a little more; Kaminsky knew that he was being watched, and not by his own people, during this time. Then he'd carefully expressed some concerns about the direction the SB would take if Gorbachev reduced the KGB to just another law-enforcement department. Encouraged, Landau invited him to meet "some friends." The friends turned out to be Vlasov and Deribas and Jurys. At this point, Kaminsky knew he couldn't draw back; Landau was sure of him, much surer than Kaminsky had intended him to be. He knew that if he tried to wiggle out of whatever they were going to propose, he'd face serious consequences, the least of which would be the loss of his job.

So he'd listened. They hadn't given him details at that first meeting five months ago, only the general principles; nor had they named the target, or how the operation would proceed. But he'd known well enough that it was Gorbachev they were after. He had also known very clearly that the Russians would kill him before he left the meeting, if he showed any signs of reluctance.

So when they were finished he'd said enthusiastically, "I'm very glad somebody's decided to take serious countermeasures at last. This sort of thing can't be allowed to continue. It would be fatal."

Which was not at all what he was feeling. What Landau didn't know, what none of them knew except Adam Kaminsky, was that the head of Branch 7 of Department 1 of the Security Bureau was a communist. A real one.

He was also far more astute politically than they believed. He'd graduated from Warsaw University in 1972, having seen what had happened to the workers' attempt to gain some freedom for themselves in 1970. They'd gotten rid of Gomulka, and had received Gierek as a replacement. Meet the new boss, same as the old boss. Kaminsky had been recruited by the SB upon graduation and had gone willingly, although not for the reasons they construed.

Adam Kaminsky wanted a second revolution.

He knew how the Tsarist police had been infiltrated by the revolutionaries before 1917, even as the revolutionary organizations in turn were infiltrated by Tsarist agents. Revolutionaries had acted like policemen, and policemen had acted like revolutionaries. When the time for testing came, the police had lost. It was enough for Adam Kaminsky to work with. When the SB asked him to join them, he did, with a good deal of silent humor.

But Kaminsky also knew, from the events of 1970 and after, that there wasn't going to be a revolution from the bottom up, not this time. Solidarity's rise and fall had only confirmed this belief; he'd been tempted to help them, naturally, but he'd resisted the temptation. If they went as far as they were saying they would, there'd be Russian tanks in the streets in no time, and God knew what would happen to Poland then. The revolution would have to come from the top down, and it would have to come from Moscow.

If Kaminsky had been a member of the Catholic Church, he would have lit candles to the Madonna when Gorbachev came to power. He'd been right to wait. There really was going to be a second revolution, one to bring socialism with a human face, and Adam Kaminsky was in a position to help lead Poland toward it.

There would be resistance, of course. Kaminsky had started gathering dossiers not only on SB-defined targets, but on members of the government and Party most likely to thwart the building of socialism as it ought to be. He knew there was going to be a reaction, and he was determined to be ready for it.

Time passed, though, and Gorbachev marched onward, apparently invincible. A year ago Kaminsky had realized that the Soviet Union's Communist Party wouldn't dare repudiate Gorbachev and his actions, unless they wanted to risk a popular uprising. He'd begun to relax.

Then, five months ago, Landau had made his approach.

Kaminsky knew now that he should have acted against them far sooner. But the Russians' security was exceptionally tight. He hadn't known, until it happened, that they were going to *kidnap* Gorbachev; in fact, he'd believed that as long as the general secretary was in the United States, he'd be safe. All Kaminsky knew was that he was to organize a series of extreme provocations, to be set in motion on this day, October 1. When it happened over there in New York, it was too late to warn anyone. And he still hadn't been able to find out who in the Polish party was acting with the conspirators; he didn't dare take his carefully prepared CONCERTO dossier to a Party member who might turn him over to the mercies of Vlasov.

He'd been prepared, as a last resort, to try to go to Moscow and warn Gorbachev in person, but he'd waited too long. Failed, in fact, after all his care and preparation.

Maybe, he thought bitterly as Vlasov ended the meeting, I'm really no good as a revolutionary after all. Maybe I should have put the dream aside, closed my eyes like so many others, done my job. What difference will it make now?

There was, of course, one thing he could still do. As Vlasov finished speaking, he decided to do it.

New York – Paris
Wednesday, October 2

THE CONCORDE'S ACCELERATION drove Brennan firmly back into his seat. Combined with the steep angle of the climbout, the thrust made it hard for him to turn his head to look out the window. They were already well out over the ocean, although he could still glimpse the brownish-green patches of the islands of South Oyster Bay as the airliner steadily changed course toward the northeast. Then the Concorde shot through a thin layer of cloud, and the islands and sea both vanished into a white haze. The sunlight through the thick glass porthole became sharper and harder as the plane thrust upward toward the region of unbreathable air which was its natural habitat.

Four hours to Paris, Brennan thought. And what will I find there? Nothing, perhaps. But it's the only thing I can do now, after yesterday's foul-up. Knight's likely relieved to have me out of the country.

He went through it again, wondering if he'd missed anything. . . .

"I ain't got much, but what there is, is yours," Ennis said as Brennan sat down opposite him. "Anything on your end?"

"Just a lot of frustration," Brennan said. They were in the back of McMullen's. The lunch crowd was mostly gone, although the aromas of grilled meat and fowl and fish still hung over the tables. Ennis was picking at a piece of chicken. Brennan wondered if he ate at every opportunity, like an old soldier, on the principle that he wouldn't know when he'd have the chance again. "No one knows anything about Galeski's contacts after he was cut loose," Brennan went on, "barring what Elizabeth Petty said about Stefan Kepa. I've looked back through all the debriefing files on Galeski, but Kepa's description doesn't fit anyone he told us about."

"Damn."

"Did your people realize I'd been checking up already?"

"Yeah. Ranelagh didn't say anything. Just looked as though he had a mouthful of eelshit. It's the look he gets when he's pissed off and planning to screw somebody into the ground."

"Why don't you apply for a transfer?"

"I like New York." Ennis chased a fragment of brown skin around his plate, stabbing futilely at it with his fork. "Anyway, all my people came up with is this. Kepa, or whoever he is, was at Kavka's Restaurant in Brighton Beach three times in the last two months. The waiter remembers him because each time he was there, he asked for pepper vodka. Pertsova, a specific Russian brand they import for the emigrés. The waiter also said he spoke fluent Russian. Like a Leningrader, he said."

"Not like a Pole?"

"Not according to the waiter."

"Sloppy of him," Brennan said. But it wouldn't be the first time an otherwise totally professional agent had been identified because of such a slip. Maybe the strain of his assignment had gotten to the man a little. When that happened, an agent sometimes became desperate for just a taste of home, to recharge his emotional batteries, so to speak. Kepa might have reasoned, because he wanted to believe it, that he'd never be spotted in Brighton Beach with its huge Russian population and their secretive ways. Two or three tastes of pepper vodka, a word or two in your native tongue with a waiter who'd never remember you, what would be the harm in that?

Plenty, as it turned out. But the human mind could always find a good reason for doing what it wanted to do, even when the action flew in the face of training and discipline.

On the other hand, it wasn't much for Brennan to work with. Kepa was possibly Russian, rather than Polish; that made sense, considering that most Poles avoided the company of Russians, if they could. But so what if he *was* Russian? It didn't prove he was working for the KGB, or that he'd set up Galeski or helped kidnap Gorbachev. Knight would laugh it out of court.

On the other hand, Kepa had vanished, leaving his car behind and no forwarding address. That meant that he didn't intend to resurface again — at least, not as Kepa — and that whatever he was doing, he was already doing it.

"God*damn* it," Brennan said, letting his frustration show at last. Maybe the Bureau, with its resources, could find the man, but Brennan couldn't; not with his hands tied as they were.

Ennis had looked up at his outburst. "Getting to you, is it?"

"It has been since it started."

Ennis gave up on the chicken skin and put his fork down. "I thought some of the guys I work with were poker-faced," he said. "But you've got them all beat to hell, with that half-grin of yours. Does the CIA issue you with a mask when you start an operation, or what?"

"It's just a quirk," Brennan said. He was thinking: I'll have to try overseas. I'll have more freedom of action. Frank Knight said we'd be hamstrung here until we have evidence of a KGB connection. And Kepa's the connection, dammit. Maybe in Europe. . .

"What're you thinking about?" Ennis queried.

"Paris," Brennan replied. "I'll tell you why, later."

Ennis fumbled for his wallet. "All right. Let's get out of here."

Brennan waited on the sidewalk for Ennis. It was another cool, bright day. Orchard Harbor would be perfect now, the leaves just starting to turn. He wondered if Molly was out painting.

Ennis joined him. "I —" Ennis began, and stopped suddenly. "Oh, fuck," he said.

Brennan looked around to follow Ennis's gaze. A very shiny black Ford was pulling up to the curb. The front passenger door opened and Ranelagh got out. He was smiling.

"Okay," he said to Ennis. "I *thought* you were up to something. I'm putting you on indefinite suspension, starting now, pending an inquiry into your actions. Go back to the office and clear up your paperwork."

"Just a minute," Brennan said. "You can't take Lee off now. Gorbachev —"

"I don't need advice from spooks," Ranelagh said. "I'm going to put your balls through the wringer, too. You were told to stay *out*."

"I was also told to provide information when requested. Lee requested some."

"Yeah. And it was supposed to go through me. Ennis, get back to the office."

"You're an asshole, Ranelagh," Ennis said.

Ranelagh's face went red. "What did you say?"

"You're an asshole," Ennis repeated obligingly, as though the question hadn't been rhetorical.

Ranelagh seemed to be having trouble getting his breath. After a moment he said, in a voice shaking with fury, "I want an apology for that. Right now. Or you're in very serious trouble."

"Okay," Ennis said agreeably. He stuck his hands in his pockets, very deliberately. "I'm sorry you're an asshole."

"Suspension *without* pay," Ranelagh snarled. "As for you. . ." he said to Brennan.

"Go on," said Brennan. "I'm waiting."

"Never mind," Ranelagh said. "You'll find out soon enough." He slammed himself back into the Ford, which accelerated rapidly away from the curb. Ennis looked after it. "I've wanted to do that for a long time," he said, with deep satisfaction.

"It may cost you a lot," Brennan told him ruefully. "You should have kept clear of me."

"It doesn't matter. Private security's always looking for people like me."

"Okay," Brennan said. "But sorry."

"Forget it. What I can't understand is how that jerk can do something like this, when we need every man we've got? How can he think that way?"

"Half-wits like that are everywhere," Brennan told him. "We have to work around them, that's all. Sometimes we can't even do that."

"I know," Ennis said. "I know it as well as you do. Sometimes, though. . ."

"Lee," Brennan said, "as far as I'm concerned, you're still in. I'm going to start looking overseas. When I get back, we'll see what we can do."

"You've got my home number," Ennis said. "I won't be going anywhere else. Christ. It'll drive my wife crazy."

The Concorde had levelled out. Cruising speed. At the forward end of the narrow tubular cabin, the NO SMOKING and FASTEN SEAT BELTS signs went dark. At this speed, well above that of sound, the ride was cream-smooth and very quiet. Far below, the sonic boom would be battering at the crests of the Atlantic rollers.

Ranelagh had been as good as his word. President Halliday had been informed that the CIA was still asking questions, getting in the way of a properly handled investigation, frightening sources of information. The president had screamed at Parr, who screamed at Reid. Reid dragged Barlow, director of Operations, over the coals for permitting his people to be so clumsy as to be caught. Barlow had bellowed at Knight, who told Brennan, figuratively, to get out of town for a while. Brennan told Knight what he wanted to do. Knight told him to go ahead and do it, but for Christ's sake keep his nose clean this time; Parr had wanted Barlow, Knight and Brennan thrown out of the Company for insubordination, and Reid had had to go to bat with the president for all three of them, not to mention covering for himself. Gorbachev seemed to be less important than the rule book. To top everything else off, Congress wanted to know why Galeski had been allowed within a hundred miles of the Soviet leader.

And as if that weren't enough, Knight was reserving judgement on the "Kepa business," as he called it. He said it looked pretty thin.

The flight attendants were plying up and down the narrow aisle with pillows, magazines, newspapers and refreshment carts. Brennan took a straight tonic, with lime, and a *New York Times*. The paper had some more information about the riots which had erupted yesterday all over Poland. Brennan gave a soundless whistle as he read the casualty figures: 267 dead, including 18 ZOMO riot police, 11 soldiers and an English tourist in Lublin who'd had the bad fortune to get in the way of a rifle volley. There were more than 700 injured. Leaflets had appeared throughout the major cities, issued ostensibly by the "Jan Paderewski Cell of Solidarity," urging armed revolt against the military regime and the Russians. Solidarity had denied any connection with the JPC, condemned the abduction again and appealed to the Polish people to remain calm, and not to be taken in by provocateurs. Nevertheless, Solidarity, which had been tentatively recognized as legal by the Polish government a few months ago, had been banned again. Several of its leaders had been detained. In Moscow, the Soviet press was issuing more diatribes against "Polish counterrevolutionary terrorists." Reassuringly, the articles were not linking the alleged terrorists to western intelligence organizations, as they had done with the early Solidarity movement, back in 1980. Some sanity still prevailed.

I'd like to meet the bastard who turned the ZOMO loose, Brennan thought. Christ, what a slaughter. The son of a bitch.

He scanned farther down. There had been riots in Hungary and Czechoslovakia, too, almost as bloody as those in Poland, and the authorities in Prague and Budapest were muttering about possble links to the JPC among the rioters. It was hard to tell who was in charge in Moscow; the Russians had learned over the last decade to cope with the prolonged illness of a leader, more or less, but they didn't seem to have a mechanism to handle the sudden departure of a Party chief. If Gorbachev had been killed, they could have promptly selected another general secretary, but at the moment the leadership was in limbo. As far as Brennan could tell, the country was being run by Ivan Zotin, the chairman of the Council of Minsters, and Yuri Isayev, chairman of the Secretariat of the Party's Central Committee. The *Times* gave no clues as to what the security organs or the military were thinking. There hadn't been any change in the Soviet or Polish position on negotiations, and the JPC apparently hadn't uttered another word since the abduction.

He folded the newspaper and stuffed it under the seat. Events were moving so fast that the *Times* article was probably far behind them by now.

The flight attendants brought food; Brennan ate without tasting, refusing the complimentary wine. He was tired, and didn't want to add the effects of alcohol to both that and jet lag.

He fell asleep half an hour after eating. The airliner boomed onward through the stratosphere, carrying him toward France.

At the precise moment his eyes were closing, a man pulled over to the side of a street in White Plains, New York. He looked in both his rearview and side mirrors; no followers. It was a lot easier these days; the usual surveillance teams had been pulled off to help in the hunt for the Russian leader.

Two minutes passed. The man looked at his watch, got out of the car and crossed the sidewalk to a telephone booth. As he reached it, the telephone rang.

"Yes?" he said in accented English. "Who is it?"

"This is Promenade."

"Yes. What is it?" Promenade had called an emergency. His voice in the receiver did not, however, betray it.

"They are sending a CIA man to Paris. His name is Sean Brennan. He is trying to find out who Kepa is."

The man in the telephone kiosk stiffened. "That's going too far. We expected them to uncover Kepa, but not to backtrack him this fast. Do they think Kepa is not Polish?"

"Brennan does."

"When will this Brennan reach Paris?"

"In no more than two hours. Concorde."

The man swore in Russian. "Why didn't you tell us this before?"

"I didn't know until three hours ago. Then I had to set this up."

"Very well. We will take measures. Is he travelling under his own passport?"

"I don't know. Probably not. Can he find out anything in Paris?"

"I think not," said the man in the kiosk. "Nothing of importance, anyway."

"I hope so."

"Is that all?"

"Yes." A click.

The man swore again in Russian, and then hurried to his car.

Brennan was awakened by the pressure change as the Concorde descended. He swallowed hard to clear his ears; the left one popped, then the right. The sleep hadn't refreshed him; he felt dull and stupid.

The airliner vibrated as the flaps and the swivelling nose cone assumed landing attitudes. Brennan made sure his seat belt was snug; he hadn't taken it off during the flight. Below the Concorde lay a solid layer of cloud, glistening under the moon. There was some buffeting as the aircraft passed through it, and then Brennan was looking down at the lights of a rain-washed Paris. Off in the distance, as the aircraft banked, he could make out a spiderweb of illumination; at its center was the white bulk of the Arc de Triomphe.

He wished he was arriving as an innocent traveller, and that Molly was with him. They hadn't ever had a real vacation together; a week here and there out of Washington was about all. She'd been alone for a long time. After her husband's death, she had moved back to the United States and rented a small farmhouse not far from Chesapeake Bay; as a way of coping with the loss — there had been no children — she had turned to sketching and then painting, and had discovered in herself a distinct talent. With the life insurance and the occasional sale of a canvas she had been able to make an adequate, if precarious, living. She had a wide circle of friends and acquaintances in Washington — some of them rather eccentric — but had no liaisons with men until Brennan turned up in her life, shortly after he was posted home from Bonn. They had met at a Christmas party given by mutual acquaintances two years ago. She'd gone out with him reluctantly at first, especially when she'd found out that he worked for the CIA, but they knew many of the same places in Europe, shared the same wry sense of humor and had a good many personal tastes in common. Despite the divergence of their professions, they were very much alike.

Brennan was more surprised than she to find that they'd fallen in love with each other. He'd kept his apartment in Washington, but his weekends were spent at the Chesapeake Bay farmhouse. She'd observed his growing dissatisfaction with his work at Langley, and when he decided to resign, leave Washington and write a history of intelligence operations during the Viet Nam war, she'd been relieved. There wouldn't be a great deal of money, but there would be freedom.

I'd be there in Orchard Harbor now, he thought, watching the lights slide under the leading edge of the wing. Except for Mikhail bloody Gorbachev. I don't suppose he's enjoying himself, either.

At 10:45 P.M. Paris time, the Concorde touched down at Charles de Gaulle Two, the airport reserved for Air France and Concorde flights. Brennan was travelling on a flash-alias, as one Roger Gorman, American, sales representative for a New Jersey electrical equipment firm. The firm didn't exist; a call to the number listed on his business card would be shunted through to the New York field office. He'd decided, almost automatically, not to travel on his own passport. If the French customs people made one of their random checks through the SDECE computers, it was faintly possible that the name Brennan would be there, flagged as CIA. As far as Brennan knew, his embassy cover during his Bonn station days had never been blown by anyone, particularly by the Russians, but he preferred to be careful.

He went to the main concourse as soon as he cleared customs, and found the Périgord Bar. It was full of sleep-deprived travellers whiling away the time until their Air France flights got off the ground; apparently there'd been another bomb threat from some Arab group or other, and all planes were delayed while they were searched even more thoroughly than usual. Brennan managed to squeeze himself and his single suitcase into a place at the bar and ordered a beer, which he had no intention of drinking. The exchange rate on his American currency was even worse than he'd expected.

He started nursing the drink, checking the mirror behind the bar every half-minute, out of habit. He couldn't see anyone who looked as though they might hail from Minsk or Kiev or Leningrad, but he hadn't expected to.

Someone shoved in beside him. "Sorry, Roger," the man said. "Late, as usual. How did your garden do this year?"

"The tomatoes were exceptionally good," Brennan said.

"Mine were lousy," said the man. "Let's go."

A fine, misty rain was falling outside. "City of Light," said the man as they passed through the main doors. "Kinda dim at the moment. I'm Dave Macarthur. The car'll pull up in a minute. Bart couldn't stop or the airport *flics* would've jailed him. They're antsy about car bombs this week."

"Hasn't changed much," Brennan observed.

"*Plus ça change, plus ça reste la même chose,*" Macarthur said, in atrociously accented French. He had a brush cut and a lower lip that was too large for the upper. The combination made him look like a truculent stevedore, except that he was much too thin. Brennan outweighed him by a good forty pounds. "Here's the car."

It was a Renault, perhaps gray, its color hard to define under the orange blaze of the sodium lights. Brennan and Macarthur piled into the back seat. The driver, presumably Bart, pulled away from the terminal entrance under the suspicious gaze of two airport police officers. Macarthur stretched forward to get an attaché case out of the front seat, and opened it. Inside were several sheaves of French currency, a typewritten list of street addresses and a flat automatic pistol.

"Here's the stuff you asked for," Macarthur said. "We didn't have a Browning. Walther okay?"

"It'll do," Brennan said. He shoved the gun into his raincoat pocket, took the money and started memorizing the addresses. There were only three of them.

"You're sure this is where they're living now?" he asked.

Macarthur nodded. "We keep an eye on them," he said. "They'd be safer in the States, but they won't go."

"Fine," Brennan said. He handed the list back. Macarthur looked at him. "You work fast," he commented.

"Good memory."

"I guess. You won't have any language problems?"

"Not if they speak German, Polish, Vietnamese or Russian."

"You're okay, then," Macarthur said. "Smooth as a baby's butt."

Brennan didn't know whether he was referring to him or the contact operation. He looked out the window, watching the cars and heavy trucks on the A1 as they whipped past in clouds of luminescent spray, watching the mass of the city begin to take shape. No one spoke. After a while Brennan spotted the floodlit white domes of Sacré-Coeur off to the left.

"Been here before?" Macarthur asked.

"Yeah. Some. Worked out of Bonn station."

"Dull city, Bonn."

"Sometimes." He thought about Jane for a moment, and then stopped.

"You're being put in a safe house on the Left Bank," Macarthur was saying. "I'll drop you off and then you're on your own. Station says just please take the usual precautions when you go in and out. Signal when you leave for good. I'll tell you the signals protocol when we get there."

"Okay." Brennan didn't think it would take more than a day to track down the men bearing the three names. He imagined he could feel the stiff edges of Kepa's photograph inside his jacket.

They reached the ring road at Porte de la Chapelle and Bart, the driver, who for Brennan was still no more than the back of a head and a pair of ears above a shirt collar, kept heading south. Paris slid by: the Gare du Nord, a jog left to pick up the Boulevard de Strasbourg, then straight on as far as the Ile de la Cité and across the Seine, the Renault's tires hissing on the neon-streaked pavement. The traffic, as usual, was dreadful even at this hour.

Brennan asked, as they passed the tall lighted facades of the Palais de Justice, "Where's the safe house?"

"Not a lot farther," Macarthur told him. "It's in that high-rise apartment area in the Quartier d'Italie. We've quit using walkups in the old quarters. Not anonymous enough. They've torn down a lot of the areas we used, anyway."

Brennan still didn't feel as though he were in Paris; the transition from New York had been too abrupt. It was as though he were sitting still, the city a motion picture projected onto the windows of the car. He looked at his watch, turning it to reflect the lights of the store fronts. Getting on toward midnight. Would it be worth trying for one contact, at least? He'd be more likely to catch one of them at home at this hour.

He'd decide after they reached the safe house.

"You like Paris?" Macarthur asked as they navigated around the Place d'Italie. Brennan could see the lighted slabs of the high rises to the south, not very far.

"Yeah. Prefer London, though."

"Too dingy. Give me Paris anytime. Even if it's full of the French. It took me three years here, but I finally figured out what it is about the French."

"What?"

"They've decided they've got four things down pat. Food, booze, sex and art. So why should they pay attention to anybody else?"

Brennan smiled. "It's as good an explanation as any."

"Here we are," Macarthur said after a few minutes of silence. "*Nous sommes arrivés.*"

They left Bart-the-driver, who still hadn't opened his mouth, waiting outside the front entrance with the Renault. In the elevator Macarthur said, "This is actually a hell of a lot better than a walkup. No roaches."

"Mm," Brennan replied absentmindedly. Now that he was standing, he realized how tired he was.

The apartment door was halfway along the corridor. Macarthur opened it. Light spilled into the hallway.

"What the hell?" Macarthur said. He reached under his jacket.

"It's okay," came a voice from the apartment. It made Brennan jump. He put a hand on Macarthur's arm before the man had his gun out. "I know who it is," Brennan said.

Macarthur relaxed, motioned Brennan through and closed the door behind them. "Who?" he said to Brennan. His voice was puzzled. Brennan didn't answer.

The living room was along a short hall and around a corner. The furnishings were sparse, and cheap. The drapes were closed. Knight was in a chair by the hidden windows, reading a copy of *Paris Match*. He dropped it on the floor and stood up. "Hello, Sean."

"Hello, Frank," Brennan said. He put down his suitcase and the attaché case. "What are you doing in Paris?"

"I'll take it from here," Knight said to Macarthur. "Sorry about the surprise."

"You mind telling me who you are?" Macarthur said.

"Yes."

Macarthur shrugged. "Have it your way." He turned to Brennan. "You're sure this is okay?"

"It's okay," Brennan said.

Macarthur shrugged again and left the room. Brennan heard the hall door thud closed behind him.

"You didn't come on the Concorde," Brennan said. "How long have you been here?" He'd last spoken to Knight at ten P.M. Tuesday, when he got clearance to go to Paris.

"I left early this morning," Knight said. "Very early, one A.M. New York time. Something's happened. I didn't want to tell you before you left, not until I had more information, in case it didn't pan out. But it looks as though it could."

"You're driving me crazy," said Brennan. "What the hell is *it*?"

"I'll put it in a nutshell," Knight said. "There's somebody in Warsaw who wants to talk to us about Mikhail Gorbachev. He sent us a plane ticket and papers. We can pick them up in Frankfurt in about two hours."

Frankfurt – Warsaw
Thursday, October 3 – Friday, October 4

THE FLASH WAS blue-white, blinding. After-images danced in Brennan's vision, obscuring the end of the dimly-lit room where the photographer was removing the last plate from the portrait camera.

"That's it," the photographer said. "Everything'll be ready inside of two hours."

"Okay," Brennan responded. He picked up the set of documents from the desk beside him, extracted the passport and the identity papers that needed photographs, and handed them to the technician. The man took his camera plates and left. Brennan leafed through the remaining documents again.

"They still look okay?" Knight asked. He had folded himself, like a partially closed jackknife, onto the plastic-covered sofa beside the desk. His bald head shone under the ceiling light. The room was in the basement of the American Consulate in Frankfurt; outside, the West German city lay asleep under the moon. It was four o'clock in the morning.

"They still look okay," Brennan answered, pondering the documents. "They ought to. They're real."

There was an airline ticket for LOT, the national Polish carrier; a travel permit issued by the Ministry of Internal Affairs; a West German visa with a Frankfurt entry stamp; a currency-exchange form; and employment documents in the name of Zygmunt Witczak, a fuels technologist working for Haldex in Katowice. The technician had taken away the driving license, Haldex identification card and passport, all of which required photographs. The round-trip airline ticket appeared to have been issued five days previously: Warsaw to Frankfurt, return. The return flight left Frankfurt at eleven A.M., today. The Warsaw CIA station had had the good judgement to send, in the diplomatic bag with the documents, a small suitcase containing a selection of Polish-made clothing and personal effects that a traveller from Katowice might be expected to have with him on his return, as well as currency. Some of the clothes fit Brennan, although no more than adequately.

"I know you haven't had much sleep," Knight said, "but can you bludgeon all the personal data into your head before you leave? You can't go in without knowing it back to front."

"I'm perfectly well aware of that," Brennan said irritably. He'd made a good start on it while assessing the papers' authenticity, before the photographer arrived, but Knight had never seen him work in the field, and seemed nervous about Brennan's preparations. "The person who provided these was very confident we'd send somebody," Brennan added. "And in time to catch this morning's flight. Any idea who it is?"

"No. That's why I'm still having second thoughts about letting you go. Not knowing who our friend is makes his maneuver tough to evaluate."

"I don't think it's booby-trapped," Brennan said. "Dangerous, yes. But if it'll lead us in the direction of Gorbachev, we've got to take him up on it. He's clearly somebody very high up, and with the ability to get his hands on documents like these without arousing suspicion. That says Polish SB."

"Let's go through it again," Knight said wearily. "Maybe we've missed something. Ten P.M. Tuesday, Warsaw time, one of our embassy secretaries is pulled over by a lone plainclothesman for a document check, even though she's got dip plates on her car. He flashes an ID card, but she doesn't get a good look at it. She thinks it's harassment until she gets her papers back and finds an instruction to the CIA station chief to clear a drop between one and two A.M. The cop knew who the station chief was, too, dammit.

"So after much hair-tearing, they take a chance and clear the drop. That's middle of the night Wednesday in Warsaw, late Tuesday in New York. In the drop are the documents we've got now, and a typewritten note that says, 'Send a man. Reserved Saski Hotel.' And that's it."

Knight stopped and looked at Brennan. Then he continued, "And I told you on the plane about the security blitz in Poland. Things changed the instant Gorbachev was snatched. Up until last Sunday, westerners went in and out of the country like a dose of salts. The Poles wanted us to come in and leave our hard currency behind when we left. You remember how easy it was? But since Sunday, it's been like trying to get into Russia during the worst of the Cold War. Warsaw station damn near lost a courier on Tuesday. The airport looks like a police barracks. They're checking *everybody*. Eighty percent of the tourists — the ones that persist — are being turned back. I want you to think hard about going. *Hard*. This might be a high-level provocation."

Brennan, who had sat down on the desk, rubbed his stinging eyes. He needed sleep, badly. He was only slightly consoled by the knowledge that Knight was at least as tired as he was. The division chief had flown from Washington to Frankfurt, leaving the US several hours before Brennan did, to do an initial vetting of the documents from Warsaw. He had then flown from Frankfurt to Paris to collect Brennan, and was now back in Germany again, Brennan in tow.

"I don't think so," Brennan said. "They could put together a provocation without going through these contortions. I think our friend, as you called him, wanted to make sure somebody would come. But he doesn't dare make more than one approach to our Warsaw station, because it's too closely watched, or he's afraid it is."

"And he knows who our station chief is," Knight observed glumly. "If he does, so might other people."

"Exactly," Brennan said. "Even if he's SB, and high up, he'd have to be worried about other surveillance on our station. Military intelligence, for example, or even another part of the SB. So he can't work with anybody inside the country.

"But because of the riots and whatever else is under the surface, border and airport security's very tight, as you pointed out. A flash-alias, which is all we'd have time to put together, isn't likely to get a man through that kind of barrier. But our friend needs someone from outside, and the outside man has to have help from the inside. Our friend has elected himself as the inside man. He's got access to authentic documents, ones without photographs, and knows how to neutralize border checks if he needs to. I wouldn't be surprised if one of those documents has a signal on it that tells airport security to back off."

Knight eyed him. "I know. I've thought all that through myself. But it's still dangerous as hell, Sean. And suppose the SB's internal security is watching our friend? He might be acting in good faith, but you'll both get scooped up if they've tumbled to him."

"We need to know what he knows," Brennan said.

"Yeah. Who in hell is he? You must have some ideas."

"My guess is Branch 2, US-Canada intelligence. Or he could be Branch 1, Illegals. Maybe 1A, illegals support. Possibly even Branch 7."

"Counterintelligence," said Knight.

"That's right. That'd be trickier. He'd have a harder job getting hold of external-travel documents. But he could do it, I think, if he was desperate enough. And I have the feeling he's desperate. He took a lot on faith, sending that airline ticket and hoping we'd respond in time."

"I'm taking a lot on faith, sending you in," Knight said. He looked at his watch. "Six and a half hours to plane time. You going to go on with the papers?"

Brennan nodded.

"Okay," Knight said, getting up. "I'll go and find us some coffee."

"Thanks," Brennan said. He forced his eyes open wider, and began drumming the personal attributes of Zygmunt Witczak into his reluctant memory.

Warsaw's Okecie International Airport terminal seemed to have more uniformed and heavily armed men than civilians inside it. There were both *militsia*, the regular police, and a stiffening of army men. Brennan didn't see any ZOMO, though; they'd be kept out of sight unless there was real trouble, since their presence after the slaughter in Tuesday's rioting would be a provocation in itself. Everyone moved very carefully, the civilians avoiding talk and staring straight ahead. Even the few children were hushed, sensing the apprehension of their parents.

The difference from what Brennan remembered was striking,

and disturbing. He'd been through Okecie several times during the '80s, but he'd never seen it this deserted. Hardly any foreigners were at the immigration line, and the line for returning Polish nationals was shorter than Brennan had expected it to be. He supposed that a good many Poles who had been outside the country when the violence began were delaying their return as long as possible. He suppressed the urge to scan for an overwatch; there were too many inquisitive eyes around, and he wouldn't be contacted probably until he was on his way to the hotel, or in it.

The man ahead of him was going through the document checkpoint. It was very thorough, the immigration officer referring several times to a list he kept out of sight beneath the counter. Behind the officer stood a thin, nondescript man with the eyes of a policeman: SB. He stared fixedly at the returning Pole, who was trying to look as innocent as he undoubtedly was.

The immigration officer picked up a stamp, pressed it carefully onto the man's passport, and handed it back with the rest of the papers. "Go on," he said. His eyes swivelled to Brennan. "You. Papers."

Brennan handed them over. The immigration officer referred to his out-of-sight lists again. The SB plainclothesman stared at Brennan. Brennan deliberately didn't stare back. His physical self was screaming at him, demanding fight or flight. It was an old sensation; he'd learned to deal with it long ago, never allowing it to reflect in his face.

The immigration officer was studying the passport, the page with the photograph and the passport number. The SB man's eyes swivelled downward to look at it, and then back up to Brennan's face. Brennan felt his heartbeat accelerate. Blood pounded in his ears.

The SB man gave Brennan a microscopic nod. "Clear him," he said to the immigration officer. The officer, without glancing at the rest of the papers, stamped them and the passport and handed them all back. "Please go on," he said.

Brennan's heartbeat began to slow as he left the document checkpoint. I was right, he thought. There's encoding in the passport. Probably the number. The SB man thought I was one of them. Our friend knows what he's doing. So far.

He went to the baggage delivery area and collected his suitcase. The customs officer passed it with no more than a cursory glance, unlike the attention given to several other travellers. The immigration officer must have telephoned ahead to clear his path. Better and better; for the moment, he was reasonably secure.

Now what?

A few people were waiting outside the restricted customs area for returning relatives or friends, but no one seemed remotely interested in Brennan. He glanced at the unfamiliar face of his East German watch. Nearly one P.M. A bus into the city, then.

He got the No. 145 bus as far as the intersection of Pulawska and Goworka Streets; the route went right by the building that housed SB headquarters. No one else on the bus looked at the place, and neither did Brennan.

He got off the bus and took several random taxi and tram rides before he was satisfied that there was no surveillance. There were a lot of *militsia* in the streets, and they were making sure that people kept moving, that there was no opportunity for a spontaneous demonstration to erupt. Up some of the side streets Brennan spotted armored cars and troop carriers, with soldiers leaning out of the hatches or sitting on the decks of the big vehicles: not threatening, precisely, but very much in evidence.

To Brennan, the city seemed hushed and tense, like a Caribbean island warned that it is in the path of a killer hurricane. The taxi drivers, normally garrulous, didn't talk. Brennan picked up a discarded copy of *Trybuna Ludu* on one of the trams; most of it was given over to diatribes against the "counterrevolutionaries" who had instigated Tuesday's riot, against the Jan Paderewski Cell, which was presumably behind the counterrevolutionaries, and against Solidarity, which was presumably behind both. Gorbachev, when he was referred to at all, was dealt with in carefully neutral terms. The outrage the paper expressed was not against the abduction of a reformer and a liberator, but against vaguely defined enemies of the revolution. In one brief article the writer considered the possibility that Gorbachev had made "mistakes and serious errors" in his readiness to relax the Party's vigilance against "revisionists and people with bourgeois mentalities." It was a cloud no larger than a man's hand, but it was there.

Brennan knew central Warsaw fairly well, and by the time he told the last taxi driver to drop him in front of the Grand Theater, he was only two-and-a-half blocks from the Saski Hotel. He walked slowly along Senatorska Street, past the great gray Lutheran Church with its dome and lantern turret, until he reached Dzerzhinsky Square. The square — before World War II, called Bank Square — had been renamed after the war for Felix Dzerzhinsky, founder of the Soviet secret police, who by a grim irony of history had been born a Pole. There was a square of the same name in Moscow, and on it stood the headquarters of the KGB. The Poles had suffered bitterly at the hands of their countryman's creation.

The Saski Hotel faced the southwest corner of Dzerzhinsky Square. It was an older place — for Warsaw, at least, which had been almost completely destroyed by the Nazis before the Russians drove them out in January, 1945 — and was of the kind the tourist guidebooks refer to as "moderate." It appeared to be undergoing renovation; the exterior was obscured by scaffolding. Brennan walked past the entrance and turned left along Przechodnia to inspect the hotel's rear. The workmen appeared to be adding an extension to the back of the place as well as renovating it; a board fence closed off the construction site. Brennan could hear the rumble of a cement mixer and the sound of hammering.

He went back to the main street. A café stood two doors west of the corner. Brennan went into the café and bought four pastries wrapped in a twist of newspaper; the state supply of paper bags had run out, apparently. Then he went back to the hotel. They were renovating the interior as well: the lobby floor was gritty with plaster dust, and the sparse remaining furniture was covered with drop cloths. It was impossible to tell what the place had looked like before the renovators started, or what it would look like when they finished.

The desk clerk registered his identification in meticulous detail before giving him the room key. Again, this differed from the last time Brennan was in Warsaw; on that visit the desk clerk in the Aurora couldn't have cared less if Brennan had presented a CIA identity card.

The elevator wasn't working, so Brennan walked up the three flights to his floor. The room was small, the furniture dowdy. There was no bathroom; it would be down at the end of the hall. Brennan looked out the window, peering around the dusty-smelling curtains. The room overlooked Dzerzhinsky Square to the northwest. Midafternoon sun blazed down on the buses and trams, and on the BTR-60 armored personnel carrier that was stationed with its squad of soldiers at the intersection of Senatorska and Marcelego Nowotki Streets.

Brennan left the window, and sat down on the bed. Then he got up again and searched the room thoroughly, not looking for microphones but for a direction to the next meeting place. Nothing. There was a telephone in the room, but incoming calls would have to be connected through the hotel switchboard. That meant that his man would either have to call in a message through the front desk, or come directly to the room. Either would seem to be dangerous.

He sat down on the bed again, reflecting on how long he should wait to hear from the Pole, assuming he was a Pole. The room had been reserved for two nights, which provided about thirty-six hours for making a contact. With the Witczak documents he was safe enough from random street checks, and he thought he was secure in the hotel. The SB probably wouldn't be checking hotel registrations exhaustively enough to find out that one Witczak, Zygmunt, did not actually work for Haldex. Or maybe Witczak did, or could be made to appear to do so. The man who had sent the passport might be able to arrange that depth of cover.

Thirty-six hours. After that, he'd have to use the CIA contingency route out of the country. He didn't know what it was; he'd find out if he needed it.

He was exhausted and hungry. It was a good thing he'd bought the jelly doughnuts in the café; he'd seen a sign in the lobby that said "Restaurant closed," although he wouldn't have eaten on the premises even if he'd been able to. Zygmunt Witczak was going to stay very much out of sight.

Brennan unwrapped the pastries, ate them and washed them down with tap water from the bathroom at the end of the hall. Then he returned to the room and lay down on the lumpy mattress. While he was wishing there was a shower attached to his room, he fell asleep.

Some quiet sound woke him. He lay quite still, eyes closed. From the darkness on the inside of his eyelids, he knew that evening had come.

The noise again. A soft tap at the door. Brennan opened his eyes; the room was lit only by the lights of the street outside. He turned on the bedside lamp, got up from the bed and went silently across the worn carpet. A foot from the door he paused and said, "Yes?"

"There is a message here for you, Mr. Witczak."

He shrugged mentally; if they had found him, there'd be more than one of them, and no physical heroics would allow him to escape. He unlocked the door and opened it. A young woman, hotel staff by her uniform, was standing in the hallway. She was quite pretty, in a worn sort of way, and held a brown manila envelope in one hand. Handing it to him she said, "It was left at the desk a few minutes ago."

"Thank you," he said, taking the envelope. She turned and glided away down the hall, obviously not expecting a tip from a fellow Pole. Brennan smiled wryly and closed the door.

He sat on the bed to open the envelope. It had been sealed along all the flaps with thin transparent tape, to prevent tampering, and was addressed simply to him at the hotel. No room number.

Who brought it? Brennan wondered as he slit the tape with a thumbnail. The man himself? Unlikely. Does he have someone working with him?

Inside the envelope was a single sheet of onionskin paper. On it wasn't typescript, as Brennan had expected, but a diagram. No, not a diagram, a map. He studied it in the light of the bedside lamp, trying to orient the tracings of black ink. After a few seconds he had it. The hotel's basement floor plan was shown, and the construction work behind it, as well as Przechodnia Street, which ran beside the building site. A dotted line ran through the basement of the hotel, out what must be a rear exit, and across the construction site to a spot just inside the board fence separating it from the street. The end of the dotted line was marked with a small rectangle, inside which was an X. Beside the X was written:

0200

Meet me at the X at two in the morning? Brennan thought. Out in the open, although behind a fence? Who is this guy, anyway? He's getting operatic.

I have to do it, though.

He memorized the map, tore it and the envelope into small pieces, and took the scraps along to the bathroom. Someone was using the facilities; he could hear water running. Brennan was about to go back to his room when the bathroom door opened and a man came out. He smelled strongly of plum brandy, and his eyes were glazed. He mumbled something unintelligible and weaved along the hall, having some trouble locating his door. Brennan watched until he'd found it and stumbled inside. The door slammed. Apart from the gurgling of water from the bathroom, and traffic sounds from outside, the floor was quiet. The crisis must be bad for the tourist trade.

He flushed the scraps of paper down the toilet, waiting until he was sure they were all gone. Then he went back to his room, and began to wait. There were six hours to go.

At fifteen minutes to two he decided to leave. The photograph of Kepa was inside the lining of the suitcase; after removing it and putting it in his jacket, Brennan switched off the bedroom light, silently opened the hotel room door and peeped out into the hallway. It was deserted.

Instead of turning left toward the main staircase, he went the other way. According to the map, there was a service and fire stairway at the rear of this wing of the hotel. He found it without difficulty, opened the fire door and entered the stairwell. It was badly lit. He went down three flights, and paused on a landing; more stairs travelled downward to the basement. He frowned, wondering for a moment what was waiting for him down there.

The basement corridor was unlit, but enough illumination filtered through from the stairwell for Brennan to see that he was in a part of the building that was being reconstructed; a cement-encrusted wheelbarrow stood in the center of the corridor, as well as some scraps of wooden forms for pouring concrete, and some masonry tools. He picked his way through the clutter. Beyond them was a stack of metal heating ducts, obviously destined for installation in the new part of the hotel. A breath of cooler air touched his face. He could barely see where he was going, and stopped to allow his eyes to adapt to the near-darkness.

After a minute he could make out enough of his surroundings to go on. His shoes crunched on hardened dollops of cement. Ahead of him appeared to be a blank wall. He reached out and touched it. Rough boards met his fingertips: a door or partition. The cool air was coming from between cracks in the boards. He ran his fingers over them. At the left edge he felt the cold metal of a set of hinges. A door, then. There should be a latch on the other side.

There was. It was, in fact, no more than a sliding bolt. Beside the doorframe Brennan could feel rough brickwork: the exterior wall of the original basement. They'd cut a doorway through it, probably as routing for pipes and electrical wiring.

He slid the bolt back with a gentle scrape. The door creaked open. Beyond it lay the excavation for the new basement, about ten feet below street level, dimly illuminated by the lights of the city above. Some of the concrete for the basement floor had already been poured. The excavation was littered with oil drums, hoses, cement mixers, piping, scrap lumber, steel concrete-reinforcing mesh, and bags of sand and cement. Brennan used a block of wood to prop the door open behind him, and started across the bottom of the hole toward the position marked on the map. It hadn't been clear from the drawing as to what level the X was on; to Brennan it would have made more sense to have the rendezvous down here in the basement-to-be; but if the map was to scale, the meeting place was up at street level. He should be looking for some kind of rectangle. Maybe.

He reached the side of the pit. It was hard, dry soil with a sandy feel to it, almost vertical. He searched around for a ladder until he found one leaning against the earthen wall, and climbed it slowly. At the top he tilted his wrist to reflect light from his watch. Two o'clock, right on time. He looked toward where he thought the X should be, but saw nothing against the dark backdrop of the fence.

There seemed to be something on the ground next to the fence, however. Brennan walked over to it. It was a wooden platform about a yard square, resting on the ground for no apparent reason. Brennan shoved it with his foot. It shifted slightly.

Was it covering something?

He squatted next to it and lifted. The boards were heavy, but he managed to shove the platform aside far enough to see that it was covering a circular hole in the earth. As far as Brennan could tell in the poor light, the rim of the hole was lined with crumbling brickwork. A dank smell wafted from the opening. It was a sewer entrance.

I'm supposed to go down there without a light? Brennan thought. He was becoming irritated. Just how much gear was I expected to bring on this jaunt? I don't even smoke, dammit, or I'd have a lighter with me.

He pushed the board cover all the way off the entrance and peered inside. He could just make out a set of iron rungs leading downward, disappearing into darkness. There was, however, no sound of flowing water from below. Brennan dropped a pebble into the dark. After a good three seconds he heard a *tick* as the stone hit a hard surface. It was deep, but dry.

He'd go as far as the bottom. If the mapmaker had any sense, he'd have left some form of illumination down there for Brennan; he couldn't assume that the American would bring a light with him.

Brennan levered himself into the sewer entrance and began to climb down. The rungs were very thick, scabbed with rust, and seemed endless. The circle of faint light above him contracted steadily. Finally, his foot struck solid masonry. He stepped off the ladder. The dank smell was much stronger now, and a chill damp breeze was flowing past him.

Brennan felt around with his right foot, then heard a scrape and a dull clunk. He knelt and swept his fingers through the dark until he found the object. It was a battery lantern. Brennan turned it on and the white beam, blinding to his night-adapted eyesight, shot out into the darkness. He closed his eyes for a moment, until they had time to adjust, then opened them.

He was at the intersection of three tunnels. The tunnels formed a Y, with the open end of the Y facing roughly west, away from the Vistula River. What seemed to be the main artery was well over six feet high, and formed the stem and one branch of the Y; the other branch was of smaller diameter, and debouched into the main tunnel about knee height above the latter's floor. A brick and masonry walkway, two feet wide, ran along the side of the main tunnel; it was on this walkway that Brennan was standing.

He flashed the light around. The floor of the main tunnel was damp, with a few small pools of standing water; seepage, perhaps. If the pools had been raw sewage, the smell would have been much worse, so he had to be in a storm sewer, not a sanitary one. He looked over the side of the walkway. The flow would have to be nearly two feet in depth before the platform was flooded. He sincerely hoped that didn't happen. The brickwork of both the walkway and the sewer walls was slick with moisture and it was old, very old, the mortar crumbly and black and missing in places.

What was he supposed to do now?

Cover the entrance, to start with. He left the lantern on the floor, climbed back up the ladder — it was about twenty feet long, he could now tell — and shifted the cover into place above the hole. Then he climbed back down again, and considered shouting. He didn't want to do that, however; there had to be a better strategy.

He shone the beam of light around the entrances to the three tunnels. Red pinpoints gleamed back from all of them, the eyes of sewer rats. Brennan grimaced. He didn't care about rats in ones or twos, but hundreds were enough to unnerve anybody. He thought about going back up for a length of timber to use as a club, but decided against it. Better to keep moving, and try to ignore the creatures.

He went closer to the downstream tunnel mouth and flicked the light around. Nothing obvious. Try the upper one, then.

This time he found it: a chalk mark high up on the wall. Okay, he thought. Ever onward.

He walked along for some distance, while the tunnel curved gently southward. About halfway along the curve, it began to descend gently. He was becoming disoriented. Was he heading away from the heights of the Old Town, or not?

He reached another branch. The right-hand tunnel seemed to lead upward, and was the same diameter as the one he had been following. It also had a walkway, but between it and the one he was on there was no bridge, only the sewer floor. There was no chalk mark to indicate that he should follow the downward-sloping tunnel.

He gingerly tested the sewer floor with the toe of his shoe. It was firm, although the surface was slightly resilient. There hadn't been much water in here for some time. He gritted his teeth and stepped down onto the lower surface; two careful strides and he was on the walkway of the upward branch. He shone the light around. There was the small chalk mark again, high up, as it had been before.

He set off along the tunnel. Twenty paces along, the roof began to drop, and in another twenty paces he could no longer walk fully upright. It was wetter here, and he could hear water dripping into a pool somewhere. It occurred to him suddenly that he had seen no access shafts since entering the system.

If I get lost, he thought, I could be down here for a long time. Sooner or later I'd find a shaft, though. I think. But what would it look like if I emerged from a manhole cover at noon in the middle of Nowy Swiat? Someone would probably ask questions.

Something was ahead: a glimmer. Brennan stopped and turned off the lantern. Purple and green after-images swam against his retinas. After a few seconds he was sure that what he saw wasn't an illusion. There was a faint yellow glow ahead. He couldn't be certain how far away it was.

He turned the lantern back on, shielded the lens with his palm and began walking toward the light, forced to crouch more and more by the lowering roof. Thirty paces along the walkway, he could see that the tunnel turned to the left, and that the light was somewhere around the curve. He went on. The light grew stronger.

Abruptly and surprisingly, the tunnel regained its original height, and jogged to the left in a forty-five-degree turn. Brennan stopped at the angle, thinking rapidly, and made his decision. Even though he'd shaded his lantern, its glimmer would have been visible to anyone looking for it. He stepped around the corner. A man was sitting on an overturned bucket just a few feet away. Beside him on the ground was an electric lantern angled upward to reflect its light off the roof. Beyond the man, the tunnel branched again, sliding off into enigmatic darkness.

"*Dzien dobry,*" Brennan said. He turned off his lantern to conserve the battery, noticing as he did so that the other man had a spare flashlight shoved into the pocket of his leather jacket. The leather glinted dully in the whitish light as the man surveyed him.

"Good morning," said the man. "I'm glad they sent someone who speaks Polish. Fluently, I hope."

"Yes," Brennan said. "I'm told my accent sounds as though I come from the coast."

The man considered this thoughtfully. "Yes. Perhaps. A dash of Pomeranian there. Your people were very quick to put the right person into Frankfurt. I considered sending a backup ticket, but I felt that sending only the one would better communicate my urgency."

"Was it you who brought the map to the hotel?"

"No."

"You have others working with you?"

"No," said the Pole. "I'm alone in this. I used one of our couriers. They're used to taking things from one place to another, and keeping their mouths shut. We're in no danger from that particular delivery. Although I can't make a habit of private enterprise, even in my position."

"What *is* your position?" Brennan asked. He was trying to get a good look at the man's face, but the reflected light from overhead threw the features into shadow.

"You need to know, I suppose. It's part of my credentials for this . . . maneuver. My name is Adam Kaminsky. I am a colonel in the *Sluzba Bezpieczenstwa*."

SB — just as we believed, Brennan thought. "What branch?"

"I am in charge of Branch 7, the *dziurkacze*, the watchers through keyholes. Counterintelligence."

"You're in charge of it?"

"Yes. For several years. Before that, I was in Branch 1, illegals and illegals support. I spent two years in New York, working out of our consulate. Please sit down. There's another bucket."

"Where are we?" Brennan asked as he pulled the rusty pail toward him and cautiously sat down on it. He was still somewhat apprehensive about becoming lost down here.

"Almost underneath the Evangelical Reform Church. The crypts are only a few meters through the wall behind me."

"These sewers are old."

"Yes. Very. As you can tell from the smell, they're not for sewage now, because they empty directly into the river. They carry rain runoff. After a heavy rain, some of these tunnels fill almost to the top." He saw Brennan's face and said, "Don't worry. I have kept an eye on the weather reports. And this tunnel is quite high up. It is most unlikely that we'll drown tonight."

"Good," Brennan replied brusquely. The tunnel was beginning to oppress him. "Why did you want to talk to us?"

"Yes. To business," Kaminsky said almost absentmindedly. "First of all, would you mind telling me who you are?"

"You know what I am," Brennan said. "That's enough for now."

"I suppose so," Kaminsky said. "Very well. You may suspect

that the Jan Paderewski Cell, even if it exists, which it does not, has nothing whatever to do with Mikhail Gorbachev's abduction."

"That's not hard to guess," said Brennan. "The difficulty is to prove it in the face of opposition from people who don't want it to be proven."

"Precisely," Kaminsky said. He turned the lamp so that its beam fell lower. Brennan could now see his face clearly. Kaminsky appeared to be a few years older than himself, with dark, deep-set eyes and a high forehead. His ears were prominent. To Brennan the man's face resembled that of a small, intelligent hunting animal; or it would have, if it hadn't looked so tired. "To begin with," Kaminsky went on, "there is no Jan Paderewski Cell. It is a facade devised by men who want Mikhail Gorbachev to fail, and not only to fail, but to admit that he was wrong in what he's tried to achieve."

"The KGB," Brennan said.

"Of course," Kaminsky answered, with a flash of bitterness. "Who else would it be? The plot is code-named CONCERTO. It was designed in Moscow, but operational direction is from here, in Warsaw. It has four major components. First, Mikhail Gorbachev's abduction, to allow the conspirators freedom of action and to divert responsibility for it to Poland. My luckless country, as always. The second component is to provoke violence against the authorities, especially here, and also in Czechoslovakia, Hungary and eventually East Germany. To make it look as though those nations are at the point of open revolt against Moscow."

"Yes," said Brennan. He could hear a rat chittering somewhere in the darkness of the tunnels.

"Of course, in the time-honored way, the riots and unrest provide the authorities with the excuses they need to increase repression, rid themselves of prominent dissidents, all the usual things. This time, however, there's icing on the cake. Gorbachev's enemies in Moscow — and everywhere else, including Poland — will say that the violence and rebellion are direct results of his policies of *glasnost* and *perestroika*. They will say: We gave him a chance to succeed, and what has it brought? The imminent destruction of the socialist community, of the fruits of the Revolution itself. He cannot be allowed to go on."

Brennan listened, fascinated. It was audacious beyond anything in his experience. "And he's too strong now for them to stop him by political means,'' Brennan said. ''They're left with only extreme measures. This is one of them. But why not simply have the Jan Paderewski Cell assassinate him? Oh. I see. That's not enough. They don't want a martyr.''

''Exactly,'' Kaminsky said. ''That is the third component of CONCERTO. He will be rescued, and brought back to Moscow. Then the fourth, and final part of the operation will begin. Understand that I do not know *all* these things for certain, but I am senior enough to know a great deal. All the evidence I've been able to gather points in the direction I have been describing.''

''Go on,'' Brennan said.

''The fourth component follows Stalin's tradition. You remember the show trials of the 1930s, during the Great Terror? It wasn't enough for Stalin's enemies, the real Bolsheviks who carried out the revolution, to be accused of treason, convicted and executed. They were required to confess their supposed crimes, although they were guilty only of having been at the center of the revolution, while Stalin was not. And they *did* confess, in public, at the show trials. Most of them were tortured into it. Only after their public confessions were they given the bullet in the back of the neck. You know how it was done.''

''Yes.''

''The same will happen to Mikhail Gorbachev. They *must* make him confess publicly that all his actions have been errors bordering on the criminal, if not actually being so. If they don't manage to do that, he will remain a rallying point for everyone who believes in what he was trying to do, and there are tens of millions of such people. If he repudiates his past, the heart will go out of those millions. They will be leaderless. And there is no one to take his place, no one else to follow. The people who think like Stalin will have won.''

''And then the purges will start,'' Brennan said.

''That's right. Anyone who supported Mikhail Gorbachev, whether here in Poland or in Moscow, in the Politburo or on the factory assembly line, will be suspect. The gulags will start to fill again. It will go slowly at first, as the Stalinists undermine powerful people of Gorbachev's persuasion, like Isayev and Zotin, but it will spread and pick up speed. It will spread here.''

There was a long silence, while the nightmare vision filled Brennan's mind. What kind of Russia would emerge from a new Terror? He couldn't imagine what it might look like.

One thing was certain, though. During such an upheaval, the Soviet Union would be frighteningly, dangerously unpredictable. The men behind CONCERTO would be perfectly aware that the political earthquake of Gorbachev's fall would have weakened the unity of the USSR, and they would be watching fearfully for an American attempt to take advantage of it. It was impossible to foretell exactly what men in that frame of mind would perceive as a threat of attack, or how they would respond to it. Brennan judged the response would probably be violent.

He was also afraid that there were men in Washington who would be willing to take that risk, seeing in Gorbachev's demise an opportunity to help the Soviet Union tear itself apart. There would be voices urging open support for any Warsaw Pact nation wanting to detach itself from the Russian orbit. God alone knew where that might lead. Had the conspirators in Moscow worked that into their planning? How could they? They'd have to be able to manipulate American foreign policy at the highest level, and even the KGB couldn't do that.

Brennan said to Kaminsky, "Why did Moscow choose the SB for this?"

The Pole gave a short, bitter snort of laughter. For an instant, Brennan glimpsed the pain under the man's composure. "For this signal honor, do you mean? I wasn't consulted. I suppose it could have been the AVH in Hungary, or the Czech StB. But they chose us, because we're the one nation that's tried to change the system, and *almost* managed to do it, in Solidarity. Walesa and the others had the Party on the run, it was almost powerless, hundreds of thousands of members turned in their Party cards. Even the Czechs didn't get that far, back in 1968. The Russians would have liked to invade us in 1980, but they didn't dare — they were afraid our army would fight them — so they got Jaruzelski and the officer corps to do their dirty work. But they'd still like to make an example of us. And because we've never submitted completely, it's easy to make the world believe that we could produce a mad organization like the Jan Paderewski Cell. We have a reputation for dramatic gestures and lost causes, remember? Like the old stories of Polish cavalrymen using lances to attack Nazi tanks. The world expects that sort of thing from us. If the purges come, they'll be worse here than anywhere else except Russia itself."

"And the SB went along with CONCERTO, without a blink?"

"The people who were recruited did."

"But you were among the recruits. You didn't think that way?"

"No. I *allowed* myself to be recruited. I had it in my mind even then to stop them, if I could."

"I see," Brennan said. It might be true; on the other hand, Kaminsky might simply be looking for a way out of a situation that he had approved of at first, and then found too much to handle. His motives didn't matter at this point, though. What did matter was how far he was willing to go to undermine CONCERTO.

"How far up is the SB involved?" Brennan asked.

"All the way to Witold Jurys. Jurys is the SB chief. I suppose you knew that. He's always been in the KGB's pocket. You have to remember that the SB leadership is just as much afraid of losing its power as KGB Chairman Oleg Chernysh is. Every SB man sometimes wakes up at five in the morning and sweats about what the Hungarian rebels did to the AVO men in the 1956 rebellion. Hanged them, shot them, beat them to death, burned them alive. They're afraid it might happen here, if the Party loses control because of Gorbachev's dreams. And not only the SB. There are Party leaders who don't want Gorbachev to succeed any more than the KGB does."

"Who?"

"I don't know. Yet. I'm still trying to find out, but it's dangerous for me to ask too many questions like that. But I'm getting close. A few more days' work —" He stopped and gestured vaguely. "I should know soon. I have assembled a dossier, but it's not complete yet."

"Do you have it here?"

"No. I will get it to you when it's complete."

Taking out some insurance that we'll protect him, Brennan thought. "Can you give me some names?"

"Yes. I mentioned Jurys, didn't I? The Russian in charge in Warsaw is Anastas Vlasov, head of Department 11 of the KGB First Chief Directorate."

Brennan gave a low whistle. Department 11 controlled all the

East Bloc intelligence services, from Rumania to Poland. Vlasov's presence in Warsaw meant that the conspiracy must reach almost, if not all the way, to Oleg Chernysh, the chairman of the KGB.

"I am in charge of domestic subversion and internal security," Kaminsky went on. "The logistics section is under Lieutenant-General Eduard Landau, SB. Overseas operations are under Colonel Antonin Deribas, KGB First Chief Directorate, also Department 11. He would be responsible for the kidnapping itself. I don't know who the kidnap team is. The rescue squad is controlled directly by Vlasov. They were to be sent from Moscow; they were never in Warsaw."

Brennan committed the information to memory. "And when your dossier is complete?"

"I want you to get me out, with the information. Then I want you to make it public, all of it, every detail. Once the truth is out, they'll have to give up. But before that can happen, you'll have to retrieve Gorbachev himself, and give him the dossier so that he can act on it. If you wait until the Russians go through the charade of rescuing him, it'll be too late. He'll be back in Moscow before you can blink, and my information won't be worth anything. They'll get him to say it's all a fabrication by his supporters. It'll work against him, in the end."

"We can't rescue him if we don't know where he is," Brennan said. "Even then, it won't be easy. Do you know where they're holding him?"

"I can make a good guess."

Brennan suppressed a groan of disappointment. He had been becoming more and more hopeful that Adam Kaminsky would be able to direct them straight to the Russian leader. "All right. Where?"

"The reason I don't know for certain," Kaminsky replied almost apologetically, "is that my responsibility in CONCERTO is domestic only. The security compartmentation is very strict. I am not supposed to know anything about the overseas component of the operation. But I began looking where I shouldn't about a month ago, and I came across one item of information."

"What?"

"There was a Russian who came to Warsaw at the start of the planning phases. He was furnished with Polish documents before he left, and spent time with Landau working out questions of logistics. They did this at a safe house outside the city, so I never saw him. But in one of our meetings, his name was mentioned. It was Romanenko."

"Go on," Brennan said.

"I don't know if it was Romanenko who established it, but the piece of information I managed to acquire from Landau's files is that a new safe house was to be set up in New York. It is located in Sheepshead Bay in Brooklyn. The address is 43 Voortman Avenue. Do you know where that is?"

Brennan nodded with relief. It was better than nothing, a lot better. It was what he'd come for, assuming Gorbachev was there.

"It might be for another purpose," Kaminsky admitted. "But the timing is very significant."

Brennan nodded in agreement. "Anything else about New York?"

"No. That's all."

"How far up in the KGB does the conspiracy go?" Brennan asked.

"I have no idea. As I said, the Russian controller here in Warsaw is Anastas Vlasov. Above him is Vadim Besedin, head of the First Chief Directorate, and above *him* is Oleg Chernysh. I believe it goes all the way to KGB Chairman Chernysh."

"No one in the Soviet Party?"

"I don't know. There will be hangers-on, of course, once the direction of the wind becomes certain. Russians are opportunists."

"That's a start," Brennan said. "Have you ever heard the name Stefan Kepa?"

After a moment's consideration, Kaminsky said, "No. Do you want me to check it for you?"

"Yes, please," Brennan answered. "If you can." He pulled Kepa's photograph out of his pocket. "This is Kepa. Do you recognize the face?"

Another pause. "No."

"It was worth a try," Brennan said, returning the photograph to his jacket.

"Who is Stefan Kepa?"

"Someone involved with the kidnapping. Do you remember the name Jerzy Galeski?"

"He defected last year. I don't know anything else about him, except that the Russians say he was part of the Jan Paderewski Cell, and that he was killed during the abduction."

"Do you think he was part of CONCERTO?"

"No. If he had been, they'd have taken his body away with them. They'd never have left it for identification. He was a plant, I think, to reinforce Polish complicity in the abduction."

"If you can get anything on Galeski," said Brennan, "we'd like to know. But don't endanger yourself doing it."

"I'll try," Kaminsky said.

"Thank you," Brennan responded. "Are you making arrangements for me to leave the country, or do I use other resources?"

Kaminsky reached inside his jacket and drew out a LOT ticket folder, which he handed to Brennan. "This is a ticket to Frankfurt for tomorrow afternoon, as well as other papers you need. The Witczak identity will serve one more time."

Brennan pocketed the folder. "Fine. What are your plans? How can we help you?" Knight hadn't wanted to suggest immediate defection; it would be much more useful to keep Kaminsky in place, as long as he wasn't in imminent danger.

"It depends on exactly when the Russians in Washington are told that Gorbachev is in the Sheepshead Bay house."

Brennan calculated rapidly. "Your information will be in Washington late tomorrow, depending on whether it's hand-delivered or transmitted. Then there'll be evaluation time, and time for the politicians to decide what to do. We'll need to put together a deception to make it look as though we located the safe house ourselves, without help from inside CONCERTO. That will put them off your scent for a while, depending on how willing the Russians are to believe it. Then their tactical team in New York will need six to seven hours' briefing and preparation time, studying the house and approaches, putting together the support, and so on. I doubt the Russians will be told before eleven or twelve P.M. on Saturday, Warsaw time. That's tomorrow night."

Kaminsky scowled at Brennan. "*Who* is going to tell the Russians? And why do you have to *tell* the Russians at all? Why not extract him yourselves?"

Brennan considered what was most likely to happen. "The Federal Bureau of Investigation will put together the deception, and will be responsible for telling the Russians where Gorbachev is.

But we can't just go in and get him, as you suggest. There's high-level politics involved here. President Halliday is going to insist the Russians make the rescue, the so-called rescue. I can guarantee that much."

"I don't like it. It hands him to them exactly as they wish."

"You don't have to like it. But there's nothing you or I can do about it."

Kaminsky looked resigned. "Very well. But your president's pigheadedness makes no sense. In any case, as soon as Vlasov knows the safe house isn't safe anymore, one of two things will happen. The first is that they will believe your FBI's disinformation, and think you located the safe house by yourselves. They won't look for a traitor immediately, so I'll be able to stay put for a few days. But I think the second possibility is more likely."

"Which is?"

"That despite anything you can do, they'll consider the possibility CONCERTO has been compromised. They'll start investigating immediately, but they won't be absolutely certain there's a leak, so they'll take it slowly at first. Vlasov will certainly conduct the investigation himself, but the first person he'll suspect will be Landau, because he's a Pole and because he knew the location of the safe house. That will give me some warning, if Landau is relieved of duties or put under surveillance."

"It's very dangerous," Brennan said. "How much warning?"

"I don't know. I do know I'll be walking a tightrope. And my nerve is going, and I don't know whether I'd be able to carry off a bluff." Kaminsky said this in a very matter-of-fact manner, as though admitting he had a cold. "A day's warning, at most, before Vlasov decides to start investigating further."

"And then?"

"As soon as I know I have to run, I'll load the dead drop I used before. It will tell you where I'm going, the name I'll be under, and where I'm to be collected once I'm there. I have three alternatives, either Rome, Vienna or London. The signal to unload the drop will be a numeral 3 in blue chalk on the third lamp post from the corner, in front of the Staszica Palace."

Brennan lodged the fact in his memory. "That's if you get enough warning," he said. "Suppose you don't, and they go after you right from the start?"

"Then you will have to come and get me. The emergency signal will be a double white chalk stroke on the same lamp post." Kaminsky reached into his pocket and handed Brennan a slip of paper. On it was another map, more complex than the one that had directed Brennan to this meeting. "Take this back to the hotel and memorize it. Then destroy it. It shows where I'll be if I have to bolt. I'll be hiding here, in the sewers. If you have to come, you'd better bring a light of your own. I can't risk leaving equipment about for any length of time. They might be searching through the tunnels."

"I'll bring a light," said Brennan, tucking the map away. It had the feel of water-soluble paper, tradecraft stuff. "Is there a fall-back hiding place?"

"No. And I have no time to prepare one. If I'm not where I'm supposed to be when you come, it means Vlasov has me and you can go back home."

"How long can you last if you've gone to ground?"

"Days. Long enough for you to reach me."

"All right," Brennan said. "You've no family?"

"I had a wife," Kaminsky said. "She left me two years ago to live with another man. I can't say I blame her. I was never at home." He stood up; the bucket scraped on the masonry.

"I'm to provide you with a code name," Brennan said. "Discus."

"Discus?" Kaminsky spelled it. "Is that correct."

"Yes," Brennan said. "Are we going out together?"

"No. There's another way. More than one. Can you find your way back by yourself?"

"Yes. You know this sewer system well, don't you?"

"Very well." Kaminsky seemed diffident all of a sudden. "I am fond of archaeology, you see. And of the history of Warsaw. There is very little of old Warsaw left aboveground, since the Nazis left, so I sometimes come down here to touch the city as it once was. The Home Army used the sewers to move around in when we revolted against the Germans in 1944. I've found a few things. . . ." His voice trailed off, and when he spoke again, it had regained its sardonic edge. "An appropriate place for someone of my profession, wouldn't you say?"

"Perhaps," Brennan answered. He paused, looking up at the Pole's shadowed eye sockets. They looked empty. "Colonel Kaminsky, why are you doing this?"

"I thought you'd get around to that sooner or later," Kaminsky said. "Americans always want to know the *why* of everything. It's what makes you so good at understanding machines, and so bad at understanding human nature. You must not misunderstand me, my nameless American. I am not doing this because I want Poland to become just like the United States, which is what Americans often think when they find someone like me who is willing to work with them. I am doing it because I despise what these people have done and are planning to do to my country. And because I am a communist. A real one, not a Party member who carries a card because it's a way to obtain better housing and better food and a new car and a trip abroad, and gives him the authority to tell other people what to do. I believe that the Revolution was hijacked, first by Dzerzhinsky who began the apparatus of terror, and then by Stalin who perfected it, and then by the bureaucrats and petty officials who use the name of the Revolution to excuse their pillage of the Soviet Union and Poland and our sister nations. I believe that if Lenin had lived longer, things would have been very different. I think they still can be. Remember what Alexander Dubcek called it in Czechoslovakia, more than twenty years ago? 'Socialism with a human face.' The trouble with Marxism is that it's an idea that's almost too powerful for human beings to handle. It's like fire; it gives its possessor great abilities to build and preserve, or to tear down and destroy. So much depends on the men who wield the power. In Mikhail Gorbachev there's a person who uses it wisely. Stalin was the opposite. But you can't blame Marxism for that. Stalin would have been a criminal ruffian in any time or place; it's Russia's misfortune — and the world's — that he was given an opportunity to use the power Marxism has within it."

"I hadn't thought of it that way," Brennan said carefully. He didn't want to be drawn into an ideological discussion thirty feet beneath the streets of Warsaw at three o'clock in the morning.

"You must excuse me," Kaminsky said tiredly. "I've never been able to say this to anyone before."

"Why did you accept recruitment to CONCERTO?" Brennan asked.

"Because I wanted to find out what they were planning to do," Kaminsky replied. "I'd been expecting something like this for five years, more or less."

"Why come to us? Why not go to someone in the Kremlin?" Brennan asked.

"Because I don't know who I can trust in my own government, let alone in Moscow," Kaminsky said. "There was no one else but you."

There was a thread of hopelessness in the words. For a moment, Brennan saw the world as the Pole must see it: a world full of betrayals, deceits and compromises; of camouflage, and deception, and sometimes imprisonment and death, made bearable only by the intensity of his belief.

As though Brennan had been speaking aloud, Kaminsky said: "I was responsible for arranging Tuesday's riots. I was monitoring the one here. I saw a woman half-crushed by an armored vehicle. You know how many dead there were that day. And a few days earlier I was present when Vlasov tortured to death a young woman who tried to defect, here in Warsaw. She worked in the SB registry, and Vlasov was afraid she might have come across some hint of CONCERTO. It was my men who picked her up, and I who handed her over to Vlasov. She knew nothing. And I knew what would happen to her, if Vlasov took her. *But I had no choice.* Can you understand?"

"I understand," Brennan said. He also stood up. This is the man I cursed on the airliner on the way to Paris, he thought. The bastard I wanted to meet, the one behind the slaughter of the riots. I've met him. Nothing is ever as you expect. "Be careful," he told Kaminsky. "We'll stop them."

"Heroes don't always win," Kaminsky said.

He picked up his lantern, turned, and walked away from Brennan into the dark labyrinth of the tunnels.

Paris
Friday, October 4

THE LUFTHANSA AIRLINER bobbed up and down on its undercarriage as the pilot taxied toward the huge gray disk of the de Gaulle One airport terminal. Brennan looked out the window; the jet was nearing one of the seven passenger debarkation subterminals, which were arranged in a vast circle around the central building. A Pan American 747 was loading at the subterminal, its corporate colors brilliant in the early afternoon light. The Lufthansa plane passed into the shadow of the 747's vast tailfin and the interior of the cabin became suddenly dim.

Frank'll be well on his way to the States by now, Brennan thought. Carrying Kaminsky's information in his head. I hope nothing goes wrong with his plane.

Brennan's return from Warsaw to Frankfurt, on the Witczak papers, had been tense but uneventful. Knight had debriefed him immediately, but instead of going straight to the consulate cipher room to transmit the information to Langley, Knight had remained sitting at the desk, deep in thought.

"What's the matter?" Brennan had asked.

"I'd trust our signals security for anything but this," Knight said. "But there's always the faintest of chances they've broken into some of our codes. If they know we know, they'll move Gorbachev. And we might never catch up with him again."

"You're going to hand-deliver the location data?"

"Yeah. To Barlow, and nobody else. I think Barlow will agree that the security's worth the delay. There's an air force MAC flight leaving here for Washington in less than an hour. I'll be on it. But we can't go back on the same plane. You're the backup if anything happens to me."

"Okay," Brennan had said. Then: "Frank, I've still got unfinished business. Stefan Kepa. That's still on the to-do list. I ought to go home by way of Paris, and clear it up."

Knight had looked doubtful. "That means you won't reach the States till well after I do."

"It doesn't matter, as long as Kaminsky's information does. Anyway, what can I do over there at the moment? I'm persona non grata with everybody from the president through Simon Parr on down."

"Not with me," Knight. "And not with Barlow or Reid, either, after they know what you've gotten out of Kaminsky."

"I'll wait for the medal," Brennan had said. "In the meantime, what about Paris?"

"Okay. But call Langley to make sure I made it."

"When will you be there?"

Knight had told him, and had then headed for the NATO airbase to catch his flight. Brennan checked plane times, called the Paris station to ask for Macarthur to collect him at de Gaulle, and then went out to the Frankfurt airport and caught the next Lufthansa airbus to Paris.

The airbus was now trundling up to one of the subterminal gangways; passengers around him were stirring, getting up. Brennan heard the engines whine to a stop, and then the thud of the gangway connecting to the plane's fuselage. He pulled his travel bag from under the seat in front of him, draped his raincoat over his arm and joined the slowly moving line of travellers in the cabin's aisle.

Once inside the terminal he cleared customs and went to the lower concourse, where he found Macarthur waiting for him in one of the lounge areas.

"You get around," Macarthur said. "Sorry, but no door-to-door service this time. Bart wasn't available, and I had to park at the back of beyond. You didn't say it was urgent, so. . ."

"It's not urgent," Brennan said. "Thanks for coming."

"This way to the parking lot," Macarthur said.

Macarthur was driving the same Renault as before. As he turned onto the A1 toward Paris he said, "You want to drop your bag at the safe house? Or I can do it for you."

"If you wouldn't mind," Brennan said. "I'd like to get started."

"I've got a wad of francs for you." Macarthur reached inside his jacket and handed them over. "Do you need the list of addresses again?"

"No. They're in my head."

"How about the Walther?"

Brennan considered. "Might not be a bad idea."

"Reach under the seat, and up."

The gun was clipped to the springs under the seat. Brennan extracted it, looked it over, and slipped it into the inside pocket of his raincoat.

"Where do you want me to drop you?"

Brennan consulted the list, to refresh his memory concerning the three men and their addresses. The first man was Czech, the second East German and the third, Rumanian. The trouble, from the point of view of timing, was that they were all over the place.

"Do any of them work these days?" he asked.

Macarthur maneuvered the Renault around a sixteen-wheel Mercedes transport. As before, the domes of Sacré-Coeur were just in view, their outlines blurry in the autumn haze. "How do you mean, working? At the trade?"

"No. Ordinary jobs."

"The second two. You won't get them at home till after six. The Czech —"

"He's nearly seventy," Brennan said. "Retired."

"You know him?"

"Yes." He remembered going to Vienna to extract Leopold Bittner, who'd been deputy head of the disinformation department of the Czech StB. It had been very smooth; Bittner had been on his way to the United States almost before the Czechs realized he'd even left Prague. That was ten years ago, not long after Jane was killed. Bittner had stayed in the US for a while, and then had gone to live in Paris, using the new identity manufactured for him by the Americans. He'd been there ever since, living quietly, almost a recluse.

He'd try Bittner first.

"I want to see the Czech," he said. "Twentieth *arrondissement*.

Could you drop me at the corner of rue des Amandiers and rue Duris?''

''Okay. You want me to wait?''

''Is there a Métro stop near there?''

''Fairly. Menilmontant.''

''I'll use the subway to get to the others, then. Have you got a set of keys to the safe house?''

Macarthur drove one-handed while he dug in a pocket. ''Here you are. Just leave it on the kitchen counter. Here's a few Métro tickets, too. Save you frigging around getting them at rush hour.''

''Thanks.''

They drove for a while in silence. Brennan began to doze, head against the back of the seat. Eventually he heard Macarthur say, ''Almost there.'' Brennan sat up, realizing that he'd dropped off to sleep for almost forty minutes.

''Long day?'' Macarthur asked.

''Kind of.'' The Renault was on the rue de Menilmontant, about to turn right onto Amandiers. ''You sure we're clean?''

''As sure as I can be,'' Macarthur said. ''I didn't spot anything on the way down from de Gaulle.''

''Good.'' Brennan had thought there was no possibility of being tracked, given the precautions he'd taken and the broken trail he'd left; in fact, there was no way the KGB would even connect him with the search for Gorbachev. At the moment, he possessed the priceless asset of anonymity.

''Here you are.''

''Thanks.'' Brennan got out, feeling the Walther bump against his hip, and closed the car door. The Renault pulled away from the curb and disappeared around the curve of the street. On the corner where Brennan stood was a shop with a sign reading *Alimentation Générale*. An Algerian girl of twelve or thirteen was standing in the doorway, which had an elaborate ironwork filigree above it. She eyed Brennan curiously as he passed and called out something in a street argot, full of long *a*'s and nasals, which he couldn't understand.

He started up rue Duris, passing a small restaurant with the menu written directly on the window in white poster paint: *plat du jour 25F, couscous à emporter*. The restaurant's facade was covered with the mosaic tiles brothels used in the 1930s; Brennan vaguely remembered that there had been an army barracks in the *arrondissement*. The soldiers were gone now, and the brothels had become Algerian restaurants with take-out couscous. Before long the street would join des Amandiers and de Menilmontant under the hammers of the developers, and the old buildings and courtyards would be razed and replaced by blocks of apartments for the professionals of the middle class. Some of the old shops might survive: they'd be gutted and renovated and turned into smart boutiques and cafes for the tourists. Brennan wondered where people like the Algerian girl and her family would go.

Or where Bittner would go, for that matter. The address was here somewhere. Brennan looked around in perplexity at the crumbling facades, until he saw the numbers "7-9" above a dark passageway leading back into the block. He went in. There was a narrow courtyard at the end of the passage, its cobbles set into broad grouts of mortar. After some searching, Brennan found a small plate next to a peeling door: *F-bis*. There were small glass panes in the upper half of the door, covered with a faded blue curtain. Brennan knocked.

He heard scraping from inside, as though a chair was being pushed across the floor. After a moment the door curtain was drawn aside a couple of inches, and an old man looked out. It was Bittner. He was much shorter than Brennan recollected from their encounter in Vienna.

"*Bonjour,*" Brennan said. Bittner looked puzzled for an instant, and then recognition dawned in his watery eyes. The door rattled and creaked as he opened it. "Come in," he said, in English. He must have remembered that Brennan's Czech wasn't very good.

It was dim inside. The windows were covered with the same fabric as the glass in the door. Brennan was standing in a combination kitchen-sitting room, none too clean, piled with books and papers. A wooden table stood near the ancient gas stove; on the table was a loaf of bread, partly sliced, a fragment of a round of cheese and a half-empty bottle of red wine with a glass beside it. There was wine on Bittner's breath, as well.

Bittner lowered himself, with the painful care of the arthritic, onto the lumpy sofa under the window and gestured at one of the wooden chairs at the table. "Sit down," he invited. He was taking Brennan's sudden appearance very matter-of-factly, almost as though he'd expected it. "There is wine, if you'd like some."

"No, thank you," Brennan replied. He felt awkward and unsure of how to begin. "Gorbachev," he said. He realized that bone disease had bent Bittner's spine into a shallow curve; this was why he'd looked so short when he opened the door.

"Yes," Bittner said. "You've come because of Gorbachev. I thought to myself, 'If they're ever going to ask me for more information, now is the time they'll do it.' I was right. Wasn't I?"

"Yes," Brennan said. "You were. I'd like to show you a photograph."

"Show it." Bittner had been an intelligence officer once; he didn't waste time.

Brennan took the picture of Kepa out of his wallet and handed it to Bittner. The old Czech studied it for about forty seconds, turning it this way and that to catch the light diffusing through the curtains behind him. Finally he said:

"It's been a long time, but it's him, all right. He's aged, but it's him."

"Do you know who he is?" Brennan asked.

"Oh, yes. He is KGB. Or was, when I knew him in Prague. Let me see. That would have been 1980. He would be in his early forties now, I think. The Russians were very nervous about what was happening in Poland at the time, and they sent us what they were pleased to call advisers. To make sure we didn't get ideas similar to those of the Poles. We didn't, of course. After 1968, when the tanks of our fraternal socialist allies rolled into Prague, we were wiser than that."

"I see. But you knew him personally?"

"Yes. He was a hard one, even for a Russian. Eleventh Department. His name is Vasily Romanenko."

Got it, Brennan thought. Kepa is KGB. One more bit of rope to hang Chernysh and his crew. "Do you know anything else about him?"

"No. He left after two months. I have no idea where he went. I came across shortly afterward, as you remember. Did I ever thank you for that?"

"Yes," Brennan said. He looked around at the small, squalid room. "You did."

Bittner followed his gaze. "It isn't a lot, is it?" he said. "I could have stayed in America, of course. But to tell you the truth, I didn't like it there. I am much happier in Paris. There are plenty of exiles here." He paused. "Do my old compatriots have any idea where I am?"

"No. You're quite safe."

Bittner smiled for the first time. It was a very faint smile, with an equally faint trace of sadness. "Yes, I'm safe. As safe as anyone is. Was there anything else?"

"No," Brennan said, putting the photograph away. "That was all." It was a difficult moment; he wasn't sure how to take his leave.

"You might," Bittner said, "arrange to have some money sent to me. I find it difficult to afford the heat, in winter."

Used and dropped, Brennan thought. Like so many of the others. "I'll make sure you get something," he said, and added silently: Even if I have to send it myself.

"Thank you." Bittner stood up. "I'm sure you need to let people know what I've told you, as soon as you can. But you're sure you won't take some wine before you go?"

He's a lonely old man, Brennan thought, and he'd very much like some company. Someone to reminisce with, without having to conceal who he is, and was. But I haven't enough time. "I'd like to," he said, meaning it. "But I'm afraid can't." He got up and moved toward the door.

"Good luck," Bittner said. There was disappointment in his voice. "I think you're going to need it." He opened the door and let Brennan out. The latch clicked shut. The sun had long since left the courtyard, and the shadows were cold. The air smelled of autumn.

Brennan went back along the passageway to rue Duris, pondering what to do next. He wasn't likely to get any clearer identification from the other two men. The best thing to do was go along to the safe house, call Langley to make sure Knight had arrived safely, collect his baggage and head for de Gaulle airport. Off to the Métro, then.

It was ten to five by the time he reached the Menilmontant station. Brennan glumly contemplated the prospect of a long ride in a packed rush-hour Métro car, and then the trudge from the Porte d'Italie station to the apartment block containing the safe house. On impulse, he began scanning the street. Not fifteen meters away was a taxi whose sign read *Libre*. Brennan waved his arms vehemently at it, at exactly the moment a woman with three angry-looking children in tow did the same thing. She was five steps closer to the cab than Brennan.

The taxi driver looked at each potential fare and made up his mind without the least difficulty. The cab pulled over to the curb in front of Brennan. The woman was pursuing it, the children trailing in her wake. One of them had started to wail. Brennan yanked the door open, threw himself into the cab, and said, "*Quartier d'Italie*." He slammed the door as the woman shouted an infuriated "*Cochon*!" after him.

The driver was grinning, not very chivalrously, Brennan thought. "*Vous êtes chanceux, monsieur*," the driver chuckled. "*Ainsi que moi.*"

Yes, we're both lucky, Brennan thought. He said as much in his stilted French; he was nowhere near fluent, although he could get along.

"Where in the Quartier?" the driver asked.

Brennan pondered. He'd have to get out well away from the block containing the safe house anyway, despite his earlier reservations about walking from the Métro station. He didn't know the names of the cross streets down there. "Just go down the avenue Choisy," he said. "I'll tell you where I want to get out."

Brennan relaxed against the seat. He felt a deep, professional satisfaction. He had not only identified Kepa, almost as an afterthought, but had managed to make contact with a man at the core of the plot to overthrow Mikhail Gorbachev. This was beginning to take on the dimensions of an intelligence coup. And he might even have time to take advantage of French cuisine before he went to the airport.

Or, better yet, find a present for Molly. She had a passion for fine scarves, which she collected at every opportunity. And she'd be surprised; she was under the impression that he was still in New York. Or would it break security if she knew he'd been in Paris?

He was annoyed with himself for even having entertained the thought. She'd understand why he hadn't been able to tell her he was leaving the country, although she wouldn't like it. And she was hardly the kind of person who would broadcast his movements. She knew better than that, although, again, she disliked the necessity for it. The secrecy was one of the many reasons he'd decided to resign. He'd been able to imagine all too clearly how she'd feel if something happened to him overseas, when she'd thought he was safely at work in Washington.

He'd check the plane schedules. Then, if he could possibly make the time, he'd snatch a bite to eat and look for a scarf for her. He could let her know he'd been in Paris, although he couldn't tell her about Warsaw. Not yet, anyway. Someday, when all this was over and Gorbachev was safe, he'd be able to describe to her what he'd done. Brennan, like most men, wanted the woman he loved to be proud of his achievements, even if they had to remain hidden from the public.

The taxi was now swinging out of the boulevard Richard Lenoir, into the traffic circle of the place de la Bastille; through the window on his left, Brennan could see the great bronze-clad base of the Colonne de juillet. The traffic was heavy, and slowing down. Dammit, he thought. I should have taken the Métro after all. It probably would have been faster. Although not as comfortable.

The cab stopped, hemmed in on both sides by other vehicles. "*Qu'est-ce qui arrive*?" Brennan asked.

"*Trop de camions, trop de voitures. Le traffic-jam,*" said the driver over his shoulder. Presumably this last was for Brennan's benefit; the driver would have spotted his accent as American.

Brennan waited. The cab chugged ahead briefly, and stopped again. The driver rolled down the window, admitting a gust of chill autumn air mixed with exhaust fumes, and stuck his head out for a look. "*Et maintenant . . . un accident,*" he observed, withdrawing his head, and raved on in a stream of argot that Brennan couldn't follow.

Two or three minutes passed. Becoming more and more impatient, he started looking for a Métro sign, and then remembered that there was a station on the other side of the square, by the Gare de Lyon. In one more minute, he thought, I'll pay the driver and head over to the subway.

The door on his left opened suddenly. Startled, Brennan looked around. A man was leaning into the cab, a big smile plastered over his face, which was distinctly not French. He was wearing a Homburg and had a gray raincoat draped over his right arm and hand.

"Monsieur Brennan," he said jovially in accented French. "I thought it was you we saw get into the cab. I think we're going the same way. I'd be happy to offer you a lift."

The cab driver half turned, scowling at the prospect of losing a profitable fare. The man in the Homburg dropped a couple of bills over the back of the driver's seat and the scowl vanished. The driver couldn't see what Brennan saw: the round muzzle of a pistol just visible under the fold of the raincoat. The man knew Brennan could see it. He wanted him to.

The shock was paralyzing. Everything Brennan had been thinking for the past half-hour was wrong, his security was blown wide open. It took him several seconds to begin to adjust to this realization.

"My car's just three back," the man said. The smile was not so broad, and the pistol muzzle jerked emphatically toward the rear of the cab. "Please accept."

"Very well," Brennan responded. He couldn't have sounded pleased enough, for the man's eyes narrowed. They were Slavic eyes above broad cheekbones. "Thank you," he added.

The man inclined his head fractionally and stood back to let Brennan climb out of the car. Brennan slid across the seat, feeling the Walther bump against his thigh. They'd suspect he was armed, and take no chances. The pistol muzzle under the raincoat was pointing at his breastbone, never wavering.

If I get into their car, Brennan thought, as his captor closed the cab door with his left hand, I'll never get out. They want to know who I saw here. Or was I followed from Warsaw? Was Kaminsky a plant, for some purpose I can't imagine? They'll take me somewhere and question me, and sooner or later, I'll break. Molly. Poor Molly.

"Go back to the car," the man with the Homburg said. "The green Peugeot. Be very careful. Keep your hands in sight. I'll be right behind you."

Brennan turned and started to walk. He was finding his wits again, as he instinctively began to survey the traffic jam for a way out. None was evident. He could see the Peugeot, the third car behind the cab. There were two men in it, one behind the wheel, the other in the rear seat. Behind the Peugeot was a large truck.

Around him, the place de la Bastille was a huge expanse of motionless vehicles. Despite the city ordinances against horn-blowing, there was a rising din of honks and beeps. Somewhere ahead, a motorcyclist was gunning his engine in short bursts, the sound angry and waspish.

One more car to pass, and he'd be at the Peugeot. He glanced at the lines of traffic on either side of him. The bumpers were almost touching. No ideas, nothing. They were going to take him.

A sudden movement jerked his attention to the way ahead. The motorcycle he'd heard a moment ago had swerved from behind the truck at the Peugeot's rear; the rider had decided to wriggle through the traffic jam. The man hadn't expected pedestrians in front of him, and he was irritable and in a hurry. The bike was already accelerating hard when its rider saw Brennan. Alarm and astonishment flew into the adolescent face under the black helmet, and its owner slammed on the brakes, but far too late to stop. The lane between the stalled cars was too narrow for him to swerve around the two men in his path. He was going to hit them.

"Look out!" Brennan yelled in Russian, hoping that the man behind him had seen what was happening. He had. Brennan felt a violent push on his left shoulder as the Russian shoved him toward the hood of the Volvo on their right. Brennan glimpsed a woman's shocked face behind the windshield, and then his feet were on the Volvo's front bumper as he twisted to see what the Russian was doing. The man was right behind him, the gun muzzle aimed into Brennan's face, as he climbed into the gap between the two automobiles, whose bumpers were only about four inches apart.

The Russian slipped. His foot went into the narrow gap and he fell sideways. At the instant he lost his aim, Brennan kicked. His toe struck the Russian under the rib cage and toppled him backward into the aisle between the lines of cars.

The motorcycle was still travelling fast when it hit him. The driver tried frantically to skid it sideways, but because of the constricted space he couldn't drop the machine and let it slide to a stop. The cycle slammed into the half-prostrate Russian, stalled, spilled its rider, and fell on top of both men.

The other two Russians were vaulting out of the Peugeot. Brennan didn't wait to see if they had guns in their hands; he leaped onto the hood of the Volvo and jumped from there onto the hood of the adjoining car. The traffic jam was so tight that there was hardly room on the ground to walk, much less run.

Because of his positioning, Brennan saw he would have to go clear across the width of the place de la Bastille in order to evade his pursuers. He flew across another gap, and then was forced to go around an articulated truck, via the car roofs this time. He risked a glance behind. All three men were after him now. Infuriated yells rose in their wake as the trapped drivers realized that something was denting their bodywork.

Brennan reached the last file of cars before the broad, round terrace at the base of the Colonne de juillet. He jumped down onto the pavement and sprinted for the other side of the terrace. At least they weren't shooting at him yet, although they'd be stupid to: a handgun wasn't accurate enough at this range, against a moving target. And there'd be *flics* on the way to the car accident the taxi driver had mentioned; the Russians wouldn't want to attract police attention with gunshots. Neither did he. Maybe he could reach the Métro far enough ahead of them to get onto a train, and get away. . . .

He risked another glance. There they were, all three of them, forty yards behind, but not gaining. They'd abandoned their car; stolen, probably. His left calf, where the shell fragment had hit him at Da Nang, was beginning to ache fiercely.

He ran by the plinth of the Colonne de juillet, jumped off the terrace and headed for the frozen river of cars on the west side of the square. The Russians weren't giving up. Onto a Renault's hood, angry yell from the driver, now a Peugeot, another Renault, a Mercedes, up on the roofs because of that truck in the way, a big *jump*, goddamn it that's a Citroen 2CV I'm coming down on, fabric —

Brennan's left foot went through the canvas of the car top and the other slammed down onto the curving hood, leaving a huge dent right in front of the windshield wipers. Brennan lost his balance and sprawled forward.

His leg wouldn't come out of the tear for an instant. The scar tissue hurt as though it were ripping apart. He felt the driver grab at his shoe, and then he was free and running again. A glance back. He'd lost some of his lead; they were still in pursuit. Determined but stupid, or desperate. How were they going to drag him off in broad daylight?

There was more space between the cars now. Three more lanes of traffic. . . . He leaped to the ground and kept running. His leg hurt, but it was beginning to loosen up, as it sometimes did. Behind him he heard car doors slamming; outraged drivers getting out. His breath was coming in huge burning gasps. He reached the curb. Have to figure out what to do next, where are they? Look over your shoulder, stupid.

They were in trouble. A couple of angry Parisians had grabbed one of the men, and the other two were fighting to get him loose. No wonder. They couldn't afford to be held for the *gendarmes*. Brennan plunged into the crowd on the sidewalk, heading for the Métro entrance; once there he could decide whether to enter the subway or head into the Gare de Lyon and try to escape in the twists and turns of the railway station. People were eyeing him curiously as he ran. No good. He had to stop attracting this much attention before he entered either the Métro or the railway station.

He stopped for a moment to look back. His pursuers had broken free, but there were other drivers after them. The three Russians were pelting toward the sidewalk, using almost the same route Brennan had, but they were a lot farther behind him than they had been.

Brennan made an instant decision, and ran for the Métro. He pounded down the stairs, where he had to slow, however, because of the rush-hour crowd. Now he looked, he hoped, simply like a man in a desperate hurry to make an appointment. He rammed his hand into his pocket, feeling for the tickets Macarthur had given him. With luck, his pursuers wouldn't have thought to provide themselves with tickets and they'd have to either buy some or risk jumping the barriers in full view of the clerks.

There were lineups at the automatic barriers. Brennan joined the line he thought was the shortest. No one behind him yet. His palm, the ticket clenched inside, was sticky with sweat. The woman in front of him reached the barrier and began fumbling in her purse, looking for her *carnet*, without success.

"*Excusez*," Brennan said, and shoved past her. The woman looked shocked for a moment, and then snarled at him, but he was already through. The platforms were just ahead. He made it to the southbound one just as a departing train was beginning to close its doors. Brennan rammed himself into the car, feeling the doors nip at his heels, and ignored the angry looks of the passengers he'd shoved aside. He scanned the reflections in the opposite windows.

The Russians were just now hurrying onto the platform. He'd made it.

Except that they shouldn't have been there at all.

Brennan reached the safe house two hours later, after doubling back on his trail several times, and calling in a Mayday in to Macarthur during one of his changeovers. He'd wondered at first if Macarthur had set up the ambush in the place de la Bastille, but when he thought about it, it didn't fit. Macarthur knew Bittner's address, as well as the addresses of the other three men Brennan wanted to see. If Macarthur had told the KGB where Brennan was going, they'd have had men waiting for him at each place, and they'd have gotten him at Bittner's. They wouldn't have risked a snatch in the open street if they'd had an alternative.

Nevertheless, when he left the Métro at the Porte d'Italie he took a bus farther north than he needed to, and then another one across the street grid, and finally walked an interminable two blocks to the apartment building. His left calf was aching like a rotten tooth.

He let himself in to find Macarthur waiting for him. "Jesus!" Macarthur exclaimed. "You look like hell. What happened?"

"I was spotted," Brennan said. "They tried to grab me on the way back from Bittner's. I expect they were going to do it on Menilmontant, but I got a cab before they could pull it off. Did you send somebody over to Bittner's?"

"Yeah. He's not there. No sign of a struggle, though. We're looking."

"Ah, fuck," Brennan said, and dropped wearily into a chair. He felt as though he'd been awake and running for a week. Bittner taken, after all these years. They might never have found him if it hadn't been for Brennan's carelessness. And Macarthur's.

Macarthur was standing over him with a glass. "Scotch? You look like you could use one."

"Yeah. Thanks." Brennan took the glass. "On the way down from de Gaulle, did you see *anything* at all? A green Peugeot 705?"

"No," Macarthur said. "I was watching, but I didn't. There was no pattern."

"They must have been using more than one car. We didn't make it hard for them, God*damn* it.'' He suppressed an urge to throw the glass at the wall, and drank from it instead. Macarthur sat down again, expressionless. If he was upset at the mess they were in, he didn't show it.

''Can you tell me what's going on?'' Macarthur asked.

''No,'' Brennan responded shortly. His own head was full of questions, the most worrisome being the puzzle of how the KGB — if it *was* the KGB, and not one of the other Bloc services — had known he was in Paris. And how they knew what he looked like, if that was how they'd picked him up at de Gaulle.

Brennan shook his head. The questions couldn't be answered yet, not without a lot of thinking, and more information.

''I have to call Langley,'' he said. ''Is it secure enough from here?''

''I brought a scrambler unit.''

''Would you hook it up for me?''

Brennan finished the Scotch while Macarthur connected the scrambler. ''Go ahead,'' he said after a minute and a half. ''I'll get out of your hair.''

He left the living room. Brennan picked up the receiver and dialled. The numbers seemed to go on forever. Finally he got the Soviet Division duty officer, who put him through to Knight's office. Knight, fortunately, was there. At least that part was all right.

''Sean here,'' Brennan said. ''Scramble.''

''Okay,'' Knight said. ''Now.''

Brennan pressed the button. ''Okay there?''

''Okay.'' The voice was fuzzy around the edges from the scrambling. ''I got here fine. Any luck your end?''

''Kepa is definitely a big brother,'' Brennan said. ''I have a positive ID.''

''Hell's bells,'' Knight said. Brennan knew exactly what he was thinking, because Brennan had already thought it through himself. Kaminsky had said that Galeski was a bona fide defector, never part of CONCERTO. Kepa had befriended Galeski in the United States, according to Mrs. Petty. Then Galeski turned up dead at Killenworth, looking very much like a Polish terrorist. But as Bittner had said, if he'd really been part of the operation they'd have removed his body.

And finally, Kepa was KGB. This provided the independent

cross-check needed to validate what Kaminsky told Brennan: that there *was* no Jan Paderewski Cell, and that the KGB was orchestrating events to remove Gorbachev.

"You still there, Frank?"

"Yeah."

"What'll you do with it?"

"Christ. I don't know. Kick it upstairs. It's too big for this level." Knight paused, ruminating. Then he said, "Okay. Anything else?"

"Yes," Brennan said. "Two things. Bad ones. First, somebody tried to pick me up. Second, they took Bittner."

"Holy shit."

"Somebody knew I was here, Frank."

Another long pause. "Not Macarthur?"

"No. It didn't work that way. But Frank, don't let anybody except Barlow and Reid know what we've found out. Something's badly wrong."

"I'll say it is." Knight's voice had regained its even calm. "You can't come back commercial. They may be watching the airports. Probably are. Stay there. I'll make arrangements for a secure flight. Get some sleep."

"Okay. Bye."

He hung up. Macarthur came back into the living room. "All finished?" he asked.

"No," Brennan said. "It's far from finished. Where did you put the Scotch?"

Moscow – Zhukovka
Saturday, October 5

YURI ISAYEV, chairman of the Secretariat of the Communist Party of the Soviet Union, was looking pensively out his office window. From the window, which was on the top floor of the Central Committee building on Staraya Square, he could count over two dozen uniformed KGB guardsmen. They had been patrolling the square for the past six days, and there were many more of them watching the other approaches to the building. At first, the patrols had been army troops; but on Tuesday, and at Oleg Chernysh's insistence, they had been replaced by KGB men: Ninth Directorate troops, the blue-tabbed Kremlin Guards. Isayev hadn't liked the move at the time, and he disliked it still.

He let the curtain fall back into place as his aide entered the office. "Ready?" Isayev asked.

"We're ready, Secretary."

"Let's be off, then."

He followed the aide out into the corridor, where more Ninth Directorate Guards stood motionless and watchful. It was ridiculous to have them posted all over the interior of the building like this; Isayev didn't believe for an instant that counterrevolutionaries could do the same thing here that Chernysh insisted they'd done in the United States, but Chernysh had been adamant. Too adamant, for Isayev's peace of mind.

Isayev and the aide went down the back stairs to the courtyard where his Zil and the Chaikas and motorcycles of the escort were waiting. There'd been frost in the night, and the air had a snap to it; the late morning sun hadn't yet penetrated into the courtyard. It wasn't going to be long until they saw snow again.

He got into the Zil and the aide closed the door on him. The courtyard reverberated as the motorcycle riders gunned their engines, and the line of vehicles rumbled out into the side street and then turned into Staraya Square. Down here at ground level, the security precautions were even more evident than from above. There wasn't a civilian to be seen.

The KGB driver on the other side of the glass partition picked up his microphone. Isayev heard the man's tinny voice through the rear-seat loudspeaker.

"Secretary, my orders are to respectfully request that you draw the curtains, for your own safety."

He and his orders can respectfully go to hell, Isayev thought. It's been bad enough working in an armed camp for the past week, but I'm damned if I'm going to ride around Moscow in a sealed box, as though a member of the Party didn't dare show his face to the world. Anyway, the windows were bulletproof. He toggled the intercom switch. "Your orders are countermanded," he said, and released it.

"Yes, Secretary," the driver said.

If only everything else were so simple, Isayev thought.

The Zil swept along the boulevards. Moscow was already looking grayer, as though in preparation for the long winter ahead. Despite his refusal to close the curtains, Isayev wasn't really looking at the streets as the car rushed along. He was thinking about the encounter he was going to have, out in the *dacha* near Zhukovka.

The Zil turned onto Volgogradsky Prospekt, heading southeast, out of the city. Huge blocks of apartments rose into the sky, which was a brilliant, cold blue. The traffic was being cleared away ahead of them, and the Zil kept up a steady eighty miles an hour. If you followed this road to its end, you would find yourself in a city that was once called Tsaritsyn, and later Stalingrad, where the German Sixth Army bled to death in the winter of 1942-1943. Now it was called Volgograd. Isayev wondered whether its name might change again.

The procession roared past the intersection of Volgogradsky Prospekt and the outer Moscow ring road, and drove on southeast. Now the road was called the M7 motorway; the Zil passed through Kotelniki, Tokarova, Okt'abr'sky, and then arrived at an unobtrusive turnoff a hundred yards short of the intersection of the M7 and the Zhukovka road. At least, the turnoff would have been unobtrusive if it hadn't been surrounded by guards, these supported by a BMP armored personnel carrier. There were many *dachas* hidden within the birch and fir woods, which, despite their apparent emptiness, were heavily patrolled.

Isayev pulled himself out of his reverie as the Zil slowed, swung left past the BMP onto the side road, and drove a third of a mile along it to a fork, where the driver turned right. After a couple of minutes the woods thinned out and Isayev could see the windows and front door of the *dacha* amid the tree trunks. The Zil followed the lead Chaika and two motorcycles into the clearing, pulled around the curving, gravelled driveway to the front of the house, and stopped. The driver got out and opened Isayev's door. The Secretary joined him on the gravel, as did all eight men in the two Chaikas. The motorcycle engines grumbled noisily, echoes rebounding from the front wall of the house. The officer in charge of the security detachment walked over to Isayev and opened his mouth to speak.

Isayev cut him off. "Get these men of yours out of sight," he snapped. "And have them turn off the engines. How much noise do you think she needs to hear?"

The major flinched. "Secretary, we are ordered to protect you. I —"

"You personally may stay by the front door here, and guard *that*, if you like. There are patrols all over these woods. What do you imagine's going to happen to me? Never mind, I don't want an answer. Do as I've ordered."

The major looked as though he were trying to swallow a live hedgehog. "Yes, Secretary."

Isayev turned away from him and surveyed the *dacha* and its surroundings as he approached the front door. He'd been here many times, but the charm of the place grew with each visit. The house was pine, with a steeply pitched, shingled roof, its two stories arranged in an L-shape, with the driveway curving into the angle of the L. Birch trees and aromatic firs crowded the grassy area beyond the drive; many of the birches, sheltered here from the wind, still retained their slender golden leaves. Behind the house there was a flagstone terrace, and a stretch of lawn which sloped down to more fir stands. Inside the woods, at the bottom of the slope, was a small stream that eventually flowed into the Pechorka River.

The door opened just as he reached it; she'd come to greet him herself. She was perfectly made-up as always, the large dark eyes outlined so that they looked even larger, the auburn hair immaculately arranged. She was wearing a plain navy-blue suit and white shoes, and a white scarf around her throat. Only when he looked closely did Isayev see that the eye shadow was not all cosmetic. Under the careful makeup her face was worn and drained.

"Raisa Gorbacheva," he said. "I've come out to talk with you."

"Thank you, Yuri Ilyich," she said. "Come in." She frowned at the clusters of men out in the driveway. Engines rumbled.

"It's all right," he said. "I've told them to get out of sight."

"Thank you."

He followed her into the *dacha*. Inside was a foyer, with more pine panelling. The living room, which looked out onto the front drive, had a huge fieldstone fireplace at one end. Mikhail had had — *has*, Isayev corrected himself — his study at the rear of the house, with a traditional tiled Russian stove in it.

"Is the house staff around?" Isayev asked as he followed her into the living room. This room displayed her flair and taste: good art, colorful rugs and wall hangings, graceful western furniture. Her private tastes deviated from the traditional Russian style, which tended toward the ornate and heavy. He remembered the fuss over her American Express credit card, and how annoyed Mikhail had been with her about it; after that, she'd been more careful to keep her personal preferences discreet.

"They're here," she said. "They're always here. I had difficulty preventing Comrade Chernysh from filling the house with guards." Her tone was sardonic. "They have installed additional security measures," she added, as an apparent afterthought.

So there are microphones now, Isayev thought. If there weren't before. Any instability in the government or the Party caused everyone to start maneuvering for positions of advantage, and Oleg Chernysh wasn't one to leave any chinks in his information system. Isayev would have to get her outside, down by the stream. There'd be surveillance devices in the woods, but there was a better chance of wind or water noise muffling a conversation.

"Is there any news?" she asked, sitting down on the raised hearth and folding her arms across her knees.

Isayev admired her self-control. She'd had that surgery which kept her — thank Heaven — from accompanying Mikhail to New York, and now she had to cope as well with the catastrophe of his abduction. "No," he replied. "Everyone is still looking, but they've found no leads."

"That's ridiculous," she retorted angrily. "If it had happened here, we'd have caught them by now. How can the Americans be so disorganized? They don't know what's going on in their own backyard. Damn them."

"The KGB team is there to assist," Isayev reminded her. "Oleg Chernysh says he's sent the very best he has. They'll keep the Americans up to the mark."

"It couldn't have been the Americans behind it?" she asked, calm again. The only sign of her inner tension was the way she was kneading the hem of her skirt between her manicured fingertips. "Could it?"

"No. It's not possible. They would never chance anything like this. They've always favored Mikhail above other possible holders of his office."

"Or so they would have us believe."

"Don't misunderstand me," he told her. "We mustn't trust the Americans an inch, not at a time like this. Any misfortune of ours causes them great delight. And they would take advantage of us, if they thought they could get away with it. But we are ready for any such attempt, and they know it."

She glanced up at him, seeing, he knew, a small, fat man with a mop of gray hair and rimless spectacles on a pink, round face. Ever since middle age Isayev had looked like everyone's favorite uncle, benign and harmless. He could be benign, but he could also be far from harmless. His docile and unassuming mask had seriously misled more than one political enemy, including Yegor Ligachev, who had been secretary for ideology and cadres before him. Ligachev had lost his post in the shakeup that drove many of the antireform people out of the Politburo and the Secretariat, or at least persuaded them to shut their mouths and go along with the mainstream. And like Ligachev before him, Isayev was now the second most powerful voice in the Party, after Mikhail Gorbachev.

Except that, as matters stood now, he was the *most* powerful voice. If Mikhail didn't come back, he'd be naturally the next in line to carry on the restructuring of Soviet society.

If he was allowed to. He had the voice, but not the weapons. Unless Stepanov, the defense minister, cast in his lot with Mikhail. That wasn't certain.

''It was the Poles, then,'' she said. ''Damn the Poles. They've always been a threat. Right through our history.''

She was referring, he knew, to the thousand years of attack and counterattack that ran like a bloody thread through the tapestry of Polish-Russian history, beginning with the Poles' conquest of the Ukraine and the taking of Kiev in 1018, and ending with the 1919-1920 war between Poland and the Soviet Union. In the latter conflict the Poles were nearly defeated at first, but then rallied and drove the Red Army back to the Dvina River in the north, and far into the Ukraine in the south. It wasn't until 1945 that the Soviet Union regained the lost territories, and a communized Poland into the bargain. Now the Poles were causing trouble again. In fact, they'd never stopped, even after 1945. Solidarity, up until now, had been the most glaring example of Polish refusal to submit.

''Perhaps we could go for a walk,'' Isayev said. ''I've been sitting down at a desk for days.''

She glanced at him and nodded. Raisa Gorbachev was far from a fool; Isayev suspected that she had nearly as much political acumen as her husband, although, being a woman, she'd find it far more difficult to put that skill to formal use. He'd often wondered how much she advised Mikhail about his courses of action, and how much of the advice he took. At the very least her status — as long as Mikhail remained alive — made her a useful ally, and Isayev knew he needed allies.

She stood up. ''Let me get a wrap. It's cold outside under the trees.''

She came back with a peasant shawl, which, on most other women, would have appeared incongruous when combined with the carefully tailored suit; on Raisa Gorbachev, it looked perfect. She led him through the house and out onto the rear terrace.

Cloud shadows swept over the woods and the lawn; a cool, steady wind was blowing from the northeast, swishing among the fir branches and shaking the gold leaves of the birches.

"There's a path down to the stream," she said. "Let's go down there."

He followed her. The wind was less strong inside the woods, although it still made plenty of noise in the branches above them. Isayev couldn't hear the sound of running water until they'd almost reached the stream, which was about ten feet wide but only inches deep at this time of year. Exposed rocks lay in the streambed, the water splashing around and between them. Raisa Gorbachev leaned against a birch trunk, watching the sun glitter on the broken surface of the stream.

"Was it the Poles?" she asked.

So her comments about Poland had been for the benefit of the microphones. She was, indeed, no one's fool.

"I don't know," Isayev told her. "It's possible." Without proof, he was unwilling to say more than that. He wasn't sure how she'd react if he said he suspected Chernysh.

"What are we going to do if Mikhail . . . does not come back?" she asked.

"I will carry on his work," Isayev said.

"If you're permitted to. Forgive me, Yuri Ilyich, but you do not have the stature my husband does."

"I know."

"If Mikhail dies in America, there will be a lot of people who will try to put things back the way they were."

"Things can't be put back the way they were," Isayev said. "It's gone too far."

"I think you are wrong," she told him. "Mikhail was worried that it could happen. He said, just before he left, that if he could have five more years, then the people would begin to notice a real difference in the way they lived. But so many things still have to be changed before that can happen. He has always been worried that the people would be too impatient, that they'd expect huge differences overnight. And he was right. They *do* expect them, and they're not getting them as fast as they convinced themselves they would. Even some senior Party members, ones who followed Mikhail in the beginning, have doubts about whether it's possible. You of all people should know that."

"I know it," Isayev said. "But I'm not one of them."

"I know. What will the Army do if Mikhail dies?"

"I have been trying to sound out Defense Minister Stepanov. He remains elusive."

"Does he believe the Poles did this thing?"

"He is evasive on that point, as well. But I know he is worried about the army having to intervene in Poland, and perhaps in Hungary and Czechoslovakia as well. Those three countries are powder kegs of counterrevolution. Look at the riots. Although I think we can depend on the East Germans."

"They're all trimming their sails," she said. "Vitali Stepanov, I mean, and the rest of them."

"I want to make a suggestion to you," he said.

"What?"

"If Mikhail does not come back from New York, I think that you and your daughter and grandchildren should leave the country. Yugoslavia would be best. Or at least get away from Moscow."

"No," she said. "I won't go. I will try to persuade Irina to take the grandchildren away, if it's absolutely necessary, but I won't leave Moscow."

"It could be very dangerous to stay."

"You're exaggerating. Without Mikhail, I'm no danger to anyone. They'd pension me off in an apartment in the Lenin Hills somewhere and forget about me. So would everyone else."

He hoped she was right, but he wasn't sure. If the men who hated Mikhail gained power, any reminder of his existence might be an embarrassment, or worse, an accusation. Already there were undercurrents in some of the press articles about the unrest within the Eastern European allies; they were using phrases like "serious errors of policy." The policies weren't being attributed to anyone specific, but no one could mistake the real target of the allegations. Isayev had ordered the suppression of such articles yesterday, but he wasn't sure his orders would be carried out. He sensed already that some of his power was slipping from his grasp. If Mikhail were killed, and Eastern Europe burst into flame with counterrevolution, the accusations of errors might become accusations of crimes. And everyone knew that Raisa Gorbachev was a strong influence on Mikhail. The accusations would fall on her head, as well.

"I'd like you to consider the suggestion anyway," he told her.

"Matters could become worse than either of us have imagined."

"Do you think so?"

"Yes."

She pondered that, and then said, "How I wish, sometimes, that I were a man. I would be able to take a hand in this, instead of doing nothing but wait."

Isayev nodded in agreement. And then Raisa Gorbachev surprised him. She leaned forward, her lips almost at his ear. He could smell her perfume, some delicate Parisian scent. "Yuri Ilyich," she breathed. "Please tell me. Is it the KGB? Oleg Chernysh?"

Isayev drew back. It was a horribly dangerous question. He had considered the possibility; sometimes, over the past few days, especially at five o'clock in the morning, he had even found the idea plausible. But he dared not voice it aloud to anyone, although he knew without a doubt that it must have occurred to others. To speak such a thing would admit to its possibility, and that was too strong a drink even for the men at Isayev's level. Moreover, even to suggest it would amount to an accusation against the KGB, and God alone knew how Chernysh and the security organs would react. At best, the accusation would weaken everyone's confidence in both the leadership and the security organs; at worst, and if it were true, it could precipitate violent action by the KGB. With Mikhail's fate still uncertain, Isayev couldn't risk that. There was still a chance he'd come back safe. If the KGB — assuming it *was* Chernysh behind the abduction — felt threatened enough to try to depose him while he was still alive, the worst might happen.

A second civil war.

How the Americans would love that, Isayev thought. It would prove everything they've always believed about us.

"I can't believe it," he said. "And it mustn't be said. Do you understand me?"

She nodded. She must have thought it through for herself, and come to much the same conclusion as he had.

It was time to move on. "Raisa Gorbacheva," he said, "I need to know how Mikhail felt about the rest of the leadership. He may have said things to you that he wouldn't have told anyone else.

I need to know who he really felt he could trust. He must have judged that there were some among us who were more committed than others."

That was a delicate way of putting it. She surveyed him, debating, he knew, just how far she could trust him. He hoped he hadn't misjudged Mikhail's opinion of him.

"You, of course," she said, to his great relief. "And Alexander Finenko. Ivan Zotin. Valentin Pokrovsky."

He nodded. The secretary for International Affairs, the chairman of the Council of Ministers, the foreign minister, as he'd suspected. She went on through the list of Politburo members and the Secretariat, Isayev keeping mental notes as she spoke. When she ended, she asked:

"Have I missed anyone?"

"Grigori Yermakov and Dmitri Averin."

"Yes. Mikhail thought they would change direction, if the wind was right."

That wasn't so good, especially in the case of Yermakov, who was head of the General Department of the Secretariat. That department handled all Secretariat administration, and the scope of its responsibility gave its chief a great deal of behind-the-scenes influence. Averin, as head of the Party Control Commission, was responsible for Party discipline, ensuring that the machine ran in an orderly fashion and that the hierarchy was preserved all the way down to the local level.

"But you say he wasn't worried about Oleg Chernysh?" Isayev said. He spoke very softly, despite the rush of the wind and the bubbling of the stream over the stones.

"He said that Oleg was too short on support to be a problem anymore."

The words caused Isayev a spasm of doubt. He wanted to believe that the KGB had nothing to do with the abduction, but he couldn't rid himself of the fear that the security organs were involved. The KGB had supported Mikhail for quite a long time — he was, after all, Andropov's protégé — but not without reservations. Mikhail had been concerned that the reservations might become overt opposition, and so he had been skillfully maneuvering to reduce Chernysh's influence in the Politburo. That fact wouldn't have escaped Chernysh. But only Isayev, as far as Isayev knew, was aware of Mikhail's intention of demoting Chernysh to nonvoting Polituro membership.

"I have to go back to Moscow," Isayev said. "There is a lot to keep track of, at the moment."

"Yes." She started back up the path, Isayev following. At the path's end, where it entered the clearing, she stopped. Isayev stopped also.

"Yuri Ilyich," she said, "I want my husband back. Do you think he'll come back?"

"Of course," Isayev said. "They'll find him soon, and then we'll be able to get back to our proper business."

Oleg Chernysh pressed the STOP button of the tape player and gazed into space. He was staring, as it happened, at the west wall of his office and roughly in the direction of New York, but for the moment he wasn't thinking about what was happening in the American city.

There was nothing useful on the tapes that Vadim Besedin, head of the First Chief Directorate of the KGB and second in command of operation CONCERTO, had brought to Chernysh half an hour earlier. Chernysh hadn't really expected the tapes to tell him anything; Isayev was too clever for that. So was Raisa Gorbachev. Taking Isayev down to that stream. . . . The technical people would have to install better microphones in the woods, especially by the water. They *might* be able to extract something intelligible from the tape recorded at that position, if they digitized it and worked it over with computer filtering. But it was out of the question to have more people fiddling around on the periphery of CONCERTO, even if they had no idea why the head of the KGB was so interested in a tape recording of Yuri Isayev speaking with Raisa Gorbachev. Chernysh had hoped the recordings would reveal whether Isayev actively suspected the KGB, and what, if anything, he was planning to do with his suspicions, but there was nothing solid.

Chernysh unlocked his desk safe and put the tapes into it. He was a large man, well-formed, without the fatty thickening of the body that usually afflicted Russian men of middle age. His face gave an appearance of cheerful openness without actually revealing anything; the nose was long and aquiline, the eyes blue, the hair above his broad forehead still red-brown and thick. Chernysh was, in fact, an exceptionally handsome man. Women also detected in him a whiff of elemental sexuality, which, combined with his good looks, made him a difficult proposition to resist. In his early days of fieldwork he'd specialized in female recruitment, his crowning achievement being the seduction of the wife of a major western ambassador to Moscow. They'd run her for six years, even after her husband returned home to a cabinet post, until she was killed in a car accident. If it had been an accident; it might have been suicide.

He was middle-aged now, and neither the looks nor the charm had deserted him. Neither had his appetite for power. He'd put up with most of Mikhail Gorbachev's reform movement for a long time, although he'd been duty-bound to point out the hazards of that famous *glasnost*; too much of it was an invitation to chaos. Mikhail was entirely too willing to trust the Soviet masses. He'd never seen them from the underside, the way Chernysh had during his years in the KGB, and Chernysh trusted neither their self-control nor their good nature. That was doubly true for the Warsaw Pact states; they'd turn on the Soviet Union in an instant if they thought they could get away with it, and God only knew where that would end. Both the allies and the Soviet masses needed a strong hand to keep them within bounds, and Mikhail wanted to remove far too many of the restraints. He'd obviously decided to remove Oleg Chernysh as well; that much was clear from the calculated political slights and the bypassing of KGB authority that had been occurring for the past eighteen months. Mikhail was going to succeed in reducing the KGB to just another police force, and that had been more than Chernysh could stomach. Fortunately, there were men under Chernysh whom he could trust, and he and Vadim Besedin and Anastas Vlasov, head of the Eleventh Directorate, had designed CONCERTO. They hadn't started out with such a drastic solution in mind, but after some discussion it was obvious that there was no way to remove the man by political means. CONCERTO was the only realistic solution; it dealt not only with Gorbachev, but also with the perennial problem of controlling the Warsaw Pact nations.

The only fly in the soup was the appearance of this American — what was his name? — Sean Brennan

The dossier concerning him was lying on Chernysh's desk. He

flipped it open and scanned it again. There wasn't much to read. Brennan had spent several years in the US embassy in Bonn, according to the dossier, but hadn't been identified as CIA at that time. His cover must have been good; the usual photographs had been taken, but after that, nobody had been very interested in him. He'd dropped out of sight, presumably returning to the United States, but had now reappeared as a full-fledged CIA man snooping around CONCERTO.

On Wednesday, Promenade reported him on the way to Paris, apparently on the trail of Stefan Kepa. That wasn't worrisome, because the identification of Kepa had been planned; it was a Polish identity intended to reinforce the cover of the CONCERTO abduction team. But the Paris trip was a surprise; it appeared that Brennan had access to unknown sources of information. Vlasov, at CONCERTO operational headquarters in Warsaw, ordered a watch kept for him at de Gaulle, but the Paris residency missed him at the airport because he'd been using a false passport, and they didn't yet have a photograph.

But they'd kept up the watch, fortunately, because yesterday he turned up at de Gaulle again, disembarking from a plane from Frankfurt. By that time they'd dug the Bonn photos out of the archives, and the watchers were able to spot him. He'd been picked up by an American embassy man named Macarthur, who might or might not be CIA. The pair of them hadn't taken any precautions — sloppy, that — and had been tracked to that address in the rue Duris.

By this time, back in Warsaw, Vlasov had been getting really worried. The American was on to something, and it might be more than Stefan Kepa. Brennan hadn't been underground in Paris. as Vlasov had believed; he'd been somewhere else. Vlasov consulted by radio with Chernysh and Vadim Besedin in Moscow, and they'd decided to order the heavy-duty section of the Paris residency to pick Brennan up. If it had been any operation other than CONCERTO they'd have let him run, but this one was different. They had to put Brennan out of circulation, get him back to Warsaw as soon as they could, and find out what he knew and where he'd been before he caught that plane out of Frankfurt. It was precarious, because Besedin was issuing orders to Paris on pretexts: the Paris residency had no idea that CONCERTO existed.

Then it all fell apart. The Paris team failed to grab Brennan, which was worse than leaving him alone, because it put the Americans on their guard. They might even — and this was infuriating to contemplate — suspect the existence of Promenade, the agent in the United States. As if that weren't enough, they'd fouled up the second priority as well. The Czechs would have been glad to get their hands on Bittner for the damage he'd caused years ago, but they never would, now. By the time they'd gotten him to the safe house he was dead, and they'd had to haul the body out of Paris and dump it in the Somme.

He must have always believed we'd catch up with him, Chernysh thought. Imagine living like that, with a cyanide pill constantly in your pocket. Why would anyone defect, with that kind of life ahead of them?

He dragged his thoughts back to the matter at hand, trying to look at the situation without exaggerating its dangers. Promenade, to start with. Promenade, actually, wouldn't be compromised easily. He'd be one of the last people to fall under any sort of suspicion; and anyway, the Americans might well believe Brennan had been blown when he went to see the Czech.

As for Gorbachev, the Americans would certainly suspect the KGB of having a hand in the kidnapping, but they'd be fools to suggest it without iron-clad proof, and even if they had the proof, they might be unwilling to interfere. As far as the internal component of CONCERTO was concerned, the pot was nicely on the boil in Poland, Hungary and Czechoslovakia, and within a few days there'd be no need for provocations to set off violent conflict between the authorities and the people; the violence would be self- sustaining. It wouldn't be long before military action to control the unrest would be appropriate. The longer Mikhail was out of the way, the more likely Stepanov would be to see which side his bread was buttered on, and he couldn't put off the necessity of Soviet intervention in Poland much longer, anyway. And Mikhail Gorbachev would be rescued, brought home and made to face the consequences of his misjudgement of both the Russian people and of Oleg Chernysh.

Chernysh leaned back against the padded leather upholstery of his chair. He disliked taking even the minor risk of leaving Brennan on the loose. Vlasov, quite rightly, had subjected that female clerk in Warsaw to rigorous questioning on no more than the ghost of a suspicion. But Brennan was different. He was obviously highly trained, and now very much on his guard. It wouldn't be easy to neutralize him. Besedin's report stated that the American hadn't left Paris by air, at least not by commercial air. He could be anywhere in the French capital; on the other hand, he might have left France by any number of clandestine routes. Washington? New York? Who knew? He was almost certainly back in the United States by now.

Those idiots at the Paris station, Chernysh thought. If they'd kept surveillance on that CIA man Macarthur after he dropped Brennan off, they might have been able to pick Brennan up again before he left France. Should we look for him back in the US?

No, Chernysh decided. Hunting him down in the United States, although doing so was quite within the KGB's capabilities, wouldn't accomplish anything useful. Brennan would have been debriefed by now, anyway. And Chernysh wanted his resources concentrated on CONCERTO, not on a search for Sean Brennan.

He shrugged and closed Brennan's dossier.

Washington, DC
Saturday, October 5

THE HOTEL CORRIDOR was dim and empty and silent. The silence of four o'clock in the morning, Brennan thought, as he trudged wearily along the red carpet, dragging his suitcase behind him. The door numbers were indistinct in the low yellow light from the wall sconces; he had to peer carefully at each one as he passed.

He spotted the right number around a turn: 1215. The year King John signed the Magna Carta in England, a voice recalled in a far corner of his mind. The beginning of western democracy.

He told the voice to shut up, and tapped gently on the door. His mind was numb from the two-hour debriefing Knight and Barlow had put him through as soon as he arrived at Langley; he'd slept for four hours on the chartered jet crossing the Atlantic, but whatever refreshment the sleep had provided had slipped away.

Reid had come into Barlow's office as they were finishing up. Because of what had happened to Brennan in Paris, he'd agreed to sit on Kaminsky's information as long as he could, but the time was up; he had to inform the president that Gorbachev's location was now known. The DCI had looked down at Brennan as he slumped, exhausted, in the chair across from Barlow's desk, and demanded:

"You're sure they were KGB?"

"I'm sure," Brennan said. "They knew I was in Paris. Somehow."

"Do you think it was a leak from somewhere over here?"

"I did at the time. I'm still worried about it. That's why I warned Frank."

Reid turned to Barlow. "Might it have been Kaminsky? Or someone watching him?"

"I don't think so," Barlow said. "Frank?"

"I don't, either," said Knight. "If they wanted Sean, he'd never have gotten out of Warsaw. They picked him up at de Gaulle the second time he was there, which means their Paris residency was watching for him. They didn't try to grab him on the way to Bittner's place, maybe because he wasn't alone. Although it's possible they were keeping an eye on Bittner, and Sean fell into a net."

"I can't believe that," Brennan said. "Trying a snatch in broad daylight like that, that tells me they were worried as hell. They wanted to find out where I'd been before Paris. Which also means they weren't able to pick me up when I arrived there the first time, either because they weren't looking for me, or because they didn't know how to identify me. But they made me *somehow*, dammit, between the time I arrived in Paris first, and the time I went back there from Frankfurt." He felt his temper fraying, and lowered his voice. "And what made them move so fast and hard after I saw Bittner is that they knew I was working on CONCERTO. They were worried I'd got too close to them while I was out of their sight. Why would they think that, unless they were warned about me?"

"But Sean," Barlow said, "you've got to look at the other possibilities as well. Maybe they made you in Frankfurt after you came back from Warsaw, and let you run as far as Paris. It could be a leak over there in Germany. They *couldn't* have been warned about your first arrival in Paris, or they'd have followed you to the meeting with Kaminsky and picked you both up. You'd never have got out of Poland. As Frank said. That tells me they didn't spot you until you were already on the way back."

"Unless the leak here knew I was going to France, but told the KGB too late for them to nail me at de Gaulle. Who knew I was going?"

"We three did," said Reid. "I also informed the president, to cool him off about you. He probably told the FBI director, as well as his national security adviser, Simon Parr, and they could have mentioned it to others. If there was a leak, it could have been any of a couple of dozen people."

"Do me a favor," Brennan said. "If I have to go out again, don't tell the president."

It was almost insubordination. Reid's eyelids flickered, but he said only, "We'll look into it, both here and in Europe. Sean, you've done an excellent job. Now you better get some sleep. Do you have somewhere to stay?"

"Yes." He didn't tell them he'd called Molly from Paris, and that she'd said she'd fly down to Washington from Boston and check into the Watergate Hotel. After the KGB's near-miss in Paris, he'd wondered about the risks of doing this, but had concluded that they'd drop the pursuit once they realized he'd been debriefed. "I'll be fine," he said. "I'll be at the Watergate, if you need to get in touch with me."

"Okay. Can you report back here at noon tomorrow, I mean today? There may be more for you to do, depending on how the briefings with the NSC and the president go."

"Okay. Noon."

That had been an hour ago. Frank had gotten him a car from the pool and he'd driven into Washington. He hadn't had a chance to call the hotel to make sure Molly had checked in, and he was relieved to find out at the front desk that she had.

He tapped at the door of the hotel room. The sound reverberated down the corridor. After a moment a voice on the other side of the door said, "Yes? Sean?"

"Molly, it's me."

He heard the rattle of the security chain being withdrawn, and the door opened wide. "I made it," he said.

She was fully dressed, but was blinking sleep from her eyes. "My God, Sean!" she exclaimed. "You look exhausted. Where on earth have you been?"

"Paris." He closed the door and dropped his suitcase just as she threw her arms around him. They stood like that for a full half-minute, not speaking. Then she said, her voice muffled by his shoulder, "I was really getting worried. I hadn't heard from you for three days. Why couldn't you tell me where you were calling from yesterday? Was it Paris?"

They released each other. "Sorry," he said. "Yes, it was. But I couldn't."

"Dangerous?"

He wasn't sure how much to say. "No."

"Come and sit down. I can have something sent up to eat."

"I'm not really hungry," he replied, following her into the suite and sagging into one of the armchairs near the bed.

"How about a stiff drink? You look as though you could use one. I brought some Glenlivet for you."

"That's the best idea I've heard for days."

She poured two fingers of the Scotch into a glass and gave it to him. He never diluted the liquor with ice or soda, preferring the glossy dark taste by itself. She curled up on the bed at his elbow while he sipped at the drink. The spirit flowed into him, warming his stomach. He felt himself begin to relax, and realized that he hadn't been able to relax for nearly a week.

"Was it only Paris you were in?" she asked.

"No. I was somewhere else, too, but I'm afraid. . ."

"That you can't tell me."

"I'm sorry. Later, maybe, but not now."

She sighed. "I was hoping this sort of thing was over. I know you have to do it, and I'm on your side when you're doing it, but I think you understand how I feel."

"I know. I'm not doing it by choice. I'd rather be home, believe me. Once this is over, I'm out for good."

"When *will* it be over?"

"It's close. I think."

"Are you going to be involved anymore?"

"It's unlikely. It'll be domestic from here on in. FBI, not us. I didn't tell you I had the president himself pissed off at me. That's why I went overseas. It was kind of get-out-of-town-till-they've-forgotten-you."

"What happened?"

"I crossed bureacratic lines. The FBI honcho in New York didn't like me on his territory. The bastard suspended the guy I was working with. Lee Ennis."

"Ennis is the honcho or your opposite number?"

"Opposite number. That reminds me. I was going to call him. In the morning. It was me that got him suspended, the poor devil."

"What happened?"

He told her as much as he could. When he'd finished, she said, "The half-wits. Here's Mikhail Gorbachev in the hands of a bunch of Polish terrorists, and everybody's worrying about jurisdiction."

"They're not Poles," Brennan said.

"What?"

"It's the KGB."

Her eyes widened. "Oh, my God. I wondered. But really?"

"Really."

"Do you know this for certain?"

"Yes." He finished the Scotch and put the glass down.

"What will you do if they ask you to do some more?"

"I don't know." He was suddenly, desperately, tired. "I can't think about it right now. It would depend on what it was. I just don't know. I've got to be back out at Langley at noon today. I'll find out then."

"Okay," she said. "You'd better get to bed. I'll wake you at ten."

President Halliday had lost control of the meeting, if indeed he had ever controlled it. He was utterly bewildered by the tangle of possibilities, probabilities and almost-certainties his advisers were arguing over and describing to him, and he had given up trying to understand them two hours after the meeting started at five A.M. He'd hardly opened his mouth for the last hour. Parr was wondering whether the president might be asleep with his eyes open; he'd barely stirred for the last fifteen minutes. A shaft of sunlight fell through a gap in the window curtains and gleamed on the coffee cups, teaspoons, sugar bowls, cream pitchers and silver water decanters that littered the table. Halliday had called the meeting in the same White House dining room that President Johnson had used for his cabinet's breakfast meetings during the Viet Nam war; Parr wondered whether the blunt old Texan's ghost was grimacing over the indecisive confusion of his successor.

"Mr. *President,*" Reid was saying, startling Halliday into a semblance of alertness, "the fact remains that we now know where Mr. Gorbachev is most likely to be, and as the FBI director has said, the place is already under surveillance to verify his presence there. We also know that the KGB is keeping him there, and we know what they intend to do with Mr. Gorbachev after he's rescued, if I may use the term. We've considered every possible way of dealing with the situation, and I respectfully suggest that we have to make some decisions very soon. Do we permit the Russians to carry on as they please, do we have the FBI intervene on Mr. Gorbachev's behalf without allowing the Russian tactical team in New York to participate, or do we let the tactical team retrieve Mr. Gorbachev and then make sure that he has an opportunity to act freely before he returns to the Soviet Union?"

Halliday said, "Well . . . " and looked desperately around the table, first at the director of the FBI, and then at Parr, at the secretary of state, and then at the rest of the National Security Council members. They all looked back at him.

Strike while the iron's hot, Parr thought. "Mr. President," he said, his voice soothing, "the director of Central Intelligence has presented our options very succinctly. But the larger question is this: do we want to interfere in what is, after all, a domestic power struggle *inside* the Soviet Union? In effect, we would be saying to the men in the Kremlin that our choice of Russian leaders is better than their choice. You and I and all the other gentlemen here know how we would react if the USSR made the same kind of suggestion to us.

"Director Reid's information states that the KGB is attempting to remove Mr. Gorbachev by force. Director Reid is unwilling to tell us where that information came from, and who provided it. I understand that; sources have to be protected. *I* don't want to know who the source is. But obviously, if he's able to get this sort of information, he's very high up indeed.

"If," he went on, "we let the Russians know that we know Gorbachev's hiding place, they'll immediately realize they have a traitor. They'll catch him sooner than later, and we lose a very valuable asset for the future. Also, they'll realize that we're aware of their operation. What's it called, by the way, Stephen?"

"Sorry," Reid said.

"Well, then, the operation. I —"

"Wait a minute," interrupted the FBI director. "There's no need for them to know we found out from a leak in Poland. We can fabricate enough evidence, if we need to, to show that we found the location ourselves. They won't need to know we've found out their dirty little secret."

Damn his eyes, Parr thought. He should never have been let in here. "They'll suspect," he said. "It'll be enough to make them start hunting for a traitor. Since there is one, they'll find him. There goes our source. I'm looking at worst-case scenarios here."

"Just another minute," Reid responded. "They don't give a

good goddamn whether we know they did it or not. They're *assuming* we'll keep our mouths shut, they'll assume we won't dare interfere. Doesn't it annoy you a *little*, being manipulated like that?"

"We have to put that sort of thing aside," Parr said. "This is far too big for personal grievances to get in the way."

"A federal crime's been committed," the FBI director said. "Kidnapping. Whoever did it has to be brought to book."

Dunce, Parr thought. Reid was pink with fury. "That's not the point at issue," Parr said blandly. "Look. I think we should keep our hands off. Absolutely off. We know, from Director Reid's own information, that Gorbachev's life isn't in danger. They're going to return him to the USSR as soon as they're ready, and that'll certainly be in just a few days' time. If we decided to preempt the KGB, and go plunging in there to rescue him by ourselves, the kidnappers may overreact. They might, possibly, kill him. *Then* we'll have a mess on our hands. We *have* to let them work out their political problems in their own way."

"Jesus Christ," Reid huffed. "I thought I was cynical, but you take the cake, Simon." He turned to the president, who was frowning in perplexity. "Mr. President, I want to suggest a compromise. The FBI director has said we can make it appear that we found out Mr. Gorbachev's location by ourselves. Let's do that. It'll force their hand. They'll have to look eager to rescue him, and we'll let Timoshkin and his men do the assault. But we'll have enough FBI and police backup to make sure the Russians don't bundle him off to a plane unless he wants to go. He'll have to be checked medically, just to start with, and we can make sure it's done in an American hospital. We can't be faulted for any of that. And we must tell the Russians we know where he is as late as possible, not before six P.M. today. That will give them time to 'prepare' for the rescue, but not enough to take serious preemptive action. Especially as they'll be told the house is already under surveillance."

"Mr. President," Parr began, and then stopped abruptly as the familiar stubborn expression slid onto Halliday's face. That bastard Reid, Parr thought, realizing from the set of Halliday's mouth that he'd had enough and would accept any suggestion, even the worst possible one, to get the meeting over with. Reid had sensed the perfect moment, and had used it before Parr could get in. He dared not push against Reid anymore. But there would be other opportunities.

"That's what we'll do," Halliday was saying. "Thank you, Director Reid. Thank you, gentlemen. You'd better get started. There's no time to lose."

Parr stood up with the rest of them as Halliday hurried out. Probably has to go to the bathroom, he thought. So do I; too much coffee.

He caught a glimpse of his face in the mirror over the sideboard. It was disturbing how much the strain of the last week — no, the last few years in Washington, topped off by this last week — had bitten into his face. He looked ten years older than he was. Lately, along with the insomnia, had come the nervous tic of his left index finger; so severe, occasionally, that he was careful to keep his hand below the table during meetings. He felt stretched and dry, as though his skin would crack like parched leather if he moved too quickly.

Perhaps I should have stayed a political history professor at Harvard, he thought. But it wasn't possible. I wanted to do so much more than that.

Reid was waiting by the door. As Parr started to push by him, the CIA director said, "Nice try, Simon."

Parr felt his index finger begin to jerk. Grasping the handle of his briefcase tightly to still the movement, he said, "What exactly do you mean by that?"

"Leave Gorbachev to the wolves," answered Reid.

"You know goddamned well it makes sense," Parr said. "As I would have said if the president hadn't needed to. . ." He realized he was about to say *go piss*, and stopped himself. "Adjourn the meeting. If Gorbachev's deposed, there's a good chance the Soviet Union will turn itself inside out for the next few years. Maybe civil war. They'd be too busy shooting each other to shoot at anybody else. We'd have a free hand in the world, for the first time since the Russians found out how to make a nuclear bomb."

"You know it's not that simple . . . Simon."

Parr felt himself flush at the insult. "It's simpler than letting Gorbachev turn the USSR into a powerhouse, which your own analysts say he may do."

"You really *are* cynical. Why not let the Russians have a few of the luxuries we all enjoy?"

"Because there's room for only one dominant power on the planet, and I don't want it to be Marxist. The president would agree with me. So do you, deep down."

"Yeah," Reid replied. "But I don't think helping the USSR tear itself apart is the way to do it. Do you want to risk a real nut at the top? Maybe another Ivan the Terrible? You think that makes the United States more secure?"

Parr ignored him. "Anyway, you're a hell of a one to talk about throwing people to the wolves. What about that poor bastard who told you where Gorbachev is? You know damn well they'll look for a leak, even if they'd like to believe that song and dance the FBI's going to put together. That Pole, if it is a Pole, is as good as dead."

"I know. I'm trading the Pole for Gorbachev."

"The problem won't go away even if you get Gorbachev loose from the KGB over here. He'll have to go back to Moscow sooner or later, and they'll be waiting for him."

"We'll deal with that when the time comes," Reid responded, and turned away.

Brennan woke at half-past nine by Molly's travel alarm, which was staring at him from the night table. For a moment he was disoriented, believing that he had somehow returned to the Saski Hotel in Warsaw, and that Kaminsky was waiting deep in the storm sewers to meet him again. Then he realized that he was in the Watergate, with the curtains drawn against the morning sun.

There was a glass of water on the night table. He drank some, swirling it around in his mouth to remove the aftertaste of the Scotch, and put his head back on the pillow. On the other side of the bed, Molly stirred and muttered in her sleep. Brennan wondered whether he should try to go back to sleep for half an hour or get up, shower and call room service to have breakfast sent up. The decision was too difficult. He closed his eyes, listening to Molly's deep breathing. She seemed to be in a dream of some kind. He turned over to look at her; she was lying on her side facing him, her auburn hair spread over the pillow, the fabric of her deep-blue nightgown dark against the paleness of her skin. Brennan reached out a fingertip and touched the corner of her mouth. She looked terribly vulnerable in her sleep. He felt again the inarticulate rush of his devotion to her, a feeling that still unsettled him with its strength, for he did not think of himself as an emotional man. It frightened him a little, as it always did. He had always disciplined himself not to imagine the myriad random ways he could lose her; if he allowed himself to dwell on such possibilities, the dread they aroused in him could make him feel physically sick.

He remembered the first time they had made love, clumsily and with a curious shyness, since for both of them it had been a long drought. In that way, as in many others, they had found themselves well-matched.

Her dream seemed to have deepened; her breaths were shorter, with a ragged edge. Her hips under the bedclothes moved rhythmically for a moment. Brennan put a hand on her waist.

She stirred and opened her eyes. After a few seconds he saw them focus on his face. "Hello," she said. "Is it morning?"

"About nine-thirty. Sorry I woke you up. Were you dreaming?"

"Yes." She turned her face partly into the pillow, a faint blush spreading over her cheekbones.

"What about?"

"It's embarrassing."

"Us?" He turned her face back up to his.

"Yes."

"Did I interrupt things by waking you up?"

"Yes."

"Should we continue?"

"You'd better, or I won't be responsible for my actions."

He put his arm around her waist and drew her toward him. After a moment she reached past him to switch off the alarm clock, murmuring, "This isn't the time for prosaic interruptions."

They had showered and were drying each other off when the telephone rang. "Dammit," Brennan said. He draped one of the towels around his waist and went to answer it. He heard his stomach growl as he sat down on the bed; his appetite was back, and he was ravenous. He picked up the receiver. Maybe Knight was calling to tell him to go home, that the resignation was accepted, that his part was finished.

"Hello?" he said, feeling the tension rise within himself.

"Sean Brennan?"

"Yeah, Frank, it's me."

"Good. Listen, don't come out here this morning. Take the next shuttle to New York and go to the station. There are things to take care of. I'll brief you there."

I thought it might be over, Brennan thought. I hoped it might be over. "What for, Frank? Why should we still be mixed up in it?"

"We're not, not operationally. But because of the, ah, overseas connections, we're to stand by for use as needed."

"What's 'use as needed,' Frank?"

"Just get back to New York. I'll explain there. See you in a few hours."

He hung up before Brennan could say anything else. Brennan sat on the bed, looking at the black telephone receiver in his hand. He heard Molly padding barefoot out of the bathroom and put the phone back in its cradle. "Shit," he said.

She sat down on the bed beside him, smelling of soap and bath powder. "They want you back," she said, without expression.

"Yeah."

"Why?"

"I don't know yet. I'm supposed to go to New York. I'll find out there."

"You know," she said, "you don't *have* to go."

"I know I don't."

"But you're going to."

"It's not finished," he replied.

She looked down at the carpet. "You know," she reflected, "one of the things I've always found so good about you is that you're always determined to finish what you start. I know I can depend on you, for anything you decide to do. I suppose I shouldn't bitch if other people feel the same way."

She was crying, silently. Brennan stared helplessly at the closed drapes.

"If it were just me," he said. "But there's so much depending on it. So many other people."

"I know. I guess. But it's hard, Sean. It's — really — *hard*. It wouldn't be so hard if you hadn't been almost out. But you've been snatched away from me. At the last moment.'' She straightened. ''Quit snivelling, Molly,'' she chastised herself. ''I hate women who snivel. Look. I'll fly back up with you to New York and go on home from there. Will that be okay?''

''Yes,'' he said. ''I'll be back as soon as I can.''

''I'll be there,'' she said.

Moscow – New York
Saturday, October 5

OLEG CHERNYSH and Vadim Besedin leaned over the platen of the teleprinter, watching as the number groups chattered onto the paper. When the output stopped, Besedin flicked the switch that isolated the machine from the Warsaw landline and keyed in the day's decoding sequence, which was based on the 1866 text of Dostoevski's *Crime and Punishment*; the system was an electronic version of the one-time pad. After a pause, the machine began to clatter out the decoded text.

PRIORITY CRASHPAD ALPHA URGENT URGENT URGENT
PROMENADE REPORT FILED: WASHINGTON TIME 1245:
WASHINGTON DATE 10/05
AMERICANS HAVE LOCATED MUSKET SAFE HOUSE. NOT REPEAT NOT BY POLICE WORK. LOCATION IS REPEAT IS FROM UNKNOWN LEAK IN WARSAW. PROMENADE DOES NOT KNOW IDENTITY OF LEAK. LEAK HAS GIVEN OPPOSITION FULL EXTENT OF CONCERTO. AMERICANS INTEND TO ALLOW OUR RETRIEVAL OPERATION TO PROCEED AS AGREED USING OUR TACTICAL TEAM BUT THEY WILL THEN REMOVE MUSKET FROM OUR CUSTODY TO THEIRS. AMERICANS WILL REQUIRE US TO MOUNT RETRIEVAL OPERATION AT: NEW YORK TIME 0200: NEW YORK DATE 10/06. ADVISE IMMEDIATELY. REMAINING ON-LINE.

VLASOV

Chernysh tore the teleprinter sheet loose and looked at Besedin. The head of the First Chief Directorate couldn't take his eyes off the message printout. His face, which was normally as expressionless as a slab of concrete, had turned gray. "A pig in Warsaw," Besedin said. "Do we abort?"

Could we? wondered Chernysh. Rescue Gorbachev, bring him back, destroy all the evidence, pretend it never happened? Impossible. He's much too astute not to suspect, he'd go looking. . . . Someone would take advantage, to curry favor with him if for no other reason. And the leak in Warsaw. Even if we abort, the Americans will tell Gorbachev what the leak told them. *Who is the pig? How did he get the information out?*

Sean Brennan. The CIA officer with the Irish name. That's where he was before he turned up in Paris and those idiots at the residency missed him, he was in Warsaw talking to . . . whom?

"We have to go on," he said to Besedin. He forced calm and decisiveness into his tone. It was desperately important that he not betray any failure of nerve to his subordinate. A loss of confidence at this stage would be disastrous.

He bent over the keyboard and typed back to Vlasov:

QUERY: WHEN DID PROMENADE DETERMINE EXISTENCE OF LEAK?

A pause, while the computer coded from the pad. Then:

0700 WASHINGTON TIME APPROXIMATE.

Chernysh consulted the first message. Promenade hadn't reported until 1245. Infuriated, Chernysh asked Vlasov why.

MEETINGS. COULD NOT REACH SECURE LINK.

Fucking bureaucracies, Chernysh thought. Fine, we'll have to play it a little differently. But carefully, so the Americans don't suspect *they've* got a leak. We'll preempt them, just a bit.

His back hurt from leaning over. He straightened up and shoved a chair into position in front of the teleprinter. Besedin typed a lot better than Chernysh did, let him do it.

"Sit down at that keyboard and tell Vlasov what I want Timoshkin and his men to do,'' Chernysh ordered. ''When that's under way, Vlasov is to start hunting for the pig. It's got to be one of the section chiefs in Warsaw, to have known as much as Promenade says.''

''But Chairman,'' Besedin objected, ''how can we proceed if whatever we do is going to be broadcast to the Americans? You know how long it can take to do the cross-checking necessary to identify a pig. Days. We can't put all the Warsaw section heads under arrest for that long, not now, there's too much to do. We have to get the pig out of there *now,* whoever he is.''

''Yes,'' Chernysh said. ''Exactly. Now sit down at that keyboard, damn you, and don't tell me my business.''

Brennan stabbed at the elevator DOWN button in a fury. Goddamn Knight. Goddamn Reid and Barlow. Goddamn the president. Goddamn *everybody*. Except Molly.

The elevator door opened and Brennan stalked inside. A pair of young women from one of the upper floors saw his face and instantly stopped chattering. Brennan stood at the back and watched the indicator lights as the elevator glided toward the ground floor. The two secretaries got out at the floor above, with unmistakable relief. Probably thought I was going to strangle them both and drop them down the shaft, Brennan thought as he went through the lobby and out onto Park Avenue. Back up in the office, Knight was undoubtedly fuming at him for taking the news so badly. Although Knight should — *did* — know better than to agree with the arrangement Reid had brought back from the White House. As if the Russian rescue unit would obligingly hand Gorbachev over to the Americans, for hospital treatment or for anything else. They were living in a dreamworld down there in Washington, even Reid. Maybe when you got that high in the power structure — the White House, the National Security Council and all of that — you forgot about the realities of fieldwork and started to believe that because you wanted a thing to be so, it would be.

To hell with them, Brennan thought. But at least I haven't been cut out of the game yet.

There was a phone booth, not too badly vandalized, across from the Bedford Hotel on East 40th Street. Brennan still had Ennis's home number in his wallet. He dialled it, half-consciously trying to make some sense out of the spiderweb of graffiti scratched into the plastic of the telephone box. A woman answered.

"This is Sean Brennan. Could I please speak to Lee?"

"He's at the office."

Oh? Ranelagh must have relented. "Thanks. I'll call him there."

Brennan was still carrying the number of the direct line to Ennis's desk. He dialled it and waited, instinctively watching the foot and vehicle traffic passing by outside the phone booth. Nobody was taking any interest in him.

A click. "Ennis here."

"This is Figleaf."

A pause. "Right. How are you?"

"Fine. They took you off the clothesline?"

"Yeah. Except that I'm not to have anything to do with our old project. The man has handed me everybody's job except that one. I'd still be hung out to dry if we weren't so short of people. That's why I'm here on a Saturday. Never mind all that crap. Listen, there's stuff going on *right now* you should know about. If you don't already."

"Got a few minutes to talk? Can you get away?"

"You bet," Ennis said. "Everybody's lost interest in me, thank Christ. How about the Gramercy Park Hotel? The piano bar. If that's close enough to you."

"It's okay. Fifteen, twenty minutes?"

"Okay. See you then," Ennis said.

Brennan hung up, and went looking for a taxi.

The bar had once been opulent, and had recently been redecorated in an attempt to recapture that opulence. Nevertheless, it still looked faintly seedy, as though its slow decay had been only temporarily masked by a thin coat of gilt and paint. The singer at the badly-tuned piano didn't seem to have been replaced, either; at the moment, she was torturing "The White Cliffs of Dover."

Ennis grimaced as the piano hit a particularly out-of-tune chord. "Christ," he complained. "Why don't they fix that thing?"

"And spoil the ambience?" Brennan asked. "It's been this way for years. An island of tradition in a sea of change."

"You're pissed off about something," Ennis said. "You don't look cheerful. Like you usually do, even when the world's falling down around your ears." He set his glass down; they were both drinking beer at the bar. The pre-theater crowd was making almost enough noise to drown out the piano, except in the *fortissimo* passages. The noise also drowned out their conversation, even three feet away. Brennan had to lean forward to catch everything Ennis was saying.

Brennan eyed the FBI man's glass doubtfully. "Won't you get fired and depensioned if somebody sees you with me? I thought Ranelagh was adamant about keeping us apart."

"Nobody'll see us," Ennis answered cheerfully. "Besides, it's Saturday and anyway I don't give a hoot at this point. In the two days I was off, I had two offers from private security firms." The cheerfulness faded. "Although I admit I'd miss working for the Bureau, if it came to that. For all we bitch about it, it gets into your blood. Is it the same in the . . . in your business?"

"It has its ups and downs," Brennan said. "I think we've got more morale problems than you do."

"Like now, for instance?" Ennis asked, raising his glass again and examining Brennan's face over the rim.

"Like now."

"What's happened?"

He's not cleared for this, Brennan thought, and if I tell him and it's ever found out, I'll be dragged over the coals. They wouldn't likely jail me, but I wouldn't ever get my pension. Oh, hell, I may not live long enough to collect it, anyway. And I could use Lee's help. I'll tell him. He nearly got himself fired for me, after all.

"I'll tell you," Brennan said, "but first off, what's going on at the Bureau? Are the people on the — project — busy all of a sudden?"

Ennis started to answer and stopped suddenly as a redheaded woman in silk and pearls pushed in beside Brennan to order a drink from the bartender. Brennan found himself looking into a pair of green eyes, which evaluated him frankly and clearly liked what they saw. She gave him a brief smile and opened her purse to extract money. Ennis waited stolidly while she received her drink, got her change and returned to her table. Her hip brushed against Brennan's side as she left.

"Working girl?" Brennan asked when she was out of earshot.

"Could be," Ennis shrugged. "Let's find another spot."

They relocated at a corner table, and sat facing into the corner itself. "Anyway," Ennis continued, "this morning the place started to turn itself inside-out like I don't know what. It was a madhouse before, what with the hunt going on, but even I never saw it like this. Ranelagh had all the SAC and assistants in his office for a good half-hour — except me, of course — and when they came out they started pulling files out of Registry like there was a Congressional committee on the way. Then the FBI commissioner himself turned up from Washington, and a couple of characters I think were from the Justice Department. They all came up the internal elevator from the secure entrance. You wouldn't happen to know what they're all doing here, would you?''

''Yes,'' Brennan said. ''They're putting together a false dossier to make it look as though they've found out where the target is.''

''What?''

''They already *know* where he is,'' Brennan said. ''But it has to look as though they found out for themselves. Then the Russian, Timoshkin, turned up, right?''

''How the hell did you know that? Yeah, he came in with one of his heavies at five past six. I gather he and his tactical rescue team are holed up in the Russian consulate, armed to the teeth. There was another Russian, too, I think from the Washington embassy. What the hell's going on? Who found out where the, ah, abducted person is?''

''I did,'' said Brennan. ''Only we don't want the Russians to know how it was done. Langley's known since yesterday, but we only told the president and the FBI early this morning. CIA people were watching the kidnappers' place until then, but nobody's supposed to know that. As far as the president and the Bureau know, we didn't find out where Gorbachev is until an hour before Reid contacted the White House and the FBI director.''

''Ye gods,'' Ennis said. ''Why the delay?''

''I can't go into the details, but there may be a leak to the Russians somewhere up above us.''

Ennis digested this for a moment, and then hid his mouth with the palm of a hand and said, ''And you've got somebody inside the opposition, over in Europe, somebody you'd like to protect.''

''That's right.''

''Just a minute,'' said Ennis. ''Are you telling me the Russians have known where Gorbachev is *all along*? And are going to fake a rescue in their own sweet time?''

Brennan nodded. "Jesus Christ," Ennis said. "So it *was* the KGB. Do they know we know?"

"They may, depending on who and where the leak is, if there is one. But according to Frank Knight, nobody cares if they *do* know we know. Welcome to the world of realpolitik, Lee. The White House just wants the whole business out of the way as soon as possible. It's getting embarrassing as hell, just look at the newspapers."

"But look," Ennis said, "if the White House really doesn't give a damn what happens to poor old Gorbie, why don't they just let the Russians play out the charade, and the less said the better?"

"I'm told it was suggested. I don't know by who. But apparently it was too much to swallow, going along with them like that, so we're trying to play both ends against the middle. Get him rescued as soon as possible, *before* the KGB wanted it to happen, and see if Gorbachev can pull his own chestnuts out of the fire. If he doesn't, too bad, but at least we're no longer involved."

"Even if it means your person in Europe gets hacked because the KGB figures out that he told us where Gorbachev is?"

"He may survive if the leak doesn't find out about him, and if the KGB believes we located the safe house without help. If the leak does find out, well . . . if it's a choice between rescuing Gorbachev and preserving the source, the source is expendable."

"That's hard cheese for the source. You want another beer?"

"Okay."

Ennis bought this time. "So what's going to happen?"

"Gorbachev's in a house not far from Brighton Beach. In Sheepshead Bay, to be exact. The plan is to let the Russian tactical team go in at two A.M. tomorrow, extract him, and then we'll get hold of him and pack him off to a hospital where he can decide for himself what he wants to do next. That's if Timoshkin and his crew allow it. My bet is that they won't. There'll be an Aeroflot jet at Kennedy by that time and he'll be on it half an hour after they've got him. They'll take the kidnappers, too, you watch. They won't leave a damn thing behind."

"How will they get away with that? The crime was committed on American soil. If we got one of the JPC members, and persuaded him to talk —"

"That's what they'll be afraid of. So they'll haul the JPC people off to Moscow right away, along with Gorbachev, and then argue that Moscow has criminal jurisdiction because the crime was committed in an ambassadorial compound, which is Soviet soil. The criminals will be duly tried, convicted, sentenced and shot, while our Justice Department is still preparing briefs. Except that the coffins will be empty when they're buried and the men who were supposed to be in them will be happily settled under new identities somewhere comfortable on the Black Sea coast. Or maybe the KGB *will* shoot them, I don't know. But they won't be left here for us to question, you can bet your last dime on it."

"This sounds like a goddamn political minefield to me," Ennis remarked gloomily. "I'm just a gumshoe. How're the bright lights in Washington going to handle it?"

"Carefully. Lots of protocol and precedence. The Russian tac team actually makes the assault. Since we can't have armed Soviet troops operating independently on American soil, there will be twelve FBI men supporting them in the immediate area, but they won't be allowed to enter the JPC safe house. Two blocks away will be the perimeter seal, a couple hundred more FBI men, NYPD guys and a few token people from the New York CIA field office, like me."

"To make it look good to the press and so on. Nobody but the Russians has any real function in the rescue itself."

"Right. As soon as the Russians bring Gorbachev out, the twelve FBI men are supposed to get him into an ambulance and scoot him off to the hospital at the Floyd Bennett Field Naval Air Station just up the way. The Russians can ride escort, but none in the ambulance. That's the theory they've dreamed up in Washington."

"But you don't think it'll happen that way."

"No. Those Russians likely have the same training as the Red Army's SPETSNAZ troops. Six of them could outnumber twelve FBI men with no problems. I don't care how well the Bureau trains its agents, they're no match for those guys."

"It's a real pissoff to have to learn this from the CIA," Ennis said. "If you'll pardon me saying so. I should have been helping set it up. What're you going to do?"

"Ever do any boating, Lee?" Brennan asked.

Warsaw
Saturday, October 5

KAMINSKY SAT in his tiny kitchen, contemplating the glass of Wyborowa vodka on the table before him. The overbright ceiling light glared down mercilessly on the frost-edged glass and the dirty plates with the remains of his supper on them: a breadcrust, a heel of sausage, slender bones from a slice of marinated carp, cucumber seeds.

He'd eaten better when Jola was living with him. She'd liked making hunter's stew and was perfect at soups and pastries. He'd lost fifteen pounds after she left their marriage for that nitwit at the Ministry of Agriculture and Food Economy. If he was a sample of the bureaucrats over there, it was no wonder there were constant lineups for food. But this bureaucrat was very good at using his Party perquisites to obtain western goods; he had a Volvo and Swedish appliances and a two-bedroom apartment. Kaminsky had always made do with an East German Skoda, which was constantly breaking down, the kitchen fixtures were domestic, and the apartment had one bedroom. Jola had wanted him to use his position to obtain all sorts of luxury goods and western hard currency, which, like most of his colleagues, he could easily have done. But he'd always refused; it wasn't good communist behavior and he wasn't much interested in material goods, anyway. She'd finally got fed up and left. It had probably been a mistake to marry a woman twelve years his junior. At least there hadn't been any children to complicate matters.

He sighed, got up, put the dirty dishes to soak in the sink and brushed the breadcrumbs from the blue tablecloth into the dish-rag, which he emptied into the waste can. The kitchen, like the rest of the apartment, was without a woman's touches and clearly that of a bachelor. But it wasn't inhabited by one of the breed of sloppy bachelors; although slightly shabby, everything was tidy and clean, to the point of austerity.

Kaminsky took the glass of Wyborowa into the living room, where the curtains were pulled open to reveal the lights of Warsaw through the rain-streaked window; it had been pouring off and on all day. The apartment was on the seventh floor of a high-rise block at the intersection of Grzybowska and Ciepla Streets, and looked roughly north, away from the Palace of Science and Culture. This was a blessing to Kaminsky; he loathed the huge Stalinist wedding-cake Palace. If he'd seen it every time he looked out the window, he'd have tried to get a new apartment. Northward there wasn't much except more apartment blocks and official buildings; the long neon-lit run of Marchievskiego Avenue, which ran parallel to Ciepla on the east and was separated from it by a broad strip of treed boulevard; and, off in the distance, the spire of the Evangelical Church.

It was down there in the sewers, almost under the church itself, that he'd spoken with the nameless American. Kaminsky wondered where the man was now, and what he was doing. It was almost nine o'clock, and the CONCERTO conspirators would be finding out very soon that Gorbachev's safe house was no longer safe.

He closed the curtains and sat down on the sofa. The vodka was still cold and he drank half of it, feeling it warm his belly. He'd better get some sleep soon; he was exhausted from tension.

He'd come home to the apartment just before eight, after being on duty for eighteen straight hours. He had been working not on CONCERTO, but on his regular duties as head of Section 7. CONCERTO was in a holding pattern at the moment, as far as the strike and riot provocation operations were concerned; he had a big one planned for Lublin on Sunday, but Saturday had been specified as quiet. The student strike at Lublin University would be all the more conspicuous as a result. Several Warsaw ZOMO units had already been secretly moved out to the university town, in preparation. Kaminsky didn't think it would be long before the senior Party membership panicked, and declared martial law.

He hadn't been able to identify which ones among them, if any, were involved with CONCERTO, but last night he'd verified his suspicions about General Albin Ornat, the man who had taken over the Party leadership and the prime minister's post after General Jaruzelski's stroke. Ornat had been head of the ministry of internal affairs, as well as chief of army security, until the stroke put Jaruzelski out of power. Ornat had then moved smoothly into the position of president and Politburo chief. He was known to be highly resistant to reform, and, given his background and political leanings, he'd be well qualified to cooperate with the KGB in an attack on Gorbachev.

With the evidence pointing to Ornat, the dossier was sufficient, and more than sufficient. Obtaining the evidence, though, had been almost an act of desperation. Last night Kaminsky had taken a risk he'd never dared before; he wouldn't have risked it at all, if time wasn't growing so short.

He had bypassed the security system in Jurys's office to get at the SB chief's private files. He'd only dared spend half an hour with the dossiers, hurriedly selecting and photographing the most important ones. Jurys seemed to have been protecting his own flanks; he had maintained a file on Ornat which made it clear that the Party leader had been aware of the progress of CONCERTO from the very beginning. There was also a memorandum to Jurys, signed by Vlasov, regarding the need for exceptionally rigorous security in "the removal operation." That was Vlasov covering *his* flanks. Jurys seemingly hadn't dared to keep incriminating information about the Russians, but there were copies of a series of messages, all with an origination code of Dzerzhinsky Square. The messages were still encoded, and Kaminsky hadn't been able to locate the plain-text translations, but he was willing to believe that the signals had come from either Besedin, or Chernysh himself.

There were some other papers Kaminsky had photographed, less important, but they added pieces to the mosaic. All told, the material from Jurys's office, combined with that already in Kaminsky's dossier, was more than enough to damn the whole nest of conspirators, especially if the messages from Moscow could be deciphered. Kaminsky thought it probable that they could be. He was going to give the Americans the exit signal tomorrow morning, and he'd be on his way out of Poland by Sunday night.

He finished the vodka, and was putting the glass down when the telephone rang. He became instantly alert. It had to be the office; no one ever called him at home nowadays except the office. He'd had a few social acquaintances when Jola was around, but they'd drifted away after she left.

"Kaminsky."

"This is Poet."

Kaminsky stiffened with apprehension. Poet was the code name Jurys used for working with CONCERTO.

"Yes?"

"Come in as soon as you can. There's a staff meeting. Ten P.M. sharp."

"Yes. I will."

Jurys rang off. Kaminsky stood holding the receiver, staring down at it. Already? Had the Americans told the Russians over there in New York already?

Calm down, he told himself. It's only an hour or two earlier than the CIA man said it would be. Anything could have happened to move it up. But Mary Madonna, I hope their deception plan worked. I don't really want to start looking for a spy within the staff, even if I'm doing the looking, especially since it's me. . . .

Even if they suspect someone inside compromised us, they'll look at Landau and his people first. Or they may decide it was somewhere else, Deribas's operations branch. Internal security won't be high on their list.

Unless they know someone was into Jurys's files. They'd suspect me first, if they knew that.

He put the receiver, which was buzzing at him, back into its cradle. Then he buckled on the belt holster with its PM63 automatic, and went into the bathroom to wash his face. Hollow eyes stared back at him from the mirror. I look dreadful, he thought. Is this how Jola saw me? Old, a gun at my waist, bound up always with my work? Probably.

He went through the kitchen into the hall, feeling a small twinge of annoyance that he couldn't wash the dishes and put them away, and got his raincoat out of the closet. He'd bought it before he lost all that weight, and he had to draw the belt into the last hole. He straightened the raincoat's folds around his middle, and left the apartment.

He was unlocking the door of the Skoda down in the apartment building's parking lot when he began to feel uneasy. It was the kind of uneasiness he'd felt when he was running illegals out of the Polish consulate in New York, and suspected that he was under surveillance. The instinct had rarely betrayed him.

Someone is watching me, he thought.

He got into the driver's seat, put the key into the ignition and pressed the accelerator all the way down while he tried to start the car. It was a sure way to make the engine flood. After making a point of being unable to start the Skoda, he got out, opened the hood and puttered around underneath it. As he did so he scanned the rest of the parking lot. No one. On the other hand, if they'd had time to set up a full watch, he'd have difficulty spotting them, anyway.

He went around to the trunk, opened it and rummaged for his tool kit. This time he was looking out across Grzybowska Street, along the narrow side street that led back into the apartment complex to the north. It was starting to rain hard again, and he had to squint to keep the drops of water from blurring his vision.

There.

The lights of a car turning away from him, into the side street, illuminated it for an instant. It was one of the standard surveillance vehicles at Kaminsky's own disposal, a Czech Tatra delivery van. Behind the windshield was a pale blur, a face.

So someone is watching me, Kaminsky thought. It has to be Vlasov behind this; Jurys acting under his orders. Who are the watchers? Probably some of my own department. Not part of CONCERTO, but willing to watch the boss if ordered to do so.

He took the toolkit around to the engine compartment and removed the air cleaner. The word is out, he thought. They know the Americans have found the safe house. They don't completely believe the deception about the Americans finding it themselves, as I suspected would be the case. So they are afraid there is a leak from the CONCERTO headquarters here. But why put surveillance on me? And so quickly? Was it because of Jurys's files?

Think, he told himself. *Think.*

I worried, back in the apartment, that there was something wrong with the timing. The American said the Russians would be told about the safe house around eleven or midnight, Warsaw time. But it's not long after nine here. Information in transit from the Americans to the Soviet embassy in Washington to Moscow, an hour. Half an hour for the KGB to decide what to do. Twenty minutes to alert Vlasov and Jurys and for Jurys to issue instructions. To get a surveillance team out here, twenty minutes to half an hour. Two hours, total. If that's what's happened, the Russians have known since seven P.M. my time, one in the afternoon in Washington. Four to five hours early.

He had the air cleaner off and was jamming the carburetor butterfly valve open with a splint of wood he kept in the toolkit for that purpose. But, he told himself, as though he were conducting a lecture, the American might have easily been mistaken about the timing. The Soviets in Washington *may* have been told about the situation four or five hours ago.

Then why am I being watched?

Suppose, he thought, as he went around to the driver's seat and got into it, that Moscow somehow found out it was me who told the Americans, or, to consider the alternative possibility, that Vlasov and Jurys suspect I broke into Jurys's office. What would they do? What would I do? This is what I was trained for, counterintelligence, so *think*.

I would call the target into headquarters on some pretext. I would make sure that he was under surveillance before the call was made. Then, even if he bolted, I'd be almost certain of grabbing him, and his flight would be proof of guilt. If he tried to brazen it out by obeying the summons, he'd be walking into a mouth full of sharp teeth.

He turned the key; the engine spat out raw fuel, drew in air through the jammed butterfly valve and fired. Kaminsky pumped the accelerator gently until the Skoda was running evenly, and then got out to remove the wooden splint from the carburetor.

As he closed the hood, he thought: It's possible they only suspect there was a leak, but have no idea who it might be. They may suspect all the senior CONCERTO staff members, so all of us are being watched, to try to frighten one of us into running. I might be able to go to that meeting, and get away with it. If no one ran, they'd be stymied for a little while. But I can't risk it. If I go back to Pulawska Street, I may never get out again. I told the American my nerve was beginning to go. I can't face it.

I *have* to run. No chance of using the escape routes I prepared so carefully, no flight to London or Vienna or Frankfurt. The clandestine routes I know about will be watched. The Americans will have to get me out, somehow.

Somehow.

Kaminsky locked the tools in the trunk and returned to the driver's seat, closing the door firmly behind him. The engine, for a change, was running smoothly. He turned on the lights and the windshield wipers. The glass in front of him smeared, and then cleared a little. Rain pattered steadily on the car's roof.

He backed out of his parking space. He knew the place he had to reach, but even if he got there he was not sure he could abandon the car and get through the nearest escape hatch without being seen and then followed. He had hoped to avoid using any of the hatches with someone hot on his heels.

There was only one exit from the parking lot, onto Grzybowska Street just west of the intersection with Ciepla. There was no cover hereabouts he could use to drop out of sight and abandon the Skoda; in any case, he was too far from the nearest escape hatch to reach it on foot. They'd be on him in an instant. Much better to get as close as he could, and then make a bolt for it.

Following the route he would usually take, Kaminsky drove past Ciepla, stopped and turned right onto Marchiewskiego. There was an army watch post stationed at the intersection; he ignored it. At the moment, the army was no danger to him.

Cross-traffic behind him confused the scene in the rearview mirror for a minute, but before he reached the next major intersection, he knew that the van was there behind him. They were being careful, and if he hadn't been watching for them, they might have escaped notice. But he was watching for them, and they should have expected that. It was sloppy. Reflexively, he decided to have the entire surveillance section retested for competence starting on Monday, and then snarled derisively at himself for the thought. He wouldn't be giving any orders on Monday.

He went around the traffic circle at Swietokrzyska and Marchiewskiego, past yet another army post, the Skoda's tires swooshing on the teeming pavement. The rain would help shield him, if he could just find three or four minutes' unobserved time. The Saski Hotel entrance was no good; at this hour of the evening there would be too many people near the construction site, and he'd waste precious seconds getting inside, and there was always the possibility that the construction crew had covered the hatch over properly. Moreover, it was too far north, and he'd obviously be driving away from the office. He'd have to use the church entrance. The trouble was that he'd still have to make a run northward, although a shorter one.

Keep going and give myself some space, he thought. It might lull them a bit.

Turn right onto Emilu Plater, southbound. So far so good; the watchers would think he was going down to Jerozolimskie and then turning left to pick up Marszalkowska a few blocks on. It was a reasonable assumption; the stoplight synchronization on the latter boulevard was a great deal better than that on Emilu Plater.

The rear rotunda of the Palace of Science and Culture was now on his left, and he could see the long brilliant glass facades of the Warsaw Central railway station ahead on his right, gleaming under the rain. The van was still behind him. There'd be more than one. He searched until he found the other car, a Skoda not unlike his own but certainly better maintained, almost in his blind spot in the right rear lane. They'd start changing places shortly. There might be a third vehicle, but he couldn't see one.

He passed the railway station — there were troops in the square surrounding that, too — and made a careful, legal stop at Jerozolimskie before turning left. He didn't want to deal with the *militsia* just now, although his identification would get him past any ordinary policeman. The van passed him on Jerozolimskie and took up a station a hundred fifty feet ahead. Behind, the surveillance Skoda tried to remain in his blind spot.

He hoped there were only two of them. If there was a full team, he'd be boxed in no matter which way he went, and he'd have to abandon his car. He was too far from the church to do that.

He had almost reached the traffic circle where the two main avenues met; the huge light-speckled slab of the Forum Hotel was dead ahead. There were army vehicles and men on the far, east side near the hotel, too far away to be a problem. The van pulled into the right-hand lane for the turn.

Into the first curve of the traffic circle now, the van swinging southward, Kaminsky obediently following.

Go.

He slammed the transmission into a lower gear and tramped on the accelerator, at the same time yanking the steering wheel hard to the left. The Skoda's rear wheels skidded on the slippery pavement; the car began to spin, the back end swinging to change places with the front. He caught the spin, straightening out, the hood now pointed at the center of the traffic circle. The surveillance car shot by on his left. Kaminsky eased off the accelerator to let the tires grip, and then the Skoda was crashing over the curb and hurtling across the center of the traffic circle, across the tram tracks, *look out for the concrete flower tubs,* a scrape and bang from the right front fender as he clipped one. The suspension slammed against its stops as the car shot over the curb on the far side of the circle and then he was back on the street, heading west, the engine shrieking, the Skoda's back end threatening to fishtail on the wet pavement. Kaminsky glanced in the rearview mirror, searching for the other Skoda; the van wouldn't have had time to turn yet. There was the car, trying to do the same thing he had but slowed by having to maneuver around a tram. He'd gained a good six hundred feet.

Full throttle, shift into high gear. The surveillance Skodas were slightly more powerful than the standard ones; he didn't have much time before the pursuing Skoda started closing the gap. If there were other cars, they'd be vectoring on him now. No point in worrying.

Here was Krucza Street, on the right. No military; he'd checked that as he was coming the other way. Wrench at the wheel, the back end almost breaking loose, around the corner. Whip out and in to pass a lumbering coal truck, another set of headlights in the windshield, just missed, horns blaring behind. The fork in the road ahead. Left; maybe they'd miss the way he'd taken. Another bend, past the bank building, the Warsaw Hotel, they'd lost him for a moment. Still too far from the church. Take a chance and shoot out onto Swietokrzyska Avenue, four lanes of traffic, just missing a bus. Stoplights straight ahead, green but how long had they been that way? Yellow. Red. Never mind, keep going. Lights behind him that hadn't been there a second ago: they were coming. Through the intersection against the signals, more horns, a booming slam as somebody ran into somebody else as they swerved to miss the rocketing Skoda, glimpse of soldiers turning in astonishment at the car howling by, they wouldn't be fast enough to interfere. Next right, get ready.

He pulled the car into Zielna Street. The small park at the end of the street was on his left. Get the speed down fast, open the driver's door, ten miles an hour, straighten out, they weren't behind yet, second gear to keep the Skoda coasting, *roll.*

He hadn't dropped from a moving car for eighteen years, and he was rusty. He rolled badly and felt a jab in his left wrist as it took his weight at the wrong angle. Never mind the pain, get up, in the name of Mary.

Kaminsky struggled to his feet and fled into the shrubbery of the park as the chasing Skoda roared around the corner. His own car was still moving, weaving around the street. It would distract them for a moment. He reached the narrow lane at the north edge of the small park, the lane that led into Bagno Street. Only a few hundred yards to go. The rain was heavier, poor visibility, good. There was no time to worry about what the rain could mean later. He kept running, hoping there wouldn't be a militia patrol back here. Around the corner, the dark bulk of Wszystkich Swietych Catholic Church just ahead. No patrols. They'd be realizing, back there behind him, that he'd likely entered the park, but they wouldn't be able to bring a car through there. If he had to stay on the streets he'd never get away, and they'd know that; they wouldn't be really worried yet. The militia would be told to start looking for him.

Except that he wasn't going to stay on the streets.

He reached the church. The front doors were always unlocked, but there might be worshippers inside, and he didn't want to make his presence in the church obvious. Instead of sprinting up the front steps, he turned short of them and ran along the eastern side as far as the jut of the transept. There was a heavy iron-bound door set into the wall between two buttresses. Kaminsky stooped and felt at the base of the wall, where a cavity had been formed by mortar eroding from between the stones. The hooked steel tool he'd made several months before was still there. He drew it out and inserted it carefully into the keyhole of the wrought-iron lock, working it against the mechanism inside. Faintly, under the patter of the rain, and the rasp of his own breathing, he heard the tongue of the lock grate back.

He replaced the lock pick, stepped into the gloom of the transept and closed the door softly behind him. The sound of the rain almost disappeared. From the direction of the nave came a faint glow: a few candles burning by the saints' chapels. The church appeared deserted, although the priest might be here already, preparing for the midnight mass. Kaminsky would have to be careful.

He was beginning to regain his breath; he walked silently along the north wall of the transept, feeling water squelch inside his drenched shoes, and stopped behind a column to peer out into the crossing. The ceiling, high above, was lost in shadows; candles flickered here and there in the semidarkness, which smelled faintly of incense. There was no one near the altar; beyond it, the apse appeared equally deserted.

Good thing this didn't happen three hours earlier, Kaminsky thought. I'd have looked stupid doing this with a priest trying to conduct mass.

He'd need light. Kaminsky crossed to the table where the candles were kept, took one and lit it with the cigarette lighter he always carried, although he no longer smoked. Then he started toward the high altar, walking slowly and shielding the candle flame with his palm. An impulse struck him as he was passing in front of the altar toward the south ambulatory, and he stopped, half-knelt, and crossed himself.

I think, he told himself as he entered the ambulatory with its saints' chapels, that that is the first time in my life I've ever genuflected. It's rather strange.

The door leading to the crypt stairway was just ahead, hidden behind one of the apse columns in a thick wall forming the partition between two of the chapels of the ambulatory. Kaminsky's hand was on the latch when he heard the main doors of the church boom open. Boot heels clacked on the pavement.

Already? he thought, yanking the door open so hard that the gust of air almost extinguished the candle. Mary Madonna, help me now.

He closed the door behind him and hurried down the curve of the narrow stone staircase as quickly as he could without extinguishing the candle. He couldn't hear anything from the church above; the floors and walls were too thick.

He reached the bottom of the stairs. There were sarcophagi down here, both free-standing and set into niches in the walls. The flickering candle threw its faint light across discolored stone and eroded carvings as Kaminsky half-trotted the width of the crypt and turned behind a five-foot-high plinth, on which rested a plain marble tomb. The lid of the tomb was well above his head; the space between the plinth and the wall behind it was no more than a shoulder's width across. Kaminsky stopped, listening. There was no sound from above. It was always possible that he hadn't been spotted entering the churchyard. If that were so, there'd only be a cursory search until they could get more men.

Set into the wall, its top edge at the level of Kaminsky's knee, was a rusty iron grill three feet long. Behind the grill was blackness: a tunnel. A dank, musty smell drifted out of it. Kaminsky guessed that at some time in the previous century there'd been trouble with drainage, the crypt had flooded, and the tunnel was then cut to drain water away into the sewers in case such a thing happened again. He'd found it by accident five months ago, when he was exploring for escape hatches against just such a day as this. It was the best-concealed entrance to the storm sewer network he'd found; the others were either dangerously public, or impermanent, like the one behind the Saski Hotel.

It had one drawback, however, and he could hear it faintly through the grill: the rumble of water flowing at high speed.

A voice echoed from the staircase and funneled down into the crypt. They were coming, dammit. He'd hoped for more time, for the water to fall. Nothing to do but keep going. He propped the candle against the wall beside him, and went quickly to work.

He'd loosened the grill some time before: it pulled easily out of the wall, although in any light but a strong one the rusted metal would show no sign of having been moved. Kaminsky got down on his hands and knees and began to feed himself into the tunnel feetfirst; he had to pull the grill closed behind him, and there was no room to turn around in the narrow drainage tunnel. He could hear footsteps on the stairs, echoing through the crypt.

The grill didn't want to slip back into its holes; it took him ten seconds to manage it. By that time, a glimmer of light was sifting around the corners of the plinth. He reached back through the bars of the grill and grabbed his candle. The flame flickered and bent. They'd see it in a moment. He blew it out, stuffed it into his pocket and began to shove himself backward along the tunnel. Its floor was damp and gritty and smelled of rat droppings. The only light was that from the searchers' flashlights in the crypt beyond the grill, and that was so faint as to be almost an illusion.

He was fifteen feet along the drainage channel, which sloped at a shallow angle away from the crypt. His foot brushed something that emitted a metallic scrape. Kaminsky crawled another two feet and reached back. His fingers closed around the handle of the electric lantern he'd cached in the tunnel. Relief flooded through him. He wasn't claustrophobic, but being down here in the pitch-dark was a little too much, with the wet walls enclosing him and the cold stone underneath and the tombs back there in the crypt. Being sealed alive in one of those caskets wouldn't be unlike this, if both ends of the channel were somehow blocked off. . . .

Stop it, he told himself furiously. You're in a lot more danger of being dragged out than being sealed in.

He didn't dare turn the lantern on, so he scuffled slowly backward into the dark. The PM63 automatic in its belt holster dug into his hipbone. The rumble of flowing water became steadily louder, until it masked all sounds from the crypt above and behind. But the light up there was stronger; he could see the bars of the grill outlined against it.

If they don't decide to check the tunnel, he thought, I have no problems. If they do —

The support dropped out from under his feet. He kept going until he felt the edge of the channel under his belly, letting his legs feel down the wall beneath the tunnel mouth. His toes met a level surface. He dropped out of the channel onto the wet floor, stood up carefully so as not to bang his head on the roof, and risked a quick flash of the lantern.

What he'd been most worried about was confronting him: the storm sewer, fed by the heavy rain of the last two days, was half full. The narrow ledge on which he was perched was barely above the surface. On the far side of the sewer, with no more than five inches of its diameter showing above the roiling and filthy surface of the water, was the feed tunnel he wanted.

He'd have to wait until the water level dropped. Even if he managed to get across the width of the main trunk without being swept away, there was a good twelve-foot stretch of feed pipe to get through before he reached the manhole shaft and the other, higher channel that led to his subterranean safe house. And he'd have to force his way against the current rushing through the feed pipe, with his face pressed against the roof so that he could breath. If the current swept him back out into the main channel and he couldn't get back onto the ledge, he'd be dragged through the dark until the main trunk dived deeper underground, and he would drown.

He gave his surroundings another sweep of the lantern. The water seemed to have risen slightly. Damn. He could always escape back up into the crypt if he had to, once his pursuers were gone.

A beam of light shot out of the drainage channel into the main sewer, starkly illuminating the stained bricks of the sewer wall and striking gleams from the churning surface of the water. Kaminsky jerked away from the channel mouth, and then risked a peek back up toward the crypt.

Somebody was crawling down the channel. To his dark-adapted eyes, it was ablaze with light.

Kaminsky found himself praying, not in words but in feelings and images. He looked at the mouth of the feed pipe, calculating. The ledge ran ten feet upstream before it became lower and disappeared beneath the water's surface. How fast was the water moving? He couldn't judge easily in the reflected light streaming out of the drainage channel.

There was no time. He had to act now, or try to shoot his way out, or surrender. Shooting wouldn't work, even if he killed the man who was now descending the channel. They'd gas him out before the water dropped. And he couldn't surrender, not while there was still a chance he'd make it.

Kaminsky tore off his raincoat and threw it into the stream, which swallowed it instantly. He threaded his trousers belt through the lantern handle, rebuckled it, and ran to the end of the ledge. He took a moment to gather himself, inhaled one deep breath, and jumped.

He hit the water about two-thirds of the way across the main trunk. The chill current grabbed at his legs and sucked him under. He felt the weight of the automatic and the flashlight trying to pull him to the bottom, and he scrabbled wildly at the sewer wall, feeling his fingernails break. How close was his pursuer to the channel mouth?

He straightened, and a rush of water battered him. He swam convulsively against the torrent from the feed channel, and managed to get an arm inside the tunnel mouth before the current in the main trunk forced him past it.

His head was still underwater, and he had to stay submerged until he was inside the feed sewer. With an agonizing effort, he got a second arm into the tributary, and his fingertips found crevices between the bricks to cling to. His right bicep began to cramp with cold. After a moment he managed to get a knee inside and braced himself across the tunnel diameter. This partly blocked the tunnel, and the water pressure rose; it threatened to spit him back out into the main line. He resisted it with all his strength. He was running out of air.

Get the other knee inside. There, a little better. Now push back farther inside, slowly, slowly, there's a nose-width of air above you, you can always get to it, but be patient, *don't panic*. Now, brace hard, and work up toward the surface. Lungs bursting, burning, want something cool in them even if it's filthy water running through the bowels of Warsaw, don't think about opening your mouth and swallowing. Turn your face upward. One knee slipping on the bricks, almost lost there, press harder —

Air, four inches of it, just enough for nose and eyes, no more. A deep, gusty breath, be careful not to choke, he might hear you. Open eyes. Light across the way there, he's in the sewer now, all right, but there's no way he can see me in here unless he points the light beam directly inside.

He might, however. Kaminsky submerged again and forced himself painfully back against the rush of the water. Two yards, three. Four. Anywhere here. He surfaced again, and this time there was nothing above his head. He was in the manhole shaft, and there, just above him, was the floor of the tunnel that led to safety.

He dragged himself out of the water and into the tunnel entrance. His teeth were chattering and he shivered convulsively. I have to get warm, he thought, and soon. How long was I in? Not more than two or three minutes. But God knows what's in that water, even if it's storm water and not sewage. I can't risk pneumonia. Thank God I had time to prepare.

He struggled to his knees and unbuckled the lantern. He'd sealed it against water, and it still worked. He'd have to strip and dry the pistol as soon as he was really safe.

Just as soon as he could risk it, he'd venture aboveground and display the emergency signal, the two chalk strokes. After that, it would be up to the American.

And until he comes, Kaminsky thought, all I can do is wait.

New York
Sunday, October 6

THE BOAT ROCKED SLIGHTLY as Ennis stood up, stretched and sat down again. The three-quarters moon had sunk well into the west; it was low enough for Brennan to see it past the edge of the canvas dodger that covered the forward half of the motor launch's cockpit. The boat was moored to one of the wharfs used by the small Sheepshead Bay fishing fleet; to the west, against the moon, were silhouetted the stumpy masts and pilothouses of a few of the fishboats. There was a police launch a couple of piers away to the east; when the wind dropped for a moment, Brennan could hear the faint grumble of its engines. From time to time he could also hear the noise of the sparse late-night traffic on the Shore Parkway to the north. Up there, not far away, was the house where Gorbachev was a prisoner. Brennan wondered whether the Russian leader was awake, and what he was thinking if he was. Seven days, less a few hours, had passed since his abduction.

If it hadn't been for those bastards, Brennan thought, I'd be at home in my own bed.

There was a faint crackle from the Cougarnet transceiver that linked Brennan to the talk-through stations to the north, and ultimately to Knight. "Park Lane to all stations," the voice on the radio intoned quietly, "All stations. Shoebox. Repeat, Shoebox."

It was one of the code words Knight had given Brennan at the briefing yesterday evening, how many hours ago? Not many. Brennan tipped his wrist so that the lights on the quay illuminated its face. Two minutes to one. "It means the Aeroflot plane's landed at Kennedy," he said. "The one they'll bundle Gorbachev and Kepa and the rest onto when they've got them." *One hour to go,* he thought, imagining Knight back at the CIA station in the black glass skyscraper, monitoring the net of men and weapons and radios that was tightening around the house in the dark street where the leader of the Soviet Union lay, perhaps sleeping.

"Nervy mothers," Ennis muttered.

Ennis wasn't supposed to be here. It had been nearly impossible for Brennan or any other CIA officer to be in at the end, for that matter; it was only direct intervention by the FBI director in Washington that had forced Ranelagh to let the Agency put half-a-dozen men into the field, along with the Bureau and police forces. They were stationed at sensitive points like the IRT railyards a mile away, where Timoshkin and his men were presumably making last-minute preparations for the rescue. All the CIA watchers were linked through the Cougarnet talk-through stations to Knight, who in turn was tied into the FBI and police communications network. Brennan was one of the watchers, and the only one among them who knew about CONCERTO. It put him in an awkward position. This position wasn't quite as awkward, though, as it would have been if permission for CIA involvement had been withheld by Washington. Brennan had decided to intervene, if necessary, by himself. As it turned out, his planned use of the boat had fit neatly into the field operation. Ennis, though, was an unauthorized extra.

"Frank," Brennan had said just before leaving the station, "what do you want me to do if Timoshkin won't release Gorbachev, and the FBI people sit on their hands?"

"Don't do *anything*. If the Bureau fucks up, that's their problem. Unless Gorbachev asks for help. Then try to intervene. But don't, for Christ's sake, get anybody killed if you do that."

"Can I have some armed backup?"

"No. We've been authorized six men, and this time around we're going to play by the rules or Barlow and Reid will tear our heads off and stuff them down our throats. I can't spare you anybody. No backup."

"No FBI people that could be indoctrinated into CONCERTO to give me a hand?"

"No goddamned way. CONCERTO's too sensitive. Even Ranelagh doesn't know about it."

"Thanks a lot, Frank," Brennan had said, and left.

He'd thought it would be laid out that way. That was why he'd recruited his own FBI assistance, in the person of Ennis, who wasn't supposed to be within ten miles of Gorbachev or any CIA officer, let alone Brennan.

Again the static from the radio. Both men listened intently.

"Park Lane to all stations," Knight's voice said over the lap of water against the wharf pilings. "Drywall. Negative Rafter."

"Your people got microphones on the house windows," Brennan said to Ennis. "No luck with cameras. That was a long shot, anyway."

The microphones would be used to try to determine how many people were inside the safe house, and where they were. The fiber-optic TV cameras would have given a lot more information about exact positioning, armament and perhaps even where Gorbachev was, but for some reason the Bureau technical teams hadn't been able to drill holes to place them, probably because going through the brick siding would have been too noisy, even with the special drills.

The safe house was on Voortman Avenue, a side road north and parallel to Emmons Avenue, almost next to the Shore Parkway. It was one of the few detached dwellings in a declining residential neighborhood, and was surrounded by older houses that had been cut up into apartments for immigrant West Indians and Haitians. Tax records showed that it had been owned for the past six years by a Wilfrid Best of Newark, New Jersey, who had never lived there; he kept it as a rental property. The Bureau had gone after him as soon as they'd found that out, but he was on a fishing trip somewhere in the wilds of northern Canada, and his wife had never seen the place. She'd let them look at the rental records, though; the tenant was a Mr. James Parker, who had paid six months' rent in advance, without a lease. She had never seen Mr. Parker. She did remember that her husband had said a previous owner had constructed a bomb shelter in the basement, likely during the nuclear war scares of the late 1950s. The odds were good that Gorbachev was down in the shelter; unfortunately, the house was so old that all records of its construction had vanished, and the FBI technical men were working blind as they tried to place their surveillance gear.

''No cameras, yeah,'' Ennis said. ''It was too much to hope for. Not that it matters, though, does it? *These* guys aren't going to shoot *this* hostage. You really think this is the right house?''

''It's got all the earmarks,'' Brennan said. ''If it isn't, it should have been.''

''The Russians are going to be laughing up their sleeves if the information's wrong.''

''Yeah.''

''I'm pretty sure it's the right one, too,'' Ennis said.

''How so?''

''Remember how we first got on to Kepa, with that parking ticket a couple miles away from here in Brighton Beach? We might have figured the safe house wasn't a hell of a long way away. But Ranelagh found out you'd spotted Kepa before we did. It pissed him off. Then I found out Kepa spoke Russian like a native, told you last Tuesday in the restaurant, and then Ranelagh found us together and suspended me. I bet he delayed following up the lead because the CIA got to it before he did, and I'd told you what I'd found out about Kepa.''

Brennan found himself cursing silently. ''Is the FBI still in friendly hands?'' he asked.

''Makes you wonder sometimes, doesn't it?'' Ennis said.

Water lapped at the sides of the motor launch. Brennan thought: And what else is in unfriendly hands? Who told the Russians I was going to Paris?

''Ten past one,'' Ennis said. ''Timoshkin should be heading for his position now.''

As if to confirm the estimate, the radio relayed, ''Stetson.''

The Soviet tactical team would be near the safe house in fifteen minutes, and would be in their assault positions shortly thereafter. Then would come half an hour of monitoring the microphones, while the technical staff tried to figure out how many men were inside the house, and where.

Not that it matters, Brennan thought, echoing Ennis. But we all have to go through the motions. It's like a marriage where one of them's having an affair, and they both know the other knows it, but neither one wants to risk bringing it out into the open for fear it'll cost them both too much. Ignore it, and maybe everything will be all right.

"We'll go up ourselves as soon as the Russians are there," Brennan said. "You sure you want to stay in this?"

"I said I'd cover your back," Ennis said. "I haven't changed my mind."

"Thanks. Just checking."

"Forget it."

Minutes passed. The launch was beginning to rise and fall gently, squeaking up and down against her fenders. The swell out in Rockaway Inlet, which was open on the southwest to the Atlantic, must have been building quickly. The wind was steady and strong now, without lulls, although the moonlit sky was still clear.

Finally, Ennis said, "How about it?"

"Okay." Brennan shoved the Cougarnet transceiver into the breast pocket of his bush jacket and stood up.

The launch's foredeck was about five feet below the level of the wharf; they climbed a worn wooden ladder to the top and headed northward along the wharf to the quay. A lane led away from the quay between two frame buildings, one of which, from the smell, had to be a fish-packing plant. Brennan had thought long and hard about his positioning, even after he'd persuaded Ennis to join him in renting the motor launch; but the harder he thought about it, the more the boat made sense. It was the only way he could think of to remove the Russian leader from the hands of both the KGB and the FBI, if that seemed to be necessary. He was afraid that, at the last moment, the Bureau men on the scene might bend to Russian pressure — or Russian weapons — and hand the Soviet leader over to them.

The lane ended at Emmons Avenue; across Emmons was the street leading toward Voortman Avenue. An FBI car was stopped at the intersection, its engine running. The driver got out as they approached. His partner was covering them from the far side of the car.

"Stop right there," the driver commanded when they were thirty feet away. "Where are you going?"

"Park Lane One," Brennan said. We're lousy with codes and passwords tonight, he thought.

"Okay," the driver said. "Come over here. Let's see some ID."

They approached the driver, who shone his flashlight on Brennan's identity badge. He compared Brennan's face carefully with the photograph on the badge. "Spook, eh?" said the FBI man. "Hello, Mr. Ennis. I thought you were on other duties. You ought to be wearing your badge."

"Last-minute change," Ennis responded crisply. "Liaison with CIA. There wasn't time to make up a badge."

"Go on, then. I'll radio ahead to the next checkpoint."

They proceeded to within half a block of the cross street that led to the safe house. There had been some debate about evacuating the entire street, but in discussion with the Russians, the idea had been discarded as too likely to alert the kidnappers. Again, the charade.

Half-past one. Timoshkin's men would be just about in their assault positions by now.

Ahead, at the Voortman intersection, Brennan could see the dark, parked car that was the next checkpoint. Around him and invisible in the darkness would be dozens of police and FBI, on rooftops, behind chimneys, in alleys, in the vehicles parked along the curbs. In a few of the buildings there were still lighted windows. Mixed with the traffic sounds from the Parkway were strains of West Indian music, occasional raised voices. Nobody was out on the street, though, and there were more than enough police around to make sure that anyone who came outside would promptly retreat.

Brennan and Ennis reached the checkpoint. As before, the driver and his partner were extremely careful, despite the alert from the perimeter post on Emmons Avenue. Brennan had already taken his identification out of his pocket when the car's radio squawked faintly and relayed something Brennan couldn't make out.

The FBI man understood it, though. He said, "Jesus Christ," and then Knight's voice crackled out of Brennan's radio.

"Park Lane to all stations! All stations! The Russians are moving early! Repeat, the Russians are moving early! Park One, if you're not there already, move your ass!"

"Holy shit," Ennis said, as Brennan started to run. He heard Ennis pelting after him. The radio bumped against his chest, up and down. He reached into his bush jacket and started pulling the Browning out of his shoulder holster. A moment's thought later, he pushed the weapon back; everyone up here would be too inclined to shoot at an unidentified running man who was waving a pistol around.

He stopped ten paces past the corner. The safe house was half a short block along, and on the same side of the street as he was. The street was dark and silent, as though nothing at all had happened, as though the Russians were still waiting. Brennan couldn't make out what was going on.

Then, suddenly, four sharp cracks split the night air: concussion grenades. The Russians were on their way in, all right. He saw the unmarked panel truck that was serving as the FBI mobile command post, just ahead on the far side of the street.

"Over to the command post," Brennan said hurriedly to Ennis. "We'll have to play it by ear." Goddamn it, he thought. What a screwup. Didn't anybody consider the Russians might preempt? Why didn't I? Would anybody have paid any attention?

He raced across the street, Ennis behind him, and heard automatic weapons fired from the safe house. Making it look good. Would they actually shoot anyone? Probably only by accident, unless somebody had a flesh wound in his contract.

Brennan banged on the rear door of the panel van. The time for silence was over; from the safe house came the bang of two more concussion grenades and another burst of automatic fire. Lights were flashing on in the apartments above the scattered store fronts and in the bedrooms of the seedy apartment buildings.

The van door flew open, almost catching Brennan's nose. Inside were crammed five men: a communications technician, three agents armed with machine pistols, and a fifth man who had opened the door and whose face Brennan couldn't see clearly because it was silhouetted by the red-lit van's interior. "What the *fuck*!" snarled a voice from the invisible face. "What's going on — Jesus Christ. *Brennan*, you prick. What in hell have you done?"

It was Ranelagh.

It would have to be him, Brennan thought. He sensed Ennis hanging back; no sense in walking willingly into a meat slicer.

"I haven't done anything," Brennan said. One more bang from the safe house, and then silence. People were hanging out their windows now, yelling to each other and down into the street. Brennan couldn't see any of the other dozen men of the FBI's close-in support group. They're trying to figure out what's happened before they charge to the rescue, he thought. "The Russians'll be out in a minute with Gorbachev," Brennan said. "You'd better get your men ready to put him into the ambulance." There was always a chance that the FBI would face the Russians down, and Brennan didn't want to deal with Timoshkin and his specialists if he didn't have to.

"The ambulance isn't here yet," Ranelagh growled. Behind him, Brennan could see the startled faces of the command post personnel, the communications man with an index finger frozen in midair over a button. "And don't start giving *me* orders!"

I've screwed it, Brennan thought, damn my hasty tongue. He won't do anything now until it's too late. The Russians will have their own transport from the consulate, or they'll commandeer FBI vehicles.

He turned away from Ranelagh and ran past the flank of the van, heading for the safe house. Ennis was at his elbow. "No luck tonight," he muttered to Brennan.

Brennan slowed. Flickering red light was pouring out of the front-ground floor window of the safe house; the concussion grenades had set something on fire. The wooden front porch was suddenly crowded with men, black against the firelight. The mass split apart as individuals ran down the porch steps; Brennan could make out the dark combat clothing and body armor of the Russian tactical team. They were armed with short assault rifles. Two of them were supporting a third, shorter figure by the upper arms. They weren't being excessively gentle.

Here we go, Brennan thought. He slowed to a walk and approached the knot of men on the sidewalk. Two black panel vans were approaching from farther up the street; likely the KGB's transport, obligingly furnished by the FBI. There was no sign of the ambulance.

Three men were coming out of the burning safe house, hands clasped on top of their heads: Gorbachev's captors, with three more of Timoshkin's men behind them, covering them with assault rifles. One of the captives was limping, although whether the limp was real or cosmetic, Brennan had no idea. He counted quickly. Six Russians. Timoshkin's tactical team was all present and accounted for. As he watched, two of them sprinted off into the night. They'd be going to get their transportation.

More men began appearing out of the darkness, from doorways and alleys. These, though, were FBI agents comprising the close-in support.

"Lee," Brennan said out of the corner of his mouth. "Can you get Ranelagh's men on our side? We're going to need them."

"If Ranelagh stays out of the way, I can," Ennis said. His voice was low and tense. "I've got the rank."

Brennan risked a glance over his shoulder at the mobile command post. No sign of Ranelagh. He was probably on the radio, trying to explain to his superiors what had happened and find out what to do next. Timoshkin had done a beautiful job of spreading chaos and indecision.

The street was suddenly flooded with illumination as the drivers of half-a-dozen FBI vehicles started their engines and turned on their headlights. Brennan and Ennis were only thirty feet from the nearest Russians, who were regarding them warily. "Antonetti," Brennan heard Ennis say. "Is that you? It's Lee Ennis. I'm in charge while the AD's on the radio. Make sure these goons don't interfere with Gorbachev, no matter *what* he wants to do. Understand?"

Brennan heard doubt in the answering voice, but Bureau discipline prevailed. "Yessir. Handelman! You other guys! Get over here and back Mr. Ennis up."

"We've got five people," Ennis told Brennan.

It's not going to be enough, Brennan thought. We're going to lose. Frank said don't get anybody hurt. I'm going to have to let them leave with him.

He stopped a yard away from the nearest Russian. The man was well over six feet tall, the face triangular with a hint of Mongol in it, the eyes very dark. He looked at Brennan; the eyes dropped to the identity badge. Something like recognition flickered across his face and was instantly masked.

Oh, my God, Brennan thought. Did I see that look?

Beside the tall Russian, the two tactical team men were still holding their prize by the upper arms. There was no mistaking the dark splotch of the birthmark at the fringe of the thinning hair: it was Mikhail Gorbachev. He was unbound, wearing dark trousers and a white shirt and ill- fitting tennis shoes. Brennan noted, in the light from the growing fire, that his eyes were alert, apparently taking in every detail of his surroundings. Not drugged, then. Beyond Gorbachev and the group of KGB troopers, two black vans were drawing to a halt.

"Might I speak with Colonel Timoshkin?" Brennan said in Russian to the tall KGB man.

"I am Colonel Timoshkin," said the tall man, without a trace of surprise at being addressed with perfect fluency in his own language. Gorbachev fixed his eyes on Brennan.

"The ambulance will be here in a moment or two," Brennan said, hoping fervently that it would be. Its presence might give him and Ennis and the five FBI men an edge. He wished for a moment that he'd thought to switch the radio to continuous transmit, so that Knight could monitor what was going on, but he didn't dare do it now, not in sight of Timoshkin.

"It's not necessary to have an ambulance," Timoshkin said. "The general secretary is not harmed. We will take him directly to the airport, with the criminals who abducted him. He will be better cared for at home in Moscow. It is too dangerous for him here."

"Mr. Gorbachev," Brennan appealed in Russian. "Would you prefer to go to an American hospital for a few hours, before you leave for home? We can provide you with *any protection necessary*."

He emphasized the last three words. He couldn't be sure whether the Soviet leader had figured out the source of the plot against him; Gorbachev might be deciding right now which medals to award Timoshkin and the men who had rescued him.

Timoshkin had sensed the emphasis. He studied Brennan intently in the flickering light. The fire had a good, crackling hold now, and Brennan could hear sirens to the north. Somebody with a bullhorn was warning residents of the street to get back into their houses.

Gorbachev drew himself up, trying to push away the hands of the men holding him. "There's no need to support me like a broken marionette," he said. The voice was strong and decisive. "Comrade Colonel Timoshkin, I'm quite well, as you say, but nevertheless I would like a night's decent rest before I return to Moscow. I can remain at the consulate, if you're so concerned for my safety. I'm sure your American allies will provide additional protection, if you think it's needed."

He's guessed, Brennan thought. Clever. If he can reach the consulate, we may have a chance to talk to him, and he knows it. It'll mess up Timoshkin's plans. He's trying.

"And get your hands off me," Gorbachev snapped at the two men holding him. "Do I have to tell you twice? Have you forgotten who I am?"

The men released Gorbachev and he took a step forward, almost past Timoshkin. The KGB colonel put out a hand to restrain him, but he brushed it aside. "Can you," Gorbachev said in Russian to Brennan, "guarantee my safety if I decide to remain in New York until morning?"

"*Da,*" Brennan replied, thinking: *He knows.*

"Good," said Gorbachev. "Then I'll remain. Please have a proper car sent for me." He angrily pushed Timoshkin's hand away as the KGB man tried to intervene again.

"General Secretary," Timoshkin said woodenly, "I cannot permit this. I am under orders. Please cooperate. I *insist*." He motioned, and one of the KGB men who had been holding the Russian leader stepped forward.

"You *insist*?" Gorbachev said, and took to his heels.

It was so unexpected that everyone, except the fleeing man, remained frozen in place for an instant. Then Ennis, who didn't understand a word of what had passed among Brennan and the two Russians, and had therefore been able to concentrate on everything else, shouted to his five men:

"*Don't let them grab him!*"

He yelled a fraction of a second before Timoshkin lunged past Brennan in an attempt to snatch at Gorbachev's flying shirttail. Brennan spun sideways, brought his right knee up, and buried it in Timoshkin's crotch, feeling the body armor flex upward with the blow; the armor was designed to resist point impacts from bullets, not a bludgeoning from a blunt instrument. The shock of colliding with Timoshkin almost knocked Brennan over. He staggered backward, seeing the Russian fall, doubled up and gasping for breath, and then the men who had been holding Gorbachev started forward, only to be body-checked by two of Ennis's agents. Somebody fired a gun — into the air Brennan hoped — and then he had regained his balance and was running back along the firelit street, Ennis pounding behind him, Gorbachev fleeing ahead.

For a moment, Brennan thought the Russian was gone, but then he glimpsed the back of his shirt as he ran into an alley. Brennan pelted after him, hearing another shot behind and the crack of concussion grenades. Like the shoot-out at the OK Corral, Brennan thought, as he raced along the alley, which was full of garbage and abandoned car parts, with occasional lights over the service doors of shops. For a man near sixty, Gorbachev was a remarkable sprinter. Brennan was starting to pant, and he could hear Ennis drawing deep breaths just behind him. The radio bounced up and down against his kidneys; its weight, though light, kept throwing him off balance.

Gorbachev was slowing down, but not because he was running out of steam. A wall crossed the alley ahead of him. He stopped in front of it; it was about eight feet high.

Brennan caught up to him. Gorbachev was more winded than Brennan had realized from his speed; he bent over from the waist, dragging in rasping gusts of air. "We have to get over," he choked out.

"Up," Brennan said. "On my hands and then shoulders."

He clasped his hands together and Gorbachev used them as a step to get his hands on the top of the wall. Just then Ennis arrived; he grabbed the Russian's ankles and pushed upward. Brennan felt the man's feet heavy on his shoulders and then the weight was gone. He looked up. Gorbachev was peering down at him. "Hurry!" he panted. "There's a roof here!"

"Lee, you next."

Ennis put a foot in Brennan's hands and jumped for the top of the wall. Brennan heaved; Ennis got his belly over the edge and Gorbachev pulled him the rest of the way. Then they both reached down and grabbed Brennan's outstretched arms.

"Sean, they're coming!"

Brennan heard a clatter of garbage bins from behind and risked a glance backward as they dragged him bodily up the wall. His shoes scrabbled for a hold on the rough mortar. He saw several Russians racing into the alleyway, the man in the lead much taller than the others. Timoshkin had recovered in a hurry.

The radio banged against the edge of the roof as Brennan clambered onto it. If only he could call Knight for backup, but there wasn't time. He heard more clattering from the alley behind.

They were on the flat roof of a garage or storage shed, that spanned the alley from side to side. Ahead, at the front of the garage, were the lights of Emmons Avenue. The FBI perimeter post would be out there. Maybe they could help. But there might be shooting if they tried for it; Timoshkin could be desperate by now. Better not to involve the FBI men unless there was no other way out. The boat. Out on the water they'd be safe.

"Wait, goddamnit," Ennis urged as they reached the edge of the roof overlooking the street. "The outer post, they may fire if we drop on them —"

The lane leading down to the dock was almost across from them. Brennan peered around the corner of the building. Both agents had stepped out of the FBI car, and were looking up the street in the direction of the shots and the fire. They wouldn't know yet that there was a pursuit in progress. "We've got to get to the boat," Brennan said.

Ennis yelled at the men by the car, "This is Special Agent Ennis! Don't shoot when we come out!"

He swung himself over the edge of the roof and dropped to the sidewalk. "Go," Brennan said to Gorbachev. He could hear combat boots thudding against concrete back in the alleyway.

Gorbachev struggled painfully over the edge of the garage. Brennan heard him grunt as he hit the ground below. He's tiring, Brennan thought. God help us all if he has a heart attack.

Brennan chanced another look back. Timoshkin had stopped running, and was in full view halfway down the alley, although his men were still coming. The Russian was standing in a certain way —

Brennan threw himself flat, hearing the shot and the snap of the bullet somewhere over his head as he struck the asphalt of the roof. He's after *me*, he thought as he slid over the edge of the garage and hit the pavement below. Me in particular.

"The boat?" Ennis asked. "Or pull in more of the perimeter people to help us? If the bastards are going to start shooting —"

There would be FBI men hidden in the shadows up and down the avenue, but Timoshkin would be on Gorbachev's heels before they could be rallied. Too risky. "The boat," he panted. "We have to use it. Can't get enough people here in time. Can't risk a firefight. Might hit Gorbachev."

Ennis understood. "Don't try to stop those guys behind us," he shouted at the two bewildered agents by the car. "Put the car across the lane if you can!"

And then all three were running again, across the street, into the lane smelling of fish and seaweed and oily salt water. Out onto the quayside, wind cold off the bay, Gorbachev really in trouble now, the breath coming from him in great tearing gasps as though he'd been struck deep in the stomach.

The police boat? No, too far away, Lee and I can't commandeer it with just the two of us, we have to get away *now*, it's got to be the launch.

The Russian was limping. His feet must be in bad shape, in the ill-fitting tennis shoes. Brennan grabbed him by the arm and half-dragged him along the wharf toward the motor launch. Ennis was ahead of them now, his legs driving up and down like trip-hammers. From behind, in the direction of the lane, Brennan heard shouts and yells but, fortunately, no shots. The perimeter guards might have delayed Timoshkin a little, but it wouldn't be by much.

"Get him into the launch," Ennis gasped. "I'll cast off."

"Down the ladder here," Brennan said to Gorbachev. "Into the boat. We'll get you away by water."

Gorbachev hesitated only a moment, and then shinned down the wooden ladder into the launch's cockpit, striking the floorboards with a thump. Close behind came Brennan, struggling with the encumbrance of the radio as he searched for the ignition key. He found it, threw himself into the driver's seat and rammed the key into the ignition, praying the engines would be warm enough to start without hesitation.

The motors kicked over and stalled. From above Ennis called, "We're loose," and Brennan heard him clatter down the steps as the engines rumbled again, almost caught, and stopped once more. Boots were thudding on the planks of the wharf. Timoshkin. Brennan tried again.

The engines caught with a thunderous roar. Brennan shoved the throttles forward, slowly, not daring to risk another stall. He felt the propellers bite water and the launch's stern dug itself into the water with the thrust, the transom slamming and scraping against the wharf pilings as Brennan spun the wheel over to force the bow out. He looked back along the wharf.

Jesus Christ.

One of the KGB men, not Timoshkin, was three strides away from the top of the ladder. Brennan saw him throw aside his assault rifle and sprint for the edge of the wharf. The launch was moving faster now, spray flying up from its stern.

The Russian jumped. For an instant he was silhouetted against the shore lights, arms outstretched, reaching for the transom.

He almost made it, but not quite. The hands grasped the boat's stern and then the Russian disappeared into the welter of the launch's wake. Brennan caught a glimpse of his head surfacing in the white water; one arm rose, then dropped as he swam.

Brennan jammed the throttles all the way forward now. The launch was approaching planing speed, wind whipping around the edges of the canvas dodger and drops of water spitting from the bow wave across Brennan's face. The boat rumbled past the end of the wharf. They were away, they'd made it.

He swung the wheel, heading east toward the bay entrance. They'd head for Manhattan, and radio Knight to have somebody waiting for them. But where, exactly?

Brennan looked through the window toward the quay and the wharves jutting from it. Timoshkin's men were running parallel to the launch, toward the police boat moored at the last wharf, stern to the quay. As the launch roared past the patrol boat's bow, Brennan saw the Russians race up the gangplank to board her.

Oh, shit, he thought. We may not be out of this yet. It depends on how fast the cops react. Instinctively, he pushed at the throttles, but they were already at full speed ahead.

They were almost at the mouth of the bay. The launch's stem was beginning to slam up and down in the moonlit cross-swell running in from Rockaway Inlet. Sheets of water whacked into the windshield. Brennan left the throttles wide open, hoping that when the launch was at full plane it would ride more easily. He couldn't risk smashing the bottom out of her.

Ennis was at his elbow. "What're they doing?" Brennan shouted over the roar of the engines and the slam of water against the hull.

"I can't see!" Ennis shouted back. "Wait a minute. God*damn* it. The police boat's coming out!"

"Maybe it's the police."

"I wouldn't bet on it. Nobody was expecting anything like this. If the crew was surprised —"

He didn't need to finish. They were out of the mouth of the

bay now and Brennan swung the bow southeast, taking the heavy swell on the starboard quarter, laying a course away from the peninsula that separated Sheepshead Bay from Rockaway Inlet. The sea was much worse out here; it was sweeping around Rockaway Point from the open Atlantic and rebounding from the Coney Island beaches in a tumble of confused water. The lights of Kingsborough Community College slid away sternward.

"It's going to get even rougher in a minute," Brennan yelled. "The wind's risen since we came over. Can you handle her for a second? Steer southeast, toward those lights." He slid out of the seat, holding the wheel until Ennis could take over.

He could see the police boat behind them in the moonlight, the wings of a huge bow wave pale against the black water. It was only a half mile behind them. Brennan's launch was probably faster, but the patrol craft was larger and would prove a better boat in confused seas like these. If the water got much rougher, they'd have to reduce speed or risk pounding the bottom out of the launch. Brennan looked at the sky. Not a sign of cloud, no heaven-sent rain squalls to hide them in darkness, only this steady, seadriving wind.

Gorbachev was sitting on the floorboards, propped against the transom seat, head between his knees. "Are you all right?" Brennan asked, picking up the radio.

The Russian lifted his head. "Better. I haven't run like that for a very long time. Are we well away?"

"For the moment. But they're following us. This boat is faster, though," he said. I hope, he added to himself.

He pressed the radio's transmit button and said, "Park One calling Park Lane. Over."

Knight's voice came back instantly, although Brennan had to turn the volume all the way up and press his ear to the speaker, because of the noise from the engine and the water. "Park Lane to Park One. What in hell's going on? All hell's broken loose over there. Where are you, dammit?"

"On the water. I've got the target. They were going to snatch him. Frank, we need help. Timoshkin's got a boat and he's after us."

A short silence. Then Knight said, "Sean, you crazy son of a bitch. You mean you snatched him *yourself*?"

"Not exactly. He ran, and we helped."

"Who is *we*?"

"Lee Ennis, FBI. Frank, for God's sake, get us some help, I'll explain later."

"Where are you exactly?"

"Heading southeast through Rockaway Inlet in that launch I rented. We're heading for the Coast Guard station beside Fort Tilden on the point, at about twenty knots. I don't know if we'll be able to keep that speed if the water gets any rougher, and we've got two-and-a-half miles to go. They may catch up with us. Can you get a chopper out here with searchlights, a police boat, Coast Guard, I don't care, *anything*."

"Can you get ashore somewhere else, before they catch up?"

"The target's had it. He can't run anymore, and they're getting closer. There are five of them and only two of us. We've got to have backup, Frank. I thought we could get clean away, but we can't. Sorry."

"I'll get help. Hang on to him. I'll call back as soon as I can. Out."

"Okay. Out."

Brennan switched off the radio and peered over the transom. He wasn't sure, but he thought the police boat was closer. A quarter of a mile, maybe. It was hard to judge distances in the moonlight. A little more than two miles to go, Brennan thought. How fast is that boat?

The launch twisted and bucked as it hit a cross-swell. Gallons of water poured in over the starboard quarter, drenching both Brennan and Gorbachev.

"I've got to slow down!" Ennis shouted. "She won't take this! Where are we going?"

"Coast Guard station!" Brennan yelled back, staggering toward the pilot's seat, water dripping into his eyes. "You know where it is?"

"Only roughly. Sean, I don't know a damn thing about boats. You'd better take her. I can't handle her in this."

Brennan got behind the wheel as another wave threatened to broach the launch and fill her. "Watch Timoshkin."

"He's getting closer."

Ennis was right, in spite of his inexperience. The launch was pounding as though she'd snap her keel. Brennan pulled the throttles back until she rode a little more easily, but she lost a good five knots' speed as he did so. He realized that he was still holding the radio, and shoved it into his bush jacket. Where in hell was Knight?

"Mr. Gorbachev!" he called. "Can you come up here for a moment?"

The Russian joined him, holding tight to a grab rail on the dashboard. "Do you know what's been happening?" Brennan asked.

"I guessed. My rescuers were not rescuers. They were going to return me to Moscow, no matter what I ordered them to do. What has been happening there?"

"It's hard for us to tell. Isayev seems to be in charge."

"And Oleg Chernysh?"

"I don't know what he's been doing."

"I can well imagine," said Gorbachev. "Preparing a coup. There's been a lot of trouble in Poland and elsewhere, am I correct?"

"Yes."

"They're a hell of a lot closer!" Ennis called from behind them. "Can't we go faster?"

Brennan tried easing the throttles forward. The pounding was no better and he thought he heard something crack under his feet. He reduced power quickly. "No. She'll break her back if I do."

"We might just make it."

"Where do you want to go, Mr. Gorbachev?" Brennan asked.

"I think, my embassy in Washington."

"Will that be safe?"

"Nowhere is safe at the moment. But I think New York is more dangerous. The Washington embassy is large, and I don't think the conspirators could have persuaded everyone there to betray me."

"All right." Brennan pulled the radio out of his pocket, steering one-handed. "Frank, have you got anything yet?"

"I was just going to call you. I've got a chopper on the way over from the naval air station at Floyd Bennett field, with six of our people in it. We had them on standby, just in case. Also there are two police helicopters heading out there. One of them's got the Russian ambassador on board. Is our guest happy?"

"Very. He wants us to take him to the Soviet embassy in Washington."

"I'll tell Barlow. Have our chopper fly you back to Floyd Bennett; I'll make sure there's a plane."

"Frank," Brennan said. "Timoshkin knew who I was."

"What?"

"I'm telling you, he looked at my badge. He knew my name. His face showed it." The launch buried its bow in a trough. Sheets of water lashed at the windshield, their spatter drowning out Knight's answer. "Never mind. I'm too busy. Out."

Brennan put the radio away and concentrated on handling the boat. He spotted the red and green lights at the entrance to the Coast Guard basin and steered for them. The police launch was twenty yards behind, gaining fast now. But Timoshkin's men wouldn't shoot. They wouldn't risk harming Gorbachev.

Brennan tried to crack on more speed, but the launch wouldn't take it. The police boat was now abeam, ten yards away. Brennan saw men on its foredeck, and the bow swung toward him.

They're going to try to board, he thought. Cut us off, and board at high speed if they have to. They won't ram, though, they don't want Gorbachev in the water.

If he could only reach the calmer water inshore, the launch could outrun the police boat. But he wasn't going to make it. Still. . .

Brennan watched carefully as the police boat converged on the launch. It appeared that Timoshkin was going to try to place the police vessel's starboard bow against the port bow of the launch, using the bigger boat's mass to turn the launch away from the land even as his troopers boarded.

We'll see, Brennan thought. This launch has a better turning circle. I hope. "Hang on!" he yelled over his shoulder.

The police boat cut in at him. Brennan chopped his throttles back and twisted the wheel to port. The launch fell off its bow wave and slowed as though it had run into a sandbar. Simultaneously the stern skidded right, toward the outside of the turn, pivoting the launch almost on its axis and throwing its hull into a forty-degree left heel. Brennan hung on desperately as the boat tried to pitch him across the cockpit. He heard a yell from behind him but didn't dare look back, because the police boat was now visible beyond the launch's bows and almost dead ahead.

Brennan's maneuver had taken Timoshkin completely by surprise. The launch was now inside the police boat's turning circle, and veering the other way. With its greater mass, the police vessel could neither slow down nor turn as quickly as the launch. It swung in a wide arc well outside the launch's new course. A flick of the wheel, and Brennan would be clear and racing for the inshore calm.

"Sean, *Sean,* for Christ's sake stop! *Stop*!"

"What —?"

"Gorbachev's overboard!"

Brennan gave the launch half throttle and spun the wheel the other way. "*Where*?"

"There!" Ennis screamed, pointing. "I see him!"

The lurch as they turned must have thrown him out. Brennan saw him now, face a white blur against the dark waves and the roiled water of their wake. Ennis threw a life ring. It hit the water a yard from Gorbachev. The police boat was turning back toward them.

"Grab his arms as we go by!" Brennan shouted. They'd have one chance. Then the police boat would shove them off and Timoshkin would pluck the Russian leader from the water for himself.

Ennis was leaning over the side of the cockpit, arms outstretched. Brennan centered his helm and sent the launch foaming toward the man in the water. He'd have to almost brush Gorbachev with the hull and pray he didn't get sucked into the props if Ennis missed.

Ennis didn't miss. Brennan saw him grab Gorbachev and, with one frenzied heave, drag the Russian half over the cockpit coaming.

"Go!" bellowed Ennis.

The police boat was just yards away. Brennan rammed both throttles to their stops. Maybe she'd break her back or drive herself under, maybe she wouldn't. Sheets of black water hurled themselves at the windshield. He heard another *crack* from beneath his feet, but the keel held.

Suddenly the water smoothed out. They were inside the wind shadow of the point. The launch stopped plunging and bucking, and picked up speed. It was flying now, planing on the after-third of its hull. Brennan saw lights approaching in the sky, three sets of them to the north: the helicopters. The police boat was no longer gaining.

The launch roared into the Coast Guard mooring basin, the red and green marker lights flying by. The basin was well floodlit. Ahead was a concrete quay, clear of boats, extending about five feet above the water. Brennan maintained the speed as long as he dared and then chopped the throttles, sluing the launch broadside onto the quay in a roar and whoosh of displaced water. The side slammed against the concrete and the launch rebounded. Brennan spun the wheel again, using the rudders to drive the stern back against the quay. "Get out!" he shouted. The police launch was right behind them. He saw Timoshkin on the foredeck. The Russian wasn't giving up.

By the time Brennan reached the launch's stern, Ennis had already heaved a drenched Gorbachev onto the quay and was scrambling up himself. Unpiloted, the launch started swinging away from the concrete. Brennan lunged for a mooring bitt and caught it just as the launch's cockpit coaming slid away from under his feet. Ennis grabbed him by the scruff of the neck and dragged him ashore.

For a moment, he'd lost track of what was happening in and over the basin. The helicopters thundered overhead, invisible against the glare of the floodlights. They'd be heading for the landing pads in front of the naval base administration building, behind the shipping basin.

The police launch was bow-on to the quay fifty yards away, held there by her engines, and Timoshkin and his men were leaping ashore.

"Head for the choppers!" Brennan screamed, and started to run, almost dragging Gorbachev across the asphalt. The helicopters had landed and Brennan could see them ahead, two police machines and a green Huey with civilian markings. Some men were climbing out of them.

"Stop now!" Gorbachev gasped. "I can't run anymore. I see Tretiakov. Now we shall see what happens."

Timoshkin can't force him now, can he? Brennan thought as he slowed to a walk. His escape route's cut, and everybody knows now that Gorbachev doesn't want to go with them. They'd be crazy to try it.

Unless they have orders to kill him.

He looked back. Timoshkin and his men were striding toward them, but their weapons were slung. Nevertheless, Brennan interposed himself between the KGB men and Gorbachev. The small of Brennan's back tingled. If Timoshkin had orders to dispose of him, now was the time he might do it. If he was willing to risk the consequences.

Tretiakov was rushing toward them. He stopped just in front of Gorbachev and relief broke over his face. "Secretary, you're safe!"

"Yes," Gorbachev said. Behind Tretiakov, Knight's men had spread out into a skirmish line. They were carrying M16s, but the guns were slung. No one wanted to chance an accident. "Despite overzealous behavior from the KGB," Gorbachev added. "They were much too concerned for me." He turned around. "Colonel Timoshkin, is it?"

Timoshkin had stopped a short distance away, his men behind him. The Russian's face was inscrutable. "Yes, Comrade Secretary."

"You may put your weapons away. Ambassador Tretiakov will see that I come to no harm. I am leaving here with him, for Washington. I am sure the Americans will provide transport for you, back to your quarters. *Do you understand me*?"

Timoshkin realized that he had lost. I wouldn't like to be in his boots when he gets back to Moscow, Brennan thought. If Chernysh doesn't nail him, Gorbachev will, later if not sooner.

"Yes, Comrade Secretary," Timoshkin replied. He didn't seem unduly concerned. "I apologize for my error. I believed you to be in danger from counterrevolutionaries." He stared at Brennan, his eyes opaque. "I was afraid that this man might be part of the Jan Paderewski Cell."

No one was acknowledging the fact that Gorbachev had fled from Timoshkin. Brennan guessed that no one would, either, until the battle lines were drawn more clearly.

"Ambassador Tretiakov," Gorbachev said, "we can go now. I would like a bath and some decent food as soon as we reach the embassy." He turned to Brennan. "Thank you."

They might try again, Brennan thought. If the leak's high enough to know what's happened here, they might try again. I'm not letting him out of my sight until he goes through the embassy gates. "Mr. Secretary," he said, "I'd like to accompany you to Washington. I feel responsible for your safety."

Gorbachev laughed. He had recovered quickly; Brennan sensed

the steel in the man. "Very well. I would like that. Unfortunately, I don't know your name."

"Sean Brennan, Mr. Secretary."

"And this gentleman?"

"Lee Ennis."

"Good. I owe you both a great deal. Shall we go?"

"Yes, sir. I'll follow you in a moment."

Gorbachev started toward the helicopter, trailed by Tretiakov. Brennan pulled the radio out of his bush jacket. "Park Lane One to Park Lane."

"Park Lane," Knight responded. "Go ahead."

"We faced them down. The target's on the way to Floyd Bennett. I'm accompanying him to Washington."

Brennan heard an exhalation of relief. "I didn't think you'd pull it off. Look, that navy plane won't be ready to go for half an hour yet. I'm going to try to get over there in time to catch it. I've got to take five minutes to report in first. Barlow and Reid will be going nuts. Can you hold the plane for me without annoying a certain party?"

"I'll try to persuade him." Brennan was starting to feel giddy with relief. The world seemed faintly ridiculous. "He owes us one."

"You bet," Knight said. "Park Lane out."

Brennan put the radio away. "Lee?" he asked. "Are you coming?"

"I don't think so," Ennis said. "I'd better go home to bed. With some luck, Ranelagh won't find out what I've been up to."

"Thanks, Lee."

"No problem. It was more excitement than I normally get in an evening."

Brennan laughed and set off after Gorbachev. He looked toward the knot of policemen from the NYPD helicopters, who were standing wary guard over the KGB men.

Timoshkin was watching him. Brennan waved, and kept going.

Andrews Air Force Base, Washington
Sunday, October 6

DESPITE THE HALF-OPEN WINDOWS, the interior of the air force service truck smelled of old cigarette smoke, oil, sweat and damp cloth. Brennan, who was sitting in the front passenger seat, studied the base terminal building through the binoculars. The air force ground crew had finished refuelling the Ilyushin-76 airliner about ten minutes ago; the big machine in its blue, red and white Aeroflot livery stood silently in the drizzly night under the floodlights, apparently deserted. It was ten P.M.

"He should be here in ten minutes or less," said Paige Martin from the jump seat behind them. "Stephen, would you mind if I lit my pipe?"

"Better not to, I think," Reid replied to the secretary of state, from his position behind the steering wheel of the service truck. "I'd like a smoke myself, but we're supposed to be keeping ourselves invisible out here."

"I suppose you're right."

The truck was stopped on the grass at the intersection of the taxiway and the main runway, well away from the flare path and the marker lights. The three men had been there for half an hour. The damp, cold drizzle sifted down out of the night sky and in through the cab windows, which were partially open for ventilation.

"That's not the same plane they had at Kennedy last night, is it?" Brennan asked the secretary of state.

"No," Martin answered. "This one's direct from Moscow this evening. When I saw the president and Gorbachev this afternoon, I asked him how he was going to arrange to get back safely, and he said he was managing it. Nikolai Koblov, deputy chairman of the Council of Ministers, was coming over to get him. I expect he's on the plane over there. I suppose Isayev doesn't dare leave Moscow. There'll be some kind of security escort, but I don't think it's KGB guards on that plane, somehow."

"Probably army or paratroops," Reid said. "If he can trust the army."

"He's going to have to trust somebody," Martin said. "Or he might just as well stay here. The balance is very delicate in Moscow. Have you been watching their media?"

"No," said Reid. "Too busy."

"The key articles in *Pravda* won't be out for some hours yet," said Martin. "But radio and television simply reported he was safe, and that he was returning as soon as possible to deal with serious policy difficulties. That's a very bad sign. It means Chernysh has grabbed a lot of influence over information dissemination. The announcers should have been gushing with ecstasy that Gorbachev was okay. And there have been riots again, inside the Soviet Union this time. The Armenian nationalist movement's raised its head again, and Armenians were fighting Azerbaijanis in Karabakh. Thirty dead. A big demonstration in Kazakhstan against imposed Russification, broken up by security troops. Twelve dead, including two police. A student riot in Poland at Lublin University. The Estonians are calling for a referendum on independence. From inside the Kremlin, it must look as though the walls are about to come tumbling down."

"He's going to have his hands full," Reid said. "He may not survive if we don't give him some kind of help. If he'll take it."

"That's the tricky part. Getting him to believe we want to help."

"I wish we could have hung on to those three JPC men Timoshkin brought out of the safe house," said Reid. "We might have been able to get something out of them."

"How did that happen?" Brennan asked. He'd known about it, but not what was behind it.

"The president was so happy Gorbachev was safe, he forgot about everything else for about half an hour," Martin said. "I wasn't immediately on hand, and he got it into his head that they'd been arrested. They were supposed to be, only Gorbachev screwed up our plans by running away. Everybody was after him, and some of Timoshkin's team got the JPC men out to the Aeroflot jet before we could stop them. By the time Halliday realized the JPC men weren't under arrest, they were on the way to Moscow along with Timoshkin and his crew. We're going to try to get them back, but . . . "

"There must have been more than three JPC men," Brennan remarked. "There had to be five at least, to carry out that massacre at Killenworth, and move Gorbachev to Sheepshead Bay. They're likely out of the country now, apart from those three Timoshkin pretended to catch."

"Probably," agreed Martin glumly.

"You said Parr was there when Gorbachev came to the White House," Reid said to Martin. "He made sure I wasn't invited. What went on?"

"Not a lot. The president made a formal verbal apology for what had happened, which was the main point of the meeting, and they had a very brief lunch together. Gorbachev looked tired, and he was limping. He said that in view of what was happening in Eastern Europe and the USSR, he would have to postpone the summit meeting and return home as soon as possible. Halliday said he quite understood, and they promised to arrange the summit for later."

"Halliday didn't make any comments on the East European situation?"

"No," said Martin. "Parr wanted him to say something about human rights, the jerk, but I scotched it."

"Could you read him? Parr, I mean."

"He didn't say much during lunch, except a couple of platitudes about how glad he was that Mr. Gorbachev was safe. I'd already given him shit, in the nicest possible way, about his human-rights idea, told him that that was the State Department's prerogative and his business was security, so he kept his mouth shut. I did it in front of the president, so he won't forgive me in a hurry. You know what he really thinks."

"Yeah," said Reid sourly. "Get the USSR to the edge of a cliff, and give it a big push. Doesn't he read his goddamned briefings? They'd be a hell of a lot more dangerous if they were tearing themselves apart. Unpredictable. The idea of a civil war over there gives me the willies. But Simon won't see it. He's too fixated on this idea that Gorbachev will turn the Soviet Union into an economic giant like Japan and buy up most of the United States."

"He may be right, Stephen."

"Maybe. But shoving the Russians over a cliff, as I said, is too damned dangerous to contemplate. You're absolutely sure he doesn't know what we're up to? He'd throw a wrench in the works with the president if he could."

"I'm certain," said the secretary of state. "I saw the president alone at two P.M. today, after Gorbachev left to go back to the Soviet embassy. Parr had already gone. I told the president what you wanted to do in Poland, and that it had to be kept under the tightest possible security. He agreed. He was annoyed at Parr, for a change. Simon was too insistent about the human-rights thing before lunch. Halliday was so happy that Gorbachev was still alive he didn't want anything to spoil it. One of the few mistakes Simon's made."

"He made one with Sean, too, didn't he, Sean?" Reid said, looking across the dark cab of the truck at Brennan. "Parr tore a strip off Sean about the operation, and Sean almost popped him one."

"Really?" Martin said. He sounded delighted.

Brennan, who had been listening to the two senior men as he watched the Ilyushin, replied. "Yes. Really."

The recollection infuriated him all over again. During the flight from Floyd Bennett Field down to Washington with Gorbachev, the Soviet ambassador, Orlov, Knight and the CIA security team, he'd been feeling exhausted but wonderful. He'd done it; he and Ennis had freed Gorbachev from the KGB, against heavy odds. Then the plane landed, right here at Andrews, and Reid and Barlow and Parr and a crowd of Secret Service agents, the FBI, State Department officials and Russian diplomatic personnel, all pounced on them. Gorbachev had been spirited away within moments, together with most of the mob, leaving Brennan, Knight, the DCI, Barlow and Simon Parr standing on the tarmac in front of one of the hangars.

"You took one hell of a risk, Knight," Parr began, "sending this cowboy in the way you did. You realize what could have happened?"

"Nobody sent me in," Brennan retorted angrily. The exhilaration had dissipated, leaving him exhausted and depressed. "I was sucked in. They tried to grab him out from under our noses. He ran. I had to do something."

"*Do* something?" Parr shouted at Brennan. "You stupid son of a bitch, suppose they'd started shooting? Suppose he'd been killed. What the fuck did you think you were doing, intervening like that? What business has a low-grade spook got frigging around with the safety of the leader of the Soviet Union? You could have started a fucking *war*, you goddamned asshole!"

The attack was more than Brennan's frayed nerves could take. "You jerkoff!" he screamed back. "You ivory-tower lily-white air-head!" He stepped forward, fists clenched. "Sitting there in your office, giving orders as though —"

He felt Barlow grab him by the arm and pull him away from Parr. "Hold it, Sean," cautioned the director of operations. "Just settle down. You won't get anywhere by slugging him."

"Even if he deserves it," Reid said. His voice was brittle. "You remember the decision, Simon? Right from the White House? Make sure Gorbachev has a chance to decide what he wants to do. Well, he decided with his feet. What was Sean supposed to do? Stop him and turn him over to Timoshkin?"

Parr had regained control of himself, although his voice was shaky. "It was too dangerous. He should have let Timoshkin retrieve Gorbachev. We could still have got him away from them, later."

Reid took out a cigarette, stuck it in his mouth and lit it. "Simon, one of these days you're going to go too far. These three men all work for me. If you've got something to say to them, say it through me. *Is that clear*? Now get lost. We've got things to do."

"You're the one who's gone too far," Parr responded. He was as expressionless as a cardinal walking in a Vatican procession, the fury gone or hidden. Then he had turned and stalked away into the night.

"It's a good thing the DO stopped you from taking a swing at him," Reid was saying. "He'd have had you for breakfast this morning if you'd done that."

"I know," Brennan said, putting the binoculars back to his eyes. His vision was blurring with fatigue. He'd managed to get four hours' sleep on a cot in his office before Knight woke him to tell him that Discus was on the run; Warsaw station had spotted the emergency signal at six A.M., Washington time. Then Knight dragged him off to the meeting with Barlow and Reid to discuss Reid's plan.

At the end of the meeting, Barlow had turned to Brennan and stated:

"Frank says you think Timoshkin knew who you were."

"I don't think it," Brennan said. "I'm sure of it. And he tried to kill me. He knew who I was. Add that to the fact that the Russians knew I was in Paris. We've got a leak."

Barlow looked at Reid. "It's starting to look like it," Reid said. "Okay, we have to take the possibility into account, especially if we get the go-ahead to send Sean in. But, and I emphasize this, the likelihood of a leak is not to be mentioned to anyone without my clearance. We'll start looking, but we're going to look very quietly. That understood? Fine, now I'm going to see the secretary of state to figure out how we can get hold of Gorbachev without being obvious about it."

They *had* figured out how to connect with the Russian leader, which was why Brennan was sitting in the cab of the truck tonight, with the binocular eyepieces jammed against his burning eyelids. He hoped he wasn't too tired to translate properly. Gorbachev could probably have managed in English, but there was always the danger of undetected misunderstanding. "Slugging Parr still would have been worth it," Brennan said.

"He's tougher than he looks, behind that professorial manner," Martin said. "He was in Special Forces in Viet Nam back in '63-'64. He plays a lot of handball, I'm told."

"Did you notice he's got a bad case of eczema on one hand?" Reid asked. "It must itch like the devil. Maybe that's why he's so short in the fuse."

"Nerves," said Martin. "Tough luck."

"Maybe —" Reid began, and then peered into the night. "Something's coming," he said.

Brennan swung the field glasses to his left. Six or seven sets of headlights were approaching from the main gate of the airbase, heading for the parked Ilyushin. The third vehicle was a long black Lincoln. Gorbachev would be in that one.

"Who's handling security?" Brennan asked.

"Secret Service and some KGB officers from the embassy," Reid said. "Even if some of them are in on CONCERTO, they wouldn't dare try anything under those circumstances. It's not assassination they want for him."

"Do you really think he'll stop?" Brennan asked Martin. He kept watching.

A pause. "Is it need-to-know, Stephen?" asked the secretary of state.

"Sean's in this up to his ears," Reid said. "Tell him."

'There was a formal written note of apology as well as the president's verbal one," Martin explained. "I hand-delivered the formal note to Gorbachev myself at six this evening. There was another piece of paper with it. I watched him read both sheets. He thanked me, and put both sheets in his pocket. But he didn't respond either way."

"The door of the plane is opening," Brennan said. "I see troops coming down the stairs. Standard camouflage-pattern uniforms. Heavily armed. Can't tell what service they are from this distance. The badges aren't KGB, though."

"Assuming Chernysh is behind it," Martin said, "he'll know from that alone that Gorbachev suspects the KGB. Otherwise that plane would have Ninth Directorate men aboard, not the military."

"I wonder what Chernysh will do now," Martin said. "Too bad your source in Warsaw had to make a run for it. He might have been able to tell us something."

"These things happen," said Reid.

Brennan, who was trying not to think about Kaminsky running for his life, focused the binoculars a little more precisely and said:

"Gorbachev's getting out of the car now. The soldiers have formed a corridor for him. He's going up the steps. Orlov's waving good-bye. I can see a civilian in the doorway greeting Gorbachev. That must be Koblov." He waited while Gorbachev disappeared inside the aircraft. "Soliders going back in now. Somebody closed the door."

"There's the engines starting up," Martin said. "We'll know in a couple of minutes."

The radio under the truck's dashboard crackled; the Aeroflot pilot was requesting permission to taxi. The tower gave him clearance.

"The escort's back in the cars and leaving," Brennan said. "We'll have him all to ourselves, if he stops."

The Ilyushin was swinging toward the taxiway, the engine's note rising and falling as the pilot jockeyed the throttles to help turn her. In a moment she was rolling steadily along the dark tarmac toward the main runway, silhouetted against the floodlights surrounding the terminal. In the cab of the service truck, no one spoke.

Brennan thought: What is he going to do? Accept our offer of help, or return to Moscow and face the wolves alone?

The Ilyushin had moved almost to the intersection of the taxiway and the runway. The pilot began to turn the big machine into the northwest wind. Brennan heard the engines starting to spool up. The service truck was almost behind the airliner now, and billows of hot exhaust, stinking of jet fuel, rolled in through the cab windows.

He's not going to stop, Brennan thought.

Then, without warning, the howl of the engines lessened. The radio under the dash crackled again, this time with the Aeroflot pilot requesting a hold.

"There it is," said Martin. "He wants to talk. Let's go."

"How long will they let him hold?"

"As long as it takes," Martin said grimly. "The tower was warned to expect this possibility."

The three men got out of the truck and sprinted toward the Aeroflot jetliner. The engines were just turning over now, but the noise as they approached the plane was still deafening. The night wind reeked of jet fuel. When they were fifty yards from the airliner, the forward door, which was set low down on the fuselage, swung out and down to form the boarding steps. Martin hurried up them, followed by Reid, and then Brennan. Inside the boarding vestibule, a crew member stood at the door controls, surveying them with considerable surprise. Behind him were Gorbachev, and another man whom Brennan didn't recognize, almost certainly Koblov.

"Close the door," Gorbachev ordered in Russian. The crew member obeyed, and the door swung up behind them with a hiss and a thump of locking gear. The crewman disappeared hurriedly in the direction of the cockpit.

"Please come this way, gentlemen," Gorbachev said in his

deeply accented English. They really were going to be better off with a translator.

This particular airliner had been fitted out as a VIP machine; instead of having unbroken rows of seats stretching aft, the cabin was sectioned off into compartments. To the left of the entryway and just behind the cockpit was a space for the armed escort; through its partially open door Brennan glimpsed camouflage uniforms. The insignia were those of the paratroops, as Reid had guessed. To the right was a comfortable lounge, and at its rear was another door, which was closed. Gorbachev led them all into the lounge and stopped.

"Nikolai Andreyevich," he said to Koblov, "please wait here. I'll tell you anything of importance later."

"Secretary —" Koblov began in protest.

"*Wait*, Nikolai," said Gorbachev quietly.

"Yes, Secretary."

Gorbachev went to the stern door of the compartment and opened it, motioning the three Americans through. Inside was a working area, with built-in desks and seating. Beyond it and farther along the fuselage, Brennan guessed, would be sleeping quarters. There'd be a communications center toward the cockpit.

"Please be seated," Gorbachev said. He looked at the secretary of state. "As you see, Mr. Martin, I've decided to hear what you have to say. Mr. Brennan I have met. Who is this gentleman?"

"Stephen Reid," replied Martin. "He is the director of the Central Intelligence Agency."

Gorbachev laughed. "Our old enemy. How do you say it? 'This had better be good.' Is that how it is said?"

"Yes, Mr. Secretary," said Martin. "We have a lot to tell you. Mr. Brennan is here to translate."

Gorbachev turned to study Brennan. "I never dreamed," he said in Russian, "that I would see the day when the CIA protected the head of the Soviet Communist Party from KGB conspirators."

He paused for Brennan to translate, and went on, "It could be interpreted differently, of course. There are some who would use the fact to accuse me of being a tool of the United States. I'm taking a considerable risk in meeting you in this manner."

"We know, Mr. Secretary," Martin replied. "But there is a great deal you must know before you go home. It could save your government."

"Tell me, please."

"The director will do so immediately."

The translation was hard work. Brennan labored to pass on the exact meaning of what Reid was telling Gorbachev, which was almost everything: CONCERTO; the Pole who had told them of its existence; the suspicion of high KGB involvement in the conspiracy; the provocations in Warsaw and Prague and Budapest to incite violence and revolt; the threat of a coup in Moscow; the American decision to keep Gorbachev out of the hands of Timoshkin's rescue team if at all possible. The telling took almost twenty minutes, while the engines hummed softly outside the shaded cabin windows. When he had finished, Gorbachev's face was livid with suppressed fury.

"I suspected it," he said. "While I was captive, the possibility suggested itself. As I thought it through, it seemed more and more likely. I had intended to begin reducing Chernysh's power, and somehow he has found out. When Colonel Timoshkin tried to remove me against my wishes, I was certain. That is why I ran."

"Did you know that Timoshkin took the kidnappers back to the Soviet Union early this morning?" asked Martin.

"Yes. That is one of the first things I checked. It makes me certain that Chernysh is behind the conspiracy. If he were innocent, Timoshkin would have killed the kidnappers before Chernysh could have them interrogated. I suppose that might still happen, on the flight back to Moscow. That would cloud the issue. But only a little. I do not believe any of this could have been done without Chernysh's knowledge. Nonetheless, it is going to be very difficult to prove."

"What will you do when you return to Moscow?" Martin asked.

Gorbachev scrutinized the three Americans. "I know," he said, "that the simple answer, which you are perhaps expecting me to give, is that I will order the arrests of Chernysh and Vlasov and work from there, perhaps purge the First Directorate leadership. But I cannot do that."

He seemed to be looking into a great distance for a few seconds. The Ilyushin's engines whined softly, drinking fuel. Then he said:

"I have been trying, since I became general secretary, to enforce the rule of law in my country. Some of our laws may be harsh or arbitrary by your western standards, but there are reasons for them which we understand and you do not. I am a lawyer by training, as you are aware, and I know what happened in Stalin's day, when the law was twisted and overridden to suit his desires. I cannot override the law as he did, or my colleagues will see that I, who have demanded of them that both the spirit and the letter of the law be observed, am as willing as Stalin was to sacrifice justice to a doubtful expediency. They will say: If Mikhail will not obey his principles, why should we? And some of them will also say: If I disagree with him too strongly, will too end up someday in Lefortovo prison? From there it is only a few steps to wondering if I do not perhaps have too much power. And one conspiracy, in men's minds, sets a precedent for another.

"I know that a conspiracy exists and that a crime has been committed, but I have no evidence to give to the procurator general. Without evidence, I cannot order the arrest of these men. I can have investigations begun, and I will, but they will take time. I do not know how much time I have. There are events taking place at home that I cannot tell you about, but they make it plain that the conspirators have been busy. I know, as you have likely guessed, that my political survival hangs in the balance. My main advantage is that my enemies seem to have expected me to be gone for several days longer than this. Their preparations are not complete. I still have weapons with which to fight them."

He ended. Brennan's mouth was dry from both the translation and the tension. Here it comes, he thought.

"Would you," Martin suggested carefully, "consider using the evidence of Discus against the KGB? He says he has documents."

"Documents would be helpful," Gorbachev said. "They would not be sufficient, alone. Much more work would be needed to build a case."

"And if Discus himself were available?" Martin asked.

"If he were," Gorbachev said, "the procurator general's work would proceed much more quickly. Perhaps quickly enough."

He was waiting for us to suggest it, Brennan thought. He wouldn't do it himself; it would be too much like asking for a favor. He's a lawyer. Make the other side commit themselves first.

"I would like to make that offer of assistance," Martin said. "Like yourself, I'm a lawyer by training. I know the frustration of building a case without sufficient information. These men have conspired to commit the crime of kidnapping, after all. They ought to be brought to account for it."

"The problem at the moment," Reid pointed out, "is that Chernysh knows that there was a leak at the very center of CONCERTO. He also has reason to suspect strongly who it is. Fortunately, Discus went underground before he was identified and caught. He's on the run."

"Holy Mother Russia," Gorbachev said. For the first time, Brennan saw the mask of controlled confidence slip.

"It was unavoidable," Reid said. "If we were to find you in time."

"It is necessary to rescue Discus and get him to Moscow before Chernysh catches him," Gorbachev said, recovering swiftly. "Who is he? Where is he?"

"He's in Poland still. But —"

"I know what you are going to say," Gorbachev broke in. "That I cannot trust the KGB to find him and bring him to me. Obviously, that is true." He paused, thinking. "It might be possible to use the GRU, Military Intelligence. It's less likely to have been penetrated by the conspirators."

"It might have been possible," said Reid, "but a short time ago, as I said, Discus went into hiding. Even if you had been able to send your own people before he ran, he'd probably have refused to believe they came from you. It's even more improbable now that he'd accept help from any Russian. It's also possible he might kill himself before allowing himself to be, as he saw it, captured."

Gorbachev gazed at the three men. "Do you have any suggestions for a way out of this impasse?"

"We've discussed it," Reid said. "Mr. Brennan is willing to go in and bring Discus out, with any documentary evidence he may have. Mr. Brennan is the only person Discus is likely to trust, because Discus has met him and knows who he is."

There. It was said. He was probably going to have to go. Maybe he could finish it *this* time.

"I see," Gorbachev said. He turned his brown eyes on Brennan, assessing him. "I have great regard for Mr. Brennan's ability. Is it remotely possible for him to persuade Discus to accompany one of my people to Moscow?"

"I doubt it," Brennan told him, after translating the question.

"I know how people behave when they are running." Including myself, he thought. "They are frightened, and very suspicious. He would suspect I was acting under compulsion. I think the only way he will go to Moscow is if I bring him there. He seems to trust the ability of the CIA to protect him."

"And you are willing to do this?"

"Yes."

"Mr. Gorbachev," Martin said, "it's possible that our involvement in getting Discus to Moscow will become known to some of your colleagues; it's going to be hard for you to avoid it completely. How much harm is there for you in that?"

"If I lose this struggle," Gorbachev said, "Chernysh will use it against me at the inevitable trial. But it will simply mean execution for treason, instead of imprisonment for ideological deviation. I prefer not to rot in Lefortovo prison." He said it flatly, without drama. "On the other hand," he continued, "if Chernysh loses, it actually may do me some good. Do you remember the Reykjavik Summit, when I proposed deep strategic arms cuts, and President Reagan flatly and rudely refused to consider them?"

"Yes."

"That shook my position at home. It is ironic, but my colleagues prefer a general secretary who enjoys a certain amount of American goodwill and support. It makes the world feel less precarious for them. I will present the matter — as and when necessary — in the guise of using my influence with the American government to force the CIA to deliver a key witness in a conspiracy case, a witness who is one of the CIA's most valuable agents. My colleagues will be impressed by my ability to gain cooperation from Washington at the expense of the CIA."

A faint smile crossed his features. My God, Brennan thought as he translated. Lawyers.

Martin looked admiringly at the Russian. "Very clever," he said. "Stephen? How do you feel about that from the Agency viewpoint?" There was amusement in his voice.

"Very clever indeed," Reid said. "As long as nobody on this side of the water agrees with him."

"Only Simon might," Martin said, "and he doesn't know anything about it."

"One question I'd like to ask Mr. Gorbachev," said Brennan. "Is he planning to treat Discus as an apprehended spy?" Before Martin could intervene, he asked the question again in Russian.

Gorbachev looked thoughtful. "He was involved in CONCERTO. He is an SB member, and he worked for the CIA. That much will have to be taken into account."

"But he only approached us after it was impossible to reach you," Brennan explained, without bothering to translate the answer. Martin was frowning at him. "He was guilty of a mistake in timing, that was all. He is on *your side*, Mr. Gorbachev."

"I will take that into account in the instructions to the procurator general," said Gorbachev.

Brennan didn't dare press any further. "What was that about?" Martin asked, with annoyance.

Brennan told him.

"You're here to translate and consult!" Martin snapped. "Not to elicit policy statements."

"Mr. Secretary," Brennan pressed stubbornly, "I'm not going to deliver that man to Moscow and see him end up in Lefortovo in the cell next to Chernysh."

Martin eyed him. "All right. But let me negotiate that, when the time comes."

"Yes, sir."

There was a knock at the door. Gorbachev opened it. Brennan heard voices in a brief, low conversation. The Soviet leader closed the door and returned.

"The pilot is becoming concerned about fuel," he said. "We don't have much more time. How soon will Mr. Brennan be with Discus?"

"We will have to use a clandestine route to get Sean into Poland," Reid said. "He can't go openly, not after what's happened in the last few days. It will take seventy-two hours to reach Warsaw."

"Three days?" Gorbachev exclaimed. "Chernysh may have Discus in his hands in three days. Three days is too long to leave him unprotected."

"It's the best we can do, without unacceptable risk to Sean," Reid said. Brennan nodded. The sea route, through Sweden and the Baltic coastline. Then by train, with false documents, to Warsaw. The land route was possible, but would take even longer and was more hazardous.

Gorbachev's face was closed, pensive. ''Wait,'' he said quietly. ''There is another possibility.''

''What?'' asked Brennan. He waited.

''Mr. Brennan,'' said Gorbachev, ''why don't you try Aeroflot? I happen to have an aircraft right here.''

Moscow – Warsaw
Tuesday, October 8

THE VOLGA STAFF CAR turned off the main highway onto a tree-lined side road, and accelerated sharply. Brennan, in the rear seat behind the driver, flexed his shoulders against the unfamiliar constriction of his tunic, and craned his neck to look out the windshield. On the horizon ahead, reflecting from the low overcast, was a bluish glow.

An airbase, he thought. We came out the Mozajskoye highway and then turned south. It must be the Kubinka base, Soviet Air Defense Command.

The glow drew steadily nearer. On Brennan's left, toward the eastern horizon, was a streak of gray; dawn was coming. The Volga swung around a curve in the road, and a glitter of floodlights appeared from behind the trees.

"Slow down," commanded the major in the front passenger seat, to the driver. "They're not expecting us."

The Volga's speed dropped. Brennan could now see the brightly-lit perimeter fence of the airbase, and the main guardhouse and the gate with its striped barrier. Beyond the perimeter fence hulked the dark shapes of the hangars and the HQ building, which was topped by the squat inverted trapezoid of the control tower. A beacon flashed rhythmically from the tower's roof.

The driver of the Volga braked to a halt a few feet from the barrier. A guard came out of the gatehouse, assault rifle slung loosely over one shoulder. He was carrying a flashlight. The Volga's driver rolled down his window; cold, dry air swept into the car. The temperature wasn't much above freezing.

"Papers, please, Comrade Captain," the guard said to the driver.

"Special consignment," said the major, from the passenger seat. He reached across to the open window, past the driver, and showed the guard a document Brennan couldn't identify.

The guard's eyes flicked to the rear window and noted Brennan's steel-blue uniform and its foreign insignia: the Polish eagle on the cap badge, the three stars and the braid of a full air force colonel on the shoulderboards. "I must check, begging your pardon, Comrade Major," he said.

"Don't you see what's written there, half-wit?" snarled the major. "Are you blind? This is a STAVKA authorization, signed by the Chief of Staff. Can't you read? Do you want ten days in the glasshouse for obstruction?"

The guard stiffened and snapped a salute that would have pleased a Taman Guards Division sergeant-major. "Yes, Comrade Major. My apologies. But we've had orders —"

"Damn your orders. If your captain wants to be particular, maybe he'd like to call STAVKA himself. We'll wait while you tell him."

The guard, who wasn't much over nineteen, gulped and said, "Please drive on, Comrade Major."

He waved to a second guard, who was standing by the barrier. The striped pole swung upward.

"And keep your mouth shut," growled the major as the driver put the Volga into gear.

The guard's reply, if there was one, was lost behind the staff car as it swept under the barrier and started along the road to the HQ building. The major remained silent; he hadn't spoken to Brennan from the time Brennan got into the car, back at Vnukovo airport southwest of Moscow, where Gorbachev's plane had landed.

It had been the most extraordinary flight of Brennan's life, those twelve hours from Andrews to Vnukovo. It would have seemed even more remarkable had he not been so tired; the fatigue gave events a dreamlike cast, as though they were as imaginary as Alice's adventures behind the looking-glass. Gorbachev had shown him the Ilyushin's VIP sleeping quarters, which were just behind the office compartment, and Brennan had thrown himself onto a bunk and tried to sleep. He'd managed to drop off for a while, until the Ilyushin's pilot put down at Gander airport in Newfoundland to refuel. Brennan tried to go back to sleep after the airliner took off again, but he couldn't. He kept wondering what kind of welcome would be awaiting Gorbachev when he reached home: an honor guard and rejoicing at his safety, or a summons to a tribunal that would overthrow him? Or, in the long tradition that reached from Ivan the Terrible to Josef Stalin, both reactions, the second following the first?

Somewhere over the Canadian side of the Arctic Circle, Brennan dragged himself out of the bunk and went to the washroom that adjoined the sleeping quarters. He washed his face and inspected it in the mirror. He was getting a noticeable stubble. There were disposable Swedish razors and tubes of shaving cream in a tray under the sink, so he shaved, and felt better. Then he went back into the sleeping compartment and stood for a moment, balancing himself against the slight sway of the aircraft, and thought: What's he doing? There might be something I could do to help. And anyway, doesn't the man ever get hungry? Surely to God, if I'm going to pull Kaminsky out for him, he could offer me at least a *blini*.

He made up his mind and opened the door to the office. There was no one in it. Brennan shrugged and went through it, opening the door on the other side, the one that led to the lounge area. Koblov looked up at him sharply. The deputy minister was sitting in the chair across from Gorbachev, who was studying a sheet of scribbled notes. Other sheets were spread across the floor, with diagrams and hastily scratched handwriting on them. Koblov leaned over and started gathering up the sheets on the floor, so that Brennan couldn't see them.

"Never mind, Nikolai," Gorbachev said, looking up as well. "Mr. Brennan seems to be one of us, for the moment." He nevertheless reversed the pad he'd been writing on. "I looked in on you just after we took off, after refuelling, but you appeared to be asleep. How are you feeling?"

He's good at it, Brennan thought. Really good at it. He has a talent for making people like him, for going out of his way — or appearing to — to be a friend. But don't forget that that smile has iron teeth. He's a man with a mission, and he'd dispense with me in an instant if he believed it would help Russia.

"A lot better," Brennan said. "Thank you, Mr. Secretary."

"Good. Are you hungry?"

"Yes, I am," Brennan replied.

"Nikolai and I have already eaten. That was why I looked in on you, there was food ready. It isn't very elaborate, it's soldiers' cooking. We don't have flight attendants on board. The major of the security detachment discovered how to work the galley. I'll have another tray brought to you back in the sleeping quarters."

It was a smooth dismissal. They had matters to discuss that they did not want overheard, reasonably enough. "Thank you," Brennan said. He turned to go.

"By the way, Mr. Brennan," Gorbachev asked, "how well do you speak Polish?"

"Fluently," Brennan said. "No accent."

Gorbachev studied him. Brennan felt himself being appraised, evaluated as a tool for the task at hand. Perhaps five seconds passed. Then Gorbachev looked down at his notepad and said, "Thank you, Mr. Brennan. It's a pleasure to work with someone of your talent. We'll make plans in a little while."

Brennan returned to the sleeping quarters. The man never needs sleep, he thought, and never seems to get tired. The Soviet Union hasn't had a leader like him since Lenin, and he knows it. Men like him come along about once in a hundred years, and he knows that, too. Or am I being seduced by his charm and decisiveness and his ability to make one sense one's own worth? Maybe we should ask President Halliday to resign, and see if we couldn't lease Mikhail Gorbachev for a few years.

He grinned at the blasphemous thought, and crawled onto one of the bunks to look out the porthole. The sky was an abyss of black with a haze of stars floating in it; at this time of year, and at this latitude, the sun was rarely above the horizon. If something went wrong with the Ilyushin's engines, they'd all plummet thirty thousand feet to the polar ice cap. Brennan looked at his watch and calculated flight time and distance. Only two or three hours to the northern coastline of Russia.

Would they dare shoot the plane down? he wondered. How far are Chernysh and the conspirators prepared to go?

There was a tap at the connecting door. Brennan got off the bunk and opened it. The far door of the office was already closing, and sitting on the floor was a tray of regulation airline food. Brennan picked it up. They didn't want anyone to see him. So much the better.

He ate, and then fell asleep again, not waking until the Ilyushin was in its final descent toward Vnukovo airport. Koblov was standing over him. The deputy minister's mouth was drawn in with anxiety.

He doesn't know exactly what's going to happen, either, Brennan thought. "What do I do when we land?" he asked.

"You're to stay here," Koblov said with a touch of nervousness. "Don't leave the aircraft, and don't show yourself at any of the portholes. Someone will come for you."

"Yes," Brennan said. He sat up on the bunk. His mouth was dry, from sleep and the pressurized air. The portholes were black again; it would be about six in the evening, Moscow time. "What then?"

"Poland. Arrangements will be made. The Secretary wishes you luck. I was instructed to tell you that."

"I'll do what I can," Brennan said. He looked up at the stiff, cold face of the Russian. Koblov obviously didn't trust him, and didn't like what he was supposed to do. "Minister Koblov," Brennan said, "Please believe me. I want Mikhail Gorbachev to survive. I'll do anything I can to help that happen."

Koblov's face softened a fraction. "Why? You're an American, CIA. The old enemy."

"I'm not an enemy," Brennan said simply. "I'm your ally."

"I do not quite understand," Koblov said hesitantly, "but I realize you saved Mikhail in New York. All right. I will believe you, until you show us differently. Good luck."

"Good luck to you, too," Brennan said.

"Yes," the Russian answered. "I think we are all going to need it."

Then he was gone.

The Ilyushin landed twenty minutes later. Brennan disobeyed Koblov's orders slightly, closing one porthole blind until only a half-inch gap remained at the bottom, and watched as the airliner taxied away from the end of the runway toward the airport terminal. Vnukovo was the VIP airport, and there were no other planes visible, except for a couple of Aeroflot short-haul airliners parked under floodlights on the service aprons in front of the hangars. The place had been cleared for Gorbachev's return.

The Ilyushin swung through ninety degrees to pull up in front of the terminal. As it turned, Brennan caught a momentary glimpse of a double rank of uniformed men ranged on either side of what must be a red carpet, although its color was a deep maroon under the mercury lights of the terminal. Beyond the end of the carpet was a solid block of troops, at least a full company, and a pair of BRDM armored personnel carriers flanking a row of Zil limousines. Brennan squinted, but couldn't make out the identity of the troops. Army or KGB? Impossible to tell. There was a civilian delegation near the limousines, but that could mean anything.

The airliner stopped and the engines subsided into silence. Doors thumped open toward the nose, and a motorized boarding ladder scurried under the glare of the floodlights to disappear beneath the Ilyushin's fuselage. A long pause. Then Brennan saw Gorbachev, with Koblov on his left and a screen of the paratroops around them, walk from under the airliner and pace steadily toward the waiting limousines. One of the civilian reception committee stepped forward, embraced Gorbachev and helped the Soviet leader into one of the cars. Engines roared, and the Zils formed themselves into a column, and set off into the night. The company of troops began to disperse, moving out of Brennan's sight.

He's got this far, Brennan thought, drawing away from his improvised spyhole. Those men must have been army. Now what?

Shortly after the cavalcade departed, the Ilyushin trembled and began to move. After a moment's fright, Brennan realized that a tractor was hauling the plane toward a hangar a few hundred yards from the airport terminal. The tractor dragged the airliner inside, detached itself and left. The interior lights went out, plunging the cabin into darkness. After a few minutes had passed, Brennan found his way to the lounge and opened some of the closed porthole blinds a fraction, to admit a little light from the hangar.

He put his eye to one of the slits he'd made and looked out. There was no one to be seen. Stretching his cramped muscles, he sat down to wait.

Nothing happened after that, for nearly ten hours.

It was about half-past four in the morning when Brennan heard the door to the lounge click open. He'd been dozing in the seat Gorbachev had occupied. He looked up to see a dim shape standing in the light from the portholes.

The figure was wearing a uniform, and was carrying something. Light fell across it as the man walked into the cabin: a suitcase. Brennan stood up, tensed and waiting.

"I was sent," the figure said. "There are clothes in the suitcase. Change into them. Leave your old ones here."

Brennan took the case without speaking and started to change. The man moved restlessly about the cabin; after some observation, Brennan made out the major's insignia on the shoulderboards. Likely GRU, he thought. Gorbachev's managed to get at least some of the military on his side.

"Finished," Brennan said. "Let's go." First time I've ever worn a Polish uniform, he thought.

"This way."

They went down the exit stairs and onto the concrete floor of the hangar. The Ilyushin had been parked close to the side wall, and an outside door was less than fifty yards away. The hangar was deserted. Brennan followed the major through the door. A cold, bitter breeze was blowing outside, sweeping across the runways from the east and whistling around the hangar eaves. Hidden in the hangars' shadow was a Volga staff car.

"Get in," the major said. "We're going."

And Brennan had got in, and that was the last word the major had said to him, all the way out here to Kubinka.

The Volga was nearing the Kubinka HQ block. Somewhere out on the air base, a fighter was being given an engine test, even at this early hour of the morning. The turbines howled and quieted, howled and quieted, and then cut off suddenly. Maybe some sleepless officer had risked his pension by going out and throwing a wrench into the air intake.

Two hundred yards short of the HQ building, the major gestured and said to the driver, "That way." The captain turned left, away from the main part of the base and toward what appeared to be an outlying service area. The staff car crunched off asphalt onto gravel, and lurched along for a quarter of a mile before pulling onto a taxiway and stopping. A little distance farther on was the shape of a medium-sized aircraft. Brennan ransacked his memory for identification, and then had it, because of the way the engine nacelles humped above the high wing: an Antonov-32, a medium utility transport, serviceable and anonymous.

"Time to go," the major told Brennan over his shoulder. He got out of the car and went around to the back, where he opened the trunk. Brennan clambered out of the Volga and stood in the cold predawn air, stretching. He was keyed up, and didn't feel at all tired.

The major removed a bundle from the trunk. "Greatcoat," he said, handing Brennan the garment. "Also, documents." He indicated the briefcase in his right hand. "We will do the briefing on the plane. I will also have to take your picture."

"All right," Brennan said.

The major signalled to the Volga's driver, and the staff car pulled away into the growing dawn light. "Come with me," the major said.

The Antonov's engines began to whine as they approached the plane. The propwash tried to blow the greatcoat from under Brennan's arm; he clamped the garment to his side and followed the major up the boarding ladder to the rear fuselage door. Inside, the sound of the engines was slightly muted, but not by much. The aircraft was a military transport: bare metal floor studded with tiedowns, machinery for the loading ramp, a two-ton electric cargo hoist suspended from a central beam overhead. Toward the front, near the cockpit bulkhead, was a row of metal seats with thin cushions strapped to them.

The major dragged the ladder aboard and slammed the door closed. Brennan heard the engines boom more loudly as the pilot applied the throttle.

"Strap in," said the major. He led the way to the forward seats and settled himself; Brennan did likewise. The Antonov bumped over rough patches of tarmac, heading for the main runway. Then it slowed down and began to turn. Through the porthole next to him Brennan saw the long ribbon of concrete slide into view and then disappear beyond the Antonov's nose.

A few seconds passed, presumably while the pilot received take-off permission from the tower. Then the engines revved into take-off power, the transport rocking against its brakes for an instant, and suddenly the aircraft was hurtling down the runway. Lightly loaded as it was, the plane lifted after a short run, the wheels thumping into their wells. The noise diminished somewhat. Brennan watched the dimly-lit ground recede away beneath him: the soil of Russia.

"How long until we arrive?" he asked the major.

"Three hours, depending on head winds." The major appeared to be in his early thirties; he was blonde, his face round-cheeked and boyish, a wide mouth. But his eyes were not young; they were cool and professional, as unrevealing as a pane of frosted glass. "You will know me as Major Rybalko. It is my responsibility to take you as far as the base of the 20th Soviet Tank Division, outside Prochowice in Poland. Once I get you off the base, it is your responsibility to retrieve your shipment and bring it back to Prochowice, at which time I will arrange for your movement to Moscow." He opened his briefcase and drew out a thick envelope, which he handed to Brennan. "Please open this."

Brennan did so. Inside was a military map of Poland covering the area from Leignica to Warsaw; the Russian army base at Prochowice was marked with a small tank symbol and a red star. There was also a set of identification papers and passes for Air Force Colonel Wladyslaw Nowak.

Rybalko had taken a Polaroid camera out of the briefcase and was fitting a flash attachment to it. "Please move to the bulkhead," he said. "I must have a blank wall behind you."

Brennan unstrapped and did as he was told. The flash popped. Rybalko counted silently, extracted the film and peeled the print away from its backing. He inspected the photograph critically. "It will do. You can sit down again."

Rybalko found a pair of scissors in the briefcase and quickly trimmed the photograph to size. "Give me the paybook," he said. "Do you know which one it is?"

"This," Brennan said, handing over the document.

"Good." Rybalko eyed him speculatively. "You're familiar with papers like these?"

"A little. My knowledge may be a little out-of-date."

"Hmm. Very well." Rybalko opened a small bottle of glue and

with extreme care pasted the photograph into the paybook. "It will take five minutes to dry," he explained, setting it to one side. "Now. We have to go through your documentation."

They started the briefing, which took over an hour. Nowak was an air force liaison officer on the planning staff of the Warsaw Pact military headquarters, situated at Lvov in western Russia. He was on a seventy-two-hour leave, exclusive of travel time. His home was in Wroclaw, and he was travelling to Warsaw as a favor to his Russian commanding officer, to obtain some western goods from the hard-currency Pewex stores in the capital.

"I'm driving?" Brennan asked.

"Yes. Your commanding officer was good enough to arrange the use of a Polonez staff car from 34th Air Army headquarters just down the road, at Leignica. The markings of the car you will actually drive are appropriate."

This has GRU written all over it, Brennan thought. I always knew these people were good, but this is the first time I've seen it from the inside. They can mount an operation in one hell of a hurry, if they need to. How much does Rybalko know? No more than he needs to, of course. He may not even know I'm American, and I'm sure he doesn't know anything about Kaminsky. I'm also sure he prefers it that way.

The sun was well up when they finished the briefing. "When we land," Rybalko concluded, "it will be about 0800. I have orders to wait for you for exactly twenty-four hours, no more. If you have not reached me by eight tomorrow morning, I must assume that you are unable to do so, and you will have to make your own arrangements from then on."

Something decisive is going to happen in Moscow soon, Brennan thought. Gorbachev doesn't have much time.

"I will take you to the car as soon as we land," Rybalko continued. "You know the route to Warsaw, with the Lodz bypass. As I told you, there will be gasoline coupons in the car. The drive to Warsaw is about three-hundred-fifty kilometers, five to six hours. That means you will reach Warsaw around two in the afternoon. Is that timing suitable?"

Brennan thought about the location of Kaminsky's bolt-hole. "No. I don't want to be in Warsaw any earlier than dusk, five P.M. at the earliest. Three hours' extra exposure is too much."

"Remember your deadline," Rybalko warned. "You're losing those three hours."

"I don't want to go in until dusk," Brennan repeated. "I don't want to be in the open any longer than I have to be."

"As you wish," Rybalko said. "In that case, you can remain here in the plane from the time we land until you're ready to leave."

"That's fine. Also, I'm going to need a flashlight, a heavy-duty one. Can you arrange that?"

Rybalko nodded without surprise. "Yes. Now, if you will excuse me, I am going to sleep for a while. You might do the same."

Rybalko bundled up his overcoat, sandwiched it between his head and the side of the fuselage and closed his eyes. The engines drummed steadily; below, the landscape passed slowly by, gray-brown with the autumn haze and the stubble of wheatfields. It would still be the middle of the night over there on the other side of the world, and Molly would be sleeping in her bed in the house in Orchard Cove, high above the beach. Brennan imagined her there, the long eyelashes against her cheeks, her quiet breathing, rhythmic like the waves of the Atlantic rolling in and out against the shore. Where did she think he was? Had she given up trying to guess?

If I live through this, he thought, I'll have used up my life's ration of luck. Maybe, if I stay put in Orchard Harbor, I won't need it anymore.

Like Rybalko, he put his coat under his cheek, and eventually drifted off into a troubled, dream-fragmented sleep.

"We're landing," Rybalko said.

Brennan opened his eyes. The porthole's plastic was right in front of him, and the plane was in a bank. He was looking almost straight down at the ground, from about two thousand feet in the air. He felt a surge of vertigo, which vanished as he straightened in the seat.

"Reset your watch," Rybalko said. "It's exactly two hours earlier here."

Brennan did so. He was slightly groggy, but could sense that when he awoke thoroughly, he'd be refreshed and alert. The sleep, broken though it had been by dreams, had done him a lot of good. He tried to remember what he'd been dreaming about, but couldn't.

The Antonov was turning into its landing approach now, heading for the small airstrip that served the base of the 20th Soviet Tank Division. The 20th was one of two Russian divisions stationed permanently on Polish soil; for a long time the Poles had wanted the two big combat formations to go home, but Moscow, even under Gorbachev, had always been unwilling to take that risk. Poland was too volatile a nation, and always had been. The Russian forces were careful to keep a low profile, but they were there, fully armed and at full strength, and everyone in the Polish armed forces, Party and government was acutely aware of the fact.

The Antonov bumped to earth and the pilot instantly put the propellers into reverse pitch; the airstrip was none too long, even for a STOL transport like the Antonov. As soon as the plane had slowed to the pace of a running man, Rybalko got out of his seat, pulled on his overcoat and carefully locked up his briefcase. "Could you help me with the ladder?" he asked.

The transport was slowing to a crawl; the concrete-block structures of the tank base were visible through the portholes. Brennan spotted a medium-sized sedan in air force colors parked near the end of the taxiway; there was no one in it. "That's the car?" he asked Rybalko as they wrestled with the boarding ladder.

Rybalko ducked his head to look out. "That's it."

The transport stopped and the engines switched off. Rybalko threw the door open with a thud. Bright autumn sunlight and a chilly breeze poured into the cabin. "It goes into the catches there," Rybalko said, meaning the ladder. They maneuvered it into place. "I'll be back for you at eleven."

"I'll be here," said Brennan.

The Russian looked at him oddly, and left. Brennan returned to his seat to wait, but became restless after a few minutes. He got up and wandered around the hold of the aircraft. There was nothing of much interest in it. A metal storage bin was welded to the cockpit bulkhead over on the port side of the hold, but it was locked. Brennan resigned himself to boredom, and took his seat again.

Rybalko returned on the dot of eleven. "You have everything?"

he asked Brennan. "Papers, billfold, money, driving license, petrol coupons, sidearm?"

Brennan checked. "Yes. It's all here." There was an extra clip of ammunition for the PM63 automatic as well. He slipped the gun into the right pocket of the overcoat, and the clip into the left.

"Come on."

Brennan, breathing deeply of the crisp air, followed the Russian down the ladder. It was a perfect day; Brennan was almost looking forward to the drive to Warsaw. Rybalko had brought with him a four-cell military flashlight. It provided a good, bright beam.

"Is that satisfactory?" asked the Russian.

"It's fine."

Rybalko handed Brennan the keys and they got into the car. It was a Polonez, a recent Polish model, and most of the controls were obvious, except for the heating and ventilation. Never mind, he'd figure it out later. He started the car and let it warm up for a moment.

"The main gate's that way," Rybalko said, pointing toward a cluster of buildings half a kilometer away. Off to the right of the buildings was one of the base's vehicle parks, crowded with T-80 tanks and self-propelled artillery. A column of men was marching briskly along the fence surrounding the park. Brennan put the Polonez into gear and started off in the direction Rybalko had indicated.

"Just drive up to the gate and stop," Rybalko said as they neared it. "I'll get out there and clear you onward. When you come back, simply stop at the guardhouse and have them ask me to come out to get you."

"All right," Brennan said, letting the car slow to a stop. "Until later, then."

"Until later," Rybalko said. He got out and closed the door solidly. "Good luck."

"Thanks," said Brennan. Rybalko conferred briefly with the guard at the vehicle barrier, who snapped a salute and swung the striped pole upward. Brennan drove underneath it. He was on his own.

He picked up Highway 12 on the east side of Wroclaw, and drove without stopping almost as far as Lodz, which he skirted using the Pabianice bypass. He paid careful attention to traffic behind and in front of him, and by the time he reached the bypass, he was sure that he was not under surveillance. This was an industrial area of the country, and the air was blurred with the haze of pollution from the dozens of textile mills and electrical engineering and chemical plants. The breeze through the car's dash vents had an acrid tang, and Brennan was glad when the industries began to thin out. Eighty kilometers from Lodz he was in the Mroga river valley, and only an hour and a half from Warsaw.

He was hungry and stiff by this time, and when he reached Lowicz he decided to stop for a break. He parked just off Kosciuszko Market Square and went looking for something to eat. He wasn't the only one; all the bakeries and butcher shops he found had long lines in front of them. Since the rioting in Warsaw and the other big cities, the food supplies had become sparser, and deliveries to the state stores more erratic. The people in the lines looked glum and harried, especially the women. His air force uniform brought dark looks from some of the men. It was a mark of a fundamental change in Polish attitudes. Until recently, the military had been well-regarded by the population at large; Poland remembered the tradition of the Home Army that had fought the Germans in the Warsaw Uprising in 1944, and the valiant, doomed defense of the country in 1939. Now that was changing; the military was taking on the colors, in the popular view, of oppression.

The looks made Brennan uncomfortable, and he didn't have time to join the lines. He returned to the car — someone called quietly after him as he left, "Why don't you butt in at the front, like your Russian friends?" — and took the E8 highway out of town. There'd be more food available in Warsaw, most likely, since it was the capital.

He drew nearer to his destination as the shadows lengthened: Sochaczew with its ruined castle of the Dukes of Mazovia overlooking the river, Paprotnia, Blonie and its incongruous juxtaposition of precision instrument factories and medieval facades. Then the last stretch before Warsaw, mile after mile of vegetable fields, all barren now after the harvest, except for places where winter cabbages still grew.

He bought gas just outside Warsaw and entered the capital, still on the E8, driving in through the industrial district of Wola. It was rush hour, and the traffic was heavy; Brennan sweated his way through it, worrying about what might happen if he was involved in even a minor accident. Despite the upheavals of the last two weeks, Warsaw appeared to be carrying on business as usual, but there were army posts at all the main intersections, and several times he saw OT-65 armored cars rumbling along in the traffic, commanders standing upright and alert in their turrets. Occasionally there were also ZOMO patrols, recognizable by their dark-blue combat fatigues. The faces of the civilians were closed off, sullen. Beneath the composed and tranquil countenance of the city, Brennan sensed, was a dark lake of resentment and bitterness that could erupt into violence with very little warning.

He considered parking at the Central Railway Station, but when he drove past he saw that the building was heavily patrolled by militia. He didn't want to travel too far from the area shown on the map Kaminsky had given him in the sewer, so he drove back north and finally located a space in a parking lot near the Chlopa Hotel. There was still a lot of light in the sky; he didn't want to move toward Kaminsky yet. He went into a nearby cafe for something to eat, and discovered that all they had besides coffee and vodka was dark rye bread, a few pastries and pearl barley soup. He ate bread and soup and finished it off with coffee and a jam pastry; it was a lot better than nothing, although he had a craving for solid meat and potatoes. He wondered what Kaminsky was eating, if anything. The Pole had been on the run since Saturday, and it was Tuesday evening now. He'd said he was prepared, but by now he'd be starting to worry.

Brennan paid the bill, and went back out into the street. It was nearly dark, and by the time he'd walked to his destination, the dusky light would be completely gone. He went back to the car to get the flashlight.

Kaminsky woke to the sound of dripping water. He opened his eyes; there was no difference in what he saw. He wondered whether he had been found, drugged in his sleep and carried off to the cells under the SB building in Pulawska Street.

No. There would be a light glaring down from the cement ceiling, for one thing, and he wouldn't hear the drip of water. And they wouldn't take him to Pulawska Street, either; there were too many people there who didn't know about CONCERTO. It would be one of the safe houses in the outlying districts, where Vlasov would peel open his brain layer by layer and then — soon — execute him.

He was lying on his back, head against the bundle of clothes and supplies that formed his escape kit. Beneath the blanket on which he lay, the stone was cold and hard. He fumbled in his trousers pocket and drew out his cigarette lighter, propped himself up on one elbow and flicked the wheel against the flint. The tiny scrape echoed through the darkness, but there was only a brief spark and no flame.

He could find his way out in the dark, probably, and there were matches in the escape kit. Nevertheless, a cold, primitive fear coiled and uncoiled in his stomach. He marvelled at it in a detached way; the feeling was perhaps like having swallowed a live snake.

He tried the lighter again. This time the tiny yellow flame sprang into life. It was painfully beautiful there in the dark, the blue crescent just above the wick, the blurred triangle of flame shading to white and then yellow and orange. Its radiance glimmered on the damp roof of the sewer arching over him. Kaminsky studied the flame for a second or two before drawing the oil lamp toward him and touching the lighter to its wick. A second, larger flame illuminated the cramped stone chamber in which Kaminsky lay.

He extinguished the lighter and sat up, stretching and yawning, checking his watch. Seven in the evening. Tuesday. Three days had gone by, more than two of them since he'd slashed the pair of chalk lines on the lamp post in front of the Staszica Palace on Nowy Swiat. He'd spent a lot of the time sleeping, down here in the dark, and he felt as dirty as the sewer itself. Rats had run over him as he slept, but so far he hadn't been bitten. Surely to God the American was going to be here soon.

He opened the metal box that protected his food and water supply against the rats, unwrapped a length of kabanos sausage, and raised it to take a bite. With the food halfway to his mouth, he stopped.

A noise in the passage outside, echoing from some uncertain distance. Metal on stone.

Kaminsky instantly dropped the sausage and blew out the lantern. Pitch-blackness surrounded him. He waited, watching the mouth of the low and narrow corridor that led from his chamber out to the sewer line beyond.

He hadn't imagined it. A rat squeaked outside. A barely visible glow gradually outlined the mouth of the entrance. Someone was approaching, with a light. The American? Perhaps; perhaps not.

Kaminsky felt around among his possessions until he found the automatic, and began creeping on hands and knees up the passage. The chamber in which he was living was very old, and he had no idea why it was there. It was connected to the storm sewer line by the sloping passage through which he was now making his way; the passage was short, barely six yards long and no higher, and it exited into an alcove beyond which was the sewer walkway. The entrance to the passage was very difficult to spot if you were heading north along the main tunnel; from that approach, the alcove was hidden behind a buttress, and the passage mouth was no more than a black shadow low down on the alcove's back wall.

Kaminsky stopped crawling ten feet from the entrance, just far enough up the tunnel's slope to be able to see through the alcove into the main sewer. He waited quietly, listening. Blood thudded in his eardrums. The light outside grew stronger.

He heard footsteps, those of men trying to walk softly on stone. And then a faint whisper. More than one, then. Therefore not likely the American.

He squinted through his narrow viewing field. A light flashed brightly outside, and he saw two pairs of military-issue boots reflecting its gleams from their wet leather. Above the boots were trousers of dark ZOMO blue.

Kaminsky gritted his teeth with frustration. They had started checking the sewers much earlier than he'd hoped. But he was fairly sure that the SB men who had pursued him into the church couldn't have seen any traces of him in the drainage tunnel; the floor had been free of deposits that could have held tracks. It was much more likely the ZOMO patrol was searching the sewers purely as a matter of course, and that his original SB pursuers hadn't realized he'd gotten into the tunnel by way of the church. Jurys must have issued a political-fugitive warrant to the militia and ZOMO, as well as to the SB surveillance directorate. They'd all have been told he was a traitor and a potential defector.

The footsteps stopped, the booted legs of the searchers now out of sight. Kaminsky realized that he was holding his breath, and went on holding it. He heard an unintelligible conversation outside, the words masked by echoes. They weren't likely enjoying this; they didn't know the tunnels, and the mazes down here were perfect for ambushes. They wouldn't search any more vigorously than they absolutely had to, or so Kaminsky hoped.

The hope was justified, at least for the moment. The voices ceased and the footsteps moved on. Kaminsky exhaled very softly, and then drew several deep breaths. They hadn't found him, but that was the only good part. If the American came to get him out now, and they crossed paths. . .

Kaminsky scrambled back down his tunnel into the dark. There was only one thing to do. He'd have to move closer to the church crypt entrance, using the chamber as a support base, and keep watch there. It was more dangerous, with the searchers about, but it was better than having the American run into them before he reached Kaminsky. At least there hadn't been any rain since he came down here, and the tunnels were dry.

He waited for half an hour, lit the lamp and began to assemble the few things he'd need for his first watch.

Exhibiting a calm he did not feel, Brennan walked up the front steps of the church and tried the handle of the smaller door set into the right-hand leaf of the big wooden main ones. It wasn't locked. He opened it and stepped through. The interior was dimly lit by chandeliers hanging from the roof far above, and by the flames of candles among the columns. A few worshippers prayed here and there, most of them, at this hour, older people.

He pictured Kaminsky's map in his imagination and oriented himself. Up there, all the way to the apse, among the saints' chapels. He started to walk, his boot heels clicking on the worn flagstones, keeping to the row of columns on the right of the nave. Ten meters, twenty. An old woman lighting a candle in front of a statue of St. Alexander glanced at him curiously for a moment, but then returned to whatever prayer she was offering.

Say one for me, too, Brennan thought as he walked on. Candles. Lights. I hope that army flashlight in my pocket has fresh batteries. I wonder how long they're good for? There is no fallback, what will I do if he's not where he said he'd be?

If he isn't there, he likely didn't make it, and I'll have to go back alone.

Brennan had reached the transept now and was walking across the center of it, toward the sanctuary. He decided to use a candle for the first part of his journey into the sewers, and save the electric light as much as possible. He spotted candles on a table nearby, and lit one after dropping a couple of coins into the offering box. Then he walked steadily into the side aisle behind the choir. The saints' chapels, more candles, flames motionless in the still air, as if painted on the gloom.

He found the crypt entrance without difficulty, and opened the door. The black stairwell gaped at him. Brennan suppressed a shudder and stepped down into it, closing the door quietly behind him. The candle flame flickered on the damp walls. He went down the steps quickly; his light advertised the fact that someone was coming, and if he was awaited there was no help for it.

There was no one in the crypt aside from himself, and the dead. He consulted the map mentally again. He was supposed to go over against the far wall, behind the high platform on which a tomb rested. The silence of the crypt was abyssal; he could hear the rush of blood in his ears, and the soft whisper of his breath moving in his throat.

He saw the grill, low down in the wall. It should be loose.

It was. He pulled it out of the wall and looked into the entrance it protected.

He wants me to go into *that*? Brennan thought. He had a vision of something wet and slippery, with teeth, waiting for him at the other end of the passage.

And there are monsters under my bed at night, he told himself. He pulled the heavy flashlight out of his overcoat pocket, and checked the action of the PM63 in the candlelight. Then he switched on the flashlight and blew out the candle, slipping the stub of wax and its glass holder into his left pocket.

Like Kaminsky, he had to enter the channel backward to close the grill after him. That done, he wriggled farther back until, with a lurch of his stomach, he felt the floor disappear from under his shins. He reminded himself that the drop was shown on the map, and eased himself down until he was standing on the walkway of the tunnel. Then he flashed the light around. There'd been a lot of water in here a little while ago; he could see muddy striations running horizontally along the tunnel walls, and there were glistening black pools of water lying on the sewer floor, which was an arm's length below the platform on which he stood.

The next stage of the route, as he remembered from the map, led into the opening of the low tunnel across from him. He jumped down to the muddy sewer floor, crossed to the entrance, stooped almost double and went in. The channel sloped up a few degrees from the horizontal. Ahead, in the beam of the lamp, Brennan could see that the sewer opened up. He reached the wider area and realized that he was in a manhole shaft. He listened for traffic overhead, but heard nothing. A side street, or perhaps the shaft was closed off.

Next stage, up into that other entrance. It was beginning to look like a long night.

Kaminsky paused, listening, and turned off his flashlight. Through the soles of his feet he felt a vibration, that of some heavy vehicle on the street overhead. Military, most likely. Maybe they were sending the tanks in already.

It might have been the vibration that had touched off his internal alarm, which was becoming more sensitive with every hour he lived down here. In time, he might become eyeless and damp and pale, guided only by smell and touch and hearing, like those fish that lived in subterranean lakes.

I'm not going to be here *that* long, he thought, half amused at the random image. I hope.

The vibration ceased and he listened some more. Very faint, but unmistakable: a voice. And light, back toward the way he had come. They were coming this way, either the two policemen he'd seen before, or another search party.

He'd have to move. This trunk line ran in a long curve toward the northeast, ending at a T-junction, which contained a manhold shaft. There was nowhere to hide, unless he went all the way back to the crypt drainage channel and crawled up into the crypt. On the other hand, they might turn away from him at the T-junction. He'd have to chance it. If they came after him, the crypt would be the best bet. At worst, he could scuttle up into the church and hide there.

He shielded his light with his fingers before turning it back on, and began trotting along the curve of the tunnel. Here it was fairly low, and he had to keep his head down to avoid striking it on the roof. Mud squelched under his feet.

Just short of the T-junction he paused to listen again. They were back there still, and he could see the gleam of their lights reflecting from the wet bricks. They were moving fast, almost as fast as he was, probably on their way out and anxious to be on the surface again. Which way would they have entered? By a street manhole on Marszalskowska, most likely; they wouldn't have to worry about concealment. That would mean they'd turn away from him at the junction. Maybe.

He went on to the junction, hurrying faster now, and turned left. This section of the sewer was straight as a rule for one hundred fifty feet; he sprinted along the straight stretch and halted just around the first bend.

Christ in Heaven. They'd turned left, as he had.

He whirled and ran for the next junction, which was the manhole shaft he'd struggled into after escaping the flood. At its bottom was the passage that led down to the large trunk where the crypt drainage channel emptied. He'd have to move fast, to get through the drainage channel and replace the grill before they caught up with him.

They'd be around the bend behind him any second. He turned off his light, not daring even the faint glow that escaped from between his fingers. They might not spot him as they rounded the bend; it was a long way back now, and these dank rough walls absorbed light. He'd be into the shaft and down it before they knew he was near.

The light behind him intensified suddenly. They'd rounded the bend.

Oh, Mary, *no*!

Light was spilling from the manhole shaft ahead of him, right into the tunnel. Somebody was in there. He heard a yell from behind, and a shot. The bullet snapped by him and ricocheted off the brickwork. Kaminsky started running in a crouch, flicking the safety catch of the automatic. He'd try to shoot his way past the man in front of him, get him as soon as his head appeared in the entrance to the shaft.

The light in the shaft suddenly went out.

The American, Kaminsky thought. If it was militia, he'd be illuminating me for the ones behind. "Discus!" he shouted, and the echoes broke the cry into fragments and tossed it back and forth along the tunnels.

The American heard him. "Okay!" came a low reply, in English.

Another shot from behind, and again the whine of a ricochet.

Idiot, Kaminsky thought as he hurled himself into the manhole shaft, just managing to grab the rusty iron ladder. If he was on full automatic. . .

The militiaman might have been listening to him; there was a short burst of automatic fire from above and several bullets walloped into the brickwork over Kaminsky's head as he scrambled down the ladder. Fragments of mortar stung his scalp, but mercifully no bullets came bouncing down the shaft.

He hit bottom, disoriented. "Where are you?" he cried.

"Here!"

A light snapped on for a fraction of a second, just enough to show Kaminsky the entrance to the tunnel, and the American crouching in it, incongruous in a blue uniform. *Air Force*? Kaminsky wondered as he ran, doubled over, into the tunnel after the American. How did he manage that?

Another flash of light as the American tried to decide where they were. Almost at the main trunk. They scrambled out into the sewer line and stopped. Kaminsky heard heavy breathing in the dark, his own and the American's, and scrapes and clatters from the manhole shaft as at least one of the militiamen hurtled down the ladder.

"We have to get rid of them," Kaminsky whispered. "If the alarm's raised —" He wondered whether the American was going to make a fuss about killing.

"All right," came the answering whisper. "How?"

"Down here." He tugged at the American's arm. "Feel the wall. The walkway ends ten meters on and there's cover."

They hid behind the slab of masonry that projected into the sewer line, and waited. The militiamen were being more cautious, now; they'd assume their quarry was armed. But would they know there were *two* men waiting for them? The American had had enough sense to keep his voice down when he called out.

The light went out. There were scuffs and whispers from the side tunnel. Brennan, crouching beside Kaminsky, thought: If they're smart, they'll go for help. Tear gas. But they couldn't use it down here, unless they've got masks. Have they?

The darkness was suddenly torn apart by the muzzle flashes of a weapon firing on full automatic. Bullets slammed into the masonry protecting Brennan and the Pole, shrieked off the tunnel walls and screamed into the distance. Kaminsky emitted a gurgling cry and rolled away from Brennan onto the open tunnel floor.

Oh, Jesus, he's been hit, he must have had his head up. All this way, for nothing.

Light flooded the tunnel. Brennan scooped up mud from the floor and smeared it on his face, and then put one eye carefully around the edge of the walkway. An arm had emerged from the side tunnel, holding a lantern. Below it, a white face peeped anxiously into the open, ready to withdraw at the first sign of movement. The militiaman saw the prone body, its arms outstretched in an attitude of crucifixion on the bottom of the sewer, and relief spread over his face. "He's down!" he exulted.

"Put another one into him," replied another voice.

"No, it's all right. He's flat on his face."

The two men emerged from the side tunnel, weapons ready. They moved warily toward Kaminsky. Brennan watched, not breathing, not daring to draw back for fear the movement would reveal him despite his blackened face. They would see him as soon as they reached Kaminsky.

Wait. Wait.

They slung their weapons, careless with relief.

Brennan fired from behind the masonry pier, clutching the automatic in both hands. His first shot hit the right-hand militiaman in the chest. Brennan changed targets, and his second bullet struck the other man in the solar plexus as he tried to train his gun on the barely visible American. Brennan shot him again, this time in the forehead, and once more changed targets. His fourth bullet hit the right-hand militiaman an inch from the first, and pierced the heart. Echoes fluttered and died; the stink of explosive mingled with the dank reek of the sewer. The militiaman's fallen lantern reflected dully from the pools of water on the tunnel floor.

The two victims were quite still; Brennan lowered the gun. He looked down at Kaminsky, feeling sick. I'll see if he's wounded, Brennan thought, but I don't see how I can get him out if he can't manage on his own. He got up and leaned over the Pole.

Kaminsky raised his face from the mud. Not a head shot, then. "Where did they hit you?" Brennan asked. "Can you turn over?"

"They didn't hit me," Kaminsky answered. He sat up. "We had to draw them out, somehow. There was a good chance they didn't know there were two of us. I didn't know what else to do, and there was no time to discuss it."

"You SOB," Brennan said, in English. He didn't know whether to hit Kaminsky, or hug him.

"What?" Kaminsky said.

"Never mind," he said, switching to Polish. "You're crazy."

"I'm Polish," Kaminsky replied, with dignity. "Your face is muddy. We'd better clean up before we leave. I have to go back to the hiding place, there are things there I need. Help me get these men out of sight. They'll be missed soon."

Camp David, Maryland
Tuesday, October 8

WHAT AN ABYSMALLY STUPID TIME to go on a working retreat, Parr thought, as he watched the president tramp cheerfully up the flagstone path toward the veranda of the lodge on which Parr was standing. Beyond the president, the woods were incandescent with October color in the late afternoon sunlight. One tall maple at the edge of the woods appeared to burn without being consumed.

Parr looked down at the surgical glove on his left hand. The eczema had been much worse this morning, and the ointment caking his skin under the glove didn't seem to help. The rash was spreading up his wrist as well, and it seemed to be trying to infect his right hand. Nerves strung far too tight, like fiddlestrings, as his long-ago divorced Rose would have told him in that hectoring tone of hers. Why don't you do something about it?

Because I can't, he snapped back at her memory. I'm committed to a position, and I'm not going to change it, or feed myself tranquilizers to make it feel better, either. I just wish I could get a little sleep.

To make matters worse, he knew Reid was up to something, Reid along with the secretary of state, something to do with Gorbachev. Halliday let it slip at the Monday cabinet meeting, just before leaving for Camp David: *There are still things we can do to help Gorbachev*, he'd said. And Parr had seen the warning glance Reid shot at the president, and the president's hasty, "If we choose to do so," directed not at Reid but at Martin.

Parr had elected not to pursue the matter; Halliday was in a hurry to leave, and Parr was afraid he was still annoyed about Parr's attempt to bring up the human-rights matter at the Halliday-Gorbachev luncheon on Sunday. That had been a mistake, looking back. Poor judgement.

Today, though, the president seemed to have forgotten the incident. But Parr had to return to Washington in an hour, and he was going to have to exert some pressure on Halliday to keep the president on a consistent policy track. If only Reid would stay away for just a little longer. He was due out here soon, but maybe he'd be delayed.

The hope dwindled as Parr heard the drumming of a helicopter off to the east. That was probably Reid. Halliday had stopped halfway along the flagstone path, and was scanning the bright sky with his head thrown back and his eyes shaded with one hand.

Trying to look like the heroic captain of the ship of state, Parr thought. The nitwit.

''Hello, Simon,'' the president said cheerfully as he reached the veranda. ''About ready to be off?''

''Nearly,'' said Parr. The helicopter had set down on the pad just beyond the guest cottages to the east; the machine was out of sight, but Reid would be getting out of it right now. ''It's a beautiful day,'' Parr observed.

''Indeed it is,'' the president drawled. He was wearing a blue work shirt, and jeans with a wide leather belt and a big silver buckle with a carving of a longhorn steer's head on it. Just down-home folks out here at Camp David, Parr thought.

''Something on your mind, Simon?'' Halliday asked briskly.

''Yessir.''

''Mr. Gorbachev, isn't it?''

''Yes, Mr. President. I —''

''I don't see what we've got to worry about, Simon,'' Halliday interrupted. ''Gorbachev's home, we're in the clear as far as he's concerned, and it's his problem what happens over there next. The Russians have shut down their alert, like we have, and so what's on your mind?''

Reid was walking around the corner of one of the guest houses. ''Mr. President,'' Parr argued, ''I strongly suspect that we're still interfering with internal Soviet politics. I think that's dangerous, at this juncture.''

Halliday eyed him uncertainly. "Why?"

"You know my views, sir. That we should leave them alone to sink or swim. If we are trying to help Mr. Gorbachev in some way, and he loses and the winners find out we were assisting him . . . well, they won't look very kindly on us. And here at home we'd be accused of playing fast and loose with the nation's safety. It could lose us the next election."

That hit the target. Halliday wanted two terms in office.

"Are you saying we should pull back?" Halliday asked.

So there *was* something going on. "I think so, sir. It would have to be your decision. But I respectfully suggest, Mr. President, that I can't advise you properly if I don't have all the information I need. I am, after all, your national security adviser, and it's my job to see the largest picture possible. The DCI is a specialist, with a precise but narrow view."

Halliday looked even more doubtful. He had a latent distrust of experts, since they often gave him more information than he could use or understand. "I need to know what's happening, sir," Parr finished, weighting his tone with calm reasonableness. "I can't serve you properly otherwise."

"Well, all right, Simon," Halliday said just as Reid approached. "You've got a point. A very strong point."

"What point is that, Mr. President?" Reid asked, in a comradely manner. "If it's anything to do with me, that is."

"It is, it is," Halliday replied. He looked nervously from Reid to Parr and back again. "Simon believes we've been holding back on him, and he's upset about it. That makes sense. He can't do his job if he doesn't know what's going on. I think we made a mistake to keep him out of the Warsaw operation, even for security reasons."

Reid closed his eyes briefly, as if praying, and then opened them again. "Mr. President, we *agreed*."

"Well, I'm changing policy," Halliday said stubbornly. "I think Simon's got to know. Okay with you if I go ahead and tell him?"

"Mr. President, I respectfully request —"

"He needs to know, Director."

"Yes, Mr. President."

A squirrel chittered in the autumn woods behind Halliday; crows were calling among themselves. "Well, Simon," Halliday said, "it's like this. We did decide to give Mr. Gorbachev a helping hand. We sent an agent to Warsaw to extract the man who told us about the conspiracy. Our man should be there right about now, and will have him back in Moscow within about twenty-four hours."

"And what, Mr. President, is this supposed to achieve?" Parr managed to keep his voice even.

"It'll give Mr. Gorbachev the lever he needs to stop the plotters and clean out the KGB, everyone who was remotely connected with the conspiracy, inside and outside the Soviet Union. He'll survive. He'll have to be grateful to us, which means we'll be able to get concessions out of him."

"I see," Parr replied. He'd rarely felt such rage. He was the chairman of the National Security Council, chief security adviser to the president of the United States, and the spooks at Langley had been going over his head in nothing less than a power grab. He would have to push for complete information, and now, or he'd lose a fatal amount of bureaucratic face.

"Might I *possibly* have some more details?" he asked sarcastically. "Who's our man over there? Who's the Polish agent? How are they getting out? How are they getting to Moscow? Anything could go wrong, Mr. President, and I have to be prepared for all contingencies."

"The details aren't your concern," Reid broke in.

"Mr. President," Parr countered, "I'm your national security adviser. I think they *are* my concern. Suppose there are political factors the DCI knows nothing about? Suppose the operation fails, and it's made public over here, and it costs you the next election, as I said earlier? A Bay of Pigs, only much worse, because here we're interfering with Russia, not Cuba."

"Simon's right," conceded Halliday. "You'd better give him all the data, Stephen."

"Mr. President, I respectfully decline to do so."

"*What?*"

"That's what I said, Mr. President."

The crows cawed. Parr noticed how the sunlight was highlighting the roughness of the tree trunks at the edge of the wood.

"Tell him," Halliday commanded. "And me. That's a direct presidential order. You work for *me*, Director."

"No, sir. I won't."

"Why not?" Halliday asked, in a tone of sweet reason. Underneath it, Parr knew, he was furious.

Reid took a deep breath. "Mr. President, can I tell you alone?"

"No. We all have to work together on this. We're supposed to be a team, Director, in case you'd forgotten."

"Yes, sir. I don't want the details of the operation to go any farther, because I suspect there's a high-level leak to the Russians. The leak may be connected to the conspirators."

There was a long silence, while the crows cackled.

"You're kidding!" gasped the president. "Who?"

"We don't know. We only suspect that there is one."

"You'd better come clean, Stephen," Parr said. "This could be a *disaster*."

"The leak is high up," Reid gave in reluctantly. "Whoever he is, he knew we were sending an officer over to make the initial contact with the source in Poland. One of our earlier defectors, who also met with our officer, has disappeared. And the Russian rescue team moved to retrieve Gorbachev earlier than they should have."

"It's pretty vague," Parr said.

"Yes, it is," Reid admitted. "I told you, it's only a suspicion. But it's the reason I don't want the details of the current operation to go any farther."

"You mean to say you suspect *me*?" Halliday demanded furiously. "Or Simon, here?"

"No, sir. We have no suspects. Only suspicion."

"Under those circumstances especially, I need to know what's going on in Poland right now," said Parr. "Mr. President —"

"Okay, Director Reid," Halliday directed. "Answer the question."

"No. Sir."

"The DCI is a presidential appointment," Halliday responded slowly. "If you don't answer, you won't be DCI when you leave here. Simon's a hell of a lot more cooperative than you are."

Just one more step, Reid, thought Parr, and I'm rid of you for good.

"Very well, sir," Reid said at last. "Under protest, I'll tell you. Our officer has already removed the agent from his hiding place. He's taking him to one of the two Soviet tank bases in Poland.

How they're getting there, I don't know. From the base, both men will be flown to Moscow. In Moscow, they will be taken straight to Gorbachev. The Polish agent has compiled a dossier detailing KGB and SB involvement in the conspiracy, which is code-named CONCERTO. He will also, as a key witness, assist Gorbachev and the Soviet procurator general in preparing an indictment of the plotters. As soon as Gorbachev has the indictment, and it won't take long, all members of the conspiracy in the Soviet Union will be arrested, by the army. The Polish armed forces will deal with CONCERTO's operational headquarters in Warsaw, which is where our source worked. We also hope that Mr. Gorbachev will cooperate, later on, in determining the identity of the leak here in the United States."

"Does Gorbachev know about the leak here?" Parr asked.

"No."

"Who is this *officer*?"

"Sean Brennan," said Reid.

"That Irish cowboy who nearly got Gorbachev killed for us?" Parr said with incredulity. "Him?"

"Yes, Simon. Him."

"What cover is he travelling under?"

"I don't know. That was to be provided by Gorbachev's people."

"How did you get Brennan into Poland?"

"Via Moscow. He went there on Gorbachev's plane, Sunday night. The plan to get him into Poland via one of the tank bases was Gorbachev's. Gorbachev was hoping to use GRU resources. I don't know whether it's actually being done that way, or not. We've had no word. We didn't expect any. Either Brennan's man makes it, or he doesn't. We won't know till afterward."

"There, Simon," Halliday said. "It's going to work. Everything's been carefully prepared, don't you think?"

"It *appears* so, Mr. President," Parr answered. "But suppose those two men are caught? You can't assume they'll get from Warsaw to the tank base, let alone to Moscow. The CONCERTO plotters know by now that they've had a traitor. They'll be turning over every stone to catch him, and I'd say the odds are good that they will, whether there's a leak here or not. Then they've got not only a traitor, but a very identifiable CIA officer who's been helping him. Sean Brennan. We're playing too fast and loose. I think we ought to consider shutting down the operation."

"We can't shut it down," Reid objected. "They're on their way, and there's no means by which I can contact Brennan in the field to tell him to stop. In any case, if he was boxed in he'd be forced to disobey."

"I wouldn't be surprised at *that,*" commented Parr acidly. "He has a talent for disobedience." He turned to Halliday. "Mr. President, thank you for having this confidence in me. But I should head back to Washington very shortly. Could you excuse me, please?"

"Go ahead, Simon," the president said indulgently. "I think everything's straightened out now."

Poland
Tuesday, October 8—Wednesday, October 9

"YOU WERE IN HERE all the time?" Brennan asked, looking around the cramped stone chamber.

"Yes. Except for going outside once to make the emergency signal." Kaminsky was sorting out his small pile of stores, his movements quick and deft. "I slept, mostly. I needed sleep, and I thought I was safe down here." Kaminsky tossed the safety razor into a corner and rubbed at his chin, wincing. They'd needed the remaining drinking water to clean the mud from their faces and hands, and he'd dry-shaved.

Something had changed about the Pole. "Your hair's black," Brennan said.

"Yes. I dyed it before I went out that one time." Kaminsky was tearing open a paper bundle, removing clothes. "I can change my appearance slightly, enough to pass a cursory check, at night and in bad light. But photographs of me will have been sent out. A careful officer at a checkpoint would be dangerous." He started pulling on the clean garments. "However, there's no choice. Have you forgotten I don't yet know who you are?"

This was a surprise. Brennan had become so used to thinking of the Pole as Adam Kaminsky, that he had in fact forgotten that the Pole didn't know his name. "Sean Brennan," he said.

"Is that an American name? It sounds different."

"It's of Irish origin," Brennan said. "But there are a lot of Irish descendants in the United States."

"Yes, I remember now, from New York. They were always policemen. Never mind. How are we getting out?"

Brennan told him. "I see," Kaminsky observed. "Moscow. Well, again, I have no choice." He was dressed. He rummaged in a plastic satchel and removed a pair of eyeglasses and two plastic pads, which he inserted into his mouth, against his cheeks. "I kept these from New York," he said, working his jaw to get the pads properly positioned. "They're a good fit. I can even talk clearly with them in." He put the glasses on, fitting the earpieces carefully.

The pads had changed the outline of his lower jaw slightly, filling it out and making his face square instead of triangular. The glasses made his eyes appear smaller. "That's good," Brennan said.

"A yank on the glasses and a finger in my mouth," Kaminsky said philosophically, "and that's that. Let me look at you."

He surveyed Brennan in the lamplight, from face to shoes. "You'd better carry the greatcoat," he said. "It's too muddy to wear, it'll attract suspicion. The shoes and trousers will pass, unless we meet a general who worries about dirty uniforms. Let's hope we don't. Check me, would you?"

Brennan did so. Kaminsky's clothes were wrinkled, and there were patches of mud on his shoes that would dust off when dry, but he didn't look like a man who had spent several days in a storm sewer. He might smell like one, of course; Brennan couldn't tell because he'd become used to the odor of the tunnels. "You're fine. Is the dossier here, or do we have to go somewhere else?"

"It's here," Kaminsky said. Standing in the shadows of a corner was a small brown leather briefcase. Kaminsky went over and picked it up. He hefted it. "It's frightening, what's in here."

"Yes," Brennan said. He didn't want to think about the significance of what was in the case. It was too much responsibility.

Kaminsky clicked on his flashlight and blew out the oil lamp. "Let's go."

They started out along the tunnels. "Have you any papers?" Brennan asked.

"Army intelligence identification card. No paybook — it's not necessary for AI officers in civilian clothes. Driver's license in same name. This face is in the photographs."

"What about the identity you were using for your other escape routes?"

"Compromised. It was from our internal contingency stock, but not part of CONCERTO. The file was under my personal supervision. After I ran, the first thing they'd do would be to check the stock to see what's missing. The army intelligence cover wasn't stock. It's something I put together on my own, and it's very little to survive on for more than a few hours, but that may be all we'll need."

"I hope so."

They reached the drainage channel that led up to the crypt. Beyond the end of the walkway in the main sewer, the bodies of the two ZOMO men huddled, invisible in the dark. Brennan wondered how many hours would pass before they were found. With luck, they wouldn't have been missed yet. Brennan tried to feel guilty about killing them, but couldn't. He knew how the ZOMO behaved toward their enemies, and their captives.

Kaminsky led the way up the channel, without lights. Brennan heard the scrape of the grill being removed, and then a whispered, "Clear."

Above, the church was dim and empty, with only a few candles burning. Kaminsky took him along the east transept and out through a small door. Brennan breathed clean cold air, filling his lungs with it, but the miasma of the sewers seemed to cling to the insides of his nostrils.

"Go and bring the car here," Kaminsky whispered. "I'll wait. What should I look for?"

"Polonez, air force staff car colors."

"Good. Hurry."

Brennan did, as much as possible without risking undue attention. There was an army checkpoint, which hadn't been there before, across from the Chlopa Hotel, but the lieutenant in charge saw his uniform and motioned him on. Perhaps they hadn't been alerted to hunt for Kaminsky, but were merely helping keep the lid on Warsaw.

He put the muddy greatcoat into the trunk of the Polonez, got into the driver's seat, and started toward the church. The military insignia of the car would divert a good deal of official attention; he didn't expect much trouble from checkpoints, at least not until the bodies of the ZOMO troopers were found.

The side alley to the east of the building was dark. For a dreadful moment he thought Kaminsky wasn't there anymore, but a second later he saw the Pole walk steadily and evenly out of the shadows onto the sidewalk. Kaminsky opened the door and got in, slumping into the passenger seat. "Drive," he said. "We must get away from Warsaw as soon as we can. When they find the bodies, they'll know I've had to go into the open again. I'll take the car out of Warsaw, if you like, once we're away from the church."

"No," Brennan said. "There's always a possibility of a random check on us. It wouldn't look right if you were driving an air force car."

"Yes. I agree. I'll direct you if you go wrong."

Brennan put the Polonez into gear and started off toward Wola, heading for the E8. He'd return the way he'd come. According to the dashboard clock, it was just after eleven in the evening. With luck, they'd be at the Russian tank base, and some kind of safety, just before dawn.

Two hours passed, without incident. Kaminsky seemed to doze. A little way past Lodz he straightened up and said, "Do you want me to drive for a while?"

"I still don't think you'd better."

"All right. Unless you're too tired to go on. If there's any danger of you falling asleep, I'll drive."

"I'm fine for the moment."

A misty rain began to fall by the time they reached Kepno. Brennan switched on the wipers, listening to the hypnotic flap of the blades against the windshield. He was becoming very sleepy. Kaminsky must have sensed it, for he began to talk.

"Do you have a wife in America?"

"No," Brennan replied. "I'm not married. My wife was killed several years ago."

"I'm sorry."

"I've gotten over it," Brennan said. "As much as you ever do."

"There's no one for you now, to go home to?"

"Well, yes. A woman I met a couple of years ago. We've been together for some time."

"That's good. What is her name?"

"Molly."

"Is she also in this work?"

"No," Brennan said, smiling despite himself at the thought. "She's an artist."

"In Poland, artists don't like intelligence people."

The wipers beat steadily: *Molly, Molly, Molly*. "Often they don't in the States, either." Brennan said. "Molly's different."

"Does she mind this, what you do?"

"Yes. I was about to leave the Agency when all this happened."

"Because of her?"

"Partly. Partly because I was tired of it. I wanted to do something else."

"What?"

"Write. Write history."

"Instead of making it." There was wry humor in the Pole's voice.

"Exactly. I've noticed that people who make history often make the people around them very unhappy. As well as themselves, usually, in the long run. I didn't want to do that to Molly and myself."

"Will you marry her, do you think?"

"Yes."

"That will be good. A writer married to an artist. It will be very stimulating for you both. Are there children?"

"No. Neither of us. What about you?"

"No children. My wife left me two years after we were married. It was a mistake, she was much younger than I am."

"I'm sorry," Brennan said.

"It hurt at the time," Kaminsky said. "Now, though, it seems like a dream, not real. It turned out for the best, that I didn't love anyone when I decided to do what I'm doing. It made it much easier, not to have to worry about what would happen to anyone else."

"There's no one?"

"No. My parents are dead."

"What will you do," Brennan asked after a moment, "when this is over?"

"I know what I'd like to do. If Gorbachev doesn't jail me, I'll go back to Poland, and do what I can to make her the country she ought to be. There's been too much grief, too much destruction. Some of it I caused."

"Don't try to be a hero," Brennan said.

"I'm not," said Kaminsky. "Like you, I think heroes are bad for the people around them. The world doesn't need more heroes. It needs decent human beings. I would like to be one."

"I think you are," Brennan said.

"Thank you. We make mistakes. I never should have become what I am. What was the worst mistake you ever made?"

The car's tires hissed on the wet highway; telephone poles flickered past in the misty headlight beams. "It wasn't a mistake, really," Brennan said. "It felt like one for a long time, though. I was in Munich, with my wife. Her name was Jane. She was killed by a car bomb that some terrorists planted outside our hotel. If I hadn't left her in the lobby for those few seconds. . ."

"Terrorists." Kaminsky shook his head.

And then Brennan was telling him all of it, the long hunt, the preparations, the journey to a wintry Berlin, the killings in the warehouse. When he had finished, Kaminsky remained silent for some time. Then he said:

"So it was you."

"You knew about it?"

"Yes. The East Germans asked us to help find the assassin. We all thought it was the start of an Israeli campaign to eliminate terrorist cells, as they did after the Olympic killings in 1972. But then there were no other deaths. We never discovered who did it. But we were trying to find you." He reached over and pressed Brennan's shoulder. "I am glad we didn't."

"Likewise."

"I should tell you," Kaminsky said, "that I was never involved in that kind of thing. Almost all of it was run by the Czech StB and the East German SSD."

"I'm glad about that." Brennan had been wondering how to react if it turned out that Kaminsky had been linked to Jane's death.

"Did it help, killing them?"

"In a way. But I've always been afraid I might make the same mistake with Molly I feel I made with Jane. I know there's no sense to it, but the fear's still there."

"It will fade with time," Kaminsky told him. "Especially if you leave this work."

"I know."

A few minutes passed. Brennan's sleepiness had vanished. "We're not far from Wroclaw," Kaminsky said. "I think we should go around it, rather than through it. I have a feeling the alarm's out by now. At Olesnica, take the paved secondary road north. It curves around to the west and we can reach the tank base by that route, without losing much time."

"All right."

He did as Kaminsky suggested, following his directions through the sleeping city. There was still plenty of fuel in the Polonez's tank. They had reached the northern outskirts where the secondary road swung toward Dobroszyce when a pair of headlights appeared suddenly in Brennan's rearview mirror. A blue beacon was flashing on the roof of the car behind.

"Oh-oh," Brennan said. "*Militsia.*" He slowed the Polenez, pulled onto the shoulder and stopped. "What do you think?"

"We're travelling very late," Kaminsky said. "Sometimes they check because of that."

"Maybe that's all," Brenann said. He heard a faint metallic click: the safety of Kaminsky's automatic being snapped over, out of sight in his pocket.

Brennan rolled down the window just in time for the traffic policeman to peer into the car. "Good morning, colonel," the officer said. "You're on the road very late."

"I know," Brennan replied. "We have to be at Prochowice by dawn."

"Could I see your identification, please?"

Brennan showed him his paybook. The militiaman studied it in the beam of his flashlight and handed the document back. "And the other gentleman?"

Kaminsky handed over the army intelligence card. This time the policeman shone the flashlight full into Kaminsky's face, comparing his features to those of the photograph on the card. Kaminsky blinked in the light, grimacing.

The flashlight clicked off. Kaminsky got his card back. "Thank you," said the militiaman. "I apologize for delaying you, colonel. But there are counterrevolutionaries everywhere. We have to be alert."

"I understand," said Brennan. "You're doing well."

The militiaman saluted and returned to his car. The blue light stopped flashing, and the police vehicle pulled onto the road and made a U-turn back toward Olesnica. Brennan rolled up his window; despite the cool night air he was sweating. "False alarm," he breathed. He sensed Kaminsky putting away the gun.

"We may be lucky yet," Kaminsky said.

They drove on, through the small Polish towns: Trzebnica, Oborniki Slaskie, Wolow. Kaminsky consulted the map. At the road sign announcing Scinawa, Kaminsky said, "Turn left just ahead. That's the road that goes past the base."

The side road wasn't marked; Brennan almost missed the turn and the Polonez's front wheels scrunched on the shoulder gravel. He straightened the wheel out and asked, "How far?"

"About three kilometers."

"Just another few minutes. We're going to make it, Adam."

"Don't tempt fate."

One mile passed, then another. Five hundred feet farther on, the Polonez crested a small rise.

Lights.

Kaminsky said, "Damnation."

"I see it," said Brennan. Ahead was an oil-drum barricade lit by flickering oil pots and three generator-powered floodlights. The barricade kinked across the road, so that it was impossible to negotiate it without making a sharp dogleg turn. On the shoulder of the road were a Polish army truck, a black civilian automobile and a BRDM wheeled scout vehicle. Brennan could see half-a-dozen soldiers manning the roadblock. The intersection of the main road and the base access road was a little way beyond the barriers; on the far side of the intersection was another roadblock, also floodlit.

"What do you think?" Brennan asked. "They're not from the Soviet base, are they?" He had a wild hope that it might be a reception committee of Major Rybalko's.

"I don't think so. Those are Polish army markings on the BRDM and the truck. And that's a civilian car. KGB or SB. I think we're in trouble."

"It's too late to put you in the trunk," Brennan said. "They'd see us stop."

"It wouldn't do any good, anyway," said the Pole. "They'd look. Can you bluff it out?"

"I'll try." Now that the crisis was upon them, Brennan felt quite calm. "I'm a colonel. That'll help."

"Do what you can. If we have to, we can try to shoot our way in."

Dammit, Brennan thought. So near and yet so far. He took his foot off the accelerator and braked gently. One of the soldiers stepped out from behind the row of oil drums and stopped, pointing at the ground to show where he wanted the Polonez to halt. Brennan complied. Behind the drums, three soldiers were covering the Polonez with automatic rifles.

So much for shooting our way through, thought Brennan.

He rolled down the window. This was going to be a different matter from dealing with a traffic patrol. He projected himself into the frame of mind of a tired, hungry air force colonel who, just short of his destination, was put to great inconvenience by some overzealous hunt for counterrevolutionaries.

The soldier was a lieutenant. He eyed Brennan's insignia and said with a touch of diffidence, "I must see your papers, please, colonel."

"What's the matter?" Brennan asked as he pulled the papers out of his tunic, allowing peevishness and annoyance to seep into his voice.

"We're checking for a defector, sir." The lieutenant began to inspect the identification, very carefully. "Trying to get into the Russian tank base over there."

"A defector to the Russians?" Brennan asked in disbelief. "What the devil are you talking about?"

"Following orders, sir." The lieutenant began to look a little flustered. Nevertheless, he checked Brennan's hair and eye coloring with considerable care.

"Get on with it, man," Brennan scowled. "A plane's leaving for Lvov HQ in an hour, and if I'm not on it because of your delays, there's going to be trouble."

"Yes, sir." The lieutenant handed the papers back, with some relief. "You're going into the base?"

"No. I'm going on past it to Leignica. Why would a Polish air force colonel be going to a Russian tank base? Use your head."

"Sorry, sir. Who is your passenger?"

"Show him your papers, for God's sake, and let's get out of here," Brennan said.

Kaminsky passed over the army intelligence identity card. The lieutenant inspected it. "Do you have your paybook, major, sir?"

"Can't you see I'm in civilian clothes?" snapped Kaminsky. "Would you like to call Warsaw for information on intelligence operations? You've seen too much already. Who ordered this checkpoint?"

"I don't know, sir." The lieutenant was being stubborn, despite the pressure from two superior officers. He shone the flashlight into the car and looked at Kaminsky. Kaminsky stared back. The lieutenant was looking even more nervous, but he didn't hurry.

"Well, what about it?" Kaminsky snarled after a moment. "Either arrest us, or let us get on with our business. We've got a plane to catch at Leignica. Would you like to come and talk to the general of pact intelligence at Lvov about it?"

The lieutenant snapped the flashlight off. "I must ask you to speak with a higher officer before you can go on, sir."

"Where is he?"

"Down the road, at the other checkpoint, sir."

"Let us through, then," Brennan ordered. "Do you think we want to soak ourselves in this drizzle? We'll drive over there."

"Yes, sir."

The lieutenant stepped away from the car and waved the barricade sentries away. Brennan drove through the dogleg between the oil drums and started toward the second checkpoint. The turnoff to the base access road was fifty yards ahead, on the right. It wasn't marked; Soviet forces stationed in Poland kept a low profile. Brennan could see the guardhouse lights of the base's main gate a half mile away.

Is Rybalko there? he wondered. Does he know what's going on out here? Maybe he does, but doesn't dare interfere with Polish troops.

He speeded up a little, forcing the lieutenant into a trot. The officer began to lose ground; in a few seconds he was level with the Polonez's rear bumper.

"I'm going to make a run for it," Brennan whispered hoarsely to Kaminsky. "Hold on."

They were twenty yards from the turnoff when Brennan saw a man, outlined against the lights of the far checkpoint, his face a blur. He was waving them down. "Civilian," said Kaminsky tensely.

He was only a dozen yards away now. Brennan could see him clearly.

Timoshkin.

Brennan rammed the accelerator to the floor and spun the steering wheel over to full lock. The staff car's rear wheels broke loose on the wet asphalt and then suddenly bit, whipping the back end around almost to the middle of the pavement, the hood pointing diagonally at the entrance to the base road. Timoshkin shouted at them; he was trying to yank a gun out of the pocket of his raincoat. Brennan pulled the steering wheel back to center and the Polonez shot across the gravel shoulder of the intersection onto the rough tarmac of the access road. Timoshkin was racing toward the car as it speeded up, his gun out now, trying to intercept them.

He was a fraction of a second too late. The left tip of the front bumper hit him a glancing blow just above the knee as he tried to aim, and threw him aside. His gun went off with a bang and the bullet whacked into the windshield post where it joined the body of the car. Brennan caught a glimpse of Timoshkin's face as he fell away, and saw the shock of recognition in it.

He saw me, Brennan thought, and then the Polonez was rocketing into the darkness toward the gate of the army base. He snapped off the headlights, remembering that the road didn't curve. Five seconds later automatic fire opened up behind, but the soldiers couldn't see the darkened staff car, and the shots went wild. Another five seconds, and Brennan saw lights behind them in the rearview mirror.

"He's coming after us," Kaminsky said. He was turned in the seat, gun out, craning to see through the back window. "Don't slow down."

"I won't," Brennan promised. Adrenalin was pumping through him, exhilaratingly. The main gate was less than a minute away. Would Timoshkin try to come through it after him?

"He's gaining," Kaminsky reported. "Special engine."

The Polonez's engine screamed in third gear. Brennan felt it pass the power peak and shifted into fourth. Have to start slowing down in a few seconds, can't crash right through the barrier, the guards might start shooting. Twenty seconds to go.

He saw someone standing by the guardhouse ahead. Rybalko, Brennan thought, please let it be Rybalko.

It was. The man sprang from his stance and began heaving at the weighted end of the barrier. The pole began to sweep upward. A Russian soldier ran out of the guardhouse and knelt beside Rybalko, aiming his weapon down the road.

The rear window of the Polonez blew out in pebbles of glass that stung the back of Brennan's neck. Timoshkin was shooting. Brennan heard Kaminsky's curse, and then the bang of his gun.

Brennan decided not to slow down; the barrier was all the way up now. He kept his foot on the floor. The Polonez was doing seventy miles an hour.

Light flared ahead: muzzle flashes. The guard beside Rybalko was shooting at their pursuers. "He hit him!" Kaminsky screamed. The headlights behind went out. Brennan heard tires shriek on wet pavement, and then the Polonez flew under the barrier, inside the base perimeter. He tramped on the brakes, pulling off the main base drive so that Timoshkin, if he was still trying, couldn't get a clear shot at him. "Where is he?" Brennan yelled at Kaminsky, more loudly than he needed to.

"He stopped. I think he's turning around. Still in one piece. I can't see him now. We're behind the gatehouse."

The Polonez stopped. Brennan leaned over the wheel. He was drenched in sweat. "We made it," he said. "We made it, gooddamnit."

"Here comes somebody." Kaminsky stiffened.

"Rybalko, I hope."

The Russian major peered into the car. "Are you hurt?"

"No," Brennan replied in Russian. "What happened to them?"

"They turned around and left. They came half an hour ago. I'd left orders to be notified if anything odd happened, and when I saw them I knew you might be in a hurry. They were Poles, and as we are a Soviet base on Polish soil, I couldn't bring our troops out and order them to leave. Sorry."

Brennan brushed glass off his uniform and climbed wearily out of the car. "This is Colonel Adam Kaminsky. Adam, this is Major Rybalko."

''Good morning, Major,'' Kaminsky said, in accented Russian.

''Good morning, Colonel Kaminsky.''

The two men eyed each other warily. Brennan broke the silence by saying, ''When can we leave? They might try something else.''

''Immediately. I will get my kit. Please wait here and we will drive out to the airstrip.''

Kaminsky and Brennan sat in the car for the five minutes Rybalko was gone, both too exhausted to do more than exchange mutters of relief. Rybalko returned, got into the driver's seat, and headed for the airstrip. ''The plane's been kept on standby,'' he said. ''The crew is sleeping on board.''

''I hope they don't mind being woken up.''

''They'll wake up when told to,'' Rybalko said succinctly, ''and fly.''

When they reached the aircraft Rybalko climbed up the entrance ladder first, and shouted into the cargo space. ''Wait till the crew is on the flight deck,'' he said to Kaminsky and Brennan, who were waiting on the ground below him. ''No one is to see you unless it's necessary.''

Brennan thought that he was being overly concerned, given the pursuit they'd just endured, but he waited. ''All right,'' Rybalko said.

They climbed the ladder and settled into the forward seats, while Rybalko slammed and sealed the door. The starters grumbled outside and the engines drummed into life, one after the other. Rybalko strapped himself in, took a bottle of vodka out of his bag and unscrewed the cap. ''Here,'' he said. ''You deserve it.''

Brennan took the bottle, gulped and then passed it to Kaminsky. The clear spirit burned its way into his stomach. Kaminsky passed it back to him, but he shook his head.

The Antonov's engines had warmed, and the pilot set the plane moving along the grass taxiway. Looking through the porthole, Brennan realized that he could see the eastern horizon. Dawn wasn't far off. He wondered whether, if they'd reached the base in daylight, they'd have been able to get through. It didn't matter now.

The transport lifted from the runway and gained altitude. As it did so, the dawn light brightened. They were flying slightly north of east, and the glow of the rising sun was visible through the starboard cabin windows. The vodka was mounting to Brennan's head, and he felt relaxed and cheerful.

The plane levelled off at little more than three hundred feet. Brennan looked questioningly at Rybalko.

"We are going to fly under radar for a while," Rybalko said. "They were too close behind you. The KGB Border Guard Directorate has fighter aircraft, and they might be ordered to intercept us."

Brennan nodded. Rybalko took a good pull at the vodka bottle, shoved it back into his bag, and pulled out a length of sausage, a canteen and a loaf of dark rye bread. "Here," he said. "If you want breakfast." He put the food on the seat beside Brennan and leaned his head against the forward bulkhead. He closed his eyes. A couple of minutes later he was snoring faintly.

A good soldier, Brennan thought with amusement. Have a drink when you can, sleep when you can. Don't forget to get your hands on food whenever possible.

"Sean," Kaminsky asked suddenly and quietly, "at what time did your people tell the Russians the location of the safe house?"

Brennan tried to remember. Knight had mentioned it to him. "Six P.M. on Saturday, New York time," he answered. "Midnight over here."

Kaminsky looked past Brennan, through the porthole where the eastern sky was becoming steadily brighter, and said, "They knew in Warsaw that they'd been betrayed long before that."

"I see." It wasn't coming as a surprise. Timoshkin had been waiting for them at the tank base, and he shouldn't have been.

"They were after me at nine in the evening," Kaminsky said. "Allow two hours for the information to reach Warsaw from the Soviet embassy in Washington. Therefore, at seven P.M. Warsaw time, someone at the Soviet embassy knew that you knew about Gorbachev's location. That's one in the afternoon in Washington. Sean, you have a . . . how is it said? A mole. A mole in Washington."

Brennan nodded. Now that he had time, he was busy thinking about Timoshkin. How, exactly, did the Russian know that he and Kaminsky were heading for the Russian base at Prochowice, and nowhere else? Or were they covering both Soviet bases in Poland, and Timoshkin simply happened to be at Prochowice?

The answer was painfully obvious, regardless of whether the conspirators had known exactly which base Brennan and Kaminsky were trying to reach. Someone had told the conspirators how they were going to get out. Someone in Washington. The same person who knew Brennan was going to be in Paris, but who didn't know he'd been diverted to Warsaw for the first meeting with Kaminsky, or who was hiding his tracks by pretending not to know. Brennan had been right about the leak. He remembered clearly the discussion he'd had with Reid and Barlow and Knight, the Sunday of Gorbachev's rescue. Reid had wanted it kept quiet.

Was it Reid? Or one of the other two? If so, why hadn't Brennan and Kaminsky been caught before they left Warsaw? But there *were* ZOMO men in the sewers, looking for Kaminsky. Were they looking for Brennan as well? Was that routine checking, or something much worse? As far as Brennan knew, no one except his three superiors at Langley, the secretary of state, and the president knew what he was supposed to do.

Who else would they have told?

There was no way of knowing at the moment, and nothing he could do about it, anyway. They'd just have to keep moving, and stay alert.

"I'm afraid you're right," he said to Kaminsky. "We've been compromised. They know we're here, and maybe what we're trying to do."

"Do you think they'll be waiting for us in Moscow?"

"They won't stop trying yet."

Kaminsky made a tiny gesture at the sleeping Rybalko. "Him?"

"I don't know. I don't think so. He could have given us to Timoshkin."

"Timoshkin?"

"The tall man who tried to stop us. Timoshkin was in New York. He was in charge of the rescue team."

"I see. We shall have to be very careful, then."

"Yes." The vodka was wearing off, and Brennan's stomach was growling. "Pass me that sausage. When Rybalko wakes up, we'll tell him, and he may have some ideas about security."

"Very well."

They ate. Brennan was becoming sleepy. Outside, as the Antonov droned over the landscape of Poland, a bank of layered cloud began to slide across the sunrise. It was the color of dark clay, and looked as thick. Bad weather, Brennan thought. Well, it'll help hide us.

He let his head drop forward onto his chest, and fell asleep in seconds.

He was awakened by a lurch of the aircraft, and jerked himself upright. His neck hurt. Kaminsky and Rybalko were already awake, and looking out the portholes. Rybalko's face wore an expression Brennan didn't like. He persuaded his eyes to focus, and looked out as well. The Antonov was still very low, but the sunlight was gone. Streamers of dank cloud, mixed with precipitation that was neither snow nor rain, ripped past the engine nacelles. The land, although close below, was barely visible in the murk. What Brennan could see of it appeared marshy and uninhabited. The leading edge of the Antonov's high wing didn't look right; it was bumpy. Ice.

"Where are we?" Brennan asked.

"South of Mogilev and east of the Berezina River," Rybalko answered. "The pilot tried to go around the bad weather, but it's everywhere."

"How far to Moscow?"

"About five hundred kilometers. Only an hour away."

An hour away. He'd slept for a long time. No wonder he felt so groggy.

A slab of ice peeled from the underside of the wing and vanished in fragments. A scattershot of hail racketed on the fuselage.

"How far does this crap stretch?"

"According to the pilot, as far as Smolensk." Rybalko looked out the window again. "To hell with the radar. I'm going to tell him to climb."

He disappeared through the door onto the flight deck. When he came back, he looked grim. "The de-icers aren't working properly," he said, and lapsed into silence.

The Antonov began to ascend, but it seemed to Brennan that it did so very slowly. The engines sounded as though they were at full throttle. The swampy landscape below faded away into the undercast. Brennan studied the wing's leading edge. The ice was thicker, spoiling the smooth airflow, paring away the wing's lift. A chunk of ice separated suddenly from the side of the engine nacelle and Brennan heard a bang from aft as it struck the tail plane.

"I can see the ground again," Kaminsky announced in a matter-of-fact tone. "We're losing altitude."

"Shit," Rybalko said, and went back to the cockpit. Brennan watched as the land reappeared through the veils of freezing rain: narrow streams, patches of willows, long smooth stretches of what appeared to be turf, but was more likely swamp grass. He tried to remember his geography. South of Mogilev, east of the Berezina. They were on the northeastern fringe of the great Pripyet marshes, which stretched away to the south almost as far as Kiev. The Russians had been draining them for farmland for centuries, but there was still plenty of bog left.

Rybalko came back. "They're still trying to get the de-icers to work properly," he said. "If they can't we're going to go down, it's as simple as that. He's turning toward the main highway to the north, he thinks we might be able to set down on that. If we make it that far, that is."

A lousy hour left, Brennan reflected, and this has to happen. He thought about the brown briefcase now tucked under Kaminsky's seat, imagining its contents fluttering across the chill expanses of the marsh, drifting on the surface of its myriad channels and dissolving into the tea-brown, peaty water, lost forever.

Their altitude was now roughly a hundred fifty feet. The fuselage shuddered as ice broke away from its undersurfaces, and the Antonov seemed to rise a little. It didn't last. The wing's leading edges were now encased in a thick pebble-glass crust. Even the propellers seemed to be icing up; shards of ice from their racing tips battered at the fuselage. It sounded like lead shot sliding off a corrugated iron roof.

The flight-deck door opened and a crewman put his head out. He looked frightened. "Strap in for an emergency landing," he said. "We can't hold her up much longer."

"How far to the highway?" Rybalko asked, but the man was gone.

The three men tightened their belts. Kaminsky threaded a belt from one of the empty seats through the handle of the briefcase and pulled it tight. "I hope the locks hold," he said. Brennan didn't answer. He was very frightened, and trying not to show it.

A tree shot underneath the starboard wing, seeming to almost brush it. The Antonov was no more than fifty feet above the swamps. "Get down!" Kaminsky yelled.

Brennan leaned over into the emergency crouch. He heard a whir as the flaps came down, but the pilot wasn't lowering the landing gear. He was going to try to belly it in. Brennan prayed for slippery grass and shallow water.

The pilot chopped the throttles.

Deprived of the power that was keeping it aloft, the transport dropped like a stone. The belly of the plane slammed onto a relatively flat surface covered with swamp vegetation, bounced slightly, and came back down hard. The port wing dipped, but there was enough airflow still for the pilot to right the plane with the flaps and ailerons. It skidded a hundred yards, shot through a shallow water channel in a huge plume of spray, and struck a piece of rising ground. The port wingtip dropped. The propeller on that side, which was still free-wheeling, dug into the ground and sawed up several hundred pounds of turf, ripping off its blade tips in the process. The unbalanced drag snatched the Antonov around until it was sliding sideways at an angle to its original line of motion. Still moving fast, the plane slammed broadside into a willow. The trunk barely missed the front of the starboard engine nacelle and punched a deep V into the fuselage just aft of the flight deck, precisely at the row of seats in which Rybalko was sitting.

Mercifully, there was no fire. Inside the cabin, everything was quiet.

There were eight men in Gorbachev's private conference room in the Central Committee building in Staraya Square: Gorbachev himself; Isayev; Defense Minister Stepanov; Chief of the General Staff Antonin Tchigorin; the head of the GRU, General Vladimir Nilov; Foreign Minister Valentin Pokrovsky; Chairman of the Council of Ministers Ivan Zotin; and one of the Secretariat heads, Alexander Finenko. Gorbachev was at the head of the table, thoughtfully studying the door at the far end of the room, which led to his office. Adjoining the office were his private dining and retiring rooms. Beyond the office was the guarded corridor that led to the right-hand door of the CC building, a door closed off by black steel gates and which no one but the general secretary and his bodyguards were allowed to use. The bodyguards, Ninth Directorate KGB men hand-picked for their loyalty to the regime and the Party, were also quartered in the right-hand side of the building.

At least, Gorbachev thought, they are supposed to be handpicked for loyalty. Has Chernysh reached any of them? Perhaps, perhaps not. He's after my political death, not my assassination.

"I urge you," Isayev was saying, every word heavy with emphasis, "to take immediate action. We can't delay any longer, Mikhail. There's every indication that Chernysh intends to force your resignation at the Central Committee plenum at eight this evening. The Kremlin will be stiff with Ninth Directorate Guards. If you go there, you won't come out as secretary. I urge you to use the army. Now."

Gorbachev took a sip of water from his glass and set it back on the green cloth of the conference table. The machine that Nilov had brought to defeat radio microphones hummed quietly in the center of the table. The room had also been swept, immediately before the meeting, by a GRU specialist Nilov had brought with him. He'd found three hard-wired microphones and disabled them. Chernysh had been busy.

"I direct this question to Minister Stepanov and General Tchigorin," Gorbachev said. "What forces do you have at your immediate disposal, and how certain are you that they will obey instructions to move en masse against the KGB?"

Tchigorin looked troubled. "The Taman Guards division is available just outside Moscow," he said, "but there is always the possibility that some of its key officers are KGB Third Directorate people. Where their loyalty would be in a crisis, it's impossible to tell at the moment. As for the men themselves . . . Secretary, while you were away, there was a great deal of agitation against your leadership. It's still going on, although it's toned down since your return. I would like to say the men would refuse orders if their officers tried to turn them against you. But I cannot be sure."

In earlier years, Gorbachev knew, a question such as his would have been answered by assurances of utter loyalty, no matter what realities were. It was a mark of his progress that Tchigorin felt able to tell the truth. "Is this your estimate as well?" he asked Stepanov.

"I am afraid it is," said the defense minister. "But I concur with Secretary Isayev. We ought to move immediately, and take the risk."

"It's a risk I can't take at this hour," Gorbachev replied. "Suppose we order the Taman Guards in and Chernysh orders the KGB to fight back? And then suppose some Taman officers lead their men over to the KGB side? That begins to look like civil war. Even if the fighting didn't spread, and no matter who won, the morale of both army and KGB would be badly damaged. And what would it look like to the population at large, with the armed forces and the security service fighting over the Party leadership, like dogs in the street? What happens to their belief in the Party then, when our disputes can't be resolved without risking another civil war?"

"I agree," Isayev said grimly, "but think of the alternative. You know what will happen to the Union if Chernysh has you removed. And what will happen to all of us here in this room."

"I know," Gorbachev said. The purges would come again, he thought, the second Great Terror. He turned to Nilov. "You are sure Rybalko will be here in an hour, with the others?"

"Yes," answered the head of the GRU. "There's no reason to think otherwise. They're on radio silence, but they've been on their way for two hours now."

Gorbachev nodded, thinking. Nilov's report on the Poland operation had been first on the agenda. Brennan had reached Prochowice with the Pole, although they'd almost been stopped right outside the camp gates; they ought to be reaching Moscow in a little over an hour. The plane was to land at the old Khodinka airfield, almost in the center of Moscow and right next to the GRU headquarters. Then there'd be time to evaluate the Pole's dossier with the procurator general, and issue arrest orders.

Unless, unless. Anything could happen, still. The border guards might be able to shoot them down, for example, and Nilov wouldn't know about it until too late. Gorbachev had been a politician too long not to make contingency plans.

"How much time would we need to move against Chernysh, before the plenum meeting starts?"

"Two hours," Tchigorin answered promptly.

He would do it if he had to, if there was no other way out. The risks were great, and the possible damage incalculable, but it was better than waiting like a steer at the abattoir gate. He thought about Raisa, waiting at the *dacha* out at Zhukovka, and Irina, and the grandchildren. . . . Then he decided. He pulled a sheet of paper toward him and scribbled on it; Chernysh might have ways of listening the GRU couldn't detect. As he did so, he said:

"I dare not risk it. It's possible I can sway the CC plenum to support us, even with Chernysh's interference. I will not have fighting in Moscow."

He passed the sheet of paper to the other four men. On it was written:

IF WE DO NOT HAVE LEGAL MEANS BY SIX THIS EVENING, WE WILL MOVE AGAINST CHERNYSH WITHOUT THEM. SEE TO IT.

Isayev was the last to read it. He nodded. "Mikhail, I urge you to reconsider —"

"No," Gorbachev said. "No military intervention." He folded the sheet of paper and tucked it away in his pocket. He thought for a moment about what he'd told the Americans about the need for the rule of law when he spoke to them in the airliner in Washington. He'd meant it, at the time. Faced with the hard facts, he had to act differently; there was too much at stake. He wondered fleetingly whether Stalin had felt the same way.

Five hundred yards away and twenty minutes later, in the building on Dzerzhinsky Square, Chernysh listened as Besedin finished his report.

"They were there, the five of them?" he asked.

"Yes, Chairman."

"Stepanov's gone over to Gorbachev, then, and taken the GRU with him. Christ damn Nilov. We should have gotten a better hold on him months ago, or at least somebody in his office. Any idea what they're planning?"

"No, Chairman. All the listening devices were defeated."

"It can't be helped, now. Fine, we'll take stronger measures. Timoshkin said Kaminsky and his CIA protector left Poland by plane two hours ago, right?"

"Yes."

"If the plane is flying straight here, it'll land at Khodinka. Have the airfield watched. If an aircraft comes in, we will preempt Gorbachev. Plan to have the guards at Staraya Square move in and arrest him, and anyone else in the building, the instant any aircraft touches down at Khodinka. I especially want Stepanov, and that bastard, Nilov. If it hadn't been for Stepanov swallowing Gorbachev's line, and the GRU sticking their fingers in — Never mind. We'll present the plenum with a dose of reality, and if the Central Committee delegates don't like it, they know what will happen to them. And when Timoshkin reaches Moscow, have him report immediately to me. *Immediately.*"

Russia
Wednesday, October 9

BRENNAN WAS THE FIRST recover. His head felt as though it had been unscrewed from his neck and then screwed back on, cross-threaded. He drew it painfully from between his knees and sat up. Wind-driven sleet whipped in through the rent in the side of the fuselage, around the shattered tree trunk.

Rybalko had been sitting one seat away from the window, which was all that had saved him from being filleted by torn metal. The seat he was sitting in had been ripped from its supports, turned partly sideways, and mashed up against the tree trunk. The GRU major's head lolled on his chest. He was pinned between the tree trunk and his seat from the knees down.

Kaminsky was sitting up. "God in heaven, we made it," he said. Then he saw Rybalko. "Oh, no."

Brennan unstrapped himself. The row of seats in which he and Kaminsky had been sitting was intact, the precious briefcase still firmly secured, unopened, by its belt. That was something.

"Help me with him," he said to Kaminsky.

Rybalko's seat was loose enough to be drawn away from the trunk of the tree. Blood was seeping through the Russian's trousers. They got him out of his seat and stretched him out on the cabin floor. He was beginning to regain consciousness and was groaning softly.

Brennan heard banging from the flight-deck door, which had been warped by the impact. One of the crew had survived, at least.

After two or three more bangs the door ground open, to reveal a man in flight clothing. He was holding a fire axe, with which he'd loosened the door. He stared down at Rybalko.

"Is there medical equipment on this plane?" Brennan asked.

"One moment," the crewman answered shakily. He disappeared and returned with a metal case. Behind him was another man, wearing pilot's wings. Brennan opened the case. "Are you two all right?" he asked the pilot.

"Bruises," the pilot replied. He spoke as though his lips were numb. "I'm sorry about the tree."

"You got us down," Brennan said. "That's good enough." He was cutting slits in Rybalko's trousers with a pair of surgical scissors, so that he could look at the damage. It was bad. Both legs had been broken at the shins: multiple fractures. A splint of white bone protruded from the flesh of the right leg. "Goddamn it," Brennan said in English. "Have either of you had medical training?"

"I have," the pilot said. "First aid. But he needs a hospital."

"I know." At least the bleeding wasn't bad. But they had to keep him from going into shock. "How far are we from the highway?"

"About ten kilometers, I think. Maybe a little less."

Wind was whistling through the torn fuselage, icy and wet. "Is the flight deck holed?" Brennan asked.

"No," said the pilot. "Let's get him up there. It will be warmer."

They moved Rybalko slowly into the cockpit and put him on the floor. His eyelids flickered, but he wasn't coming out of it yet. The copilot brought fire blankets from the plane's emergency stores and spread them over the injured Russian. "He's going to be in a lot of pain," Brennan said. "Is there morphine in the medical kit?" He was trying to decide what to do next.

"I'll look," Kaminsky said.

There were several ampoules. Brennan snapped the protective cover off one of them. He was about to jab it into Rybalko's shoulder when the Russian's eyes opened.

"We crashed?" he asked faintly.

"Yes," said Brennan. "You've injured your legs. But you're going to be fine. We'll get medical attention immediately."

"How? Where are we?"

"A few kilometers from the highway. I'm giving you some morphine. You're going to start to hurt."

"Wait, damn you." Rybalko's voice strengthened a little. "What are you going to do?"

"I don't know. Get you medical attention, then go on to Moscow with you."

"Don't be a fool," Rybalko said. His face was white; the pain must be starting. "It will take too long. You have to go straight to Moscow. It's five hundred kilometers yet. You can't use up time on this."

Brennan settled back on his heels, the morphine ampoule balanced between fingers and thumb. Rybalko was right. It was brutal, but they were going to have to leave him. And they couldn't draw attention to the crash until they reached Moscow. That would be hours yet. Rybalko would survive, but he'd be in agony all that time, despite the morphine to take the edge off it.

"I know," he said. "I'm sorry. What were we supposed to do when we got there?"

"That's all off, now," Rybalko whispered. "There is a telephone number for emergencies. Memorize it. Tell the others to move away before I tell you."

Brennan motioned them back. "Go ahead."

Rybalko said it, very slowly and softly. Beads of sweat were gathering on his forehead, despite the growing chill of the flight deck. "I've got it," Brennan said.

"You mustn't use it until you are almost at Moscow. The KGB has been monitoring long-distance calls. If you reach Podol'sk, that's thirty kilometers out, it will be safe to call. When the person answers, say 'Victorine,'" and then tell him where you are and how you're entering the city. He'll send assistance. 'Victorine.' Remember."

"I'll remember."

"Weapons," Rybalko said. "My right tunic pocket. A key. Open the locker in the cargo hold."

Brennan obeyed. The top of the metal locker had been jammed by the crash, and it took both his strength and Kaminsky's to wrench it open. Inside were three AKR submachine guns, ammunition clips and a crate of RGD-5 hand grenades.

"We might need them," Kaminsky said. He took out an AKR and three clips of ammunition, as well as two of the grenades.

Brennan did likewise, stuffing the clips and grenades into the pockets of his tunic. He kept the PM63 pistol as well. They returned to the cockpit.

Rybalko raised his voice. "Captain," he said to the pilot. "These are my orders. You and your officer are to remain here with me until help arrives. That will be some hours. You are not to leave the aircraft for any reason, no matter what condition you think I am in. Someone will come. Do you understand?"

"Yes, Major."

"They'll obey," Rybalko said to Brennan. "They're GRU. Give me the morphine now. Then go."

Brennan nodded, and jabbed the needle through the cloth of the uniform. Rybalko closed his eyes.

"Take care of him," Brennan said. "Keep him warm."

"Yes, sir." Some of Rybalko's authority seemed to have rubbed off on Brennan.

Ten minutes later, he and Kaminsky were slogging through the marsh in the teeth of a freezing wet wind. The rain had lessened to a slow patter, but there was still enough to trickle from the band of Brennan's uniform cap and down the collar of the greatcoat at the back of his neck. The coat still smelled of Warsaw sewer mud.

"How far did he say?" Kaminsky asked as they sloshed though a knee-deep water channel. Around them, the bog seemed to stretch to the mist-shrouded horizon, without a sign of human presence. They were following a map and compass the pilot had given them from the Antonov's emergency kit. Kaminsky was carrying the briefcase.

"About ten kilometers," Brennan said.

"It'll take us over an hour to cover it, in this muck," Kaminsky said, squelching into a mudhole. "My feet will never be warm again. What are you planning to do when we reach the highway?"

"Commandeer a car."

"You don't think there's any chance of getting to an airbase and getting a plane? We could tell the base commander to call Gorbachev."

Brennan wasn't sure whether the Pole was joking or not. "Look at us," he said. "You're a Pole in civilian clothes, and I'm a Polish air force officer, and we're both a hundred kilometers from anywhere we ought to be. We look like drowned rats. If you were an airbase commander, what would you do with us?"

"Lock us up," Kaminsky said gloomily. "For several hours, while I checked with military district authorities, who would then check with Moscow."

"Exactly. Besides, we'd never get through to Gorbachev, even if we knew what number to call."

"I suppose you're right. We should have brought Rybalko's vodka to use as a bribe."

"I checked. The bottle was broken."

"Damn."

They sloshed onward. Fortunately, at this time of year the marsh was relatively dry, and they never encountered any channels that were more than thigh-deep. But the water in each one was icy. Brennan's teeth were chattering, and he began to worry about hypothermia. Kaminsky was older than he, and was having a harder time. Brennan carried the briefcase for a while. The AKR submachine gun on its sling bumped rhythmically against his waist.

The plodding seemed to go on for a very long time, one foot squelching in front of the other, while the rain drizzled down. After a while, the land began to rise, and there were no more water channels. The temperature was a little above freezing now, though, and the raindrops no longer clung gelatinously to the marsh grasses. After about fifty minutes, Brennan saw a line of poles off in the distance. Telephone poles.

"There's the highway," he said, stopping. "We were closer than the pilot thought."

"I wonder if anyone saw us come down."

"Not likely, out here in this weather."

They trudged onward. The poles drew slowly nearer. Finally they came to the road, which was two-lane asphalt, badly surfaced, with muddy shoulders and a drainage ditch on each side. It stretched away to a half-visible horizon. There were no vehicles in sight.

"Hell," Brennan said. "Maybe it's not the main highway."

"Look on the map," Kaminsky said, sitting wearily down on the edge of the soaked pavement. He was so wet that a little more water made no difference.

Brennan unfolded the map, trying to use his body to shield it from the rain. "Let me see. This is where the pilot thinks we went down. There's nothing between that point and the main road, and the contour lines look about right, except we were closer than he thought we were. This is it, all right. The Bobruisk-Moscow road. Dovsk should be west of here, and Cerikov east."

"I'm not going to walk to Moscow," Kaminsky said. "Not even for Mikhail Gorbachev."

"Something will have to come along soon," Brennan said doubtfully.

"I hope it's a car, and not some *muzhik* on a tractor," Kaminsky said.

Now that he was standing still, the wind cut at Brennan like a scalpel. He looked around for shelter, but there was none, not even low bushes. The only place even slightly out of the wind was the ditch. He and Kaminsky hunkered miserably down in it, arms wrapped around their knees.

"The glamorous life of an intelligence officer," Kaminsky said. "What time is it?"

Brennan consulted his watch. "Eight o'clock. Ten o'clock, Moscow time." Probably about seven hours to the city, he thought, after we get a car, if we get a car. Four P.M. at the earliest, that is, if we were starting out right now. More likely five.

"I wonder what's happening there," Kaminsky said. His tone didn't expect an answer.

Brennan was watching over the edge of the ditch, toward the west. He squinted. There was definitely something there. He waited a few seconds as it got bigger.

"Vehicle coming," he said. "Too far away to tell what it is."

"Do you want to try, or me?" Kaminsky asked.

"I will. They're more likely to stop when they see a uniform."

"Unless they see it's not one of theirs."

"I'll keep the coat partly closed."

"Go ahead, then. I'll keep out of sight. Good luck."

Brennan watched a while longer. Whatever it was, it was moving slowly. After another forty seconds he was able to make it out. It was a heavy truck, grinding along under a load of concrete piping.

Too damned slow, he thought. And too hard to maneuver if we're chased. He squatted in the ditch, keeping out of sight of the road. "Sorry," he said to Kaminsky. "Not suitable."

The truck rumbled by, shaking the ground. Brennan raised his head after it was gone, but had to duck as a car shot by on the other side of the road, going the wrong way, naturally.

"Dammit," he said. "This is ridiculous."

"Nothing we can do about it," Kaminsky replied, with Slavic fatalism.

Ten minutes passed, but no vehicles. Then Brennan heard another one, coming from the west this time. He peeped cautiously over the edge of the ditch. This one was progressing at a reasonable speed, and it was too small for a truck. He decided to take a chance, left his AKR with Kaminsky, and climbed out of the ditch. He stood in the middle of the eastbound lane, hand outstretched imperiously in an order to stop.

It was a white Zhiguli. The driver began to slow down a hundred yards away, proceeding cautiously. When he saw the unmistakable cut of a uniform coat, he slowed down even more, pulling onto the shoulder a short way from Brennan. The man behind the wheel was about Kaminsky's age, jowly and balding, with a well-fed look about him. He rolled down the window and called, as Brennan strode toward him:

"Broken down up ahead, officer? I'll be glad to help you out —"

He realized suddenly that the cap badge was a gold eagle, and not a red star. He frenziedly tried to get the Zhiguli into gear, but Brennan leaned into the window, turned off the ignition and put the muzzle of his PM63 under the driver's nose.

"Sorry," he said, and added, with a satisfying irony, "I am commandeering this vehicle, in the name of the Party and the Soviet people."

Timoshkin was on the carpet, literally and figuratively, standing rigidly at attention in front of Chernysh's desk. Besedin leaned against the wall behind Timoshkin, glowering. It was a quarter past four in the afternoon, Moscow time. Outside Chernysh's high window the air was clear; the rain had stopped some time ago.

"They're not here yet, Timoshkin," Chernysh said in a low, even voice. "Where are they?"

"Comrade Chairman, I'm afraid I don't know."

"You let them get away in Poland. You let them take the target away from you in New York. Your incompetence has endangered us all."

"Yes, Comrade Chairman. I am at fault."

"It was this man Brennan again."

"Yes, Comrade Chairman. I saw him clearly."

Chernysh tapped on the polished surface of his desk with the cap of his fountain pen, thinking. It might be possible, if there was more time, to use the CIA's involvement against Gorbachev; there might be a treason charge there, somewhere. But there wasn't enough time.

"What did Kaminsky take away from SB headquarters? Was the damage assessment complete when you left Warsaw?"

They'd almost caught the Pole; it had been obvious when he took to his heels after being called in for a "staff meeting" that he was the traitor. He'd been the only one who ran from the summons, and he must have been expecting such a trap to be laid, to judge from the speed with which he'd gotten into the sewers. He'd been well prepared from the first, damn him.

"It was still in progress, Comrade Chairman. He was very subtle, and it's hard to tell what he got away with. But he probably has a dossier with him. We think CONCERTO file indexes were duplicated, and that he managed to get a record of a good deal of signals traffic between here and Warsaw. Then there were the records he himself had access to. We must assume that copies were taken, or that he transcribed the documents from memory later on. He obviously knew about the New York safe house. There may have been lax document security at the beginning. And General Jurys thinks his files may have been broken into."

"Could Kaminsky have sufficient material to prove a connection between this office and CONCERTO?"

Timoshkin licked his lips. He seemed to have difficulty speaking. "General Vlasov thinks it's possible."

"Should I have Vlasov begin destroying the Warsaw files?" asked Besedin.

"What good will that do," Chernysh snapped at him, "if Kaminsky made copies of them?"

"He can't have copied everything," Besedin said. "Our compartmentation was better than that."

"I hope so. But if I order wholesale destruction of the Warsaw files now, it'll signal Jurys and the other Poles that we're in extreme danger here. Would you bet your life they don't jump overboard, trying to save their own skins?"

Besedin didn't answer. It was a very uncomfortable question.

"I thought you wouldn't," said Chernysh. "We have to assume, since they're not here by air, that they're coming by road or rail. Timoshkin, you've got one more chance. Besedin has the Surveillance Directorate watching the railway stations, and Brennan will know that, so he's likely coming by road. Accordingly, we have surveillance on all the routes coming into Moscow from the west and south. I want you and your men out on the streets, and I want you to monitor the watcher net. If the watchers pick him up, they're going to follow him and route communications straight through to this office. At that time I'll vector you and your men onto him. As soon as you've got him visually, I'll pull the directorate watchers off; they're not in CONCERTO and I want to keep it that way. Stop Brennan and Kaminsky and bring them here. We have to find out how much Kaminsky told the Americans, and how much they told Gorbachev." And maybe, he thought, a live CIA officer might make a treason charge against Gorbachev *just* possible.

"Yes, Chairman."

"Requisition as many Volgas as you need from Surveillance, under my authority. Now get going."

Timoshkin left. Besedin said, "It's going to be hard, if he's driving. There are thousands of vehicles moving into Moscow at any given time."

"Something went wrong for them," Chernysh said. "They would be here by now, by plane, if it hadn't. Keep that check going with the militia, for stolen cars reported west of here. Those are the ones the surveillance people are to keep a special watch for. And anything that doesn't have a Moscow plate code. Moreover . . ." He paused.

"Yes, Chairman?"

"What I said before still applies. If Brennan gets past us this time, we move against Gorbachev. He's getting too close."

Podol'sk: a gray outrider of the Soviet capital, dismal and smoky under a lowering sky. On the outskirts rose huge slate-colored concrete-slab apartment buildings to house the men and women who worked in the heavy machinery factories on the town's southern boundary. The M4 ran right through Podol'sk on the way to Moscow. Eighteen miles to go.

Brennan was driving, and looking for a telephone kiosk. The main street, being a continuation of the Moscow-Kharkov highway, was wide, with a broad concrete median down the center, and a line of mercury-vapor lamp posts down the middle of the median. The lamps would be turned on in an hour or so; already there was a hint of dusk in the eastern sky. On either side of the street were gray nondescript buildings four and five stories high, their limestone and granite facades stained dark by the rain. A few trams were rumbling along the street, half-empty; it wasn't yet rush hour.

"There's one," Kaminsky said from the back seat, where he was guarding their reluctant and still-frightened passenger.

The kiosk was on a corner, next door to a bread store. In front of the store was a line of stolid, patient women carrying string bags. They watched the Zhiguli dully as it rolled past. The passive looks didn't reassure Brennan; Russians were notorious busybodies, by North American standards.

He pulled around the corner and stopped, checking the signs carefully to make sure stopping wasn't prohibited. He'd removed the insignia from the shoulder straps of the greatcoat, and his tie was at this moment binding the wrists of the unfortunate owner of the Zhiguli. They'd had no choice but to take him with them. He'd been blustery at first, threatening them with the status of his Party position in Mogilev, but a couple of jabs in the ribs from Kaminsky's pistol and a furious tirade in Polish had put a stop to that. The man was thoroughly cowed, and had been waxing more apprehensive the closer they got to Moscow. He was clearly convinced that Brennan and Kaminsky were going to do something along the order of blowing up the Kremlin, and was equally convinced that he'd be accused of helping them.

Without the cap, tie and insignia, Brennan decided that at this distance from the bread line, he would pass as a civilian with a good, if dirty, overcoat. He turned around and said to Kaminsky, in Russian, "Watch him. If he twitches, shoot him."

Kaminsky nodded. The prisoner looked more terrified than ever. Brennan got out of the car, feeling in his trousers pocket for the change and bills he'd taken from Rybalko. There were several two-kopek coins. He closed the kiosk door after him, deposited them and waited. The answer came at the first ring.

"Yes."

"Victorine."

"Where are you?"

"Podol'sk."

"Come in via Lenino and Varshavskoye Schosse, straight up to Moskorecky Bridge. Do you know how?"

"Yes."

"Vehicle?"

"White Zhiguli, license 5246GKA."

"You will be met."

Click.

Brennan hung up the receiver. Something, finally, was going right. He returned to the car. "Home free," he said to Kaminsky, in English. The Zhiguli's owner gaped.

"What?" said Kaminsky.

"Never mind. We're off."

Besedin slammed down the telephone. "This is it," he said. "Mogilev MVD has a missing-person report, a party official who was supposed to be in Roslavl by eleven this morning, and never turned up. His car's missing, too, license 5246GKA. He was using the Mogilev-Moscow highway. It has to be them."

"Tell Surveillance," said Chernysh. "Alert Timoshkin. If Brennan's coming in from that direction, it'll be by the Podol'sk main road or the Naro-Fominsk cutoff. Probably the latter, for discretion. Send Timoshkin that way. Have communications patch Timoshkin's radio through to my secure Moscow line number three. I want to direct this myself."

They were at the intersection of Varshavskoye and Kashirskoye when Kaminsky said, "We're being followed."

"Who? Friends?"

"I don't think so. A green van, a blue Volga, changing places. It must have been put together in a hurry, or they'd have more vehicles than that, and I'd never have spotted them."

"Not far now," Brennan said. They passed a Metro station on the left. Brennan couldn't see the sign. Ahead, just to the right, he could see the huge seventeen-story bulk of the Vishnevsky Surgical Institute. In a few minutes they'd be across the river and under the Kremlin walls. Surely someone would have met them by then.

"Wait a minute," said Kaminsky. "They've gone. Peeled off."

"What the hell?" Brennan exclaimed. "Maybe they weren't after us?"

"I don't know."

"Keep hoping. We ought to have support soon."

Brennan maneuvered around a bus. Danilovsky Metro station on the right. Where was the welcoming committee?

A black Volga shot by in the outside lane, followed by another. They pulled abreast of each other, filling both lanes in front of the Zhiguli, and began to brake.

"There's another one —!" Kaminsky yelled.

Brennan tried to pull out into the oncoming traffic, but the third Volga was already beside him, boxing them in. He saw Timoshkin's face in the front passenger seat. Timoshkin was aiming a gun at him, but for some reason didn't fire.

"Jump!" Brennan shouted. He jammed on the brakes and skidded the Zhiguli sideways to slow it down. Rubber shrieked on the road. The car spun out of control, slammed over the curb onto the sidewalk, bounced off a lamp post, and slid back into the road, moving now in a straight line. Brennan grabbed the AKR from the seat beside him, flung his door open, threw himself out of the car, and rolled. Horns blared and he saw a bus tire rush by him not four inches from his eyes. Then he was on his feet, the AKR ready, searching wildly around for Kaminsky. The Pole was fifteen feet away, up on the sidewalk and sheltering behind the Zhiguli. Their passenger was nowhere to be seen. He was probably huddled on the floor in the rear.

Timoshkin's Volgas had stopped sixty feet farther on and men were pouring out of them. Brennan thought there were eight of them. Probably the same crew he had had in New York, he thought, as he ran to the car and threw himself beside Kaminsky, under the shelter of the Zhiguli's battered right-rear fender. Timoshkin and his men were also armed with machine pistols, judging by the brief glimpse he'd had of them.

Kaminsky was clutching the briefcase to his chest with his left arm, his AKR in his right hand. He raised it above the level of the trunk lid and fired a short, unaimed burst in the direction of the Volgas. "Now what?" he said, drawing back. "Except for the car, we're in the open."

Brennan looked around. The sidewalk, which had been full of

pedestrians an instant ago, was deserted. Most of them had dived into the stores lining the street, following the Russian instinct for self-preservation. But Kaminsky was right. There was an alley a dozen yards away, but the ground between it and the truck could be swept by fire. A deathtrap. Timoshkin had made one mistake; he should have left one car behind them, but he'd been too eager to box them in.

But it didn't matter. They were caught, like wasps in a bottle. Timoshkin would have realized that by now.

"If they try to take us alive —"

A long burst of automatic-weapons fire ripped into the Zhiguli. Brennan heard a shriek from inside the truck, as the bullets hit their ex-prisoner. More than one weapon was firing. From inside the stores came screams of fright, as bullets bounced and smashed into windows.

"They're keeping us down so they can get on our flanks," said Brennan.

"Yes," Kaminsky acknowledged grimly.

Another burst of gunfire. Brennan heard thuds from the Zhiguli's bodywork as the bullets hit. The shrieking from inside had stopped.

"We've got to do something before they flank us," Brennan said. "The grenades. They won't know we've got the grenades." He lay prone to peep around the rear wheel and underneath the trunk overhang, pointing the AKR ahead of him.

He was just in time to see two of Timoshkin's men break from behind the Volgas for the mouth of a narrow side street. A fusillade of bullets flew overhead as their companions provided cover, but they were aiming too high. Brennan fired a quick burst that chopped both running men off at the knees, and yanked his own head back behind the wheel as a hail of gunfire concentrated on the Zhiguli's trunk area. Luckily, the angle of the car over the curb prevented bullets from passing under its center.

"I got two," he told Kaminsky. "They've got the same problem we have. There's a fire zone on each side of their cars."

"There're more of them," Kaminsky reminded him.

Brennan smelled gasoline. The Zhiguli's tank had been penetrated and was leaking. They had to get away even more urgently now.

"I've got an idea," he muttered. "Try to get their fuel tank."

He edged the muzzle of the AKR past the rear wheel and fired a whole clip blindly in the direction of the Volgas. Shots came back. He yanked the gun back under cover and rammed a fresh clip into it. Kaminsky bobbed his head around the front bumper for a split second. "You hit it," he said. "There's gas on the road."

"Grenades," said Brennan as he yanked the pair of steel ovoids out of his coat. "A salvo. It's our only chance. Set their cars on fire, and hit them while they're coping with that."

Kaminsky nodded, freeing his own grenades. "Wait," he said. "Smoke screen."

He took out his lighter, the one he'd used to light his oil lamp in the Warsaw sewers, flicked it. Brennan watched the damp patch spreading from underneath the Zhiguli. What about the poor bastard inside, he started to say, but Kaminsky hissed, "Go!" and threw the lighter at the pool of gasoline. Flames ran along its surface.

Brennan backed away from the spreading flames, and crouched well over to keep below the level of the Zhiguli's windows. He saw Kaminsky doing the same, a yard to his right. He armed one of the grenades. The Russians fired again.

"Throw!" Kaminsky hissed, and he and Brennan sent the first pair of grenades arching toward Timoshkin's Volgas. They armed the next pair and threw again while the others were still in the air.

The flames reached under the Zhiguli. "Get back!" Brennan yelled.

He was only just clear when the Zhiguli's tank blew up with a dull *whump*. Simultaneously Brennan heard the four raggedly spaced detonations of the grenades, followed by a rolling boom from the direction of the Volgas. Heat from the Zhiguli seared his face and crisped his eyebrows. Black smoke poured from the flaming car. He plunged into the murk, sensing Kaminsky on his right, and opened suppressing fire as he burst out of the greasy cloud into the street beyond.

All three Volgas were burning. A man staggered out of a ball of flame, his clothing curling like paper in a bonfire. Kaminsky's bullets knocked him to the pavement. There were no answering shots. Brennan held his fire and raced in the infantryman's dodging crouch toward the wreckage of Timoshkin's two nearest vehicles. He glimpsed a figure stumbling from between them and the third car, and fired a round at it. The figure collapsed into the roadway. Still there was no return fire.

Brennan and Kaminsky gingerly approached the burning vehicles and checked all around them. Brennan could barely make out four bodies in the wreaths of flame, killed either by the grenades or the explosions of the Volgas' fuel tanks. An odor like burnt pork mingled with the stink of explosives and raw gasoline.

"Jesus," Brennan said. The reek made his stomach turn.

"We were lucky," Kaminsky said. His eyes were busy, checking the street and the windows above it, and he hadn't lowered his AKR. "They were overconfident, and they didn't know about the grenades."

"Yes," Brennan agreed. He stepped over to the man he had shot. It was Timoshkin, with half his uniform burned off. "We got him," Brennan said dully.

"*Listen*!"

Kaminsky was already halfway to the base of a lamp post. He flung himself into its cover, sighting the AKR down the street, although his line of fire was blocked by smoke from the Zhiguli. Brennan heard the rumble of a heavy diesel engine from the far side of the burning car, and ran for a doorway.

A shadow loomed amid the smoke and emerged as a BDRM scout car. Following it lumbered a BTR60 armored personnel carrier. Uniformed men stood in the hatches of both vehicles, weapons at the ready.

Maybe it's the reception committee, Brennan thought.

The officer in the BRDM had seen Kaminsky. He held up both arms to signal a stop, and then leaned nonchalantly on the hatch rim. "Good day!" he called over the sputtering of the flames. "Are you from Warsaw, by any chance?"

There was no possible escape from that many men and weapons, if they weren't the rescue unit. Brennan slung the AKR and stepped into the open, keeping his hands carefully away from the gun. Kaminsky was doing the same.

"The American?" the officer asked as Brennan and Kaminsky approached the BRDM.

Brennan nodded. "Yes. And the Pole."

"I am General Nilov. I was afraid you were in there." He gestured at the burning car. "Those other ones?"

"They tried to stop us," Brennan said. "Timoshkin's over there. He's dead."

Nilov's eyes narrowed. "Good. Get in here immediately. I have to take you to the Central Committee building right away."

"Where in hell is he?" Chernysh ranted. "It's been half an hour, he should have been here by now. Call him, Besedin."

Besedin got on to line three, the one patched into Timoshkin's car radio. After a minute he put the receiver down. "Communications say they can't raise him."

"To hell with it," Chernysh growled. "Give the order to the troops at Staraya Square. Start the Kremlin Guards moving."

"Comrade Chairman," Besedin said desperately, "just a little longer. It would be much better if the plenum did it —"

"Damn the plenum!" Chernysh shouted. "He's not coming, you idiot! We've been preempted." He dashed to the window, and drew the curtain aside and looked out. Then, very slowly, he let the drape fall back into place.

"What?" Besedin asked.

"The army," Chernysh said quietly. The fury in his voice was gone. "There are troops moving into the square. Get out, Besedin. See if you can organize a defense of the building. Do what you can."

Besedin scuttled out. Chernysh went to his desk and pulled out the middle drawer. He knew Besedin wouldn't be able to do anything, probably wouldn't even try.

I failed, he thought. I planned badly. I should have gone after Gorbachev this afternoon, when I had the chance. Stupid of me.

He drew the Makarov pistol out of the desk and snapped off the safety catch. Then he put the muzzle of the gun into his mouth and blew the top of his head off, from the inside.

Moscow – Washington
Thursday, October 10

BRENNAN HAD NEVER been inside a Soviet limousine before. The interior of the Zil was all red plush and smooth russet leather, and red plush curtains covered the deeply tinted windows. A faint, sweetish odor of tobacco smoke clung to the upholstery.

The Zil drew up in front of the Central Committee building and the driver jumped out to open Brennan's door. Outside the car, the late afternoon air was sharp and cold; it smelled like snow. Brennan walked up the steps to the right-hand entrance with its black iron gates, the chauffeur beside him. The guards were Soviet army men, not KGB.

The chauffeur handed one of the guards a document. After a moment's scrutiny the guard nodded and pressed a button set into the wall behind him. There was a click and the gate slid open. Brennan walked through it; the chauffeur remained behind.

Inside the gates there was another guard to meet him. They walked along the carpeted hall to an anteroom, where a male secretary was sitting behind a desk: one of Gorbachev's aides. "Mr. Brennan?"

"Yes."

"The general secretary will see you now."

The aide got up and opened the polished wooden door leading from the anteroom. Inside, Gorbachev was working at a large desk. The window curtains were open, and through the glass

Brennan could see the gray light of Moscow. A single lamp on Gorbachev's desk cast a yellow glow.

"Mr. Brennan," Gorbachev said, "please sit down." He gestured at a leather armchair near the desk, almost touching its left corner. "Your ambassador requested that I see you."

"Yes, sir. I realize you are extremely busy. Thank you for letting me come on such short notice. It was good of you to send a car for me."

"I was going to ask you here later today, in fact," Gorbachev said. "Would you like to know what has been happening?"

Which is to say, Brennan thought, would Washington like to know what is happening. This is what the State Department calls a back-channel discussion.

"Yes, Mr. Secretary." His own request could wait. Knight and the rest of them would want any information they could get about the Russian leader's position. Brennan had been in the code room of the US embassy half the night, transmitting his report and receiving instructions in return.

"Try to persuade him to find out who the leak is," Knight had signalled."We're working on this end, but we're in the dark. We haven't yet identified everyone who might have learned about your operation, and at this level we have to walk on eggs. Do as much as you dare."

"The information you brought was enough to satisfy the procurator general that there was cause for arrest," Gorbachev was saying. "Although Chernysh eluded us by killing himself when the army moved into Dzerzhinsky Square. There was no resistance at KGB headquarters; Besedin and three of his aides, who were helping with CONCERTO, were too busy trying to destroy their files. Besedin was taken into custody, and has been talking ever since. Vlasov has been arrested in Warsaw, and so has Jurys. There will be other arrests soon, among them that of the two officers who so remarkably survived at Killenworth. And without the CONCERTO provocateurs, Poland will be much calmer."

"What about the kidnappers?" Brennan asked.

"They were located in the basement of the Lubianka, and very comfortable they were, for prisoners. Chernysh's report on their initial interrogation, the report he submitted to the Central Committee on Tuesday, was a pack of lies, of course. I knew it, but if I'd accused him at that point, he might very well have taken violent measures. I wasn't sure how far his preparations had gone."

"Not far enough, evidently," Brennan said.

"No. It was very close, though, at the end." Gorbachev's face took on a distant look, as though he were thinking of something else. Then he said, "We have also unearthed one of Chernysh's men in our embassy in Washington. He has, unfortunately, committed suicide, like his master."

"I see," Brennan said noncommittally.

"Mr. Brennan, I have some bad news for your government. Besides the agent in the embassy, Chernysh had yet another man in Washington. He was not Russian. Perhaps I should not tell you this, but I have no use for this particular tool of the KGB. You will understand why, when I tell you."

"I don't think you need to," Brennan said. "We knew there was someone high up, an American who was cooperating with Chernysh and the others."

"Ah," Gorbachev said. "It doesn't come as a surprise, then."

"No, sir. But we would like to know who it is."

"Unfortunately, I don't know, either. Besedin, as I said, was busy destroying files. Among them were a number of, what are they called, key files, the master ones that give the real identities of agents operating on American soil. All we were able to retrieve was this." Gorbachev opened a desk drawer and removed an accordion folder, tied up with Kremlin red ribbon. "I give it to you, as a token of my appreciation. Perhaps it will help. Besedin doesn't know who he is, apparently. He is high enough for Chernysh to have handled him personally. Whatever his motives, this man was as determined to destroy me as Chernysh was. You are welcome to him. His code name is Promenade." Gorbachev pushed the folder across the polished wood to Brennan.

Brennan took it. "Thank you, Mr. Secretary."

The Russian leader eyed Brennan speculatively. There was a hint of amusement in his eyes. "You're a very intelligent and resourceful man, Mr. Brennan. I don't suppose you'd consider coming and working for me?"

"Thank you for your offer," Brennan said. "But I think that it might be misconstrued, both here and in the United States."

Gorbachev laughed. "Indeed it might." He stood up. "Thank you, Mr. Brennan. The car will take you back to your embassy."

A few snowflakes were drifting through the air outside. Brennan was about to get into the Zil when an army staff car pulled up behind it. Kaminsky got out of one side, and General Nilov out of the other. Kaminsky waved to Brennan and strode over to him. "Sean," he said. "How are you?"

"Fine. Are they treating you well over at GRU?"

"Very. I'm returning to Warsaw tomorrow, to help sort matters out. The Russians didn't throw me in jail, after all."

Brennan studied the Pole. There was a ruthlessness in him, a hardness, that had enabled him to survive this long; he'd set the Zhiguli alight without wondering whether the man inside was still alive. I'm glad I'm getting out of this business, Brennan thought.

"I wish you luck, Adam," he said. "When you're done, come and see me in America. You'd like the place I live in."

"Perhaps I'll be able to."

"Adam," Brennan said. "Please be careful. Don't become like the people you've been fighting."

Kaminsky's eyes clouded. "I know," he said. "It would be easy. I'll be on my guard."

"Fine. Good-bye."

"Good-bye."

He turned and followed Nilov up the steps to the iron gates. Brennan got into the Zil and rode thoughtfully through the darkening Moscow streets to the embassy. The snow was beginning to fall in big flakes now, thickening steadily.

Paulson, the CIA chief of station, was waiting for him on the seventh floor. "Any luck?"

"Yes," Brennan said.

"Use the bubble. There's no one in it. Do you want me?"

"No," Brennan said.

"Okay."

Brennan went through the double doors into the bubble, a room isolated structurally, electronically and magnetically from the rest of the embassy. It was swept daily for listening devices. The white walls were blank. In the middle of the room was a long poured-resin table with similar chairs around it. They had all been manufactured under CIA supervision in the United States, and had been sent to Moscow under diplomatic seal, to prevent tampering.

Brennan sat down at the table and opened the accordion folder. His hands were trembling. Inside were papers, a lot of them, and a small reel of audio tape. The tape would be for voiceprinting, so the KGB could ensure that voice communication from their agent wasn't an imitation.

Brennan called Paulson and obtained a tape recorder. The chances of recognizing the voice were slim, but he'd try it before going through the papers. He threaded the reel into the machine and stopped, one finger on the play button. He almost didn't want to know.

Reid? Was it Reid? He had known enough. So had Barlow. And Knight, but Brennan couldn't bring himself to believe it was Knight. And the president would have known everything.

God, not the *president*. Surely not. Surely that reportedly invincible ignorance wasn't a cover for something darker?

He pressed the key. There was a faint sizzle, and then a voice. The voice was reading something.

It is a matter of historical record that a shipload of Ulster immigrants was brought by the land speculator Colonel Alexander McNutt to Nova Scotia in October of seventeen sixty-one. The next year some of these —

Brennan pressed the stop key. He put his head in his hands and closed his eyes.

No wonder, he thought. No wonder. It was him, all along.

Promenade clutched at the telephone receiver and dialled again, his shaking fingers more clumsy than ever. The digits of the telephone number kept changing places in his head. He couldn't seem to keep things in order; his concentration had been deteriorating for three days. And when the news came in yesterday, that Gorbachev had utterly defeated his opponents, he'd had to resist a frantic urge to beat at his forehead with both fists, splitting the skull to release some of the unbearable pressure inside.

The telephone rang at the other end. It was the emergency number, the one that was supposed to be always manned, the one that would get him out. But it hadn't been manned all day. And he *had* to get out. He couldn't go on anymore, or he'd betray himself.

Another ring.

Click.

"Yes?"

"This is Promenade." He forced calm into his voice. "Vertigo. I repeat, vertigo." It was the pull-me-out emergency signal.

"There is no vertigo," the voice responded coldly. "This number is being disconnected."

Click.

The hysteria was suddenly gone, leaving him cold and suspended. They'd cut him loose. He'd never get out.

Brennan.

He hung up. His movements were coordinated and smooth now. He had decided what to do.

New York – Orchard Harbor
Saturday, October 12

THEY WERE WAITING for him beyond the JFK international-arrivals customs area: Barlow, the CIA director of operations; Knight; and somewhat to Brennan's surprise, Lee Ennis. Brennan shoved the glass door open and set down his suitcase. Ennis stuck out a hand and Brennan shook it.

"Congratulations." Ennis smiled. "You made it." Knight and Barlow were nodding and smiling.

"Hello, Lee," said Brennan. "Pardon me for asking, but what are you doing here?"

Ennis scowled. "Ranelagh's getting a promotion for setting up Gorbachev's rescue."

"I beg your pardon? He didn't have anything to do with it."

"You're telling *me*? Anyway, he decided I was reformed enough to be CIA-FBI liaison for the next stage."

Brennan stared at Ennis in astonishment and frustration. "*What* next stage? Jesus Christ, do you mean you haven't caught up with him?"

"No, we haven't," Barlow put in. "He must have realized somehow that we knew. As soon as you signalled us, Reid went to the president and Halliday called in the FBI and the attorney general. The AG authorized a full surveillance, but he was gone."

"To the Russians?" Brennan asked.

"Not likely," Knight cut in. "From what you told us from

Moscow, he wouldn't be welcome there. He's on the run, plain and simple. There's nowhere he can go."

"I hope not," Brennan snarled. "The bastard. How did they get someone into that high a position?"

"That," said Barlow, "is what we want to ask *him*. We'll get him, no matter what. There are no holds barred, this time around. But Sean, we'd like to start debriefing you as soon as possible. You might be able to give us a lead. We might as well start right here in New York, today."

"When will I get to go home?"

"As soon as the debriefing's over. Does your resignation still stand?" Barlow's voice had become distinctly chilly.

"Yes," Brennan said.

"Fine. Let's get on with it, then."

A blurred voice boomed from the air around them. "Would Mr. Richard Chambers please contact his home office as soon as possible. Mr. Richard Chambers."

"That's me," Barlow said, excitement coloring his voice for an instant. "Maybe we've got him. Can we get a secure line here, Lee?"

"The Bureau satellite office upstairs," said Ennis. "I'll take you up."

They reached the FBI office after a hurried five minutes' walk. Ennis waved identification and commandeered the station chief's office, after making sure the phone line was secure. "Go ahead," he told Barlow as he shut the door behind the other three men.

Barlow planted himself behind the desk and punched Reid's direct number. Like the phone in Ranelagh's office in Manhattan, this one had a built-in speaker.

"Stephen?" Barlow said. "Returning your call. Yeah, he's here, too. So are Frank and Lee Ennis. No, nobody else. Okay. I've got a speaker here, it'll save time." He flipped a switch. "You're supposed to listen to this," he told the others.

Reid's voice floated out of the speaker. "I'm playing you a tape of a phone call I received fifteen minutes ago. It's him. Pick it apart as you hear it." A faint click and a hum. Then:

"Hello, Stephen."

If Brennan had had any doubts about the identity of the voice he'd heard in Moscow, they were banished now. The speaker was

Simon Parr, national security adviser to president of the United States, and an agent for the KGB.

"This is Simon Parr, right?" said Reid's voice, to confirm the identification.

"You know it is."

"Where are you?"

"Never mind that for the moment. I'll let you know when it's time. I want to negotiate."

"You've nothing to negotiate with."

"Oh, but I have. Listen."

A scream broke from the speaker. It was high, a woman's scream. It cut off abruptly. After a moment, Parr's voice came back on the line. "I've gone into the hostage-taking business," he said calmly. "There's a woman here with me, and I'll kill her — slowly — if you don't cooperate."

"Okay," Reid said evenly. "What do you want?"

"I want to negotiate certain things. Among them, protection from the KGB. Gorbachev wants my head, and I don't have to tell you why that's happened. I also want other things like immunity from prosecution in return for telling you everything I know about Soviet work over here."

That wouldn't amount to much, Brennan thought. They'd have kept him so compartmented he wouldn't know anything except what he was involved in himself. It's a bluff. What we'd want to know is how much he told them about *us*.

"We might consider it," Reid said. He was clearly playing for time. "Assuming you have valuable information. We —"

"Shut up and listen. I want the negotiator to be Sean Brennan. He's got an in with the Russians. I may need that. And he got me into this. He can goddamned well help get me out. I want him face-to-face, and nobody else within twenty miles. He has to have full power to speak for you."

There was a brief silence. Within it, at the edge of hearing, Brennan heard a chime.

Bong-bong. Pause. *Bong-bong*.

A ship's clock telling the hours. The ship's clock on the wall in the house in Orchard Harbor.

He's got Molly. That was Molly screaming.

He began to speak, but a voice within him said:

Wait.

Why?

Barlow said no holds barred. They want him, preferably alive, but dead if it's the only way. As soon as they find out where he is they'll go in. A hostage won't slow them down at all, not with so much at stake.

Molly.

Wait until Reid says something about Molly.

"I want Brennan," Parr repeated, ending the silence.

"He's not here. He's still in Moscow," said Reid.

"Bullshit. He's here. You wouldn't delay this long, getting him back to pick his brains. I *want* him, Reid. Get him here."

"It'll take time."

"I don't have time. Neither does the hostage. I'm calling back in three hours. He'd better be available."

Click.

The faint hissing of the tape stopped. Reid had shut off the tape recorder. He came back on the line and said, "That's all there is at this point."

"Where is he?" Barlow asked. "What about the automatic trace?" The trace on all Langley telephones provided an immediate readout of the number from which a caller was telephoning.

"He defeated it. The readout was garbage. We've got widgets to do that, and so does the KGB. I imagine they provided him with one."

"What do you want us to do?"

"Get over to the FBI offices at Federal Plaza, if that's okay with Ennis. The Bureau's got better communications than we have at our Manahattan station. Then sit tight. When Parr comes back on, we'll patch him through so Sean can talk to him. Parr said he wanted face-to-face contact with Sean, so he's got to let us know where he is sooner or later. Maybe we can get somebody on top of him before Sean has to put in an appearance."

"We're going to negotiate?"

"Hell, no. We just have to know where he is. Then we go in and get him."

"What about the hostage?"

"If it comes to a choice . . . " Reid said. "Well, we have to nail Parr, and fast. If he gets it into his head to talk to the press, we're all going to be in a world of shit, from the president on down. This was the *national security adviser,* for Christ's sake. You take my meaning?"

Yes, Brennan thought. No holds barred. Everybody wants his ass covered. Besides that, Molly is expendable. And if I tell them Parr has her, they'll lock me up till it's over. They wouldn't trust me to do what they want.

And they'd be right.

"He hasn't got a chance, you know," said Knight. "He must realize there's no way we'd give him immunity from prosecution. Why does he think we'll do anything but lie to him?"

Ennis was looking oddly at Brennan. "I've been involved in hostage situations," the FBI man said quietly. "The perpetrator is usually playing it by ear. He makes illogical demands, and wishful thinking makes him believe he'll get away with them. In this case, though, I think there's something else."

"What?" said Reid from the speakerphone.

"I think he wants to kill Sean."

Barlow nodded thoughtfully. "Revenge. Sean pulled the rug out from under him."

"That settles it," said Reid. "Sean isn't to go anywhere near him. As soon as we find out where he is, we go in. Frank, set it up with the FBI."

"Okay," said Knight.

"Call me as soon as you're at the Bureau offices," Reid said, and hung up.

Brennan thought, *I have to get out of here*. Molly was up there with Parr. He might be torturing her even now, just for the enjoyment of it. To revenge himself on Brennan.

I can't think about that, Brennan told himself. The others were standing up. "Come on, Sean," Knight said.

"I'll ride with Lee," said Brennan.

Barlow looked surprised. "I thought we could talk in the car."

"I need a break before we start again."

Barlow paused, but seemed reluctant to issue a direct order. They needed Brennan to cooperate. "All right. We'll see you there."

Ennis's car, to Brennan's relief, was parked well out of sight of Barlow's CIA vehicle. Ennis started the engine, but didn't put the car into gear. Instead he turned to look at Brennan.

"Okay, Sean. You want to tell me what's going on?"

Brennan had no weapons, no transport and no backup. He was going to have to trust someone.

"What do you think of the hostage decision?" he asked.

"I think it stinks," Ennis said flatly. "That's not the way I was trained to do things."

"The hostage is Molly," Brennan stated. "My Molly. Parr is at our house in Orchard Harbor. Near Portland, in Maine."

"*What*? How do you know?"

"There was a bell on that tape. I don't know if you heard it. It's the clock in our living room. I've never heard another one like it."

"Jesus Christ. No wonder you didn't say anything."

"What am I going to do, Lee? If I tell them, they'll make soothing noises and lock me up till they've got Parr. Parr will kill Molly without a blink as soon as they show up, as soon as he realizes he can't get me."

"You're right," Ennis said. He drummed his fingers on the rim of the steering wheel and gazed pensively through the windshield.

"Let me try it, Lee. Give me a gun and a way to get up there."

"They might let you go and get him, if they knew about Molly."

"No, they wouldn't. They want him alive. They'd know the choice I'd make, if it came to him or Molly."

"I see," said Ennis. He looked back at Brennan. "You sure have a way of landing me in impossible positions."

Brennan didn't speak.

"What the hell," Ennis said. "Let's go."

He slammed the car into gear and roared out of the parking lot. But he didn't turn for the Manhattan exit.

"Where are we going?"

"To charter a helicopter. Sort of. How far to your place in Maine?"

"Three hundred miles. Two hours' flight time by chopper, maximum. That will give us an hour before Parr calls back. I'm hoping Reid will stall him if I'm not there."

"Reid won't have much choice. Here we are."

The FBI car was pulling up to the security gate outside the new heliport east of the main hangars. Ennis flashed his badge and the guard waved them through. They stopped outside the small administration building. Ennis said, "Wait here," and hurried inside.

Five minutes passed, with Brennan chafing at the delay. Then Ennis came back out. "Got one," he said as he restarted the car. "I commandeered it, actually. It's fast, so it'll be less than two hours to your place. It'll be a one-way trip, though. We'll be nearly out of fuel by the time we set down. The charter company doesn't know it's one-way yet. They think we're going to Portland."

"One way is all I need," Brennan said.

The car drew up to a concrete pad on which sat a spanking new Bell passenger helicopter. The main rotor was already turning.

"Guns," Ennis said, opening his door. "In the trunk."

Stowed in the trunk were a pump-action shotgun, a rifle and a Browning 9mm pistol, as well as two sets of tactical body armor, which looked more like padded ski vests than battle gear. Brennan selected the Browning and the shotgun, along with two spare Browning clips and a box of shotgun shells. Then, to his astonishment, Ennis picked up the rifle and stuffed a box of ammunition into his jacket.

"What in hell are you doing?"

"I'm going with you. I called base when I got the helicopter and told somebody else to take over liaison for the next few hours."

"Lee, you don't have to do this. They could hang you for it, if it goes wrong."

"Screw it," said Ennis. "I didn't like the way the wind was blowing, anyway. Let's take the body armor. We may be doing close-range work."

They left the car where it was and boarded the helicopter.

"Where in hell *is* he?" Barlow snarled at no one in particular. "Parr's supposed to call back in under an hour, goddamn it."

Ranelagh hung up the telephone and stared at Barlow from the other side of his desk. "Kindly watch your language in my office."

"No word on where Ennis is?" Knight asked.

"Nothing," said Ranelagh. "He called in before you got here, and told Brinsley to take over for him, and that's all. That was the comm center I was just talking to. They haven't heard from him, either."

"Nor Brennan?"

"No. I would have told you if they had."

"Does Ennis do this kind of thing often?" Barlow queried acidly.

"Not after today, he won't!" Ranelagh snapped. "He's out. Without pension, if I can manage it."

"Why in hell would Sean just disappear like that?" Knight asked plaintively. "It doesn't make any sense."

Barlow was looking thoughtful. "It has to make *some* kind of sense. Sean wouldn't go wandering off for no reason. So, assuming he and Ennis haven't been held up somewhere, there's a reason."

"Oh, Jesus," said Knight. "*That's it*. The woman. On the tape. *It was Molly Carpenter*. The woman he lives with. It must have been. Parr went to Brennan's place in Maine. Brennan realized it somehow. And when he heard Reid say we weren't going to worry about hostages —"

"He's gone there himself," said Barlow. "Christ. He'll screw up everything. I have to call Washington."

Reid put his telephone down. The news from Barlow wasn't *all* bad. At least they knew where Parr was. He could be stalled, long enough for Barlow to get a team up there to him. The trick was going to be to catch up with Brennan before he caught up with Parr. Brennan, in his present state, was as unpredictable as the traitor.

Reid settled himself to wait for the ex-national security adviser's call. Five minutes to go.

Despite himself, he jumped when the blue telephone rang. With a lurch of his stomach he recognized the calling number on the readout.

President Halliday was on the line.

The helicopter settled onto the narrow beach, the rotor downwash kicking up blasts of sand. A sullen rain had just begun to fall. The pilot switched off the engine and yanked the earphones from his head. He was still angry. "What am I going to do if this thing starts washing out to sea? I haven't got enough fuel to get as far as Portland."

"Just stay put, like we told you," Brennan said. "The tide's high right now, so the chopper's safe. If you're really worried, lift to the top of the bluffs. But don't go up the coast any farther. We'll send somebody back when we're done."

"This better be on the level," the pilot muttered at them.

"You'll get paid," Ennis said. "Quit worrying. We'll be back in less than two hours. It won't even be dark by then. But don't report your position, or I'll charge you with obstructing a federal officer."

The pilot muttered something else. Brennan and Ennis ignored him, put the body armor on and climbed out of the machine onto the sand. A cold, dank wind was whipping spray off the tops of the breakers to mix salt water with the drizzly rain.

"A mile to the path," Brennan said. "There's a climb. Then we go after him."

"He won't be expecting us," Ennis said. "At least we'll have that advantage."

"Yes," Brennan agreed. He was working it over again in his mind, as he and Ennis had planned it aboard the helicopter, figuring out their access to the house and angles of approach. Brennan knew the place better than Parr did, which was another slight advantage.

They slogged along the sand through the steady drizzle. Brennan found himself worrying about the path up to the top of the bluffs. It hadn't been in good repair when he was last on it, and if there'd been a lot of rain recently there might be washouts. How they'd get up the cliff if that was the case, he wasn't sure.

"There it is," he said at last. "That's the bottom of the path. The house is at the top."

"Okay. Hell, that's a long way up."

"The path looks okay, though."

"I hope it's the same way it looks."

They started up the steep, zigzagging path. The surface was crumbling in places, but they managed to traverse the partial washouts. The wet clay was as slippery as grease.

"Now comes the hard part," Brennan muttered to Ennis. They were about seven feet below the lip of the cliffs. They had to make their way along the steep clay face for some thirty feet to the right, to climb over the top under cover of the cedar grove on that side of the house. Brennan wondered again if they might have been better off to make their approach from the road, but once more rejected the idea. Parr would be expecting attackers to come from that direction. But if he hadn't actually looked over the top of the cliff and seen the path, he'd think his rear was secure. The trick was to avoid the open stretch of lawn between the house veranda and the clifftop, which was why they had to make their way along the face of the cliff to the cedars.

Brennan led the way. The clay was deeply channelled from erosion, which in dry weather would have provided easy going. Lubricated by the rain, it was another matter. They had clipped the rifle and shotgun to their tactical jackets, but the long weapons swung clumsily and made balancing even more difficult.

Inch by inch, they made their way along the cliff face, which here slanted inward at about fifteen degrees from the vertical. Brennan jammed a foot into a crevice, tested the hold, freed his other foot, searched for the next channel. Did it again and again.

He had a yard to go, then a foot. He could see the cedar roots thrusting out of the clifftop above him. He reached up, grabbed a root and pulled gently. It held. Gingerly, he used the root network to pull himself upward. Finally, he reached the top and was over. He turned around to help Ennis.

The FBI man was just below the roots and reaching upward when the clay projection under his feet gave way. He made a desperate lunge for Brennan's hand and missed by an inch. Ennis began sliding down the near-vertical incline, foot by foot, toward the place where the slope became a true vertical, dropping sheer to the beach sixty feet below. Brennan opened his mouth to scream advice at him.

Parr would hear. Brennan closed his mouth.

Ennis must have had the same thought, too, because he remained grimly silent as he slid. He was now only ten feet from the vertical drop.

It was a six-inch rock outcrop, almost invisible from Brennan's position, that saved Ennis. His foot hit it and he jarred to a stop, arms outstretched, fingers digging into the slimy clay. He raised a mud-streaked face to look up at Brennan.

"Can you climb back?" Brennan hissed at him.

Ennis maneuvered himself carefully so that most of his weight was on the outcrop. He kicked some dirt away from the stone to give himself a better footing, and tried to start working his way back up the cliff. He got two feet and slid back, narrowly catching the outcrop as he did so. He looked back up at Brennan and shook his head despairingly.

"Can you hang on?"

"As long as I need to," Ennis gasped up at him. "Sorry. Can you find a rope?"

There's rope in the garage, Brennan thought. But I'd never get in without him hearing me. And I don't know how much time I've got. Reid will have spoken to Parr by now. Barlow and the rest of them may be on their way, probably are on their way. I have to go on.

"No. Parr would hear."

"Go on, then. Go and get him. I'll be okay."

"I'll be back," Brennan called softly down to Ennis. Ennis nodded in agreement, or hope.

Brennan unclipped the shotgun from the armor jacket and made sure there was a shell in the gun's breech. Then he ran in a crouch along the line of cedars until he was opposite the north side of the house. On this side of the building there were no ground-floor windows, and only a small one in the upper story. There was also, however, an entrance to the old root cellar, an almost horizontal door closing off the cellar steps from the yard above. It was padlocked, and Brennan knew where the key to the padlock was.

He hadn't heard Haig bark. Had Parr killed the dog? The animal didn't have an attack dog's temperament, and he weighed only forty pounds. He might try to defend Molly, but he wouldn't have a chance against Parr. The dog could also be a problem if he was out and about. He might see Brennan before he scented him, and start barking.

There was nothing to be done about the problem. Brennan ran across the narrow lawn between the cedars and the cellar door, crouched, and dug under the turf. The key was there in its jam jar. He got it out and inserted it carefully into the padlock. The lock was well oiled, and clicked open easily.

Now to open the door. He'd oiled the hinges at the same time he did the lock. The door swung up without a squeak.

Hang on, Molly, Brennan thought. Hang on, Lee. We're almost there.

Cold air bearing the smell of damp earth and old cement wafted from the cellar below. There were five flagged steps leading down. He took every one slowly and carefully. Gray light filtered past him from the world outside. The steps leading up to the kitchen were just ahead in the gloom. Brennan peered up the stairwell. At the top of the steps, the kitchen door was open half an inch.

The telephone was in the kitchen. Odds were good that Parr was up there with it, waiting for a contact with Brennan. He'd have Molly there, too. The door opened out into the kitchen, not into the stairwell. Would Parr be on the right or the left of the door?

Right, almost certainly. That was where the phone was. And Parr was a careful man, so he'd keep well away from Molly, even though she'd be tied up. Molly would likely be over by the sink, on the other side of the kitchen. The door swung left, away from Parr. Brennan would have a clear shot at him.

If he was fast enough.

He put a foot on the first step, testing for creaks as his weight came down. The wood and its old nails remained silent.

"Do you know when he's coming back?"

Brennan stiffened. It was Parr's voice, from the kitchen above. To the right, as far as Brennan could tell, by the phone.

"No, I don't." Molly.

"If he's not there when I call again, it's all over for you. He's stalling. They're all stalling."

"I tell you, I don't know where he is." Molly's voice was frightened but strong. A wave of relief swept through Brennan.

"Listen to me," Parr said. His voice was soft. "If he's not there, if I can't reach him, I'll reach him through you. That might be even better. He'll live, but you won't, and I'll make sure he knows how you died. You know what I did in southeast Asia? I learned a lot about interrogation techniques. You'd be surprised at the pain you can produce with the most commonplace instruments. Kitchen utensils, for example."

Brennan heard the unmistakable sound of a drawer sliding and metal being moved about. "This, to start with," Parr went on. "A garlic press. Or an electric carving knife. Or something as simple as a vegetable peeler."

"Somebody will come," she said.

"Nobody knows we're here together," said Parr. "I'm tempted to start now. Maybe I will. I think I *definitely* will. Sorry, but I'll have to gag you. Can't disturb the neighbors. Where do you keep the tea towels?"

The floor creaked under Parr's weight. He was moving away from the phone, toward the wrong side of the door.

Brennan charged up the steps. His weight slammed the door wide and he hurtled into the kitchen, the muzzle of the shotgun searching for Parr.

Parr was no more than five feet away, closer to the phone than Brennan had expected, and he was already reacting. He had a heavy black automatic in his fist, and before Brennan could get the shotgun on target, he had fired.

My God, he's fast, Brennan had time to think as he saw the automatic's hammer snap down. He heard a deafening explosion and felt a violent punch in his rib cage as the heavy bullet slammed into the armor jacket and threw him backward.

But he'd already pulled the shotgun trigger when the bullet hit him. The weapon went off with a tremendous *boom* in the enclosed space, and Parr's gun hand and forearm shredded in a spray of blood and flesh. Parr screamed as Brennan, winded and stunned even with the protection of the jacket, fell partly back into the stairwell. Brennan struggled to his feet barely in time to see Parr use his left hand to tear open the kitchen door. Then the man was through it and into the front yard.

Brennan staggered over to Molly, who was staring at him in a daze of shock and horror. She was tied to a kitchen chair with a length of clothesline. "Are you all right?" he gasped at her.

"Yes. Yes. Oh, God, Sean. He's crazy. Don't let him come back."

Brennan grabbed a paring knife from the rack beside the sink and sawed her hands free. "I'm going to get him," he said as he handed her the knife. He was getting his wind back. "Call my work number at Langley. Tell them I've got Parr. Tell them to send somebody. Don't call the police."

She was already cutting her ankles free. Brennan pumped another shell into the shotgun and ran out the door after Parr. The trail was easy to follow. Even in the rain the blood was thick on the grass and on the pavement of the driveway.

Brennan was out on the road now, and there was Parr, three hundred feet ahead, weaving in a staggering run. He won't get far in that condition, Brennan thought. Shock will get him. But I want him alive, the bastard.

Brennan tried to run faster. Did Parr have another gun, and could he use it left-handed?

Brennan was gaining, but to his surprise Parr hadn't slowed down. He was still pelting along the road, just running like a wounded animal. Brennan knew the road ahead ended in an old washout, with a huge, steep-sided gully beyond it leading down to the beach. Parr wouldn't likely realize the washout was there. Unless he went into the woods inland, he was trapped.

Parr ran around the first of the two bends before the washout, and disappeared. Brennan forced himself into a faster run. He didn't want the man to go over the gully edge and fall to his death in the ravine below. It would be too easy a way out.

Brennan rounded the first bend. Parr was no more than fifty feet ahead, obviously flagging.

But he summoned a burst of speed, and vanished around the second bend, where the road narrowed under a tunnel of trees. From beyond, Brennan could hear the boom of waves along the beach. He rounded the bend himself. Parr, had used up his last reserves. He was staggering now and no longer even trying to run. Ahead of him were the checkered sign and the waist-high steel guard rails that marked the washout. On the other side of the rails was a short stretch of cracked and weed-grown asphalt, and then a void.

''Stop!'' Brennan shouted. ''There's a cliff.''

The national security adviser halted, almost fell to his knees and then straightened slowly. He turned to face Brennan. Parr was holding his right wrist with his left hand, to staunch the flow of blood. His face was gray with shock.

Brennan approached carefully, keeping the shotgun aimed. He was wary of Parr, even now.

''I ought to kill you, you son of a bitch,'' said Brennan. ''For what you did to Molly.''

''Go ahead,'' Parr said. ''I wish I'd had an hour with her. She wouldn't have been much use to you after that.''

Brennan's finger tightened on the trigger. Don't, he told himself. Don't.

''It's all over,'' he told Parr. ''You lost.''

Parr gave a feeble laugh. ''Did I? Wait till the trial. The CIA and the FBI will be hung out to dry for letting me past them. Halliday will be lucky if he doesn't get impeached. It's not over yet, Brennan.''

''Walk,'' Brennan said.

Something went *snap* by Brennan's right ear and a round black hole appeared in the center of Parr's forehead. The security adviser pitched over backward and fell in a heap onto the wet concrete of the road.

Brennan turned around, very slowly and carefully. Back at the curve, under a maple tree, stood Barlow. He was cradling a scope-sighted sniping rifle in the crook of his right arm.

Brennan didn't move or speak as Barlow walked toward him. He waited until the director of operations was an arm's length away before he said:

''What was that for?''

Barlow shrugged. ''Certain people decided it would be better if there wasn't any trial. The DCI went along with it.''

''You mean the president decided.''

Barlow shrugged again. ''You didn't hear it from me.''

''You were going to let Molly take her chances, no matter which way it was decided.''

Barlow looked down at Parr's body. ''You have to understand our position. We would have saved her if it was possible. Frank's back at the house. She's okay.''

Brennan drew his fist back and punched Barlow as hard as he could in the stomach. Barlow dropped the rifle and doubled over, gasping and retching.

''I quit,'' Brennan said. He set off down the road, breaking into a run as he went. He hadn't quite quit. He still had to retrieve Ennis.

Orchard Harbor
Monday, October 14

MOLLY WAS SITTING on the veranda when Brennan came back from the village. Indian summer had replaced the cold drizzle of the weekend, and even the breeze from the ocean was warm. Haig was half-asleep in a patch of sun in the middle of the veranda floor. He opened one eye and thumped his tail at Brennan's approach. The dog had gone off on one of his jaunts the day Parr came, which was fortunate. Parr would have killed him as a matter of course.

Brennan put the *New York Times* on the table beside Molly. She didn't move to pick it up. "Is it in there?" she asked.

"Yes. Parr was regrettably killed in an automobile crash on Sunday. Body burned beyond recognition. Identified from dental records."

She shivered. "Can they really get away with that?"

"Their chances are good."

"Lee called," she said. "He wants to know if we'll be home next weekend. I think he'd like to get out of New York."

"If it's okay with you."

"It's fine with me. I don't like being alone, after . . . what happened."

"We could move," he said. "It might be better for you."

"No," she said with determination. "I'm not going to leave a place I love because of someone's evil. It would be letting them win. I'll get over it. Anyway, the dog likes it here."

"If it's hard, tell me."

"I will," Molly answered. "Does the paper say anything about Gorbachev?"

Brennan picked up the paper and unfolded it. "He's firmly in the saddle, apparently. And according to Halliday, or so it says here on the front page, a new age of international cooperation is coming. The president says we're about to enter the broad sunlit uplands of world peace." Brennan winced.

"What's the matter?" Molly asked.

"Halliday stole that last bit from Winston Churchill." Brennan angrily tossed the newspaper onto the floor. "The man's an idiot. As well as an accessory to murder."

Molly nodded but did not speak. Brennan thought: If I hadn't heard the clock strike behind Parr's voice on that tape, she'd be dead. There wasn't one among them, from Frank Knight to Halliday himself, who was willing to lift a finger to save Molly from Parr. All they could think about was their own professional and political skins. And Halliday's come out of it looking like John F. Kennedy in the Cuban missile crisis.

"Halliday will be able to make enormous political capital out of it all," Molly observed, as though she had overheard Brennan. "From the outside, it looks as though he did everything right. Not like Carter and the hostages in Tehran, for example. Halliday's a shoo-in for the next election."

"Not necessarily," Brennan said.

Molly folded her hands in her lap and studied the distant horizon. "What do you mean, Sean?"

"Halliday is ignorant, and weak, and vicious, and has no business being president of the United States. And I know what I know."

Molly turned toward Brennan and reached out to clasp his hands between hers. Her face was calm and determined.

"Good," she said. "I didn't think you'd let him get away with it."